The Poisonwood Bible

"Kingsolver's powerful new book is actually an old-fashioned nineteenth-century novel, a Hawthornian tale of sin and redemption and the 'dark necessity' of history."
—Michiko Kakutani, *New York Times*

"A powerful new epic. . . . She has with infinitely steady hands worked the prickly threads of religion, politics, race, sin, and redemption into a thing of terrible beauty."
—*Los Angeles Times Book Review*

"Powerful. . . . Kingsolver is a gifted magician of words."
—*Time*

"Beautifully written. . . . Kingsolver's tale of domestic tragedy is more than just a well-told yarn. . . . Played out against the bloody backdrop of political struggles in Congo that continue to this day, it is also particularly timely."
—*People*

"Tragic, and remarkable. . . . A novel that blends outlandish experience with Old Testament rhythms of prophecy and doom."
—*USA Today*

"The book's sheer enjoyability is given depth by Kingsolver's insight and compassion for Congo, including its people and their language and sayings."
—*Boston Globe*

The Poisonwood Bible

The Poisonwood Bible

A NOVEL

BARBARA KINGSOLVER

HarperPerennial

A Division of HarperCollins*Publishers*

Grateful acknowledgment is made to reprint the following:

"The Red Wheelbarrow" by William Carlos Williams from *Collected Poems: 1909–1939, Volume I.* Copyright © 1938 by New Directions Publishing Corp. Reprinted by permission of New Directions Publishing Corp.

Excerpt from *The Strange Case of Dr. Jekyll and Mr. Hyde* by Robert Louis Stevenson. Copyright © 1990 by The University of Nebraska Press. Reprinted by permission of The University of Nebraska Press.

Selections from *The Complete Poems of Emily Dickinson* by Emily Dickinson (ed. Thomas H. Johnson). Reprinted by permission of Little, Brown and Company.

HarperCollins books may be purchased for educational, business, or sales promotional use. For information please write: Special Markets Department, HarperCollins Publishers, Inc., 10 East 53rd Street, New York, NY 10022.

First HarperPerennial edition published 1999.

Designed by Elliott Beard

The Library of Congress has Cataloged the hardcover edition as follows:
Kingsolver, Barbara.
    The poisonwood bible: a novel/ Barbara Kingsolver.
        p.   cm.
    ISBN 0-06-017540-0
    1. Missionaries—Congo (Democratic Republic)—Fiction.   2. Americans—Congo (Democratic Republic)—Fiction.   3. Family—Congo (Democratic Republic)—Fiction.   4. Congo (Democratic Republic)—History—1960–1997—Fiction.   5. Domestic fiction.   I. Title.
    PS3561.I496P65 1998
    813'.54—dc21   98-19901

ISBN 0-06-09-3053-5 (pbk.)

00 01 02 03 ❖/RRD 30 29 28 27 26 25

For Frances

Contents

Author's Note

THIS IS A WORK OF FICTION. Its principal characters are pure inventions with no relations on this earth, as far as I know. But the Congo in which I placed them is genuine. The historical figures and events described here are as real as I could render them with the help of recorded history, in all its fascinating variations.

Because I wasn't able to enter Zaire while researching and writing the novel, I relied on memory, travel in other parts of Africa, and many people's accounts of the natural, cultural, and social history of the Congo/Zaire. Such is the diversity and value of these sources—to me, and to any reader who might wish to know more of the facts underpinning the fiction—that I've cited many of them in a bibliography at the end of the book. Most profoundly helpful among them was Jonathan Kwitny's description of Zaire's postcolonial history, in his excellent book, *Endless Enemies,* which gave shape to my passion to write a novel on the same subject. I returned continually to that account for the big picture and countless small insights. I gleaned many kinds of instruction from Janheinz Jahn's classic text, *Muntu*; Chinua Achebe's novel, *Things Fall Apart*; Alan P. Merriam's *Congo: Background of Conflict*; and *Lumumba: The Last Fifty Days* by G. Heinz and H. Donnay. I couldn't have written the book at all without two remarkable sources of literary inspiration, approximately equal in size: K. E. Laman's *Dictionnaire Kikongo-Français*, and the King James Bible.

I also relied on help from my lively community of friends, some of whom may have feared they'd breathe their last before I was through putting new versions of a mountainous manuscript in front of them. Steven Hopp, Emma Hardesty, Frances Goldin, Terry Karten, Sydelle Kramer, and Lillian Lent read and commented invaluably on many drafts. Emma Hardesty worked miracles of collegial tact, friendship, and efficiency that allowed me to spend my days as a writer. Anne Mairs and Eric Peterson helped sort out details of Kikongo grammar and Congolese life. Jim Malusa and Sonya Norman provided insights for the final draft. Kate Turkington cheered me on from South Africa. Mumia Abu-Jamal read and commented on the manuscript from prison; I'm grateful for his intelligence and courage.

I thank Virginia and Wendell Kingsolver, especially, for being different in every way from the parents I created for the narrators of this tale. I was the fortunate child of medical and public-health workers, whose compassion and curiosity led them to the Congo. They brought me to a place of wonders, taught me to pay attention, and set me early on a path of exploring the great, shifting terrain between righteousness and what's right.

I spent nearly thirty years waiting for the wisdom and maturity to write this book. That I've now written it is proof of neither of those things, but of the endless encouragement, unconditional faith, insomnolent conversation, and piles of arcane reference books delivered always just in the nick of time by my extraordinary husband. Thanks, Steven, for teaching me it's no use waiting for things that only appear at a distance, and for believing a spirit of adventure will usually suffice.

Book One

GENESIS

And God said unto them,
Be fruitful, and multiply, and replenish the earth,
and subdue it: and have dominion
over the fish of the sea, and over the fowl of the air,
and over every living thing that moveth upon the earth.

GENESIS 1:28

Orleanna Price

SANDERLING ISLAND, GEORGIA

IMAGINE A RUIN so strange it must never have happened.

First, picture the forest. I want you to be its conscience, the eyes in the trees. The trees are columns of slick, brindled bark like muscular animals overgrown beyond all reason. Every space is filled with life: delicate, poisonous frogs war-painted like skeletons, clutched in copulation, secreting their precious eggs onto dripping leaves. Vines strangling their own kin in the everlasting wrestle for sunlight. The breathing of monkeys. A glide of snake belly on branch. A single-file army of ants biting a mammoth tree into uniform grains and hauling it down to the dark for their ravenous queen. And, in reply, a choir of seedlings arching their necks out of rotted tree stumps, sucking life out of death. This forest eats itself and lives forever.

Away down below now, single file on the path, comes a woman with four girls in tow, all of them in shirtwaist dresses. Seen from above this way they are pale, doomed blossoms, bound to appeal to your sympathies. Be careful. Later on you'll have to decide what sympathy they deserve. The mother especially—watch how she leads them on, pale-eyed, deliberate. Her dark hair is tied in a ragged lace handkerchief, and her curved jawbone is lit with large, false-pearl earrings, as if these headlamps from another world might show the way. The daughters march behind her, four girls compressed in bodies as tight as bowstrings, each one tensed to fire off a woman's heart on a different path to glory or damnation. Even now they resist affinity like cats in a bag: two blondes—the one short and fierce, the other tall and imperious—flanked by matched brunettes like bookends, the forward twin leading hungrily while the rear one sweeps the ground in a rhythmic limp. But gamely enough they climb together over logs of rank decay that have fallen across the path. The mother waves a graceful hand in front of her as she leads the way, parting curtain after curtain of spiders' webs. She appears to be conducting a symphony. Behind them the curtain closes. The spiders return to their killing ways.

At the stream bank she sets out their drear picnic, which is only dense, crumbling bread daubed with crushed peanuts and slices of bitter plantain. After months of modest hunger the children now forget to complain about food. Silently they swallow, shake off the crumbs, and drift downstream for a swim in faster water. The mother is left alone in the cove of enormous trees at the edge of a pool. This place is as familiar to her now as a living room in the house of a life she never bargained for. She rests uneasily in the silence, watching ants boil darkly over the crumbs of what seemed, to begin with, an impossibly meager lunch. Always there is someone hungrier than her own children. She tucks her dress under her legs and inspects her poor, featherless feet in their grass nest at the water's edge—twin birds helpless to fly out of there, away from the disaster she knows is coming. She could lose everything: herself, or worse, her children. Worst of all: *you*, her only secret. Her favorite. How could a mother live with herself to blame?

She is inhumanly alone. And then, all at once, she isn't. A beautiful animal stands on the other side of the water. They look up from their lives, woman and animal, amazed to find themselves in the same place. He freezes, inspecting her with his black-tipped ears. His back is purplish-brown in the dim light, sloping downward from the gentle hump of his shoulders. The forest's shadows fall into lines across his white-striped flanks. His stiff forelegs splay out to the sides like stilts, for he's been caught in the act of reaching down for water. Without taking his eyes from her, he twitches a little at the knee, then the shoulder, where a fly devils him. Finally he surrenders his surprise, looks away, and drinks. She can feel the touch of his long, curled tongue on the water's skin, as if he were lapping from her hand. His head bobs gently, nodding small, velvet horns lit white from behind like new leaves.

It lasted just a moment, whatever that is. One held breath? An ant's afternoon? It was brief, I can promise that much, for although it's been many years now since my children ruled my life, a mother recalls the measure of the silences. I never had more than five minutes' peace unbroken. I was that woman on the stream bank, of course. Orleanna Price, Southern Baptist by marriage, mother of children living and dead. That one time and no other the okapi came to the stream, and I was the only one to see it.

I didn't know any name for what I'd seen until some years afterward in Atlanta, when I attempted briefly to consecrate myself in the public library, believing every crack in my soul could be chinked with a book. I read that the male okapi is smaller than the female, and more shy, and that hardly anything else is known about them. For hundreds of years people in the Congo Valley spoke of this beautiful, strange beast. When European explorers got wind of it, they declared it legendary: a unicorn. Another fabulous tale from the dark domain of poison-tipped arrows and bone-pierced lips. Then, in the 1920s, when elsewhere in the world the menfolk took a break between wars to perfect the airplane and the automobile, a white man finally did set eyes on the okapi. I can picture him spying on it with binoculars, raising up the cross-haired rifle sight, taking it for his own. A family of them now reside in the New York Museum of Natural History, dead and stuffed, with standoffish glass eyes. And so the okapi is now by scientific account a real animal. Merely real, not legend. Some manner of beast, a horseish gazelle, relative of the giraffe.

Oh, but I know better and so do you. Those glassy museum stares have got nothing on *you*, my uncaptured favorite child, wild as the day is long. Your bright eyes bear down on me without cease, on behalf of the quick and the dead. Take your place, then. Look at what happened from every side and consider all the other ways it could have gone. Consider, even, an Africa unconquered altogether. Imagine those first Portuguese adventurers approaching the shore, spying on the jungle's edge through their fitted brass lenses. Imagine that by some miracle of dread or reverence they lowered their spyglasses, turned, set their riggings, sailed on. Imagine all who came after doing the same. What would that Africa be now? All I can think of is the other okapi, the one they used to believe in. A unicorn that could look you in the eye.

In the year of our Lord 1960 a monkey barreled through space in an American rocket; a Kennedy boy took the chair out from under a fatherly general named Ike; and the whole world turned on an axis called the Congo. The monkey sailed right overhead, and on a more earthly plane men in locked rooms bargained for the Congo's treasure. But I was there. Right on the head of that pin.

I had washed up there on the riptide of my husband's confidence and the undertow of my children's needs. That's my excuse, yet none of them really needed me all that much. My firstborn and my baby both tried to shed me like a husk from the start, and the twins came with a fine interior sight with which they could simply look past me at everything more interesting. And my husband, why, hell hath no fury like a Baptist preacher. I married a man who could never love me, probably. It would have trespassed on his devotion to all mankind. I remained his wife because it was one thing I was able to do each day. My daughters would say: You see, Mother, you had no life of your own.

They have no idea. One has *only* a life of one's own.

I've seen things they'll never know about. I saw a family of weaver birds work together for months on a nest that became such a monstrous lump of sticks and progeny and nonsense that finally it brought their whole tree thundering down. I didn't speak of it to my husband or children, not ever. So you see. I have my own story, and increasingly in my old age it weighs on me. Now that every turn in the weather whistles an ache through my bones, I stir in bed and the memories rise out of me like a buzz of flies from a carcass. I crave to be rid of them, but find myself being careful, too, choosing which ones to let out into the light. I want you to find me innocent. As much as I've craved your lost, small body, I want you now to stop stroking my inner arms at night with your fingertips. Stop whispering. I'll live or die on the strength of your judgment, but first let me say who I am. Let me claim that Africa and I kept company for a while and then parted ways, as if we were both party to relations with a failed outcome. Or say I was afflicted with Africa like a bout of a rare disease, from which I have not managed a full recovery. Maybe I'll even confess the truth, that I rode in with the horsemen and beheld the apocalypse, but still I'll insist I was only a captive witness. What is the conqueror's wife, if not a conquest herself? For that matter, what is *he*? When he rides in to vanquish the untouched tribes, don't you think they fall down with desire before those sky-colored eyes? And itch for a turn with those horses, and those guns? That's what we yell back at history, always, always. It wasn't just me; there were crimes strewn six ways to Sunday, and I had my own mouths to feed. I didn't know. I had no life of my own.

And you'll say I did. You'll say I walked across Africa with my wrists unshackled, and now I am one more soul walking free in a white skin, wearing some thread of the stolen goods: cotton or diamonds, freedom at the very least, prosperity. Some of us know how we came by our fortune, and some of us don't, but we wear it all the same. There's only one question worth asking now: How do we aim to live with it?

I know how people are, with their habits of mind. Most will sail through from cradle to grave with a conscience clean as snow. It's easy to point at other men, conveniently dead, starting with the ones who first scooped up mud from riverbanks to catch the scent of a source. Why, Dr. Livingstone, I presume, wasn't he the rascal! He and all the profiteers who've since walked out on Africa as a husband quits a wife, leaving her with her naked body curled around the emptied-out mine of her womb. I know people. Most have no earthly notion of the price of a snow-white conscience.

I would be no different from the next one, if I hadn't paid my own little part in blood. I trod on Africa without a thought, straight from our family's divinely inspired beginning to our terrible end. In between, in the midst of all those steaming nights and days darkly colored, smelling of earth, I believe there lay some marrow of honest instruction. Sometimes I can nearly say what it was. If I could, I would fling it at others, I'm afraid, at risk to their ease. I'd slide this awful story off my shoulders, flatten it, sketch out our crimes like a failed battle plan and shake it in the faces of my neighbors, who are wary of me already. But Africa shifts under my hands, refusing to be party to failed relations. Refusing to be any place at all, or any thing but itself: the animal kingdom making hay in the kingdom of glory. So there it is, take your place. Leave nothing for a haunted old bat to use for disturbing the peace. Nothing, save for this life of her own.

We aimed for no more than to have dominion over every creature that moved upon the earth. And so it came to pass that we stepped down there on a place we believed unformed, where only darkness moved on the face of the waters. Now you laugh, day and night, while you gnaw on my bones. But what else could we have thought? Only that it began and ended with *us*. What do we know, even now? Ask the children. Look at what they grew up to be. We can only speak of the things we carried with us, and the things we took away.

The Things We Carried

KILANGA, 1959

Leah Price

W E CAME FROM BETHLEHEM, Georgia, bearing Betty Crocker cake mixes into the jungle. My sisters and I were all counting on having one birthday apiece during our twelve-month mission. "And heaven knows," our mother predicted, "they won't have Betty Crocker in the Congo."

"Where we are headed, there will *be* no buyers and sellers at all," my father corrected. His tone implied that Mother failed to grasp our mission, and that her concern with Betty Crocker confederated her with the coin-jingling sinners who vexed Jesus till he pitched a fit and threw them out of church. "Where we are headed," he said, to make things perfectly clear, "not so much as a Piggly Wiggly." Evidently Father saw this as a point in the Congo's favor. I got the most spectacular chills, just from trying to imagine.

She wouldn't go against him, of course. But once she understood there was no turning back, our mother went to laying out in the spare bedroom all the worldly things she thought we'd need in the Congo just to scrape by. "The bare minimum, for my children," she'd declare under her breath, all the livelong day. In addition to the cake mixes, she piled up a dozen cans of Underwood deviled ham; Rachel's ivory plastic hand mirror with powdered-wig ladies on the back; a stainless-steel thimble; a good pair of scissors; a dozen number-2 pencils; a world of Band-Aids, Anacin, Absorbine Jr.; and a fever thermometer.

And now we are here, with all these colorful treasures safely transported and stowed against necessity. Our stores are still intact, save for the Anacin tablets taken by our mother and the thimble lost down the latrine hole by Ruth May. But already our supplies from home seem to represent a bygone world: they stand out like bright party favors here in our Congolese house, set against a backdrop of mostly all mud-colored things. When I stare at them with the rainy-season light in my eyes and Congo grit in my teeth, I can hardly recollect the place where such items were commonplace, merely a yellow pencil, merely a green bottle of aspirin among so many other green bottles upon a high shelf.

Mother tried to think of every contingency, including hunger and illness. (And Father does, in general, approve of *contingencies*. For it was God who gave man alone the capacity of foresight.) She procured a good supply of antibiotic drugs from our granddad Dr. Bud Wharton, who has senile dementia and loves to walk outdoors naked but still can do two things perfectly: win at checkers and write out prescriptions. We also brought over a cast-iron frying pan, ten packets of baker's yeast, pinking shears, the head of a hatchet, a fold-up army latrine spade, and all told a good deal more. This was the full measure of civilization's evils we felt obliged to carry with us.

Getting here with even the bare minimum was a trial. Just when we considered ourselves fully prepared and were fixing to depart, lo and behold, we learned that the Pan American Airline would only allow forty-four pounds to be carried across the ocean. Forty-four pounds of luggage per person, and not one iota more. Why, we were dismayed by this bad news! Who'd have thought there would be limits on modern jet-age transport? When we added up all our forty-four pounds together, including Ruth May's—luckily she counted as a whole person even though she's small—we were sixty-one pounds over. Father surveyed our despair as if he'd expected it all along, and left it up to wife and daughters to sort out, suggesting only that we consider the lilies of the field, which have no need of a hand mirror or aspirin tablets.

"I reckon the lilies need *Bibles*, though, and his darn old latrine spade," Rachel muttered, as her beloved toiletry items got pitched out of the suitcase one by one. Rachel never does grasp scripture all that well.

But considering the lilies as we might, our trimming back got us nowhere close to our goal, even without Rachel's beauty aids. We were nearly stumped. And then, hallelujah! At the last possible moment, saved. Through an oversight (or else probably, if you think about it, just plain politeness), they don't weigh the passengers. The Southern Baptist Mission League gave us this hint, without coming right out and telling us to flout the law of the forty-four pounds, and from there we made our plan. We struck out for Africa carrying all our excess baggage on our bodies, under our clothes. Also, we had *clothes* under our clothes. My sisters and I left home wearing six pairs of underdrawers, two half-slips and camisoles; several dresses one on top of the other, with pedal pushers underneath; and out-side of everything an all-weather coat. (The encyclopedia advised us to count on rain). The other goods, tools, cake-mix boxes and so forth were tucked out of sight in our pockets and under our waist-bands, surrounding us in a clanking armor.

We wore our best dresses on the outside to make a good impres-sion. Rachel wore her green linen Easter suit she was so vain of, and her long whitish hair pulled off her forehead with a wide pink elas-tic hairband. Rachel is fifteen—or, as she would put it, going on sixteen—and cares for naught but appearances. Her full Christian name is Rachel *Rebeccah*, so she feels free to take after Rebekah, the virgin at the well, who is said in Genesis to be "a damsel very fair" and was offered marriage presents of golden earbobs right off the bat, when Abraham's servant spied her fetching up the water. (Since she's my elder by one year, she claims no relation to the Bible's poor Rachel, Leah's younger sister, who had to wait all those years to get married.) Sitting next to me on the plane, she kept batting her white-rabbit eyelashes and adjusting her bright pink hairband, try-ing to get me to notice she had secretly painted her fingernails bubble-gum pink to match. I glanced over at Father, who had the other window seat at the opposite end of our entire row of Prices. The sun was a blood-red ball hovering outside his window, inflaming his eyes as he kept up a lookout for Africa on the horizon. It was just lucky for Rachel he had so much else weighing on his mind. She'd been thrashed with the strap for nail polish, even at her age. But that is Rachel to a T, trying to work in just one last sin before leaving civilization. Rachel is worldly and tiresome in my opinion, so I stared out the window, where the view was better. Father feels makeup and nail polish are warning signals of prostitution, the same as pierced ears.

He was right about the lilies of the field, too. Somewhere along about the Atlantic Ocean, the six pairs of underwear and cake mixes all commenced to be a considerable cross to bear. Every time Rachel leaned over to dig in her purse she kept one hand on the chest of her linen jacket and it still made a small clinking noise. I forget now what kind of concealed household weapon she had in there. I was ignoring her, so she chattered mostly to Adah—who was ignoring her too, but since Adah never talks to anyone, it was less noticeable.

Rachel adores to poke fun at everything in Creation, but chiefly our family. "Hey, Ade!" she whispered at Adah. "What if we went on *Art Linkletter's House Party* now?"

In spite of myself, I laughed. Mr. Linkletter likes to surprise ladies by taking their purses and pulling out what all's inside for the television audience. They think it's very comical if he digs out a can opener or a picture of Herbert Hoover. Imagine if he shook *us,* and out fell pinking shears and a hatchet. The thought of it gave me nerves. Also, I felt claustrophobic and hot.

Finally, finally we lumbered like cattle off the plane and stepped down the stair ramp into the swelter of Leopoldville, and that is where our baby sister, Ruth May, pitched her blond curls forward and fainted on Mother.

She revived very promptly in the airport, which smelled of urine. I was excited and had to go to the bathroom but couldn't surmise where a girl would even begin to look, in a place like this. Big palm-tree leaves waved in the bright light outside. Crowds of people rushed past one way and then the other. The airport police wore khaki shirts with extra metal buttons and, believe you me, guns.

Everywhere you looked, there were very tiny old dark ladies lugging entire baskets of things along the order of wilting greens. Chickens, also. Little regiments of children lurked by the doorways, apparently for the express purpose of accosting foreign missionaries. The minute they saw our white skin they'd rush at us, begging in French: "*Cadeau, cadeau?*" I held up my two hands to illustrate the total and complete lack of gifts I had brought for the African children. Maybe people just hid behind a tree somewhere and squatted down, I was starting to think; maybe that's why the smell.

Just then a married couple of Baptists in tortoiseshell sunglasses came out of the crowd and shook our hands. They had the peculiar name of Underdown—Reverend and Mrs. Underdown. They'd come down to shepherd us through customs and speak French to the men in uniforms. Father made it clear we were completely self-reliant but appreciated their kindness all the same. He was so polite about it that the Underdowns didn't realize he was peeved. They carried on making a fuss as if we were all old friends and presented us with a gift of mosquito netting, just armloads of it, trailing on and on like an embarrassing bouquet from some junior-high boyfriend who liked you overly much.

As we stood there holding our netting and sweating through our complete wardrobes, they regaled us with information about our soon-to-be-home, Kilanga. Oh, they had plenty to tell, since they and their boys had once lived there and started up the whole of it, school, church, and all. At one point in time Kilanga was a regular mission with four American families and a medical doctor who visited once a week. Now it had gone into a slump, they said. No more doctor, and the Underdowns themselves had had to move to Leopoldville to give their boys a shot at proper schooling—*if*, said Mrs. Underdown, you could *even* call it that. The other missionaries to Kilanga had long since expired their terms. So it was to be just the Price family and whatever help we could muster up. They warned us not to expect much. My heart pounded, for I expected everything: jungle flowers, wild roaring beasts. God's Kingdom in its pure, unenlightened glory.

Then, while Father was smack in the middle of explaining something to the Underdowns, they suddenly hustled us onto a tiny airplane and abandoned us. It was only our family and the pilot, who was busy adjusting his earphones under his hat. He ignored us entirely, as if we were no more than ordinary cargo. There we sat, draped like tired bridesmaids with our yards of white veil, numbed by the airplane's horrible noise, skimming above the treetops. We were tuckered out, as my mother would say. "Plumb tuckered out," she would say. "Sugar, now don't you trip over that, you're tuckered out, it's plain to see." Mrs. Underdown had fussed and laughed over what she called our charming southern accent. She even tried to imitate the way we said "right now" and "bye-bye." (*"Rot nail,"* she said. *"Whah yay-es, the ayer-plane is leavin rot nail!"* and *"Bah-bah"*—like a sheep!) She caused me to feel embarrassed over our simple expressions and drawn-out vowels, when I've never before considered myself to have any accent, though naturally I'm aware we do sound worlds different from the Yanks on the radio and TV. I had quite a lot to ponder as I sat on that airplane, and incidentally I still had to pee. But we were all dizzy and silent by that time, having grown accustomed to taking up no more space in a seat than was our honest due.

At long last we bumped to a landing in a field of tall yellow grass. We all jumped out of our seats, but Father, because of his imposing stature, had to kind of crouch over inside the plane instead of standing up straight. He pronounced a hasty benediction: "Heavenly Father please make me a powerful instrument of Thy perfect will here in the Belgian Congo. Amen."

"Amen!" we answered, and then he led us out through the oval doorway into the light.

We stood blinking for a moment, staring out through the dust at a hundred dark villagers, slender and silent, swaying faintly like trees. We'd left Georgia at the height of a peach-blossom summer and now stood in a bewildering dry, red fog that seemed like no particular season you could put your finger on. In all our layers of clothing we must have resembled a family of Eskimos plopped down in a jungle.

But that was our burden, because there was so much we needed to bring here. Each one of us arrived with some extra responsibility biting into us under our garments: a claw hammer, a Baptist hymnal, each object of value replacing the weight freed up by some frivolous thing we'd found the strength to leave behind. Our journey was to be a great enterprise of balance. My father, of course, was bringing the Word of God—which fortunately weighs nothing at all.

Ruth May Price

GOD SAYS THE AFRICANS are the Tribes of Ham. Ham was the worst one of Noah's three boys: Shem, Ham, and Japheth. Everybody comes down on their family tree from just those three, because God made a big flood and drowneded out the sinners. But Shem, Ham, and Japheth got on the boat so they were A-okay.

Ham was the youngest one, like me, and he was bad. Sometimes I am bad, too. After they all got off the ark and let the animals go is when it happened. Ham found his father Noah laying around pig-naked drunk one day and he thought that was funny as all get-out. The other two brothers covered Noah up with a blanket, but Ham busted his britches laughing. When Noah woke up he got to hear the whole story from the tattletale brothers. So Noah cursed all Ham's children to be slaves for ever and ever. That's how come them to turn out dark.

Back home in Georgia they have their own school so they won't be a-strutting into Rachel's and Leah and Adah's school. Leah and Adah are the gifted children, but they still have to go to the same school as everybody. But not the colored children. The man in church said they're different from us and needs ought to keep to their own. Jimmy Crow says that, and he makes the laws. They don't come in the White Castle restaurant where Mama takes us to get Cokes either, or the Zoo. Their day for the Zoo is Thursday. That's in the Bible.

Our village is going to have this many white people: me, Rachel, Leah, and Adah. Mama. Father. That is six people. Rachel is oldest, I am youngest. Leah and Adah are in between and they're twins, so maybe they are one person, but I think two, because Leah runs everywhere and climbs trees, but Adah can't, she is bad on one whole side and doesn't talk because she is brain-damaged and also hates us all. She reads books upside down. You are only supposed to hate the Devil, and love everybody else.

My name is Ruth May and I hate the Devil. For the longest time I used to think my name was Sugar. Mama always says that. *Sugar, come here a minute. Sugar, now don't do that.*

In Sunday school Rex Minton said we better not go to the Congo on account of the cannibal natives would boil us in a pot and eat us up. He said, I can talk like a native, listen here: Ugga bugga bugga lugga. He said that means, I'll have me a drumstick off'n that little one with the curly yellow hair. Our Sunday-school teacher Miss Bannie told him to hush up. But I tell you what, she didn't say one way or the other about them boiling us in a pot and eating us up. So I don't know.

Here are the other white people we had in Africa so far: Mister Axelroot that flies the plane. He has got the dirtiest hat you ever saw. He lives way on down by the airplane field in a shack by himself whenever he comes over here, and Mama says that's close enough quarters for *him*. Reverent and Misrus Underdown, who started the African children on going to church way back years ago. The Underdowns talk French to each other even though they are white people. I don't know why. They have their own two boys, the Underdown boys, that are big and go to school in Leopoldville. They felt sorry for us so they sent us comic books to take on the airplane with us. I got almost all of them to myself when Leah and them all went to sleep on the airplane. *Donald Duck. Lone Ranger.* And the fairy-tale ones, *Cinderella* and *Briar Rose*. I hid them in a place. Then I got to feeling bad and upchucked on the airplane, and it got all over a duffel bag and the *Donald Duck*. I put that one under the cushion so we don't have it anymore.

So this is who all will be in our village: the Price family, Lone Ranger, Cinderella, Briar Rose, and the Tribes of Ham.

Rachel Price

MAN OH MAN, are we in for it now, was my thinking about the Congo from the instant we first set foot. We are supposed to be calling the shots here, but it doesn't look to me like we're in charge of a thing, not even our own selves. Father had planned a big old prayer meeting as a welcome ceremony, to prove that God had ensued us here and aimed to settle in. But when we stepped off the airplane and staggered out into the field with our bags, the Congolese people surrounded us—*Lordy!*—in a chanting broil. Charmed, I'm sure. We got fumigated with the odor of perspirating bodies. What I should have stuffed in my purse was those five-day deodorant pads.

I looked around for my sisters to tell them, "Hey, Ade, Leah, aren't you glad you use Dial? Don't you wish everybody did?" I couldn't find either one of the twins but did catch sight of Ruth May fixing to executrate her second swoon of the day. Her eyes were rolled back with mostly the whites showing. Whatever was pulling her under, I knew she was opposing it with all her might. Ruth May is surprisingly stubborn for a child of five and unwilling to miss out on any kind of a spree.

Mother took hold of her hand and also mine—something I would not have tolerated in the slightest back home in Bethlehem. But here in all the hubbub we would have lost track of each other, with how we were just getting swept along on a big dark river of people. And the dirt, law! There was dirt everywhere like red chalk dust, and me with my good green linen suit on the outside, wouldn't you know. I could just feel the grit in my hair, which is so extremely fair it is prone to get stained. Boy, what a place. Already I was heavy-hearted in my soul for the flush commodes and machine-washed clothes and other simple things in life I have took for granite.

The people were hurrying us on down toward some kind of open dirt-floor patio with a roof over it, which as it turned out was going to be our father's church. Just our luck, a church made of dirt. But worship was not on the docket that night, let me tell you. We ended up there in the throng under the thatched roof and I almost screamed when I realized the hand I held was not my mother's but a thick brown claw, a stranger! What I trusted was gone. I just plumb let go, and the earth reeled beneath me. I threw my eyes around in panic like Black Beauty trapped in the flames. Finally I spotted my mother's white shirtwaist like the flag of "We Give Up!" waving near Father. Then, one by one, I found the pastel shapes of my sisters like party balloons but in the wrong party, man oh man. I knew right then I was in the sloop of despond. Father, on the other hand, was probably all deeply gratified, just gratified up one side and down the other. Praising Jesus for this occasion to which we were all going to have to rise.

We needed desperately to change—the extra underwear and dresses were dragging us down—but there was no chance whatso-ever for that. None. We just got shoved straight into the heathen pandemony. I have no idea where our suitcases and canvas bags had gone to. My embroidery hoops and a pair of pinking shears in an oilcloth sheath hung around my neck, threatening myself and others in the push and shove. Finally we were allowed to sit down about as close together as humanly possible at a table, on an oily bench made out of rough logs. Day one in the Congo, and here my brand-new tulip-tailored linen suit in Poison Green with square mother-of-pearl buttons was fixing to give up the goat. We had to sit so close to other people there wasn't room to breathe, if you even wanted to, being in the position to contract every kind of a germ there was. Another thing we should have brought: Listerine. Forty-five percent fewer colds. A roar of voices and weird birds lombarded my ears and filled my head to the brink. I am sensitive to noise of any kind—that and the bright sunlight both give me tension headaches, but the sun at least by then had gone down. Otherwise I probably would have followed Ruth May's example and passed out or upchucked, her two big accomplishments of the day. The back of my neck felt pinched, and my heart smote like a drum. They had made a horrible roaring fire in one end of the church. Oily smoke hung above us like a net, drooping under the thatched roof. The scent of it was strong enough to choke any animal you can think of. Inside the bright orange rim of the fire I could see the outline of some dark thing being turned and pierced, with its four stiff legs flung out in a cry for help. My woman's intuition told me I was slated to die here and now, without my mother's palm even to feel the sweat on my forehead. I thought of the few occasions in my life up to now when I had tried—I admit—to bring on a fever to avoid school or church. Now a real fire beat in my temples, all the fevers I'd ever begged for, caught up to me at last.

All at once I understood the pinch on my neck was Mother. She had all four of us within the reach of her long arms: Ruth May, me, and my sisters Leah and Adah—Ruth May just small, of course, but Leah and Adah being a pretty good-sized pair of twins, although with Adah being the shorter because of her handicap. How Mother managed to keep a grip on us all like that is beyond me, I'm sure. And the beat of my heart was not my heart, I finally figured out, but the drums. The men were pounding on big loggedy-looking drums, and women were singing high, quavery tunes like birds gone crazy in the full moon. They called the songs back and forth in their own language between a leader and the rest of the group. They were such weird songs it took me a while to realize they followed the tunes of Christian hymns, "Onward Christian Soldiers" and "What a Friend I Have in Jesus," which made my skin crawl. I guess they have a right to sing them, but here's the thing: right in front of our very eyes, some of the women stood up there in the firelight with their bosoms naked as a jaybird's egg. Some of them were dancing, and others merely ran around cooking, as if nakedness were nothing special. They passed back and forth with pots and kettles, all bare-chested and unashamed. They were very busy with the animal in the fire, pulling it to pieces now and mixing it with something steaming in a pot. Whenever they bent over, their heavy breasts swung down like balloons full of water. I kept my eyes turned away from them, and from the naked children who clung to their long draped skirts. I kept glancing over at Father, wondering, Am I the only one getting shocked to smithereens here? He had that narrow-eyed, lockjawed look like he was starting to get steamed up, but you never know exactly where that's going to lead. Mostly someplace where you wish you were anyplace *but*.

After a good long hootenanny of so-called hymns shouted back and forth, the burnt offering was out of the fire and into the frying pan so to speak, all mixed up into a gray-looking, smoldering stew. They started plunking it down in front of us in tin plates or bowls. The spoons they gave us were big old metal soup ladles, which I knew would never fit into my mouth. I have such a small mouth, my wisdom teeth are coming in all sigoggling. I looked around for someone to trade spoons with, but lo and behold, nobody but our family even had any kind of a spoon at all! What the others aimed to do with their food, I wouldn't hazard to guess. Most of them were still waiting to get served, like birds in the wilderness. They held up their empty metal bowls or hubcaps or whatnot and cheerfully beat them like drums. It sounded like an entire junkyard orchestra, because everybody's plate was different. Ruth May just had a little tiny cup, which I knew she would resent because it made her seem more of a baby.

In all the ruckus, somebody was talking English. It just dawned on me all of a sudden. It was near about impossible to make out what was going on, because people all around us were singing, dancing, banging their plates, waving their arms back and forth like trees in a hurricane. But up by the bonfire where they were cooking, a coal-black man in a yellow shirt with the sleeves rolled up was gesturing towards us and hollering at the top of his lungs: "Welcome! We welcome you!"

There was another man behind him, much older and dressed just out of this world, with a tall hat and glasses and a cloth drapery dress and swishing an animal's tail back and forth. He hollowed something in their language and everybody began to pipe down just a hair.

"Reverend and Mrs. Price and your children!" cried the younger man in the yellow shirt. "You are welcome to our feast. Today we have killed a goat to celebrate your coming. Soon your bellies will be full with our *fufu pili-pili*."

At that, why, the half-naked women behind him just burst out clapping and cheering, as if they could no longer confine their enthusiasm for a dead goat.

"Reverend Price," the man said, "please offer with us a word of thanks for this feast."

He gestured for Father to come forward, but Father needed no invitation, it seems. He was already on his feet, away up on his chair, so he looked ten feet tall. He was in his shirtsleeves, which was not an unusual sight as he's one of those men that's easy in his body and in the heat of a sermon will often throw off his suit jacket. His pleated black trousers were belted tight but his chest and shoulders looked just huge. I'd almost forgotten, he still carried numerous deadly weapons under that clean white shirt.

Slowly Father raised one arm above his head like one of those gods they had in Roman times, fixing to send down the thunderbolts and the lightning. Everyone looked up at him, smiling, clapping, waving their arms over their heads, bare bosoms and all. Then he began to speak. It was not so much a speech as a rising storm.

"The Lord rideth," he said, low and threatening, "upon a swift cloud, and shall come into Egypt."

Hurray! they all cheered, but I felt a knot in my stomach. He was getting that look he gets, oh boy, like Here comes Moses tromping down off of Mount Syanide with ten fresh ways to wreck your life.

"*Into* Egypt," he shouted in his rising singsong preaching voice that goes high and low, then higher and lower, back and forth like a saw ripping into a tree trunk, "and *every* corner *of* the earth where *His light*," Father paused, glaring all about him, "where His *light* has *yet* to *fall!*"

He paused for breath and began again, swaying ever so faintly as he sang out: "The Lord *rideth* in the person of His *angels of mercy,* His emissaries of *holiness* into the *cities* on the plain, where *Lot* dwelled amongst the *sinners!*"

The cheers were slowing down. He had everybody's attention now.

"And Lot *said* unto the *sinners* who *crowded* at his door, I *pray* ye, *brethren*, do not do so *wickedly!* For the *sinners* of *Sodom* pressed their *evil will* against the entrance to his *household.*"

I shuddered. Naturally I knew Chapter 19 of Genesis, which he'd made us copy out time and again. I detest the part where Lot offered his own virgin daughters to the rabble of sinners, to do with as they might, just so they'd forget about God's angels that were visiting and leave them be. What kind of a trade is that? And his poor wife, of course, got turned to a pillar of salt.

But Father skipped over all that and went straight to the dire consequences: "The *emissaries* of the Lord *smote* the sinners, who had come *heedless* to the sight of God, *heedless in their nakedness.*"

Then he stopped, just froze perfectly still. With one of his huge hands he reached out to the congregation, pulling them in. With the other, he pointed at a woman near the fire. Her big long breasts lay flat on her chest like they'd been pressed down with an iron, but she did seem heedless of it. She was toting a long-legged child all straddly on her hip, and with her free hand was scratching at her short hair. She looked around nervously, for every pair of eyes in the place had followed Father's accusing gaze straight to her nakedness. She bounced her knees, shifting the big child upwards on her hip. His head lolled. He had hair that stood out in reddish tufts and he looked dazed. For an eternity of silence the mother stood there in the spotlight, drawing her head back on her neck in fear and puzzlement. Finally she turned around and picked up a long wooden spoon and went to poking at the stew kettle.

"Nakedness," Father repeated, "and *darkness* of the *soul!* For we shall *destroy* this place where the *loud clamor* of the *sinners* is waxen *great* before the *face* of the Lord."

No one sang or cheered anymore. Whether or not they understood the meaning of "loud clamor," they didn't dare be making one now. They did not even breathe, or so it seemed. Father can get a good deal across with just his tone of voice, believe you me. The woman with the child on her hip kept her back turned, tending to the food.

"And Lot went out and *spake* unto those that were *worthy*." Now Father was using his gentler, simmering-down tone. "And Lot said unto them, '*Up*! Get ye *out* from this place of *darkness*! *Arise* and come forward into a *brighter land!*'

"O Lord, let us pray," he concluded, landing abruptly back down on earth. "Lord, grant that the worthy among us here shall rise above wickedness and come out of the darkness into the wondrous light of our Holy Father. Amen."

All faces were still set on my father, as if they all were shiny, dark plants and his red head was the sun. But their expressions had fallen in slow motion from joy to confusion to dismay. Now, as the spell broke, people began to mutter and move about. A few women lifted up their wraparound sarongs and tied them in front, to cover their breasts. Others gathered up their bare-bottomed children and moved out into the darkness. I guess they were going home to bed without any supper.

The air above our heads grew perfectly quiet. There was not a peep to be heard but katydid noises outside in the deep, black night.

Well, there was nothing now but to dig in. With everyone's eyes upon us, my sisters and I picked up our big metal spoons. The food they'd set before us was a stew that tasted like pure nothing, just wet clumps stuffed in my mouth that I would have to chew into glue. Once I took it in, though, the very first bite slowly grew to a powerful burn on my tongue. It scorched my eardrums from the inside. Tears ran from my eyes and I couldn't swallow. This was going to be the start of a real crying jag, I had the feeling, for a girl whose only hopes for the year were a sweet-sixteen party and a pink mohair twin set.

Ruth May choked out loud and made a horrible face. Mother leaned over, to slap her on the back, I thought, but instead she whispered at us in the awfulest, hissing voice: "Girls, you be polite, do you hear me? I'm sorry but if you spit that out I will thrash you to an inch of your lives."

This was *Mother*, who'd never laid a hand on us in all our lives! Oh, I got the picture, right there, our first night in Africa. I sat breathing through my nose, holding in my mouth the pure, awful slavor of something on fire and a bristle of stiff hairs from the burnt hide of a dead goat. I shut my eyes tight, but even so, the tears ran down. I wept for the sins of all who had brought my family to this dread dark shore.

Adah Price

SUNRISE TANTALIZE, evil eyes hypnotize: that is the morning, Congo pink. Any morning, every morning. Blossomy rose-color birdsong air streaked sour with breakfast cookfires. A wide red plank of dirt—the so-called road—flat-out in front of us, continuous in theory from here to somewhere distant. But the way I see it through my Adah eyes it is a flat plank clipped into pieces, rectangles and trapezoids, by the skinny black-line shadows of tall palm trunks. Through Adah eyes, oh the world is a-boggle with colors and shapes competing for a half-brain's attention. The parade never stops. Into the jangled pieces of road little jungle roosters step from the bush, karkadoodling. They jerk up their feet with cocky roosterness as if they have not yet heard about the two-legged beasts who are going to make slaves of their wives.

Congo sprawls on the middle of the world. Sun rises, sun sets, six o'clock exactly. Everything that comes of morning undoes itself before nightfall: rooster walks back into forest, fires die down, birds coo-coo-coo, sun sinks away, sky bleeds, passes out, goes dark, nothing exists. Ashes to ashes.

Kilanga village runs along the Kwilu River as a long row of little mud houses set after-one-the-other beside a lone red snake of dirt road. Rising up all round us, trees and bamboo. Leah and I as babies had a long, hodgepodge string of unmatched beads for dress-up which would break when we fought over it and fly into a snaking line of odds and ends in the dirt. That is how Kilanga looked from the airplane. Every red mud house squats in the middle of its red dirt yard, for the ground in the village is cleared hairless as a brick.

The better to spy and kill our friends the snakes when they come calling, we are told. So Kilanga is a long low snake break clearing. In a long row the dirt huts all kneel facing east, as if praying for the staved-off collapse—not toward Mecca exactly but east toward the village's one road and the river and behind all that, the pink sunrise surprise.

The church building, scene of our recent feast, resides at one end of the village. At the other end, our own house. And so when the Price family strolls to church we are able en route to peer straight into each and every villager's house. Every house has only a single square room and a thatched roof, under which might dwell the likes of Robinson Crusoe. But no one here stays under a roof. It is in the front yards—all the world's a stage of hard red dirt under bare foot—where tired thin women in every thinkable state of dress and disrepair poke sticks into their little fires and cook. Clumps of children stonethrowing outflowing rush upon terrified small goats, scattering them across the road so that the goats may tiptoe back and be chased again. Men sit on buckets and stare at whatsoever passes by. The usual bypasser is a woman sauntering slowly down the road with bundles upon bundles balanced on her head. These women are pillars of wonder, defying gravity while wearing the ho-hum aspect of perfect tedium. They can sit, stand, talk, shake a stick at a drunk man, reach around their backs to fetch forth a baby to nurse, all without dropping their piled-high bundles upon bundles. They are like ballet dancers entirely unaware they are on stage. I cannot take my eyes from them.

Whenever a woman leaves her wide-open-to-the-world yard to work her field or saunter off on an errand, first she must make her-self decent. To do this, even though she is already wearing a wrap-around skirt, she will go and get another large square of cloth from the house, which she wraps around her first skirt—covering her legs right down to the instep of her foot—into a long, narrow sarong tied below her bare breasts. The cloths are brightly printed and worn together in jangling mixtures that ring in my ears: pink gingham with orange plaid, for example. Loose-joint breaking-point colors, and whether you find them beautiful or find them appalling, they do make the women seem more festive, and less exhausted.

Backdrop to the Kilanga pageant, rising up behind the houses, a tall wall of elephant grass obscures our view of anything but the distance. The sun suspended above it in the afternoon is a pink, round dot in the distant white haze you may stare at and never go blind. The real earth where the real sun shines seems to be somewhere else, far from here. And to the east of us, behind the river, a rising rumple of dark green hills folded on each other like a great old tablecloth, receding to pale hazy blue. "Looming like the Judgment," says our mother, pausing to wipe her damp forehead with the back of her hand.

"It's a place right out of a storybook," my twin sister, Leah, loves to declare in response, opening her eyes wide and sticking her short hair behind her ears as if to hear and see every little thing oh so much better. "And yet this is our own family, the Prices, living here!"

Next comes this observation from my sister Ruth May: "Nobody here's got very many teeth." And finally, from Rachel: "Jeez oh man, wake me up when it's over." And so the Price family passes its judgments. All but Adah. Adah unpasses her judgments. I am the one who does not speak.

Our Father speaks for all of us, as far as I can see. And he is at the moment not saying much. His hammer turned out to be a waste of two or three good pounds, because there appear to be no nails in the mud-and-thatch town of Kilanga. The wide-open building that serves as church and school was built of concrete-block pillars holding up a roof of palm thatch and billowy clouds of scarlet bougainvillea. By now it all seems more or less welded together by its own decay. Our house is also mud, thatch, cement, and flowering vines. Leah in her earnest way helped him scout around for a project, but alas he found nothing worth pounding at, anywhere. This was a great disappointment to Our Father, who likes to repair things between Sundays.

Yet here we are to stay. The bush plane that dropped down into the field to leave us here went right away again, and there will be no more coming-going until that same plane returns again. We asked about the dirt road through the village and were told it stretched all the way to Leopoldville. I doubt it. A short way on either side of our village the road falls into a frenzy of hard dirt ruts that look like ocean waves frozen solid in the middle of a tempest. Our Father says in the great beyond nearby there are probably swamps you could sink a battleship in, not to mention a mere automobile. We do see vestigial signs of automobiles in our village, but they resemble the signs of life you would dig up in a graveyard if you were inclined to that pastime. Which is to say: parts dead and rusted, scattered around and used not for transportation but for anything but. On a walk one day with Our Father he pointed out for his daughters' edification a carburetor air-filter lid boiling a family's dinner over a cookfire, and a Jeep muffler being put to use by six boys at once, as a drum.

The Kwilu River is the throughway here: Kwilu, a word without a single rhyme. Nearly a prelude, but not quite. Kwilu. It troubles me, this dubious escape route. It sits unanswered like a half-phrase of music on my ear.

Our Father claims the Kwilu is navigable downstream from here all the way to where it joins the Congo River; upstream, one may go only as far as the high, scenic cataracts that thunder just to the south of us. In other words, we have arrived very nearly at the end of the earth. We sometimes do see the odd boat passing by, but only carrying people from nearby villages exactly like this one. For news or mail or evidence of what Rachel calls The Pale Which We Are Way Beyond, we wait for the rough-and-ready airplane pilot, Mr. Eeben Axelroot. He is reliable in the following way: if they say he is coming on Monday, it will be Thursday, Friday, or not at all.

Like the village road and the river, nothing here really continues to its end. The Congo is only a long path that takes you from one hidden place to another. Palm trees stand alongside of it looking down at you in shock, like too-tall, frightened women with upright hair. Nevertheless, I am determined I will walk that path, even though I do not walk fast or well. My right side drags. I was born with half my brain dried up like a prune, deprived of blood by an unfortunate fetal mishap. My twin sister, Leah, and I are identical in theory, just as in theory we are all made in God's image. Leah and Adah began our life as images mirror perfect. We have the same eyes dark and chestnut hair. But I am a lame gallimaufry and she remains perfect.

Oh, I can easily imagine the fetal mishap: we were inside the womb together dum-de-dum when Leah suddenly turned and declared, Adah you are just too slow. I am taking all the nourishment here and going on ahead. She grew strong as I grew weak. (Yes! Jesus loves me!) And so it came to pass, in the Eden of our mother's womb, I was cannibalized by my sister.

Officially my condition is called hemiplegia. *Hemi* is half, hemisphere, hemmed-in, hemlock, hem and haw. *Plegia* is the cessation of motion. After our complicated birth, physicians in Atlanta pronounced many diagnoses on my asymmetrical brain, including Wernicke's and Broca's aphasia, and sent my parents home over the icy roads on Christmas Eve with one-half a set of perfect twins and the prediction that I might possibly someday learn to read but would never speak a word. My parents seem to have taken this well in stride. I am sure the Reverend explained to his exhausted wife that it was the will of God, who could plainly see—with these two additional girls so close after the first one—our house had enough females in it now to fill it up with blabber. They did not even have Ruth May yet, but did have a female dog that howled, Our Father still likes to say, Like One Too Many Sopranos in Church. The Dog that Broke The Camel's Back, he also calls it. Our Father probably interpreted Broca's aphasia as God's Christmas bonus to one of His worthier employees.

I am prone to let the doctors' prophecy rest and keep my thoughts to myself. Silence has many advantages. When you do not speak, other people presume you to be deaf or feeble-minded and promptly make a show of their own limitations. Only occasionally do I find I have to break my peace: shout or be lost in the shuffle. But mostly am lost in the shuffle. I write and draw in my notebook and read anything I please.

It is true I do not speak as well as I can think. But that is true of most people, as nearly as I can tell.

Leah

IN THE BEGINNING my sisters bustled indoors, playing the role of mother's helper with more enthusiasm than they'd ever shown for housework in all their born days. For one reason only: they were scared to set foot outside the house. Ruth May had the bizarre idea that our neighbors desired to eat her. Rachel, who sighted imaginary snakes at the least provocation, said, "Jeez oh man," rolled her eyes, and announced her plan to pass the next twelve months in bed. If they gave out prizes for being sick, Rachel would win the gold bricks. But soon she got bored and dredged herself up to see what all was going on. She and Adah and Ruth May helped unpack and set up housekeeping. The first task was to pull out all the mosquito netting and stitch it into tents to cover our four identical cots and my parents' larger one. Malaria is our enemy number one. Every Sunday we swallow quinine tablets so bitter your tongue wants to turn itself inside out like a salted slug. But Mrs. Underdown warned us that, pills or no pills, too many mosquito bites could still overtake the quinine in our blood and spell our doom.

I personally set myself apart from the war on blood parasites. I preferred to help my father work on his garden. I've always been the one for outdoor chores anyway, burning the trash and weeding, while my sisters squabbled about the dishes and such. Back home we have the most glorious garden each and every summer, so it's only natural that my father thought to bring over seeds in his pockets: Kentucky Wonder beans, crookneck and patty-pan squash, Big Boy tomatoes. He planned to make a demonstration garden, from which we'd gather a harvest for our table and also supply food and seeds to the villagers. It was to be our first African miracle: an infinite chain of benevolence rising from these small, crackling seed packets, stretching out from our garden into a circle of other gardens, flowing outward across the Congo like ripples from a rock dropped in a pond. The grace of our good intentions made me feel wise, blessed, and safe from snakes.

But there was no time to waste. About as soon as we'd knelt on our own humble threshold in a prayer of thanks, moved in, and shed our kitchen goods and all but the minimum decent requirement of clothing, Father started clearing a plot of ground out of the jungle's edge near our house, and pacing off rows. He took big goose steps—giant steps, we'd have called them, if he had first asked, "Mother May I?" But my father needs permission only from the Saviour, who obviously is all in favor of subduing the untamed wilderness for a garden.

He beat down a square of tall grass and wild pink flowers, all without once ever looking at me. Then he bent over and began to rip out long handfuls of grass with quick, energetic jerks as though tearing out the hair of the world. He wore his cuffed, baggy work khakis and a short-sleeved white shirt, and labored at the center of a rising red cloud of dust like a crew-cut genie who'd just appeared there. A fur of red dust gathered on the curly hairs of his forearms, and rivulets of perspiration ran down his temples. The tendon of his jaw was working, so I knew he was preparing a revelation. The education of his family's souls is never far from my father's thoughts. He often says he views himself as the captain of a sinking mess of female minds. I know he must find me tiresome, yet still I like spending time with my father very much more than I like doing anything else.

"Leah," he inquired at last, "why do you think the Lord gave us seeds to grow, instead of having our dinner just spring up out there on the ground like a bunch of field rocks?"

Now *that* was an arresting picture. While I was considering it, he took up the hoe blade that had crossed the Atlantic in our mother's purse and shoved it onto a long pole he'd whittled to fit its socket. Why *did* the Lord give us seeds? Well, they were sure easier to stuff in our pockets than whole vegetables would have been, but I doubted if God took any real interest in travel difficulties. I was exactly fourteen and a half that month, and still getting used to the embarrassment of having the monthly visits. I believe in God with all my might, but have been thinking lately that most of the details seem pretty much beneath His dignity.

I confessed I didn't know the answer.

He tested the heft and strength of his hoe handle and studied me. He is very imposing, my father, with broad shoulders and unusually large hands. He's the handsome, sandy-haired type that people presume to be Scottish and energetic, though possibly fiery-tempered.

"Because, Leah, the Lord helps those that help themselves."

"Oh!" I cried, my heart rushing to my throat, for of course I had known *that*. If only I could ever bring forth all that I knew quickly enough to suit Father.

"God created a world of work and rewards," he elaborated, "on a big balanced scale." He brought his handkerchief out of his pocket to ream the sweat, carefully, out of one eye socket and then the other. He has a scar on his temple and poor vision on the left side, from a war injury he doesn't ever talk about, not being one to boast. He refolded the handkerchief and returned it to his pocket. Then he handed me the hoe and held his hands out from his sides, palms up, to illustrate the heavenly balancing act. "Small works of goodness over here," he let his left hand drop slightly, "small rewards over here." His right hand dropped just a mite with the weight of an almost insignificant reward. "Great sacrifice, great rewards!" he said then, letting both hands fall heavily from the shoulders, and with all my soul I coveted the delicious weight of goodness he cradled in those palms.

Then he rubbed his hands together, finished with the lesson and with me. "God merely expects us to do our own share of the perspiring for life's bounty, Leah."

He took back the hoe and proceeded to hack out a small, square dominion over the jungle, attacking his task with such muscular vigor we would surely, and soon, have tomatoes and beans coming out our ears. I knew God's scale to be vast and perfectly accurate: I pictured it as a much larger version of the one at the butcher's counter in the Bethlehem Piggly Wiggly. I vowed to work hard for His favor, surpassing all others in my devotion to turning the soil for God's great glory. Someday perhaps I shall demonstrate to all of Africa how to grow crops! Without complaint I fetched bucket after bucket of water from the big galvanized tub on the porch, so he could douse the plot a little at a time ahead of his hoe, to hold down the awful dust. The red mud dried on his khakis like the blood of a slain beast. I walked behind him and found the severed heads of many small, bright orange orchids. I held one close to my eye. It was delicate and extraordinary, with a bulbous yellow tongue and maroon-spotted throat. Nobody had ever planted these flowers, I felt sure, nor harvested them either; these were works that the Lord had gone ahead and finished on His own. He must have lacked faith in mankind's follow-through capabilities, on the day He created flowers.

Mama Bekwa Tataba stood watching us—a little jet-black woman. Her elbows stuck out like wings, and a huge white enameled tub occupied the space above her head, somewhat miraculously holding steady while her head moved in quick jerks to the right and left. Mama Tataba's job, we were surprised to learn, was to live with us and earn a small stipend by doing the same work she'd done for our forerunner in the Kilanga Mission, Brother Fowles. He'd left us two boarders, in fact: Mama Tataba and a parrot named Methuselah. Both had been trained by him in the English language and evidently a good deal else, for Brother Fowles left some mystery in his wake. I gathered through overhearing my parents that Brother Fowles had entered into unconventional alliances with the local people, and too he was a Yankee. I heard them saying he was New York Irish, which tells you a lot, as they are notorious for being papist Catholics. Father explained to us that he had gone plumb crazy, consorting with the inhabitants of the land.

That's why the Mission League finally allowed us to come. At first they'd insulted my father by turning us down, even after our Bethlehem congregation had done special tithes for a whole year to fly us here for the perfusion of Jesus' name. But no one else volunteered for the Kilanga post, and the Underdowns had requested that it be taken by someone steady, with a family. Well, we were a family all right, and my father is steady as a stump. Still, the Underdowns insisted that our mission last no more than one year—not enough time for going plumb crazy but only partway, I guess, even if things went poorly.

Brother Fowles had been in Kilanga six years, which really when you think about it is long enough for about any kind of backsliding you could name. There was no telling how he might have influenced Mama Tataba. But we needed her help. She carried all our water up from the river and cleaned and lit the kerosene lamps and split wood and built the fire in the cookstove and threw buckets of ash down the hole in the outhouse and paused to kill snakes more or less as a distraction between heavier jobs. My sisters and I stood in awe of Mama Tataba, but were not quite used to her yet. She had a blind eye. It looked like an egg whose yolk had been broken and stirred just once. As she stood there by our garden, I stared at her bad eye, while her good eye stared at my father.

"What you be dig for? Worm grub?" she demanded. She turned her head slightly from side to side, surveying my father's work with what he calls her "acute monocular beam." The galvanized bucket remained perfectly still on top of her head—a great, levitating crown.

"We're cultivating the soil, sister," he said.

"That one, brother, he bite," she said, pointing her knuckly hand at a small tree he was wresting from his garden plot. White sap oozed from the torn bark. My father wiped his hands on his trousers.

"Poisonwood," she added flatly, emphasizing the descending syllables as if she were equally tired of all three.

My father mopped his brow again and launched into the parable of the one mustard seed falling on a barren place, and the other one on good soil. I thought of the bright pointy-nosed mustard bottles we used in abundance at church wiener suppers—a world apart from anything Mama Tataba had ever seen. Father had the job of his life cut out for him, bringing the Word to a place like this. I wanted to throw my arms around his weary neck and pat down his rumpled hair.

Mama Tataba seemed not to be listening. She pointed again at the red dirt. "You got to be make hills."

He stood his ground, my father, tall as Goliath and pure of heart as David. A film of red dust on his hair and eyebrows and the tip of his strong chin gave him a fiendish look untrue to his nature. He ran his large, freckled hand across the side of his head, where his hair was shaved close, and then through the tousled crown, where Mother lets it grow longer. All this while inspecting Mama Tataba with Christian tolerance, taking his time to formulate the message.

"Mama Tataba," he said at last, "I've been tending the soil ever since I could walk behind my father."

When he says anything at all, even a simple thing about a car or a plumbing repair, it tends to come out like this—in terms that can be interpreted as sacred.

Mama Tataba kicked the dirt with her flat, naked sole and looked disgusted. "He won't be grow. You got to be make hills," she stated, then turned on her heel and went in the house to help my mother slosh Clorox water across the floor to kill the hookworms.

I was shocked. In Georgia I'd seen people angered by my father before, or intimidated, but not contemptuous. Never.

"What does she mean, make hills?" I asked. "And why did she think a plant could bite you?"

He showed no trace of concern, though his hair blazed as if it had caught fire in the late-afternoon light. "Leah, our world is filled with mystery" was his confident reply.

Among all of Africa's mysteries, here were the few that revealed themselves in no time flat. My father woke up the next morning with a horrible rash on his hands and arms, presumably wounded by the plant that bites. Even his good right eye was swollen shut, from where he'd wiped his brow. Yellow pus ran like sap from his welted flesh. He bellowed when Mother tried to apply the salve. "I ask you, how did I earn this?" we heard him roar in their bedroom, through the closed door. "Ow! Great God almighty, Orleanna. How did this curse come to me, when it's God's own will to cultivate the soil!" The door flew open with a bang, and Father barreled out. Mother chased him with bandages but he batted her roughly away and went outside to pace the porch. In the long run, though, he had to come back in and let her tend to him. She had to bind his hands in clean rags before he could even pick up a fork, or the Bible.

Right after prayers I went out to check the progress of our garden, and was stunned to see what Mama Tataba had meant by hills: to me they looked like graves, as wide and long as a regular dead human. She had reshaped our garden overnight into eight neat burial mounds. I fetched my father, who came walking fast as if I'd discovered a viper he meant to behead. My father by then was in a paroxysm of exasperation. He squinted long and hard with his bad eye, to make out the fix our garden was in. Then the two of us together, without a word passing between us, leveled it out again as flat as the Great Plains. I did all the hoeing myself, to spare his afflicted hands. With my forefinger I ran long, straight furrows and we folded into them more of our precious seeds. We stuck the bright seed packets on sticks at the ends of the rows—squash, beans, Halloween pumpkins—to remind us what to expect.

Several days later, once Father had regained his composure and both his eyes, he assured me that Mama Tataba hadn't meant to ruin our demonstration garden. There was such a thing as native customs, he said. We would need the patience of Job. "She's only trying to help, in her way," he said.

This is what I most admire about Father: no matter how bad things might get, he eventually will find the grace to compose himself. Some people find him overly stern and frightening, but that is only because he was gifted with such keen judgment and purity of heart. He has been singled out for a life of trial, as Jesus was. Being always the first to spot flaws and transgressions, it falls upon Father to deliver penance. Yet he is always ready to acknowledge the potential salvation that resides in a sinner's heart. I know that some-day, when I've grown large enough in the Holy Spirit, I will have his wholehearted approval.

Not everyone can see it, but my father's heart is as large as his hands. And his wisdom is great. He was never one of those back-woods ministers who urge the taking up of copperhead snakes, baby-flinging, or the shrieking of nonsense syllables. My father believes in enlightenment. As a boy he taught himself to read parts of the Bible in Hebrew, and before we came to Africa he made us all sit down and study French, for the furtherance of our mission. He has already been so many places, including another jungle over-seas, in the Philippine Islands, where he was a wounded hero in the Second World War. So he's seen about everything.

Rachel

ON CONGO EASTER SUNDAY there were no new clothes for the Price girls, that's for sure. We tromped off to church in the same old shoes and dresses we'd worn all the other African Sundays so far. No white gloves, it goes without saying. And no primping, because the only mirror we have in the house is my faux-ivory hand mirror brought from home, which we all have to share. Mother set it on the desk in the living room, propped against the wall, and every time Mama Tataba walks by it she yelps like a snake bit her. So: Easter Sunday in dirt-stained saddle oxfords, charmed I'm sure. As far as my sisters are concerned I have to say they didn't care. Ruth May is the type to wear rolled-up Blue Bell jeans to her own funeral, and the twins too, they've never cared a hoot what they looked like. They spent so much time staring at each other's faces before they were born they can go the rest of their lives passing up mirrors without a glance.

While we're on the subject, you should see what the Congolese run around in. Children dressed up in the ragbags of Baptist charity or else nothing at all. Color coordination is not a strong point. Grown men and women seem to think a red plaid and a pink floral print are complementary colors. The women wear a sarong made of one fabric, with another big square of a different fabric wrapped over the top of it. Never jeans or trousers—not on your life. Bosoms may wave in the breeze, mind you, but legs must be strictly hidden, top secret. When Mother steps foot out of the house in her black Capri pants, why, they all just gawk and stare. As a matter of fact, a man walked into a tree in front of our house and knocked out a tooth, thanks to Mother's stretch pants. Women are expected to wear just the one style of garment and no other. But the men, now that is a course of a different color. They dress up every different way in the world: some have long shirts made from the same flowery African cloth that is attired by the women. Or they'll wear a bolt of it draped over one shoulder in the style of Hercules. Others wear American-style buttoned shirts and shorts in drab, stained colors. A few of the smaller men even go gallivanting around in little undershirts decorated with childish prints, and nobody seems to notice the joke. The one that knocked his tooth out has got himself a purple, steel-buttoned outfit that looks like a cast-off janitor uniform. As for the accessories, I hardly know where to begin. Sandals made of car tires are popular. So are antique wing tips curling up at the toes, black rubber galoshes unbuckled and flapping open, or bright pink plastic thongs, or bare feet—any of these can go with any of the before-mentioned outfits. Sunglasses, plain glasses, hats, no hats, likewise. Perhaps even a knit woolen cap with a ball on top, or a woman's bright yellow beret—I have witnessed all these wonders and more. The attitude toward clothing seems to be: if you have it, why not wear it? Some men go about their daily business prepared for the unexpected tropical snowstorm, it seems, while others wear shockingly little—a pair of shorts only. When you look around, it appears that every man here was fixing to go to a different party, and then suddenly they all got plunked here together.

So that is how Easter Sunday looked in our church. Well, anyhow it was hardly the church for crinolines and patent leather. The walls were wide open. Birds could swoop in and get your hair for their nest if they felt like it. Father had put up an altar made of palm leaves in front, which looked presentable in a rustic way, but you could still see black char and stains on the floor from the fire they made on our first night here, for the welcome feast. It was an unpleasant reminder of Sodom, Gomorrah, and so forth. I could still choke on the memory of goat meat if I thought about it. I never swallowed it. I carried one bite in my mouth all evening and spat it out behind the outhouse when we went home.

So all right, no new dresses. But I was hardly allowed to complain about *that* because, guess what. It wasn't even real Easter. We arrived smack dab in the middle of summer, far from the nearest holy day. Father was disappointed about the timing, until he made the shocking jet-age discovery that days and months do not matter one way or another to people in this village. They don't even know Sunday from Tuesday or Friday or the twelfth of Never! They just count to five, have their market day, and start over. One of the men in the congregation confided to Father that having church just every old now and then, as it seems to them, instead of on market day, has always bamfuzzled everybody about the Christians. That sure gave us a hoot! So Father had nothing to lose by announcing his own calendar and placing upon it Easter on the Fourth of July. Why not? He said he needed a focal point to get the church geared up.

Our great event for counterfeit Easter Sunday was a pageant, organized by Father and whoever else could drum up the enthusiasm. So far, for our first few weeks in Kilanga, attendance in church had been marked by almost total absence. So Father saw this pageant as a splectacular mark of things being on the upswing. Four men, including the one in the janitor uniform and another with only one leg, performed the roles of soldiers and carried real spears. (There weren't any women at the services to speak of, so they weren't going to be caught dead in any play.) At first the men wanted to have someone play out the role of Jesus and raise up from the dead, but Father opposed that on principle. So they merely dressed up as Roman guards, standing around the tomb laughing with pagan satisfaction because they'd managed to kill God, and then in the second act, leaping about, showing great dismay to find the stone rolled back.

I didn't much care for looking at those men in the pageant. We aren't all that accustomed to the African race to begin with, since back home they keep to their own parts of town. But here, of course, with everyplace being their part of town. Plus, these men in the pageant were just carrying it to the hilt. I didn't see there was any need for them to be so *African* about it. They wore steel bracelets on their black arms, and loose, flapping cloths tucked half hazardly around their waists. (Even the peg leg one!) They came running or hopping into the church, carrying the same heavy spears they would use later in the week to slew the animals. We knew they did it. Their wives came to our door daily with whole, dripping legs of something not ten minutes dead. Before the great adventure is all over, Father expects his children to eat rhinoceros, I suppose. Antelope is more or less our daily bread. They started bringing us that the very first week. Even, once, a monkey. Mama Tataba would haggle with the women at the door, and finally turn to us with her scrawny arms raised up like a boxing champ, holding up our dinner. Jeez oh man, tell me when it's over! Then she'd stomp out to the kitchen hut and build such a huge fire in the iron stove you'd think she was Cape Carniveral launching a rocket ship. She is handy at cooking anything living or dead, but heaven be praised, Mother rejected the monkey, with its little dead grin. She told Mama Tataba we could get by on things that looked less like kinfolk.

So when the men with their bloodstained spears came jingling down the aisle of our church pageant on Easter Sunday it represented progress, I'm sure, but it wasn't what Father really hoped for. He had envisioned a baptism. The whole point of Easter in July was supposed to be an altar call, followed by a joyful procession down to the river with children dressed all in white getting saved. Father would stand waist deep out there like the Baptist Saint John and hold up one hand, and in the name of the Father and the Son and the Holy Ghost he would dunk them under, one by one. The river would be jam-packed with purified souls.

There is a little stream that runs by the village, with small pools where people wash clothes and get water for drinking, but it isn't deep or wide enough for anything near the proper baptismal effect. For Father it's the wide Kwilu River and nothing less. I could see exactly how he meant the ceremony to go. It could have been, really, a pretty sight.

But the men said no, that was not to be. The women were so opposed to getting dunked in the river, even on hearsay, they all kept their children extra far from the church that day. So the dramatic points of Father's pageant were lost on most of Kilanga. What with my sisters and me, our mother, and Mama Tataba being the only females in attendance, and all the men that could walk being in the play, a higher proportion of the audience than you'd care to think was either daydreaming or examining the contents of their nostrils.

Afterwards, instead of the baptism, Father lured people down as near as he could get them to the river by means of the age-old method of a church supper. We had a picnic down on the bank of the Kwilu, which has the delightful odor of mud and dead fish. The families that would not darken the door of the church, which by the way doesn't have any door, did manage to join us for the picnic. Naturally, since we brought most of the food. They seem to think we are Santa Claus, the way the children come around begging us for food and things every single day—and us as poor as church mice! One woman who came trying to sell us her handmade baskets looked in our door and spied our scissors and asked right flat out if she could have them! Imagine having the nerve.

So they all came grandly down to the picnic: women with their heads wrapped in print cloth like birthday presents. Children wearing what few clothes they had—which even that was only for our benefit, I knew, after Father's blowup over the little dress-code problem. In a certain way they seemed naked irregardless. Some of the women had newborn babies too, teeny fawn-colored frowning things, which the mothers wrap up in great big bundles of cloths and blankets and even little woolly caps, in all this heat! Just to show how prized they are, I guess. In all this dust and dirt with hardly anything ever coming along that's shiny and new, a baby does seem like quite an event.

Of course, everyone kept staring at *me*, as they always do here. I am the most extreme blonde imaginable. I have sapphire-blue eyes, white eyelashes, and platinum blonde hair that falls to my waist. It is so fine I have to use Breck Special Formulated and don't care to think what I'll do when my one bottle that Father allowed runs out: beat my hair on a rock like Mama Tataba does with our clothes, charming. On their own initiative the Congolese seem unable to produce much in the way of hair—half of them are bald as a bug, even the girls. It is a disturbing sight to see a good-sized little girl in a ruffly dress, and not a hair on her head. Consequently they are all so envious of mine they frequently walk up boldly and give it a yank. It's surprising that my parents allow the situation to present itself. In some ways they are so strict you might as well have a Communist for your parents, but when it comes to something you really wish they'd notice, oh, well! Then parental laxity is the rule of the day.

The Easter picnic on the Fourth of July was one long, drawn-out eternity of a Congolese afternoon. The riverbank, though it looks attractive from a distance, is not so lovely once you get there: slick, smelly mudbanks framed by a tangle of bushes with gaudy orange flowers so large that if you tried to put one behind your ear like Dorothy Lamour you'd look like you were wearing a Melmac soup bowl. The River Kwilu is *not* like the River Jordan, chilly and wide. It is a lazy, rolling river as warm as bathwater, where crocodiles are said to roll around like logs. No milk and honey on the other side, either, but just more stinking jungle laying low in the haze, as far, far away as the memory of picnics in Georgia. I closed my eyes and dreamed of real soda pop in convenient throwaway cans. We all ate fried chicken that Mother had cooked, southern style, starting from scratch with killing them and lopping off their heads. These were the self-same chickens Ruth May had chased around the house that very morning before church. My sisters moped somewhat, but I nibbled my drumstick happily! Considering my whole situation, I was not about to be bothered by the spectrum of death at our picnic. I was just grateful for a crispy taste of something that connected this creepy, buzzing heat with real summertime.

The chickens had been another surprise for us, like Mama Tataba. There was just the biggest flock of black-and-white-checkered hens here waiting for us when we arrived. They were busting out of the henhouse, roosting in the trees and wherever they could find a spot, for after Brother Fowles left, they'd all gone to hiding their eggs and raising up babies during the backslide between missions. People in the village had thought of helping us out by eating a few before we got here, but Mama Tataba, I guess, kept them warded off with a stick. It was Mother who decided to contribute most of the flock for feeding the village, like a peace offering. On the morning of the picnic she had to start in at the very crack of dawn, to get all those hens killed and fried up. At the picnic she walked through the crowd passing out thighs and drumsticks to the little children, who acted just as pleased as punch, licking their fingers and singing out hymns. Yet, for all her slaving over a hot stove, Father hardly noticed how she'd won over the crowd. His mind was two million miles away. He just mostly stared out at the river, where no one was fixing to get dunked that day, whatsoever. Just big mats of floating plants going by with stilty-legged birds walking around and around on top, every one of them no doubt thinking he's king of the world.

I was sore at Father all right, for us having to be there in the first place. But it was plain to see he was put out, too, something fierce. When he gets his mind set on something you'd just as well prepare to see it through. The picnic was festive, but not at all what he'd had in mind. It was nothing, in terms of redemption.

Ruth May

IF SOMEBODY WAS HUNGRY, why would they have a big fat belly? I
don't know.

The children are named Tumba, Bangwa, Mazuzi, Nsimba, and
those things. One of them comes in our yard the most and I don't
know his name at all. He's near about big, like my sisters, but doesn't
wear a thing on God's green earth but an old gray shirt without any
buttons and baggy gray underpants. He has a big old round belly
with his belly button sticking out like a black marble. I can tell it's
him because of the shirt and underpants, not because of the belly
button. They all have those. I thought they were all fat, but Father
said no. They're hungry as can be, and don't get their vitamins. And
still God makes them look fat. I reckon that's what they get for
being the Tribes of Ham.

One of them is a girl, because of her dress. It's purple plaid, and
it's ripped right open on the bodice so one of her nipples shows,
but she just runs around a-wearing it anyway like she never noticed
and neither did anybody. She has shoes too. They used to be white
but now they're dirt-color. Anything that ever was white is not
white here. That is not a color you see. Even a white flower opening
up on a bush just looks doomed for this world.

I only got to bring me two toys: pipe cleaners, and a monkey-
sock monkey. The monkey-sock monkey has done gone already. I
left him out on the veranda and come the next morning, he was
gone. One of those little children stole, which is a bad sin. Father
says to forgive them for they know not what they do. Mama says

you can't hardly even call it a sin when they need ever little thing as bad as they do. So I don't know which one, if it was a sin or it wasn't. But I sure got mad and had a fit. I accidentally peed in my britches. My monkey-sock monkey was named Saint Matthew.

The grown-up Congo men are all named Tata Something. That one, name of Tata Undo, he is the chief. He wears a whole outfit, cat skins and everything and a hat. Father had to go see Tata Undo to pay the Devil his do. And the women are all Mama Something, even if they don't have children. Like Mama Tataba, our cooking lady. Rachel calls her Mama Tater Tots. But she won't cook those. I wish she would.

The lady in the little house that's pretty close to ours is Mama Mwanza. One time her roof caught on fire and fell on her and burnt up her legs but not the rest of her. That happened way back years ago. Mama Tataba told Mama about it in the kitchen house and I was listening. They won't talk about the bad things in front of my sisters, but me I can listen all the livelong day while I'm getting me a banana in the kitchen house and peeling it. Mama Tataba hangs the whole big family of bananas up in the corner all together, so the tarantula spiders that use it for their house can just move on out when they take a notion. I sat real still on the floor and peeled my one banana like Saint Matthew would if he was a real monkey and not gone, and I heard them talking about the woman that got burned up. The roofs burn up because they are all made out of sticks and hay like the Three Little Pigs. The wolf could huff and puff and blow your house down. Even ours. It's a right smart better than the other ones, but it's not bricks. Mama Mwanza's legs didn't burn all the way off but it looks like a pillow or just something down there she's sitting on wrapped up in a cloth sack. She has to scoot around on her hands. Her hand bottoms look like feet bottoms, only with fingers. I went over there and had me a good look at her and her little girls with no clothes on. She was nice and gave me a piece of orange to suck on. Mama doesn't know.

Mama Mwanza almost got burnt plumb to death when it happened but then she got better. Mama says that was the poor woman's bad luck, because now she has got to go right on tending after her husband and her seven or eight children. They don't care one bit about her not having any legs to speak of. To them she's just their mama and where's dinner? To all the other Congo people, too. Why, they just don't let on, like she was a regular person. Nobody bats their eye when she scoots by on her hands and goes on down to her field or the river to wash clothes with the other ladies that work down there every day. She carries all her things in a basket on top of her head. It's as big as Mama's big white laundry hamper back home and seems like she's always got about ten hundred things piled up in there. When she scoots down the road, not a one of them falls out. All the other ladies have big baskets on their heads too, so nobody stares at Mama Mwanza one way or another.

What they do is, they all stare at *us*. They look at Rachel the worst. First Mama and Father were thinking it might do Rachel some good to be cranked down a notch or two. Father said to Mama: "A child shouldn't think herself better than others because she is blonde as a white rabbit." He said that. I told it to Leah and she laughed out loud. I am blonde too but not as much as a white rabbit. Strawberry blonde, Mama says. So I hope I don't have to get cranked down a notch or two like Rachel. I like strawberries about better than anything. You can keep a rabbit for a pet or you can eat it. Poor Rachel. Everwhen she goes out, whole bunches of little Congo children run after her on the road a-reaching and a-yanking on her long white hair to see if they can get it to come off. Sometimes even the grownups do too. I reckon they think it's a right good sport. Leah told me it's because they don't believe it is her hair and think she's got something strange draped over her head.

Rachel gets her the worst sunburns, too. I get burnt but not like her. Pink is Rachel's favorite color and it's a good thing because that's what she is. Father says it is the lot of every young woman to learn humility and God plots for each her chosen way.

Mama says, "But must they look on us as freaks of nature?"

Rachel was Miss Priss and now she is a freak of nature. Used to be, Adah was the only one of us in our family with something wrong with her. But here nobody stares at Adah except just a little because she's white. Nobody cares that she's bad on one whole side because they've all got their own handicap children or a mama with no feet, or their eye put out. When you take a look out the door, why, there goes somebody with something missing off of them and not even embarrassed of it. They'll wave a stump at you if they've got one, in a friendly way.

At first Mama got after us for staring and pointing at people. She was all the time whispering, "Do I have to tell you girls ever single minute don't stare!" But now Mama looks too. Sometimes she says to us or just herself, Now Tata Zinsana is the one missing all the fingers, isn't he? Or she'll say, That big gouter like a goose egg under her chin, that's how I remember Mama Nguza.

Father said, "They are living in darkness. Broken in body and soul, and don't even see how they could be healed."

Mama said, "Well, maybe they take a different view of their bodies."

Father says the body is the temple. But Mama has this certain voice sometimes. Not exactly sassing back, but just about nearly. She was sewing us some window curtains out of dress material so they wouldn't be looking in at us all the time, and had pins in her mouth.

She took the pins out and said to him, "Well, here in Africa that temple has to do a hateful lot of work in a day." She said, "Why, Nathan, here they have to use their bodies like we use *things* at home—like your clothes or your garden tools or something. Where you'd be wearing out the knees of your trousers, sir, they just have to go ahead and wear out their *knees*!"

Father looked at Mama hard for talking back to him.

"Well, sir," she said, "that is just what it looks like to me. That is just my observation. It appears to me their bodies just get worn out, about the same way as our worldly goods do."

Mama wasn't really sassing back. She calls him *sir* the way she calls us *Sugar* and *Hon*, trying to be nice. But still. If it was me talking back that way, he'd say, "That is a fine line you are walking there, young lady." And he appeared to be fixing to say just such a thing to Mama. He was debating about it. He stood there in the front doorway with the sun just squeaking by him on all sides. He is so big he near about filled up the whole doorway. His head almost touched. And Mama was just sitting down short at the table, so she went back to sewing.

He said, "Orleanna, the human body is a sight more precious than a pair of khaki trousers from Sears and Roebuck. I'd expect you to comprehend the difference."

Then he looked at her with his one eye turned mean and said, "You of all people."

She turned red and breathed out like she does. She said, "Even something precious can get shabby in the course of things. Considering what they're up against here, that might not be such a bad attitude for them to take."

After that Mama put pins back in her mouth, so no more talking.

He didn't say anything, Yes or No, just turned his back and went on out. He doesn't approve talking back. If that was me, oh, boy. That razor strop burns so bad, after you go to bed your legs still feel stripedy like a zebra horse.

I'll tell you one thing that Father has sure wore out bad: his old green swivel rocker in the living room of our house where we live in Bethlehem, Georgia. You can see white threads in the shape of a bottom. It doesn't look very polite. And nobody but him did it, either. He sits there of an evening and reads and reads. Once in a while he reads to us out loud when we have our scripture stories. Sometimes I get to picking my scabs and think about cartoons instead of Jesus, and He sees me doing that. But Jesus loves me and this I know: nobody can sit in that green swivel rocker but Father.

Mama says there's another man and lady with two little girls and a baby living in our house in Bethlehem, Georgia. The man is the minister while we're gone. I hope they know about Father's chair because if they sit in it, oh, boy. They'll get it.

Adah

I T WAS NEITHER DIABOLICAL NOR DIVINE; *it but shook the doors of the prison house of my disposition; and like the captives of Philippi, that which stood within ran forth.* So feel I. Living in the Congo shakes open the prison house of my disposition and lets all the wicked hoodoo Adahs run forth.

To amuse my depraved Ada self during homework time I wrote down that quote from memory on a small triangular piece of paper and passed it to Leah, with the query: *FROM WHAT BOOK OF THE BIBLE?* Leah fancies herself Our Father's star pupil in matters Biblical. *Star Pupil: Lipup Rats.* Miss Rat-pup read the quote, nodding solemnly, and wrote underneath, *The book of Luke. I'm not sure which verse.*

Hah! I can laugh very hard without even smiling on the outside.

The quote is from *The Strange Case of Dr. Jekyll and Mr. Hyde,* which I have read many times. I have a strong sympathy for Dr. Jekyll's dark desires and for Mr. Hyde's crooked body.

Before we fled Bethlehem's drear libraries I had also recently read *The Pilgrim's Progress* and *Paradise Lost,* which have weaker plot lines than *Dr. Jekyll,* and many other books Our Father does not know about, including the poems of Miss Emily Dickinson and *Tales of the Grotesque and Arabesque* by Edgar Allan Poe. I am fond of Mr. Poe and his telltale Raven: *Erom Reven!*

Mother is the one who notices, and tells naught. She started it all, reading the Psalms and various Family Classics aloud to Leah and me. Mother has a pagan's appreciation for the Bible, being devoted to such phrases as "purge me with hyssop," and "strong bulls of Bashan have beset me round," and "thou hast put off my sackcloth and girded me with gladness." Likely she would run through the fields dressed in sackcloth, hunting hyssop amongst the wild bulls, if not obligated to the higher plane of Motherhood. She is especially beset by Leah's and my status as exceptional children. When we entered the first grade, we were examined by the spinster principal of Bethlehem Elementary, Miss Leep, who announced that we were *gifted*: Leah, on account of her nonchalant dazzling scores on reading-comprehension tests, and myself by association, as I am presumed to have the same brain insofar as the intact parts go. This was a shock to Mother, who up to that point had offered us no education higher than the names of the wildflowers growing in the roadside ditches where we walked barefoot (when Our Father's scorching eyes were not upon us: *Sun o put o not upon us!)* from the parsonage to the corner market. My earliest Mother memories lie laughing blue-eyed in the grass, child herself, rolling side to side as Rachel and Leah decorated her all over with purple-clover jewelry. Once Leah and I were gifted, though, everything changed. Mother seemed sobered by this news from our teachers, as if she had earned a special punishment from God. She became secretive and efficient. She reined in our nature walks and settled down to business with a library card.

She need not have troubled with secrecy, for all Our Father noticed. On first hearing Miss Leep's news he merely rolled his eyes, as if two dogs in his yard had reportedly been caught whistling "Dixie." He warned Mother not to flout God's Will by expecting too much for us. "Sending a girl to college is like pouring water in your shoes," he still loves to say, as often as possible. "It's hard to say which is worse, seeing it run out and waste the water, or seeing it hold in and wreck the shoes."

And so I shall never have opportunity to have my leather wrecked by college, but I do owe a great debt to Miss Leep for saving me from the elementary discard heap. A principal less observant would have placed Leah in Gifted, and Adah in Special Ed with the mongoloids and all six of Bethlehem's thumb-sucking, ear-pulling

Crawley children, and there would I remain, to learn how to pull my own ear. Overjoyed, null and void, Mongoloid. I still have a fellow feeling for that almond-tasting word.

Oh, but it did unsettle the matrons of Bethlehem to see the poor thing boosted into a class ahead of their own children, there to become dazzling slick-quick at mathematics. In third grade I began to sum up our grocery bill in my head, silently write it down and hand it over, faster than Delma Royce could total it on her cash register. This became a famous event and never failed to draw a crowd. I had no idea why. I merely felt drawn in by those rattling, loose numbers needing their call to order. No one seemed to realize calculating sums requires only the most basic machinery and good concentration. Poetry is far more difficult. And palindromes, with their perfect, satisfying taste: Draw a level award! Yet it is always the thin gray grocery sums that make an impression.

My hobby is to ignore the awards and excel when I choose. I can read and write French, which in Kilanga is spoken by all who ever passed through the Underdowns' school. My sisters seem not to have slowed down long enough to learn French. Speaking, as I said—along with the rest of life's acrobatics—can be seen in a certain light as a distraction.

When I finish reading a book from front to back, I read it back to front. It is a different book, back to front, and you can learn new things from it. It from things new learn can you and front to back book different a is it?

You can agree or not, as you like. This is another way to read it, although I am told a normal brain will not grasp it: *Ti morf sgniht wen nrael nac uoy dna tnorf ot kcab koob tnereffid a si ti.* The normal, I understand, can see words my way only if they are adequately poetic: *Poor Dan is in a droop.*

My own name, as I am accustomed to think of it, is Ecirp Nelle Hada. Sometimes I write it this way without thinking, and people turn up startled. To them I am only Adah or, to my sisters sometimes, the drear monosyllabic *Ade*, lemonade, Band-Aid, frayed blockade, switchblade renegade, call a spade a spade.

I prefer *Ada* as it goes either way, like me. I am a perfect palindrome. *Damn mad!* Across the cover of my notebook I have written as a warning to others:

ELAPSED OR ESTEEMED, ALL ADE MEETS ERODES PALE!

For my twin sister's name I prefer the spelling *Lee*, as that makes her—from the back-court position from which I generally watch her—the slippery length of muscle that she is.

The Congo is a fine place to learn how to read the same book many times. When the rain pours down especially, we have long hours of captivity, in which my sisters determinedly grow bored. But are there books, books there are! Rattling words on the page calling my eyes to dance with them. Everyone else will finish with the singular plowing through, and Ada still has discoveries ahead and behind.

When the rainy season fell on us in Kilanga, it fell like a plague. We were warned to expect rain in October, but at the close of July—surprising no one in Kilanga but ourselves—the serene heavens above began to dump buckets. *Stekcub pmud!* It rained pitchforks, as Mother says. It rained cats and dogs frogs bogs then it rained snakes and lizards. A pestilence of rain we received, the likes of which we had never seen or dreamed about in Georgia.

Under the eave of the porch our charge Methuselah screamed like a drowning man in his cage. Methuselah is an African Grey parrot with a fine scaly look to his head, a sharp skeptical eye like Miss Leep's, and a scarlet tail. He resides in a remarkable bamboo cage as tall as Ruth May. His perch is a section of a sturdy old-fashioned yardstick, triangular in cross-section. Long ago someone broke off the inches nineteen through thirty-six and assigned these to Methuselah for the conduct of his affairs.

Parrots are known to be long-lived, and among all the world's birds, African Greys are best at imitating human speech. Methuselah may or may not have heard about this, for he mumbles badly. He mumbles to himself all day long like Grandfather Wharton. Mostly he says incomprehensible things in Kikongo but also speaks like Mr.

Poe's Raven a desultory English. On the first day of rain, he raised his head and screeched through the roar of the storm his best two phrases in our language: first, in Mama Tataba's side-slant voice, "*Wake up, Brothah Fowels! Wake up, Brothah Fowels!*"

Then in a low-pitched growl, "*Piss off, Methuselah!*"

The Reverend Price looked up from his desk by the window and made note of the words "Piss off." The morally suspect ghost of Brother Fowles was thick upon us.

"That," the Reverend declared, "is a Catholic bird."

Mother looked up from her sewing. My sisters and I shifted in our chairs, expecting Father to assign Methuselah "The Verse."

The dreaded Verse is our household punishment. Other lucky children might merely be thrashed for their sins, but we Price girls are castigated with the Holy Bible. The Reverend will level his gaze and declare, "You have The Verse." Then slowly, as we squirm on his hook, he writes on a piece of paper, for example: Jeremiah 48:18. Then say ye good-bye to sunshine or the Hardy Boys for an afternoon as you, poor sinner, must labor with a pencil in your good left hand to copy out Jeremiah 48:18, "*Come down from your throne of glory and sit in the mire, O daughter that dwells in Dibon,*" and additionally, the ninety-nine verses that follow it. One hundred full verses exactly copied out in longhand, because it is the final one that reveals your crime. In the case of Jeremiah 48:18, the end is Jeremiah 50:31, "*Lo! I am against you, O Insolence! saith the oracle of the Lord, the God of hosts; For your day has come, your time of reckoning.*" Only upon reaching that one-hundredth verse do you finally understand you are being punished for the sin of insolence. Although you might well have predicted it.

He sometimes has us copy from Old King James, but prefers to use the American Translation that includes his peculiarly beloved Apocrypha. That is one pet project of the Reverend's: getting other Baptists to swallow the Apocrypha.

I have wondered, incidentally: does Our Father have his Bibles so entirely in mind that he can select an instructive verse and calculate backward to the one-hundredth previous? Or does he sit up nights searching out a Verse for every potential infraction, and store this ammunition at the ready for his daughters? Either way, it is as impressive as my grocery sums in the Piggly Wiggly. We all, especially Rachel, live in terror of the cursed Verse.

But in the case of the cursing parrot that first long rainy day, Methuselah could not be made to copy the Bible. Curiously exempt from the Reverend's rules was Methuselah, in the same way Our Father was finding the Congolese people beyond his power. Methuselah was a sly little representative of Africa itself, living openly in our household. One might argue, even, that he was here first.

We listened to parrot prattle and sat confined, uncomfortably close to Our Father. For five solid hours of downpour we watched small red frogs with immense, cartoonlike toes squeeze in around the windows and hop steadily up the walls. Our all-weather coats hung on their six pegs; possibly they were meant for all weather but this.

Our house is made of mud-battered walls and palm thatch, but is different from all other houses in Kilanga. In the first place it is larger, with a wide front room and two bedrooms in back, one of which resembles a hospital scene from Florence Nightingale's time, as it is chock-full of cots under triangles of mosquito net for the family surplus of girls. The kitchen is a separate hut, behind the main house. In the clearing beyond stands our latrine, unashamed, despite the vile curses rained upon it daily by Rachel. The chicken house is back there too. Unlike the other villagers' houses, our windows are square panes of glass and our foundation and floor are cement. All other houses have floors of dirt. Curt, subvert, overexert. We see village women constantly sweeping their huts and the barren clearings in front of their homes with palm-frond brooms, and Rachel with her usual shrewdness points out you could sweep a floor like that plumb to China and never get it clean. By the grace of God and cement our family has been spared that frustration.

In the front room our dining table looks to have come off a wrecked ship, and there is an immense rolltop desk (possibly from the same ship) used by Our Father for writing his sermons. The desk has wooden legs and cast-iron chicken's feet, each clutching a huge glass marble, though three of the marbles are cracked and one is gone, replaced by a chink of coconut husk in the interest of a level writing surface. In our parents' room, more furniture: a wooden bureau and an old phonograph cabinet with no workings inside. All brought by other brave Baptists before us, though it is hard to see quite how, unless one envisions a time when other means of travel were allowed, and more than forty-four pounds. We also have a dining table and a rough handmade cupboard, containing a jumble-sale assortment of glass and plastic dishes and cups, one too few of everything, so we sisters have to bargain knives for forks while we eat. The cabinet also contains an ancient cracked plate commemorating the World's Fair in St. Louis, Missouri, and a plastic cup bearing the nose and ears of a mouse. And in the midst of this rabble, serene as the Virgin Mother in her barnful of shepherds and scabby livestock, one amazing, beautiful thing: a large, oval white platter painted with delicate blue forget-me-nots, bone china, so fine that sunlight passes through it. Its origin is unfathomable. If we forgot ourselves we might worship it.

Outdoors we have a long shady porch our mother in her Mississippi-born way calls a veranda. My sisters and I love to lounge there in the hammocks, and we longed for refuge there even on the day of our first downpour. But the storm lashed sideways, battering the walls and poor Methuselah. When his screaming got too pathetic to bear, our grim-faced mother brought in his cage and set it on the floor by the window, where Methuselah continued his loud, random commentary. In addition to papism, the Reverend probably suspected this noisy creature of latent femaleness.

The deluge finally stopped just before sunset. The world looked stepped on and drenched, but my sisters ran out squealing like the first free pigs off the ark, eager to see what the flood had left us. A low cloud in the air turned out to be tiny flying antlike creatures by the millions. They hovered just above the ground, making a long, low hum that stretched to the end of the world. Their bodies made clicking sounds as we swatted them away from us. We hesitated at the edge of the yard, where the muddy clearing grades into a long grass slope, then charged on into the grass, until our way was barred by the thousand crossed branches of the forest's edge: avocado, palms, tall wild sugar-cane thickets. This forest obscures our view of the river, and any other distance. The village's single dirt road skirts our yard and runs past us into the village to the south; on the north it disappears into the woods. Though we watch Mama Tataba vanish that way and return again, intact, with her water buckets full, our mother did not yet trust the path to swallow and deliver her children. So we turned and tromped back up the hill toward the pair of flowery round hibiscus bushes that flank the steps to our porch.

What a landing party we were as we stalked about, identically dressed in saddle oxfords, long-tailed shirts, and pastel cotton pants, but all so different. Leah went first as always, Goddess of the Hunt, her weasel-colored pixie haircut springing with energy, her muscles working together like parts of a clock. Then came the rest of us: Ruth May with pigtails flying behind her, hurrying mightily because she is youngest and believes the last shall be first. And then Rachel, our family's own Queen of Sheba, blinking her white eyelashes, flicking her long whitish hair as if she were the palomino horse she once craved to own. Queen Rachel drifted along several paces behind, looking elsewhere. She was almost sixteen and above it all, yet still unwilling for us to find something good without her. Last of all came Adah the monster, Quasimodo, dragging her right side behind her left in her body's permanent stepsong sing: *left . . . behind, left . . . behind.*

This is our permanent order: Leah, Ruth May, Rachel, Adah. Neither chronological nor alphabetical but it rarely varies, unless Ruth May gets distracted and falls out of line.

At the foot of the hibiscus bush we discovered a fallen nest of baby birds, all drowned. My sisters were thrilled by the little naked, winged bodies like storybook griffins, and by the horrible fact they were dead. Then we found the garden. Rachel screamed triumphantly that it was ruined once and for all. Leah fell to her knees in a demonstration of grief on Our Father's behalf. The torrent had swamped the flat bed and the seeds rushed out like runaway boats. We found them everywhere in caches in the tall grass at the edge of the patch. Most had already sprouted in the previous weeks, but their little roots had not held them to the Reverend Farmer's flat-as-Kansas beds against the torrent. Leah walked along on her knees, gathering up sprouts in her shirttail, as she probably imagined Saca-jaweah would have done in the same situation.

Later Our Father came out to survey the damage, and Leah helped him sort out the seeds by kind. He declared he would make them grow, in the name of God, or he would plant again (the Reverend, like any prophet worth his salt, had held some seeds in reserve) if only the sun would ever come out and dry up this accursed mire.

Even at sunset, the two of them did not come in for supper. Mama Tataba bent over the table in our mother's large white apron, which made her look counterfeit and comic, as though acting the role of maid in a play. She watched him steadily out the window, smiling her peculiar downturned smile, and made satisfied clicks with her tongue against her teeth. We set ourselves to the task of eating her cooking, fried plantain and the luxury of some canned meat.

Finally he sent Leah in, but long after dinner we could still hear the Reverend out there beating the ground with his hoe, revising the earth. No one can say he does not learn his lesson, though it might take a deluge, and though he might never admit in this life-time that it was not his own idea in the first place. Nevertheless, Our Father had been influenced by Africa. He was out there push-ing his garden up into rectangular, flood-proof embankments, exactly the length and width of burial mounds.

Leah

I T ONLY TAKES FIVE DAYS in hot weather for a Kentucky Wonder bean to gather up its vegetable willpower and germinate. That was all we thought we needed. Once the rains abated, my father's garden thrived in the heat like an unleashed temper. He loved to stand out there just watching things grow, he said, and you could believe it. The beanstalks twisted around the sapling teepees he'd built for them, and then they wavered higher and higher like ladies' voices in the choir, each one vying for the top. They reached out for the branches of nearby trees and twined up into the canopy.

The pumpkin vines also took on the personality of jungle plants. Their leaves grew so strangely enormous Ruth May could sit still under them and win at "Hide and Seek" for a very long time after the rest of us had stopped playing. When we squatted down we could see, alongside Ruth May's wide blue eyes, yellow blossoms of cucumber and squash peering out from the leafy darkness.

My father witnessed the progress of every new leaf and fat flower bud. I walked behind him, careful not to trample the vines. I helped him construct a sturdy stick barricade around the periphery so the jungle animals and village goats would not come in and wreck our tender vegetables when they came. Mother claims I have the manners of a wild animal myself, as I am a tomboy, but I never fail to be respectful of my father's garden. His devotion to its progress, like his devotion to the church, was the anchoring force in my life throughout this past summer. I knew my father could taste those Kentucky Wonder beans as surely as any pure soul can taste heaven.

Rachel's birthday came in late August, but the Betty Crocker cake mix let us all down. Normal cake production proved out of the question.

To begin with, our stove is an iron contraption with a firebox so immense a person could climb right in if they felt like it. Mother yanked Ruth May out by the arm, pretty hard, when she found her in there; she dreaded that Mama Tataba in one of her energetic fits might stoke up the stove with the baby inside. It was a sensible concern. Ruth May is so intent on winning Hide and Seek, or any game for that matter, she would probably go ahead and burn up before she'd ever yell and give herself away.

Mother has figured out how to make bread "by hook or by crook," she likes to say, but the stove doesn't really have a proper oven. In fact, it looks less like a stove than a machine hammered together out of some other machine. Rachel says it was part of a locomotive train, but she is famous for making things up out of thin air and stating them in a high, knowing tone.

The stove wasn't even the worst of our cake troubles. In the powerful humidity the powdered mix got transfigured like Lot's poor wife who looked back at Gomorrah and got turned to a pillar of salt. On the morning of Rachel's birthday I found Mother out in the kitchen house with her head in her hands, crying. She picked up the box and banged it hard against the iron stove, just once, to show me. It clanged like a hammer on a bell. Her way of telling a parable is different from my father's.

"If I'd of had the foggiest idea," she said very steadily, holding her pale, weeping eyes on me, "just the foggiest idea. We brought all the wrong things."

The first time my father heard Methuselah say, "Damn," his body moved strangely, as if he'd received the spirit or a twinge of bad heartburn. Mother excused herself and went in the house.

Rachel, Adah, and I were left on the porch, and he looked at each one of us in turn. We had known him to forbear with a silent grimace when Methuselah said, "Piss off," but of course that was the doing of Brother Fowles. The mote in his brother's eye, not the sin of his own household. Methuselah had never said "Damn" before, so this was something new, spoken right out very chipper in a feminine tone of voice.

"Which one of you taught Methuselah to say that word?" he demanded.

I felt sick to my stomach. None of us spoke. For Adah that's normal, of course, and for that very reason she often gets accused when none of us speaks up. And truthfully, if any of us was disposed to use curse words, it would be Adah, who could not care less about sin and salvation. That's the main reason I got Mother to cut my hair in a pixie, while Adah kept hers long: so nobody would get our attitudes mixed up. I myself would not curse, in or out of Methuselah's hearing or even in my dreams, because I crave heaven and to be my father's favorite. And Rachel wouldn't—she'll let out a disgusted "Jeez" or "Gol!" when she can, but is mainly a perfect lady when anybody's listening. And Ruth May is plain too little.

"I fail to understand," said Father, who understands everything, "why you would have a poor dumb creature condemn us all to eternal suffering."

I'll tell you what, though, Methuselah is not dumb. He imitates not just words, but the voices of people that spoke them. From Methuselah we have learned the Irish-Yankee voice of Brother Fowles, whom we picture as looking like that Father Flanagan that runs the Boys Town. We could also recognize Mama Tataba, and ourselves. Furthermore, Methuselah didn't just imitate words, he *knew* them. It's one thing simply to call out, "Sister, God is great! Shut the door!" when the spirit moves him, but he'll also call out "banana" and "peanut" as plain as day, when he sees these things in our hands and wants his share. Oftentimes he studies us, copying our movements, and he seems to know which words will provoke us to laugh or talk back to him, or be shocked. We already understood what was now dawning on my father: Methuselah could betray our secrets.

I didn't say so, of course. I haven't contradicted my father on any subject, ever.

Rachel finally blurted out, "Father, we're sorry."

Adah and I pretended to be fascinated by our books. We brought our schoolbooks with us and study them whenever Mother threatens we're going to fall behind and wear the dunce cap when we go home, which there's no chance of really, except for Rachel, who is the one stubbornly mediocre mentality in our family. I think our mother is really just afraid we're going to forget about normal things like George Washington crossing the Delaware and autumn leaves and a train speeding west toward St. Louis at sixty-five miles per hour.

I peeped up from my book. Oh, dear Lord. He was staring directly at me. My heart palpitated fiercely.

"The Lord will forgive you if you ask," he said, very disgusted and quiet, the tone of voice that makes me feel worse than any other. "Our Lord is benevolent. But that poor African bird can't be relieved of what you've taught it. It's an innocent creature that can only repeat what it hears. The damage is done." He started to turn away from us. We held our breath as he paused on the steps and looked back, right in my eyes. I burned with shame.

"If there's anything to be learned from this," he said, "it's about the stink and taint of original sin. I expect you'd better think about that while you do The Verse." Our hearts fell. "All three of you," he said. "Book of Numbers, twenty-nine thirty-four."

Then he walked off abruptly, leaving us like orphans on the porch.

The thought of spending the rest of the day copying out the tedious Book of Numbers sobered me deeply as I watched my father go. He directed his stride toward the river. He'd been going down there nearly every day, tearing his walking stick into the elephant-ear leaves that curtained the riverbank. He was scouting out baptismal sites.

I already knew how Numbers 29:34 came out, as I'd gotten it before. The hundredth verse winds up at 32:32, with how when you sin against the Lord you get found out, and to watch what proceeds out of your mouth.

I hadn't even considered the irreversible spoiling of Methuselah's innocence, which just goes to show I have much to learn. But I'll admit I prayed that afternoon that Father had taken Rachel's apology as a confession, so he wouldn't think the sin was mine. It was hard, accepting his accusations by keeping silent. We all knew very well who'd been the one to yell that word *Damn!* She'd said it over and over when she wept over the wreck of her useless cake mixes. But none of us could let him in on that awful secret. Not even me—and I know I'm the one to turn my back on her the most.

Once in a great while we just have to protect her. Even back when we were very young I remember running to throw my arms around Mother's knees when he regaled her with words and worse, for curtains unclosed or slips showing—the sins of womanhood. We could see early on that all grown-ups aren't equally immune to damage. My father wears his faith like the bronze breastplate of God's foot soldiers, while our mother's is more like a good cloth coat with a secondhand fit. The whole time Father was interrogating us on the porch, in my mind's eye I was seeing her slumped over in the kitchen house, banging in mortal frustration against that locomotive engine of a stove. In her hand, Rachel's Angel Dream cake mix, hard as a rock; in her heart, its heavenly, pink-frosted perfection, its candles ablaze, brought proudly to the table on that precious bone-china platter with the blue flowers. She'd been keeping it a secret, but Mother was going to try and have a real sweet-sixteen party for Rachel.

But Angel Dream was the wrong thing, the wrong thing by a mile. I'd carried it over in my own waistband, so it seemed like some part of the responsibility was mine.

Adah

HOLY FATHER, bless us and keep us in Thy sight," the Reverend said. Sight Thy blessed father holy. And all of us with our closed eyes smelled the frangipani blossoms in the big rectangles of open wall, flowers so sweet they conjure up sin or heaven, depending on which way you are headed. The Reverend towered over the rickety altar, his fiery crew cut bristling like a woodpecker's cockade. When the Spirit passed through him he groaned, throwing body and soul into this weekly purge. The "Amen enema," as I call it. My palindrome for the Reverend.

Mama Tataba's body next to mine in the pew, meanwhile, was a thing gone dead. Her stiffness reminded me of all the fish lying curved and stiff on the riverbanks, flaking in the sun like old white bars of soap. All because of the modern style of fishing Our Father dreamed up. The Reverend's high-horse show of force. He ordered men to go out in canoes and pitch dynamite in the river, stupefying everything within earshot. Shot ears. Now, where did he get dynamite? Certainly none of us carried it over here in our drawers. So from Eeben Axelroot, I have to think, for a large sum of money. Our family receives a stipend of $50 a month for being missionaries. This is not the regular Baptist stipend; Our Father is a renegade who came without the entire blessing of the Mission League, and bullied or finagled his way into this lesser stipend. Even so, it is a lot of Congolese francs and would be a Congolese fortune if that were that, but it is not. The money comes in an envelope on the plane, brought by Eeben Axelroot and to Eeben Axelroot it mostly returns. Ashes to ashes.

To Kilanga's hungry people Our Father promised at summer's end the bounty of the Lord, more fish than they had ever seen in their lives. "The word of Christ is beloved!" he cries, standing up precariously in his boat. "*Tata Jesus is bangala!*" So determined he is to win or force or drag them over to the Way of the Cross. Feed the belly first, he announced at dinner one night, seized with his brilliant plan. Feed the belly and the soul will come. (Not having noticed, for a wife is beneath notice, that this is exactly what our mother did when she killed all the chickens.) But after the underwater thunder, what came was not souls but fish. They came rolling to the surface with mouths opened wide by that shocking boom. Round shocked bubbles for eyes. The whole village feasted all day, ate, ate till we felt bug-eyed and belly-up ourselves. He performed a backward version of the loaves and fishes, trying to stuff ten thousand fish into fifty mouths, did the Reverend Price. Slogging up and down the riverbank in trousers wet to the knees, his Bible in one hand and another stickful of fire-blackened fish in the other, he waved his bounty in a threatening manner. Thousands more fish jerked in the sun and went bad along the riverbanks. Our village was blessed for weeks with the smell of putrefaction. Instead of abundance it was a holiday of waste. No ice. Our Father forgot, for fishing in the style of modern redneck Georgia you need your ice.

He was not going to bring up the loaves and fishes in today's sermon, was a good guess. He would merely give out the communion with the usual disturbing allusions to eating flesh and drinking blood. Perhaps this perked up congregational interest, but we Price girls all listened with half an ear between us. And Adah with her half a brain. Hah. The church service lasts twice as long now because the Reverend has to say it once in English, and then the schoolteacher Tata Anatole repeats it all in Kikongo. Our Father finally caught on, nobody was understanding his horrible stabs at French or Kikongo, either one.

"It was *lawlessness* that came forth from Babylon! *Law less ness!*" declared the Reverend, waving an arm impressively toward Babylon as if that turbulent locale lurked just behind the school latrine.

Through the bedraggled roof a ray of sun fell like God's spotlight across his right shoulder. He paced, paused, spoke, and paced behind his palm-leaf altar, giving every impression he was inventing his Biblical parables on the spot. This morning he was spinning the tale of Susanna, beautiful and pious wife of the rich man Joakim. *Annasus ho!* While she bathed in the garden, two of Joakim's advisors spied her naked and cooked up their vile plan. They leaped from the bushes and demanded that she lie down with them. Poor Susanna. If she refused they would bear false witness against her, claiming they caught her in the garden with a man. Naturally the righteous Susanna refused them, even though this meant she would be accused and stoned for adultery. Stoning moaning owning deboning. We were not supposed to wonder what kind of husband was this Joakim, who would kill his own lovely wife rather than listen to her side of the story. No doubt the Babylonians were already out scouting around for their favorite rocks.

The Reverend paused, resting one hand flat on the altar. The rest of his body rocked almost imperceptibly inside his white shirt, marking time, keeping his rhythm. He scrutinized his parishioners' blank faces for signs that they were on the edge of their seats. There were eleven or twelve new faces now, a regular stampede to glory. A boy near me with his mouth hanging open closed one eye, then the other, back and forth. We all waited for Tata Anatole the school-teacher-translator to catch up.

"But God would not let this happen," the Reverend growled, like a dog awakened by a prowler. Then rising an octave like "The Star-Spangled Banner": "God *stirred* up the holy *spirit* of a man named *Daniel!*"

Oh, hooray, Daniel to the rescue. Our Father loves Daniel, the original Private Eye. *Tata* Daniel (he called him, to make him seem like a local boy) stepped in and demanded to question the two advisors separately. Tata Daniel asked them what kind of tree Susanna was supposedly standing under when she met this man in the garden. "Um, a mastic tree," said one, and the other, "Well, gee, I guess it was a live oak." How stupid, that they had not even conspired to get their story straight. All the evildoers in the Bible seem spectacularly dumb.

I watched Tata Anatole, expecting him at least to stumble over "mastic" and "live oak," as there could not possibly be words for these trees in Kikongo. He did not pause. *Kufwema, kuzikisa, kugambula,* smoothly the words rolled forward and I realized this slick trick schoolteacher could be saying anything under the sun. Our father would never be the wiser. *So they stoned the dame and married two more wives apiece and lived happily ever after.* I yawned, uninspired yet again by the pious and beautiful Susanna. I was unlikely ever to have her problems.

In my mind I invented snmyhymns, as I call them, my own perverse hymns that can be sung equally well forward or backward: *Evil, all its sin is still alive!* Also I made use of this rare opportunity to inspect Mama Tataba at close range. Normally she moved much too fast. I considered her my ally because, like me, she was imperfect. It was hard to say what she ever thought of Our Father's benedictions, in church or out, so I pondered more interesting mysteries, such as her eye. How did she lose it? Was she exempt from marriage because of it, as I presumed myself to be? I had little idea of her age or hopes. I did know that many women in Kilanga were more seriously disfigured and had husbands notwithstanding. *Standing with naught. Husbands.* Here, bodily damage is more or less considered to be a by-product of living, not a disgrace. In the way of the body and other people's judgment I enjoy a benign approval in Kilanga that I have never, ever known in Bethlehem, Georgia.

We finished off Susanna by singing "Amazing Grace" at the speed of a dirge. The ragtag congregation chimed in with every sort of word and tune. Oh, we were a regular Tower of Babel here at the First Baptist Church of Kilanga, so no one noticed that I mouthed my own words to the proper tune:

> *Evil, all . . . its sin . . . is still . . . alive!*
> *Do go . . . Tata . . . to God!*
> *Sugar don't . . . No, drag us*

drawn onward,
A, he rose . . . ye eyesore, ha!

When church was over Mama Tataba took us back to the house, while the clever Reverend and his wife stayed behind to smile and shake hands and bask in the general holiness. Mama Tataba stomped down the path ahead of my sisters and me. Bringing up the rear, I concentrated on trying to pass up the dawdling Rachel, who walked with her hands held out slightly from her thighs as if she had once again, as usual, been crowned Miss America. "Hold your hands like you've just dropped a marble," she instructs us generally as she fashion-models her way through the house. In spite of all that stateliness, I could not catch up. So I watched an orange-and-white butterfly that hovered over her and finally lit on her white head. The butterfly poked its tiny proboscis down into her hair, probing for nurture, then flew away unsatisfied. Mama Tataba saw none of these events. She was in a bad mood and shouted at us confidentially, "Reverant Price he better be give that up!" Flesh eating and blood drinking, did she mean? The sermon had meandered from the pious Susanna to Rahab, the harlot of Jericho. So many Biblical names sound backward, like Rahab, I wonder sometimes if the whole thing was written by a mental freak like me. But in the end he got around to emphasizing baptism, as always. This was likely what disturbed Mama Tataba. Our Father could not seem to accept what seemed clear enough even to a child: when he showered the idea of baptism—*batiza*—on people here, it shrunk them away like water on a witch.

Later on at the dinner table he was still animated, though, which is the status quo on Sundays. Once he gets wound up in the pulpit he seems unwilling to give up center stage.

"Do you know," he asked us, tall and bright-headed like a candle in his chair, "last year some men drove here all the way from Leopoldville in a truck with a broken fan belt? A Mercedes truck."

Ah, me. One of his Socratic moods. This was not dangerous, for he rarely actually struck us at the table, but it was designed to show us all up as dull-witted, bovine females. He always ended these interrogations with an exasperated, loud private conversation with God concerning our hopelessness.

Methuselah was definitely in the girls' camp. He made a habit of prattling at the top of his lungs through Sunday dinners at our house. Like many human beings, he took the least sign of conversation as his cue to make noise. Our mother sometimes threw a tablecloth over his cage in frustration. "*Mbote! Mbote!*" he screamed now, which in Kikongo means hello and good-bye, both. This symmetry appeals to me. Many Kikongo words resemble English words backward and have antithetical meanings: *Syebo* is a horrible, destructive rain, that just exactly does not do what it says backward.

We listened vaguely to Our Father's tale of the putative Mercedes truck. Our only material goods from the outside world of late were comic books, which my sisters cherished like Marco Polo's spices from China, and powdered eggs and milk, to which we felt indifferent. All brought by Eeben Axelroot. As for this truck-and-fanbelt story, the Reverend loved to speak in parables, and we could surely spot one coming.

"That road," said our mother, bemused, gesturing with a lazy bent wrist out the window. "Why, I can't imagine." She shook her head, possibly not believing. Can she allow herself not to believe him? I have never known.

"It was at the end of a dry season, Orleanna," he snapped. "When it's hot enough the puddles dry up." You brainless nitwit, he did not need to add.

"But how on earth did they run it without a fanbelt?" our mother asked, understanding by the Reverend's irritation that she was expected to return to the subject at hand. She leaned forward to offer him biscuits from the bone-china platter, which she sometimes, secretly, cradled like a baby after the washing and drying. Today she gave its rim a gentle stroke before folding her hands in submission to Father's will. She was wearing a jaunty shirtwaist, white with small red and blue semaphore flags. It had been her outermost dress when we came over. Its frantic little banners seemed to be signaling distress now, on account of Mama Tataba's vigorous washings in the river.

He leaned forward to give us the full effect of his red eyebrows and prominent jaw. "Elephant grass," he pronounced triumphantly.

We sat frozen, the food in our mouths momentarily unchewed.

"A dozen little boys rode on the back, weaving fan belts out of *grass*."

Leah blurted out all in a rush, "So the plain simple grass of God's creation can be just as strong as, as rubber or whatnot!" She sat ram-rod straight as if she were on television, going for the sixty-four-dollar question.

"No," he said. "Each one wouldn't last but two or three miles."

"Oh." Leah was disconsolate. The remaining nitwits ventured no other guesses.

"But just as soon as it gave out," he explained, "well, they'd have another one at the ready."

"Keen," Rachel said, unconvincingly. She is the most dramatic member of the family, and the worst actress, which in our family is a crucial skill. All of us were giving diligent attention to our pow-dered potatoes. We were supposed to be reaching an understanding here about the elephant-grass fan belt illustrating God's vast great-ness; nobody wanted to be called on.

"A Mercedes truck!" he said finally. "The pinnacle of German invention, can be kept in business by twelve little African boys and some elephant grass."

"Sister, shut the door! *Wenda mbote!*" Methuselah called out. Then he shouted, "*Ko ko ko!*" which is what people in Kilanga shout in someone's doorway when they come visiting, since gener-ally there is no door to knock on. This happened often at our house, but we always knew it was Methuselah, since we did have a door and did not, as a rule, have visitors. If anyone actually ever came, usually in the hope of selling us food, they did not knock on the door but merely hung about the yard until we took notice.

"Well, I expect you could keep anything going with enough lit-tle boys and enough grass," our mother said. She did not sound all that pleased about it.

"That's right. It just takes adaptability."

"Damn damn damn!" observed Methuselah.

Mother shot the bird a worried glance. "If that creature lives through nine hundred Baptist missions he will have quite a lot to say."

She stood up then and started stacking the plates. Her Living Curl had long since been pronounced dead, and on the whole she appeared to be adapted to within an inch of her life. She excused herself to go boil the dishwater.

Unable to work either the dishwater or Methuselah's long memory into a proper ending for his parable, Our Father merely looked at us all and heaved the great sigh of the put-upon male. Oh, such a sigh. It was so deep it could have drawn water from a well, right up from beneath the floor of our nitwit household. He was merely trying, that sigh suggested, to drag us all toward enlightenment through the marrow of our own poor female bones.

We hung our heads, pushed back our chairs, and filed out to help stoke up the firebox in the kitchen house. Cooking meals here requires half the day, and cleaning up takes the other half. We have to boil our water because it comes from the stream, where parasites multiply in teeming throngs. Africa has parasites so particular and diverse as to occupy every niche of the body: intestines small and large, the skin, the bladder, the male and female reproductive tracts, interstitial fluids, even the cornea. In a library book on African public health, before we left home, I found a drawing of a worm as thin as a hair meandering across the front of a man's startled eyeball. I was struck through with my own wayward brand of reverence: praise be the lord of all plagues and secret afflictions! If God had amused himself inventing the lilies of the field, he surely knocked His own socks off with the African parasites.

Outside I saw Mama Tataba, on her way to the kitchen house, dip in a hand and drink straight out of the bucket. I crossed my fingers for her one good eye. I shuddered to think of that dose of God's Creation going down, sucking her dry from the inside.

Leah

MY FATHER had been going to the garden alone, every day, to sit and think. It disturbed him that the plants thrived and filled the fenced patch with bloom like a funeral parlor, but would not set fruit. I knew he was praying about it. I sometimes went out to sit with him, even though Mother held it against me, saying he needed his solitude.

He speculated that there was too much shade from the trees. I thought long and hard about this explanation, as I am always eager to expand my understanding of horticulture. It was true, the trees did encroach on our little clearing. We constantly had to break and hack off branches, trying to win back our ground. Why, some of the bean vines had wound themselves all the way into the very treetops, striving for light.

Once he asked me suddenly as we sat mulling over the pumpkins, "Leah, do you know what they spent the last Bible convention in Atlanta arguing about?"

I wasn't really expected to know, so I waited. I was thrilled by the mere fact of his speaking to me in this gentle, somewhat personal way. He didn't look at me, of course, for he had much on his mind, as ever. We'd worked so hard for God's favor, yet it seemed God was still waiting for some extra labor on our part, and it was up to my father to figure out what. With his stronger eye he stared deeply into a pumpkin blossom for the source of his garden's disease. The flowers would open and close, then the green fruits behind them would shrivel and turn brown. There wasn't a single exception. In exchange for our honest sweat we'd so far earned flowers and leaves, but nothing we could actually have for supper.

"The size of heaven," he finally said.

"I'm sorry?" My heart skipped a beat. Here I'd been trying to second-guess Father, working out the garden business. He is always two steps ahead of me.

"They debated about the size of heaven, at the Bible convention. How many furlongs it is. How many long, how many wide—they set men with adding machines to figuring it out. Chapter twenty-one of Revelation sets it out in reeds, and other books tell it in cubits, and not a one of them quite matches up." Inexplicably, he sounded put out with the men who brought their adding machines to the Bible convention, and possibly with the Bible itself. I felt extremely uneasy.

"Well, I sure hope there'll be room enough for everybody," I said. This was a whole new worry to me. Suddenly I began to think of all the people already up there, mostly old, and not in particularly good shape either. I pictured them elbowing each other as if at a church rummage sale.

"There will always be room for the righteous," he said.

"Amen," I breathed, on safer ground.

"Many are the afflictions of the righteous, and the Lord delivers him out of them all. But you know, Leah, sometimes He doesn't deliver us *out* of our hardships but *through* them."

"Heavenly Father, deliver us," I said, although I didn't care for this new angle. Father had already bent his will to Africa by remaking his garden in mounds, the way they do here. This was a sure sign to God of his humility and servitude, and it was only fair to expect our reward. So what was this business of being delivered through hardships? Did Father aim to suggest God was not obligated to send us down any beans or squash at all, no matter how we might toil in His name? That He just proposed to sit up there and consign us to hardships one right after another? Certainly it wasn't my place to scrutinize God's great plan, but what about the balancing scales of justice?

Father said nothing to ease my worries. He just plucked up another bean flower and held it up to the sky, examining it in the African light like a doctor with an X-ray, looking for the secret thing gone wrong.

His first sermon in August waxed great and long on the subject of baptism. Afterward, at home, when Mother asked Mama Tataba to go put the soup on the stove, Mama Tataba turned and walked smack dab out the front door in between the words "soup" and "stove." She went out and gave my father a good talking to, shaking her finger at him across a row of tomatoless tomato plants. Whatever it was he'd done wrong in her opinion, it was really the last straw. We could hear her voice rising and rising.

Naturally it shocked us half to death to hear somebody caterwauling at Father this way. It shocked us even more to see him standing there red-faced, trying to fit a word in sideways. With all four of us girls lined up at the window with our mouths gaping open, we must have looked like the Lennon Sisters on Lawrence Welk. Mother shooed us from the window, ordering us to go hunt up our schoolbooks and read them. It wasn't the proper time for school, or even a school day, but we did everything she said now. We'd recently seen her throw a box of Potato Buds across the room.

After a quiet eternity of the Trojan War, Mama Tataba burst in and threw her apron on a chair. We all closed our books.

"I won't be stay here," she declared. "You send a girl get me at Banga you be need help. I go show you cook eel. They got a big eel downa river yesterday. That fish a good be for children."

That was her final advice for our salvation.

I followed her out the door and watched her tromp down the road, the pale soles of her feet blinking back at me. Then I went to track down my father, who had wandered a little distance from the fenced garden and was sitting against a tree trunk. In his fingers he carefully stretched out something that looked like a wasp, still alive. It was as broad as my hand and had a yellow *8* on each clear wing, as plain as if some careful schoolchild or God had painted it there.

My father looked like he'd just had a look down Main Street, Heaven.

He told me, "There aren't any pollinators."

"What?"

"No insects here to pollinate the garden."

"Why, but there's a world of bugs here!" An unnecessary remark, I suppose, as we both watched the peculiar insect struggling in his hands.

"African bugs, Leah. Creatures fashioned by God for the purpose of serving African plants. Look at this thing. How would it know what to do with a Kentucky Wonder bean?"

I couldn't know if he was right or wrong. I only faintly understand about pollination. I do know that the industrious bees do the most of it. I mused, "I guess we should have brought some bees over in our pockets too."

My father looked at me with a new face, strange and terrifying to me for what it lacked in confidence. It was as if a small, befuddled stranger were peering through the imposing mask of my father's features. He looked at me like I was his spanking newborn baby and he did love me so, but feared the world would never be what any of us had hoped for.

"Leah," he said, "you can't bring the bees. You might as well bring the whole world over here with you, and there's not room for it."

I swallowed. "I know."

We sat together looking through the crooked stick fence at the great variety of spurned blossoms in my father's garden. I felt so many different things right then: elation at my father's strange expression of tenderness, and despair for his defeat. We had worked so hard, and for what? I felt confusion and dread. I sensed that the sun was going down on many things I believed in.

From his big cage on the porch, Methuselah screeched at us in Kikongo. "*Mbote!*" he said, and I merely wondered, Hello or goodbye?

"What was Mama Tataba so mad about just now?" I dared to ask, very quietly. "We saw her hollering."

"A little girl."

"She has one?"

"No. A girl from here in the village that got killed last year."

I felt my pulse race ahead. "What happened to her?"

He did not look at me now, but stared off at the distance. "She got killed and eaten by a crocodile. They don't let their children step foot in the river, ever. Not even to be washed in the Blood of the Lamb."

"Oh," I said.

My own baptism, and every one I have witnessed so far, took place in something like a large bathtub or small swimming pool in the Baptist Church. The worst harm that could come to you might be that you would slip on the stairs. I hoped there would be room in heaven for that poor little girl, in whatever condition she'd arrived there.

"I fail to understand," he said, "why it would take six months for someone to inform me of that simple fact." The old fire was seeping back into this strange, wistful husk of my father. I felt gratified.

"*Ko ko ko!*" Methuselah called.

"Come in!" my father retorted, with impatience rising in his craw.

"Wake up, Brother Fowles!"

"Piss off!" my father shouted.

I held my breath.

He shoved himself straight to his feet, strode to the porch, and flung open the door of Methuselah's cage. Methuselah hunched his shoulders and sidled away from the door. His eyes in their bulging sockets ticked up and down, trying to understand the specter of this huge white man.

"You're free to go," my father said, waiting. But the bird did not come out. So he reached in and took hold of it.

In my father's hands Methuselah looked like nothing but a feathered toy. When he hurled the bird up at the treetops it didn't fly at first but only sailed across the clearing like a red-tailed badminton shuttlecock. I thought my father's rough grip had surely got the better of that poor native creature, and that it would fall to the ground.

But no. In a burst of light Methuselah opened his wings and fluttered like freedom itself, lifting himself to the top of our Kentucky Wonder vines and the highest boughs of the jungle that will surely take back everything once we are gone.

Book Two

THE REVELATION

And I stood upon the sand of the sea,
and saw a beast rise up. . . .
If any man have an ear, let him hear.

REVELATION 13:1,9

Orleanna Price

SANDERLING ISLAND, GEORGIA

ONCE EVERY FEW YEARS, even now, I catch the scent of Africa. It makes me want to keen, sing, clap up thunder, lie down at the foot of a tree and let the worms take whatever of me they can still use.

I find it impossible to bear.

Ripe fruits, acrid sweat, urine, flowers, dark spices, and other things I've never even seen—I can't say what goes into the composition, or why it rises up to confront me as I round some corner hastily, unsuspecting. It has found me here on this island, in our little town, in a back alley where sleek boys smoke in a stairwell amidst the day's uncollected refuse. A few years back, it found me on the Gulf Coast of Mississippi, where I'd returned for a family funeral: Africa rose up to seize me as I walked on a pier past a huddle of turtle-headed old fishermen, their bait buckets set around them like a banquet. Once I merely walked out of the library in Atlanta and there it was, that scent knocking me down, for no reason I can understand. The sensation rises up from inside me and I know you're still here, holding sway. You've played some trick on the dividing of my cells so my body can never be free of the small parts of Africa it consumed. Africa, where one of my children remains in the dank red earth. It's the scent of accusation. It seems I only know myself, anymore, by your attendance in my soul.

I could have been a different mother, you'll say. Could have straightened up and seen what was coming, for it was thick in the air all around us. It was the very odor of market day in Kilanga. Every fifth day was market day—not the seventh or thirtieth, nothing you could give a name like "Saturday," or "The First of the Month," but every thumb if you kept the days in your hand. It makes no sense at all, and then finally all the sense in the world, once you understand that keeping things in your hand is exactly how it's done in the Congo. From everywhere within walking distance, every fifth day, people with hands full or empty appeared in our village to saunter and haggle their way up and down the long rows where women laid out produce on mats on the ground. The vendor ladies squatted, scowling, resting their chins on their crossed arms, behind fortresses of stacked kola nuts, bundles of fragrant sticks, piles of charcoal, salvaged bottles and cans, or displays of dried animal parts. They grumbled continually as they built and rebuilt with leathery, deliberate hands their pyramids of mottled greenish oranges and mangoes and curved embankments of hard green bananas. I took a deep breath and told myself that a woman anywhere on earth can understand another woman on a market day. Yet my eye could not decipher those vendors: they wrapped their heads in bright-colored cloths as cheerful as a party, but faced the world with permanent vile frowns. They slung back their heads in slit-eyed boredom while they did each other's hair into starbursts of astonished spikes. However I might pretend I was their neighbor, they knew better. I was pale and wide-eyed as a fish. A fish in the dust of the marketplace, trying to swim, while all the other women calmly breathed in that atmosphere of overripe fruit, dried meat, sweat, and spices, infusing their lives with powers I feared.

One particular day haunts me. I was trying to keep track of my girls but could see only Leah. I recall she was in the pale blue dress with the sash that tied behind her back. All the girls but Rachel generally ran ragged, so this must have been—for our family—a Sunday, a coincidence of our big day and the villagers'. Leah had a basket in her arms, carrying for me some burden that held her back from her preferred place at the head of the pack. The others had moved out of sight. I knew Nathan would be impatient for our return, so I beckoned to Leah. She had to cross over a row of produce to get to me. Without a thought, as the twin whose legs never failed her, she shifted the basket to her left hip and took a giant step over a pyramid of oranges. I stretched out my hand to her. Right there as she reached for it, though, she got stuck somehow, mid-straddle over the oranges, unable to bring the other foot over. *Phhffff!* The woman squatting beside the oranges leaped up hissing, slicing her hands like scissors blades at the two of us, scorching me with eyes so hot the angry chocolate irises seemed to be melting into the white. A row of men on a bench looked up from their bowls of new beer and stared at us with the same clouded eyes, all motioning for me to move my child: *stupid ghost! nonperson!* straddling a woman's market-day wealth. I can't stop being embarrassed by the memory of myself and Leah there with her genitals—bare, for all anyone knew—suspended over a woman's oranges. A foreign mother and child assuming themselves in charge, suddenly slapped down to nothing by what they all saw us to be.

Until that moment I'd thought I could have it both ways: to be one of them, and also my husband's wife. What conceit! I was his instrument, his animal. Nothing more. How we wives and mothers do perish at the hands of our own righteousness. I was just one more of those women who clamp their mouths shut and wave the flag as their nation rolls off to conquer another in war. Guilty or innocent, they have everything to lose. They *are* what there is to lose. A wife is the earth itself, changing hands, bearing scars.

We would all have to escape Africa by a different route. Some of us are in the ground now and some are above it, but we're all women, made of the same scarred earth. I study my grown daughters now, for signs they are resting in some kind of peace. How did they manage? When I remain hounded by judgment? The eyes in the trees open onto my dreams. In daylight they watch my crooked hands while I scratch the soil in my little damp garden. What do you want from me? When I raise up my crazy old eyes and talk to myself, what do you want me to tell you?

Oh, little beast, little favorite. Can't you see I died as well?

Sometimes I pray to remember, other times I pray to forget. It makes no difference. How can I ever walk free in the world, after the clap of those hands in the marketplace that were plainly trying to send me away? I had warnings. How can I bear the scent of what catches up to me?

★ ★ ★

There was so little time to ponder right and wrong, when I hardly even knew where I was. In those early months, why, half the time I would wake up startled and think I was right back in Pearl, Mississippi. Before marriage, before religion, before everything. Mornings in the Congo were so steamy you couldn't see a thing but cloud come to earth, so you might as well be anywhere. Mama Tataba would appear to me standing in the bedroom doorway in her olive-green cardigan half buttoned up, with the five-dollar holes in the elbows, a knit cap of pilled wool pulled down to her eyebrows, her hands thick as hide; she could have been a woman standing in the alley door of Lutton's General Store in the year of our Lord and my childhood, 1939.

Then she'd say, "Mama Prize, a mongoose be got in the white flour," and I would have to hold on to the bed frame while the landscape swirled like water down a drain and pulled me back to the center. Here. Now. How in the world did a person get to be where I was?

Everything turned on the day we lost them both, Mama Tataba and the accursed parrot, both released by Nathan. What a day *that* was. For the native members of our household, Independence Day. The bird hung around, casting his vexed eye down on us from the trees, still needing to be fed. The other, she on whom our lives depended, vanished from the village. And the rain poured down and I wondered, Are we lost right now without knowing it? It had already happened so many times in my life (my wedding day comes to mind) that I thought I was out of the woods, not realizing I'd merely paused on the edge of another narrow precipice in the midst of a long, long fall.

I can still recite the litany of efforts it took to push a husband and children alive and fed through each day in the Congo. The longest journey always began with sitting up in bed at the rooster's crow, parting the mosquito curtain, and slipping on shoes—for there were hookworms lying in wait on the floor, itching to burrow into our bare feet. Shoes, then, sliding me across the floor to greet the day.

Dreaming of coffee. I'm afraid I didn't miss the physical presence of my husband in his absences as much as I missed coffee. Out the back door, into the shock of damp heat, straining for a look at the river: resisting the urge to run.

Oh, that river of wishes, the slippery crocodile dream of it, how it might have carried my body down through all the glittering sand-bars to the sea. The hardest work of every day was deciding, once again, to stay with my family. They never even knew. When I pried open the lock meant to keep the beasts and curious children out of our kitchen hut, I nearly had to lock it again behind me, to keep myself in. The gloom, the humidity, the permanent sour breath of rainy season all bore down on me like a bothersome lover. The fresh stench of night soil in the bushes. And our own latrine, which was only one step removed.

Standing at the work table I would leave my own thoughts and watch myself murdering oranges with our single dull knife, slitting their bellies and squeezing out the red blood. But no, first the fruit had to be washed; these strange, so-called blood oranges were gath-ered wild from the forest. When I bought them from Mama Mokala I knew they'd passed through the hands of her boys, all of whom bore white crusts on their eyes and penises. Washed, then, with a drop of precious Clorox bleach, measured out like the Blood of the Lamb. It's comical, I know, but I carried through those days the image of a pop-ular advertising campaign from home that pictured teams of very soiled children under the bold invocation: CLOROX NEEDED HERE!

Very well then, the juice wrenched from the disinfected skin, and then the pulpy liquid had to be diluted with water if I hoped to make the precious oranges last at all. It's hard to say which cost me more dearly: bleach, oranges, or water. Bleach and oranges both I had to bargain for, or beg for in the case of supplies flown in to us by the awful man Eeben Axelroot. Every few weeks he turned up without warning, a sudden apparition in rotten boots and sweat-stained fedora, smoking Tiparillos in my doorway and demanding money for things that were already ours, donated by the Mission League. He even sold us our mail! But then nothing came to us free. Not even water. It had to be carried a mile and a half, and boiled. "Boiled," a small word, meant twenty minutes over a roaring fire on a stove that resembled the rusted carcass of an Oldsmobile. "Fire" meant gathering up a pile of sticks in a village that had already been gathering firewood for all the years since God was a child, picking its grounds clean of combustibles as efficiently as an animal combing itself for lice. So "fire" meant longer and longer forays into the forest, stealing fallen branches from under the blunt-eyed gaze of snakes, just for one single bucket of drinkable water. Every small effort at hygiene was magnified by hours of labor spent procuring the simplest elements: water, heat, anything that might pass for disinfectant.

And food, that was another song and dance. Finding it, learning its name, cutting or pounding or dashing its brains to make it into something my family would tolerate. For a long time I could not work out how all the other families were getting by. There seemed to be no food to speak of, even on a market day when everybody came around to make the tallest possible pile out of what they had. It didn't seem to stack up to enough sustenance for the two dozen families in our village. Yes, I could see there was charcoal for cooking it, and shriveled red *pili-pili* peppers for spicing it, and calabash bowls to put it in, but where was the *it*, whatever it was? What on God's earth did they eat?

At length I learned the answer: a gluey paste called *fufu*. It comes from a stupendous tuber, which the women cultivate and dig from the ground, soak in the river, dry in the sun, pound to white powder in hollowed-out logs, and boil. It's called manioc, I was informed by Janna Underdown. It has the nutritional value of a brown paper bag, with the added bonus of trace amounts of cyanide. Yet it fills the stomach. It cooks up into the sort of tasteless mass one might induce an American child to try once, after a long round of pulled-up noses and double-dog dares. But for the people of Kilanga *fufu* was the one thing in life, other than time, that appeared to be taken for granted. There will always be manioc. It is the center of life. When the tall, narrow women dressed in their sarongs returned serenely from the fields, they toted it in huge parcels impossibly balanced on their heads: manioc-root bundles the size of crumpled horses. After soaking and peeling it, they arranged the long white roots into upright sprays in enamel tubs and passed single file through the village like immense lilies on slender, moving stalks. These women spent their days in the steady labors of planting, digging, and pounding manioc, though the dreamy way they moved through that work made it seem entirely separate from any end product. They reminded me of the groups of black men called *gandy dancers* in the Old South, who would come along the railroad track chanting, nodding, stepping forward and back in unison, banging out a rhythm with their steel rods, captivating children and moving on before you realized they had also, incidentally, repaired the track. That is how these women produced manioc, and that is how their children ate it: with no apparent thought to the higher purposes of production and consumption. *Fufu* was simply another word for food. Any other thing a person might eat—a banana, an egg, the bean called *mangwansi,* a piece of fire-blackened antelope flesh—was just the opposite, and its consumption was seen as a remarkable, possibly uncalled-for occasion.

My family required remarkable occasions three times a day. They couldn't understand that the sort of meal they took for granted, a thirty-minute production in the land of General Electric, translated here to a lifetime of travail. A family might as well sit waiting for Mother and her attendants to come out of the kitchen with three Thanksgiving dinners a day. And Mama Tataba managed to do it, complaining all the while. She muttered while she worked, never resting, only pausing from time to time to hike up the waist of her wraparound *pagne* underneath her wool sweater. She rolled her eyes whenever she had to undo my mistakes: the tin cans I forgot to wash out and save, the bananas I failed to check for tarantulas, the firebox I once stoked entirely with sticks of *bängala*—the poison-wood tree! She slapped the match out of my hand as I bent to light it, then pulled out the green sticks one by one with a potholder, explaining tersely that the smoke alone would have killed us all.

In the beginning I knew no Kikongo beyond the practical words she taught me, so I was spared knowing how she cursed our mortal souls as evenhandedly as she nourished our bodies. She pampered my ungrateful children, and resented us utterly. She could reach her fingers deep into a moldy bag, draw out a miraculous ounce of white flour, and slap out biscuits. She rendered goat fat into something like butter, and pulverized antelope meat into hamburgers with a device I think had been rigged from the propeller of a motorboat. She used a flat rock and the force of her will to smash groundnuts into passable peanut butter. And at the terminus of this long labor sat Rachel at the foot of the table: sighing, tossing her white hair from her shoulders, announcing that all she wished for in this world was "Jiffy, smooth. *Not* crunchy."

Fufu nsala, Mama Tataba called us. I gathered this had to do with *fufu*, the food staple, not yet knowing Kikongo is a language that is not exactly spoken but sung. The same word slanted up or down the scale can have many different meanings. When Mama Tataba incanted this hymn to all of us, under her breath, she was not calling us *fufu* eaters or *fufu* shunners or anything I could have guessed. *Fufu nsala* is a forest-dwelling, red-headed rat that runs from sunlight.

I'd thought I was being brave. The very first time I went into the kitchen house, a snake slithered away from the doorstep and a tarantula eyed me from the wall, hunkering down on his bandy legs like a football player on the offensive line. So I carried a big stick. I told Mama Tataba I'd grown up knowing how to cook, but not to be a circus trainer. Heaven only knows how she must have despised her pale rat of a cowering mistress. She couldn't have imagined the likes of an electric range, or a land where women concerned themselves with something called *waxy yellow buildup*. As much as she held me in contempt, she may never have had any real inkling of my true helplessness. I like to think she wouldn't have left us had she known. As it was, she left a pitched wake in which I felt I would drown.

Strange to say, it was Nathan's frightful confidence in himself that drove her off. He believed, as I did, we were supposed to have come prepared. But there is no preparing for vipers on the doorstep and drums in the forest, calling up an end to a century of affliction. By the time summer trailed off into the season of endless rains, it was clear there was going to be trouble. I couldn't stop imagining the deaths of my children. I dreamed them drowned, lost, eaten alive. Dreamed it, and woke in a stone-cold fright. When sleep refused to return, I lit the kerosene lamp and sat alone until dawn at our big dining-room table, staring at the words of the Psalms to numb my mind: *Lord, I have loved the habitation of thy house, and the place where thine honour dwelleth. Gather not my soul with sinners, nor my life with bloody men.*

Redeem me.

At sunrise I sometimes left the house to walk. To avoid the river, I took the forest path. More than once I startled elephant families browsing in the clearings. Woodland elephants are different from their grand cousins who stomp across the grasslands: they're smaller and more delicate, nuzzling through the leafy soil with rosy-pink tusks. Sometimes in the dawn light I also saw families of Pygmies moving among the shadows, wearing nothing but necklaces of feathers and animal teeth, and on rainy days, hats made of leaves. They were so small—truly less than half my size—and so gaily decorated, I thought for a long time they were children. I marveled that whole bands of boys and girls were out in the forest all on their own, with knives and spears and infants strapped on their backs.

Perhaps it was reading the Bible that had set my mind in such an open frame, ready to believe in any bizarre possibility. That, and the lack of sleep. I needed to tie myself down by some kind of moorings, but there was no one at all to talk to. I tried poring over the American news magazines sent to us via the Underdowns, but I only found them disturbing. President Eisenhower spoke of having everything under control; the Kennedy boy said Uncle Ike was all washed up and we need look no farther than the Congo—*Congo!*—for evidence of poor U.S. leadership, the missile gap, and proof of the Communist threat. The likes of Eleanor Roosevelt declared we ought to come forth with aid and bring those poor children into the twentieth century. And yet Mr. George F. Kennan, the retired diplomat, allowed that he felt "not the faintest moral responsibility for Africa." It's not our headache, he said. Let them go Communist if they feel like it.

It was beyond me to weigh such matters, when my doorstep harbored snakes that could knock a child dead by spitting in her eyes.

But Nathan wouldn't hear my worries. For him, our life was as simple as paying in cash and sticking the receipt in your breast pocket: we had the Lord's protection, he said, because we came to Africa in His service. Yet we sang in church "*Tata Nzolo*"! Which means *Father in Heaven* or *Father of Fish Bait* depending on just how you sing it, and that pretty well summed up my quandary. I could never work out whether we were to view religion as a life-insurance policy or a life sentence. I can understand a wrathful God who'd just as soon dangle us all from a hook. And I can understand a tender, unprejudiced Jesus. But I could never quite feature the two of them living in the same house. You wind up walking on eggshells, never knowing which *Tata Nzolo* is home at the moment. Under that uncertain roof, where was the place for my girls? No wonder they hardly seemed to love me half the time—I couldn't step in front of my husband to shelter them from his scorching light. They were expected to look straight at him and go blind.

Nathan, meanwhile, wrapped himself up in the salvation of Kilanga. Nathan as a boy played football on his high school team in Killdeer, Mississippi, with great success evidently, and expected his winning season to continue ever after. He could not abide losing or backing down. I think he was well inclined toward stubbornness, and contemptuous of failure, long before his conscription into the war and the strange circumstances that discharged him from it. After that, hounded by what happened in a Philippine jungle and the ghosts of a thousand men who didn't escape it, his steadfast disdain for cowardice turned to obsession. It's hard to imagine a mortal man more unwilling to change his course than Nathan Price. He couldn't begin to comprehend, now, how far off the track he was with his baptismal fixation. The village chief, Tata Ndu, was loudly warning people away from the church on the grounds that Nathan wanted to feed their children to the crocodiles. Even Nathan might have recognized this was a circumstance that called for reconciliation.

But reconciliation with Tata Ndu was a mighty cross to bear. When he granted us an audience, he sat in a chair in his front yard looking away from us. He adjusted his tall hat made of sisal fibers. He took off and examined his large black glasses frames (which bore no lenses), and made every other effort at scholarly disinterest, while Nathan talked. He flicked at flies with the official staff of his office—some sort of stiffened animal tail that ends in a silky white tassel. During the second interview, Nathan even retracted baptism as a specific program, and suggested we might organize some kind of sprinkling.

We eventually received a formal reply, via the elder Ndu son, stating that sprinkling was all very well but the previous Brother Fowles had disturbed the chief with peculiar ideas about having only one wife at a time. Imagine, Tata Ndu said, a shamefaced chief who could only afford one single wife! The chief expected us to disavow any such absurdities before he could endorse our church.

My steadfast husband tore his hair in private. Without the chief's blessing he could have no congregation. Nathan burned. There is no other way to say it. *Many are the afflictions of the righteous: but the Lord delivereth him out of them all,* he declared to the sky, squinting up at God and demanding justice. I held him in my arms at night and saw parts of his soul turn to ash. Then I saw him reborn, with a stone in place of his heart. Nathan would accept no more compromises. God was testing him like Job, he declared, and the point of that particular parable was that Job had done no wrong to begin with. Nathan felt it had been a mistake to bend his will, in any way, to Africa. To reshape his garden into mounds; to submit to Tata Ndu on the subject of river baptism; to listen at all to Tata Ndu or even the rantings of Mama Tataba. It had all been a test of Nathan's strength, and God was displeased with the outcome. He would not fail again.

He noticed the children less and less. He was hardly a father except in the vocational sense, as a potter with clay to be molded. Their individual laughter he couldn't recognize, nor their anguish. He never saw how Adah chose her own exile; how Rachel was dying for the normal life of slumber parties and record albums she was missing. And poor Leah. Leah followed him like an underpaid waitress hoping for the tip. It broke my heart. I sent her away from him on every pretense I knew. It did no good.

While my husband's intentions crystallized as rock salt, and while I preoccupied myself with private survival, the Congo breathed behind the curtain of forest, preparing to roll over us like a river. My soul was gathered with sinners and bloody men, and all I was thinking of was how to get Mama Tataba to come back, or what we should have brought from Georgia. I was blinded from the constant looking back: Lot's wife. I only ever saw the gathering clouds.

The Things We Learned

KILANGA, JUNE 30, 1960

Leah Price

I N THE BEGINNING we were just about in the same boat as Adam and
Eve. We had to learn the names of everything. *Nkoko, mongo, zulu*—
river, mountain, sky—everything must be called out from the void by
the word we use to claim it. All God's creatures have names, whether
they slither across our path or show up for sale at our front stoop:
bushbuck, mongoose, tarantula, cobra, the red-and-black monkey
called *ngonndo*, geckos scurrying up the walls. Nile perch and *nkyende*
and electric eel dragged from the river. *Akala, nkento, a-ana*: man,
woman, and child. And everything that grows: frangipani, jacaranda,
mangwansi beans, sugarcane, breadfruit, bird of paradise. *Nguba* is
peanut (close to what we called them at home, goober peas!); *malala*
are the oranges with blood-red juice; *mankondo* are bananas. *Nanasi* is
a pineapple, and *nanasi mputu* means "poor man's pineapple": a papaya.
All these things grow wild! Our very own backyard resembles the
Garden of Eden. I copy down each new word in my school notebook
and vow to remember it always, when I am a grown-up American
lady with a backyard garden of my own. I shall tell all the world the
lessons I learned in Africa.

We've learned from the books left behind by Brother Fowles,
field guides to the mammals and birds and the Lepidoptera, which
are the butterflies. And we've learned from anyone (mostly children)
who will talk to us and point at the same time. We've even had a
surprise or two from our own mother, who grew up way deeper in
Dixie than we did. As the buds on the trees turn to flowers, she
raises her black eyebrows in surprise above her wide blue eyes and

declares: bougainvillea, hibiscus, why, tree of heaven! Who would have thought Mother knew her trees? And the fruits—mango, guava, avocado—these we had barely glimpsed before, in the big Kroger store in Atlanta, yet now the trees reach right down and deliver such exotic prizes straight into our hands! That's one more thing to remember when I'm grown, to tell about the Congo: how the mango fruits hung way down on long, long stems like extension cords. I believe God felt sorry for the Africans after putting the coconut so far out of reach, and aimed to make the mango easier to get a hand on.

I look hard at everything, and blink, as if my two eyes were a Brownie camera taking photographs to carry back. At the people, too, who have names to be learned. Gradually we've begun to call out to our neighbors. Closest by is poor lame Mama Mwanza, who scurries down the road on her hands. And Mama Nguza, who walks with her head held strangely high on account of the giant goiter nestled like a goose egg under her chin. Tata Boanda, the old fisherman, goes out in his boat every morning in the brightest red pair of trousers you ever saw in your life. People wear the same thing day in and day out, and that's how we recognize them, by and large. (Mother says if they really wanted to put one over on us, they'd all swap outfits for a day.) On cool mornings Tata Boanda also wears a light green sweater with a white border on the placket—he's quite a sight, with his muscular chest as manly as all get-out framed by the V-neck of a ladies'-wear sweater! But if you think about it, how would he or anyone here ever know it's a lady's sweater? How do I even know? Because of the styling, though it's nothing you could plainly describe. So is it even a lady's sweater, here in the Congo? I wonder.

There is something else I must confess about Tata Boanda: he's a sinner. Right in the plain sight of God he has two wives, a young and an old one. Why, they all come to church! Father says we're to pray for all three of them, but when you get down to the particulars it's hard to know exactly what outcome to pray for. He should drop one wife, I guess, but for sure he'd drop the older one, and she already looks sad enough as it is. The younger one has all the kids, and you can't just pray for a daddy to flat-out dump his babies, can you? I always believed any sin was easily rectified if only you let Jesus Christ into your heart, but here it gets complicated.

Mama Boanda Number Two doesn't seem fazed by her situation. In fact, she looks like she's fixing to explode with satisfaction. She and her little girls all wear their hair in short spikes bursting out all over their heads, giving an effect similar to a pincushion. (Rachel calls it the "haywire hairdo.") And Mama Boanda always wraps her *pagne* just so, with a huge pink starburst radiating across her wide rump. The women's long cloth skirts are printed so gaily with the oddest things: there is no telling when a raft of yellow umbrellas, or the calico cat and gingham dog, or an upside-down image of the Catholic Pope might just go sauntering across our yard.

Late in the fall, the milky green bushes surrounding every house and path suddenly revealed themselves as poinsettias. They bloomed their heads off and Christmas rang out in the sticky heat, as surprising as if "Hark the Herald Angels" were to come on your radio in July. Oh, it's a heavenly paradise in the Congo and sometimes I want to live here forever. I could climb up trees just like the boys to hunt guavas and eat them till the juice runs down and stains my shirt, forever. Only I am fifteen now. Our birthday, in December, caught me off guard. Adah and I were late-bloomers in terms of the bad things, like getting breasts and the monthly visit. Back in Georgia when my classmates started turning up in training brassieres, one after another, like it was a catching disease, I bobbed off my hair and vowed to remain a tomboy. With Adah and me doing college algebra and reading the fattest books we could get our hands on, while the other kids trudged through each task in its order, I guess we'd counted on always being just whatever age we wanted to be. But no more. Now I'm fifteen and must think about maturing into a Christian lady.

To tell the truth, it's not purely paradise here, either. Perhaps we've eaten of the wrong fruits in the Garden, because our family always seems to know too much, and at the same time not enough. Whenever something big happens we're quite taken aback, but no one else is the least bit surprised. Not by a rainy season come and gone where none was supposed to be, nor by the plain green bushes changing themselves bang into poinsettias. Not by butterflies with wings as clear as little cats-eye glasses; not by the longest or shortest or greenest snake in the road. Even little children here seem to know more than us, just as easily as they speak their own language.

I have to admit, that discouraged me at first: hearing the little kids jabbering away in Kikongo. How could little babies smaller than Ruth May speak this whole other language so perfectly? It's similar to the way Adah will sometimes turn up knowing some entire, difficult thing like French or the square root of pi when I'd been taking for granted I knew everything she did. After we first arrived, the children congregated outside our house each and every morning, which confused us. We thought there must be something peculiar, such as a baboon, on our roof. Then we realized the peculiar thing was *us*. They were attracted to our family for the same reason people will pull over to watch a house afire or a car wreck. We didn't have to do a thing in the world to be fascinating but move around in our house, speak, wear pants, boil our water.

Our life was much less fascinating from my point of view. Mother gave us a few weeks leeway on the schoolbooks, what with all the confusion of our settling in, but then in September she clapped her hands together and declared, "Congo or not, it's back to school for you girls!" She's determined to make us scholars—and not just the gifted among us, either. We were all chained together in her game plan. Each morning after breakfast and prayers she sat us down at the table and poked the backs of our heads with her index finger, bending us over our schoolbooks (and Ruth May her coloring), getting us in shape for Purgatory, I'd reckon. Yet all I could concentrate on was the sound of the kids outside, the queer glittery syllables of their words. It sounded like nonsense but carried so much secret purpose. One mysterious phrase called out by an older boy could rout the whole group in shrieks and laughter.

After lunch she'd allow us a few precious hours to run free. The children would scream and bolt in terror when we came out, as if we were poisonous. Then after a minute or two they'd creep forward again, naked and transfixed, thrilled by our regular habits. Before long they'd have reassembled themselves in a semicircle at the fringe of the yard, chewing on their pink sugarcane stalks and staring. A brave one would take a few steps forward, hold out a hand and scream, "*Cadeau!!*" before running away in horrified giggles. That was the closest thing to fellowship we had achieved so far—a shrieked demand for a gift! And what could we give them? We hadn't given a single thought to *them* wanting earthly goods, in our planning ahead. We'd only brought things for ourselves. So I just tried to ignore the whole business as I lay in the hammock with my nose in the same book I'd already read three times. I pretended not to care that they watched me like a zoo creature or potential source of loot. They pointed and talked among themselves, lording it over me that their whole world left me out.

My mother said, "Well, but, sugar, it goes both ways. You know how to speak English and they don't."

I knew she was right, but I took no consolation from that. Speaking English was nothing. It wasn't a skill like being able to name all the capitals and principal products of South America or recite Scripture or walk on top of a fence. I had no memory of ever having had to work hard for my native tongue. For a time I did work hard to learn French, but then Adah ran away with that prize so I dropped the effort. She could know French for the both of us, as far as I was concerned. Though I do have to say it seems an odd talent for someone who just on general principles refuses to talk. Back home, the idea of French had seemed like a parlor game anyhow. After we got here, it still did. These children have nothing to do with *je suis, vous êtes*. They speak a language that burgles and rains from their mouths like water through a pipe. And from day one I have coveted it bitterly. I wanted to get up from my hammock and shout something that would flush them up like a flock of scared ducks. I tried to invent or imagine such a stout, snappy phrase. "Bukabuka!" I imagined myself shouting. "We like Ike!" Or, from a spaceship movie I had seen once: "Klatu barada nikto!"

I wanted them to play with me.

I suppose everyone in our family wanted the same, in one way or another. To play, to bargain reasonably, to offer the Word, to stretch a hand across the dead space that pillowed around us.

Ruth May was the first one among us to get her way.

That should have been no surprise, as Ruth May appears to be capable of leaping tall buildings with the force of her will. But who'd have thought a five-year-old could establish communications with the Congolese? Why, she wasn't even allowed out of our yard! It was my job to keep her there, usually, with one eye always on the lookout for her to fall out of a tree and crack her head wide open. That really is the kind of thing Ruth May would do, just for the attention. She was bound and determined to run off, and sometimes I had to threaten her with catastrophe just to keep her in check. Oh, I said awful things. That a snake might bite her, or that one of those fellows walking by and swinging his machete might just cut her gizzard out. Afterward I always felt guilty and recited the Repentance Psalm: "Have mercy upon me, O God, according unto the multitude of thy tender mercies." But really, with all those multitudes of tender mercies, He has got to understand sometimes you need to scare a person a little for her own good. With Ruth May it's all or nothing.

As soon as I had her good and terrified I'd slip away. I'd go hunt for the Pygmies, who are supposed to be dwelling right under our noses in the forest, or for monkeys (easier to spot). Or I'd cut up fruit for Methuselah, still hanging around begging, and catch grasshoppers for Leon, the chameleon we keep in a wooden crate. Mother lets us keep him on the condition we never bring him in the house. Which is funny, because I *found* him inside the house. His bulging eye sockets swivel whichever way they please, and we love to get his eyes going so one looks up and the other down. He catches the grasshoppers we throw in his box by whipping out his tongue like a slingshot.

I could also try to talk Father into letting me tag along with *him*. There was always that possibility. Father spends his days making rounds through the village, trying to strike up chats with the idle old men, or venturing farther afield to inspect the state of grace in the neighboring villages. There are several little settlements within a day's walk, but I'm sorry to report they all fall under the jurisdiction of our same godless chief, Tata Ndu.

Father never lets me go that far, but I beg him anyhow. I try to avoid the drudgery of housekeeping chores, which is more up Rachel's alley *if* she can stoop to being helpful on a given day. My view of the home is, it is always better to be outside. So I loiter at the edge of the village, waiting for Father's return. There, where the dirt road makes a deep red cut between high yellow walls of grass, you never know what might be coming toward you on dusty feet. Women, usually, carrying the world on their heads: a huge glass demijohn full of palm wine, with a calabash bowl perched on top like an upside-down hat; or a bundle of firewood tied up with elephant grass, topped off with a big enamel tub full of greens. The Congolese sense of balance is spectacular.

Most of the girls my age, or even younger, have babies. They appear way too young to be married, till you look in their eyes. Then you'll see it. Their eyes look happy and sad at the same time, but unexcited by anything, shifting easily off to the side as if they've already seen most of what there is. *Married* eyes. And the younger girls—if they are too young to be married and too old to be strapped on someone's back (which is not a wide margin)—why, they come striding along swinging their woven bags over their shoulders and scowl at you, as if to say, Out of my road, can't you see I'm busy! They may only be little girls tagging after their mothers, but believe you me, with them it's all business. The girls are usually just about bald, like the boys. (Mother says it's from not getting their proteins.) But you can tell the girls by their stained, frilly dresses, castoffs from some distant land. It took me aback for months that they look so much like little boys in ruffly dresses. No girl or woman wears pants, *ever*. We are the odd birds here. Apparently they think we're boys, except maybe Rachel, and can't tell a one of us apart from the other. They call us all *Beelezi*, which means

Belgians! I mean to tell you, they call us that right to our faces. It's how they greet us: "*Mbote, Beelezi!*" The women smile, but then cover their mouths, embarrassed. The little babies take one look and burst out crying. It's enough to give you a complex. But I don't care, I'm too fascinated to hide indoors or stay cooped up in our yard. Curiosity killed the cat, I know, but I try to land on my feet.

Right smack in the middle of the village is a huge kapok tree, which is where they get together and have their market every fifth day. Oh, that's something to see! All the ladies come to sell and bicker. They might have green bananas, pink bananas, mounds of rice and other whitish things piled on paper, onions or carrots or even peanuts if it's our lucky day, or bowls of little red tomatoes, misshapen things but highly prized. You might even see bottles of bright orange soda pop that someone walked here all the way from Leopoldville, I guess, and will walk a long way more before they're all sold. There's a lady that sells cubes of caramel-colored soap that look good to eat. (Ruth May snitched one and took a bite, then cried hard, not so much from the bad taste as the disappointment, I imagine. There's so little here for a child in the way of sweets.) Also sometimes we'll see a witch doctor with aspirins, pink pills, yellow pills, and animal pieces all laid out in neat rows on a black velvet cloth. He listens to your ailments, then tells you whether you need to buy a pill, a good-luck charm, or just go home and forget about it. That's a market day for you. So far we've only purchased things from around the edges; we can't get up the nerve to walk in there whole hog and do our shopping. But it's fascinating to look down the rows and see all those long-legged women in their colorful *pagnes*, bent over almost double to inspect things laid out on the ground. And women pulling their lips up to their noses when they reach out to take your money. You watch all that noise and business, then look past them to the rolling green hills in the distance, with antelopes grazing under flat-topped trees, and it doesn't fit together. It's like two strange movies running at the same time.

On the other days when there's no market, people just congregate in the main square for one thing and another: hairdos, shoe repair, or just gossiping in the shade. There's a tailor who sets up his foot-pedal sewing machine under the tree and takes their orders, simple as that. Hairdos are another matter, surprisingly complicated, given that the women have no real hair to speak of. They get it divided into rows of long parts in very intricate patterns so their heads end up looking like balls of dark wool made of a hundred pieces, very fancily stitched together. If they've got an inch or two to work with, the hairdresser will wrap sprigs of it in black thread so it stands up in little spikes, like Mama Boanda Number Two's. The hairdo business always draws an audience. The motto seems to be, If you can't grow your own, supervise somebody else's. The elderly women and men look on, working their gums, dressed in clothes exactly the same color as their skin, from all the many ground-in years of wash and wear. From a distance you can't tell they have on anything at all, but just the faintest shadow of snow-white hair as if Jack Frost lightly touched down on their heads. They look as old as the world. Any colorful thing they might hold in their hands, like a plastic bucket, stands out strangely. Their appearance doesn't sit square with the modern world.

Mama Lo is the main hairdresser. She also runs a palm-oil business on the side, getting little boys to squash it out of the little red oil-palm nuts in her homemade press and selling it to the other villagers just a little each day, for frying their greens and what not. Mama Lo doesn't have any husband, though she's as industrious as the day is long. With the way they do here, it seems like some fellow would snap her up as a valuable add-on to his family. She isn't a whole lot to look at, I'll grant you, with her sad little eyes and wrinkled mouth she keeps shut, morning till night, while she does everybody's hair. The state of her own hair is a mystery, since she always wraps her head in a dazzling cloth printed with peacock feathers. Those lively feathers don't really match her personality, but like Tata Boanda in his ladies'-wear sweater, she seems unaware that her outfit is ironic.

If I settle down on a stump somewhere at the edge of the village square, they'll forget about me sooner or later, I've found. I like to sit there and keep an eye out for the woman with the great big white purse, exactly like what Mamie Eisenhower might take shopping, which she carries proudly through the village on her head. And I love to watch the boys climb up palm trees to cut down the oil nuts. Way high up there with the sunlight falling reddish-brown on the palm trunks and the boys' narrow limbs, they look beautiful. They seem touched by the Lord's grace. In any event, they never fall. The palm fronds wave around their heads like ostrich plumes.

Twice I've seen the honey man who comes out of the forest carrying a block of honeycomb dripping with honey—sometimes bees and all!—in his bare hands. A smoking roll of leaves juts from his mouth like a giant cigar. He sings softly to the bees as he walks through the village, and the children all run after him, mesmerized by the prospect of honey, their eagerness for a sweet causing them to vibrate and hum like the bees.

On the rare days when Eeben Axelroot is in his shack at the end of the airplane field, I've been known to go down there and spy on him, too. Sometimes Adah comes, although she generally prefers her own company to anyone else's. But Mr. Axelroot provides a grave temptation, as he is such an abominable curiosity. We hide amongst the banana trees that have sprung up all around his latrine, even while it gives us the creeps knowing all this lush growth is fertilized by such a disgusting man's night soil. The big banana-tree leaves grow right up against the shack's filthy back window, leaving narrow gaps perfect for spying. Mr. Axelroot himself is boring to watch; on a typical day he sleeps till noon, then takes a nap. You can just tell he isn't saved. But his clutter is fascinating: guns, tools, army clothes, even a radio of some kind, which he keeps in an army footlocker. We can hear the faint static emanating from the trunk, and the spooky, distant voices speaking French and English. My parents told us there was not a radio within a hundred miles of our whole village (they wanted to get one for safety's sake, but neither the Mission League nor the Lord has so far provided). So they aren't aware of Mr. Axelroot's radio, and since I only learned of it through spying, I can't tell them about it.

My parents shun him completely. Our mother is so sure none of us would want to go near his house she hasn't bothered to forbid it. That's good luck for me. If no one has said outright that spying on Mr. Axelroot is a sin, then God probably couldn't technically hold it against me. The Hardy Boys did spying for the cause of good, and I have always felt mine is in this same vein.

It was midway through September when Ruth May made her inroads. I came back from my spying foray one afternoon to find her playing "Mother May I?" with half the village's children. I was flabbergasted. There stood my own little sister in the center of our yard, the focal point of a gleaming black arc of children strung from here to there, silently sucking their sugarcane sticks, not even daring to blink. Their faces concentrated on Ruth May the way a lens concentrates sunlight. I half expected her to go up in flames.

"You, that one." Ruth May pointed and held up four fingers. "Take four scissors steps."

The chosen child opened his mouth wide and sang a rising four-note song: "Ma-da-meh-yi?"

"Yes, you may," Ruth May replied benevolently.

The little boy crossed his legs at the knees, leaned back, and minced forward twice plus twice more, exactly like a crab that could count.

I watched for a long while, astonished to see what Ruth May had accomplished behind my back. Every one of these children could execute giant steps, baby steps, scissors steps, and a few other absurd locomotions invented by Ruth May. She grudgingly let us join the game, and grudgingly we did. For several afternoons under the gathering clouds, all of us—including the generally above-it-all Rachel—played "Mother May I?" I tried to picture myself in a missionary role, gathering the little children unto me, as it was embarrassing to be playing this babyish game with children waist-high to me. But we were so tired of ourselves and each other by then the company was irresistible.

We soon lost interest, though, for there was no suspense at all: the

Congolese children always passed us right by on their march to victory. In our efforts to eke the most mileage out of a scissors step or whatever, my sisters and I sometimes forgot to ask (or Adah to mouth) "Mother May I?" Whereas the other children never, *ever* forgot. For them, shouting "Ma-da-me-yi" was one rote step in a memorized chain of steps, not a courtesy to be used or dropped the way "yes, ma'am" and "thank you" are for us. The Congolese children's understanding of the game didn't even take courtesy or rudeness into account, if you think about it, any more than Methuselah did when he railed us with hell and damnation. This came as a strange letdown, to see how the game always went to those who knew the rules without understanding the lesson.

But "Mother May I?" broke the ice. When the other children got wise to Ruth May's bossy ways and drifted off, one boy stayed. His name was Pascal, or something near it, and he captivated us with frantic sign language. Pascal was my *nkundi*: my first real friend in the Congo. He was about two-thirds my size, though much stronger, and fortunately for us both he owned a pair of khaki shorts. Two frayed holes in the back gave a generous view of his buttocks, but that was all right. I rarely had to be directly behind him except when we climbed trees. The effect was still far less embarrassing to me than pure nakedness. I think I would have found it impossible to be friends with a purely naked boy.

"Beto nki tutasala?" he would ask me by way of greeting. "What are we doing?" It was a good question. Our companionship consisted mainly of Pascal telling me the names for everything we saw and some things I hadn't thought to look for. *Bängala,* for example, the poisonwood tree that was plaguing us all half to death. Finally I learned to see and avoid its smooth, shiny leaves. And he told me about *ngondi,* the kinds of weather: *mawalala* is rain far off in the distance that doesn't ever come. When it booms thunder and beats down the grass, that is *nuni ndolo,* and the gentler kind is *nkazi ndolo.* These he called "boy rain" and "girl rain," pointing right to his private parts and mine without appearing to think a thing in the world was wrong with that. There were other boy and girl words,

such as *right* and *left*: the man hand and the woman hand. These dis-
cussions came several weeks into our friendship, after Pascal had
learned I was not, actually, a boy, but something previously unheard
of: a girl in pants. The news surprised him greatly, and I don't like to
dwell on how it came about. It had to do with peeing in the bushes.
But Pascal quickly forgave me, and it's a good thing, since friends of
my own age and gender were not available, the girls of Kilanga all
being too busy hauling around firewood, water, or babies. It did
cross my mind to wonder why Pascal had a freedom to play and
roam that his sisters didn't. While the little boys ran around pretending to shoot each other and fall dead in the road, it appeared that
little girls were running the country.

But Pascal made a fine companion. As we squatted face to face, I
studied his wide-set eyes and tried to teach him English words—
palm tree, house, run, walk, lizard, snake. Pascal could say these words
back to me all right, but he evidently didn't care to remember
them. He only paid attention if it was something he'd never seen
before, such as Rachel's Timex watch with the sweep second hand.
He also wanted to know the name of Rachel's hair. *Herr, herr*, he
repeated over and over, as if this were the name of some food he
wanted to make sure he never got hold of by mistake. It only
dawned on me later, I should have told him "blonde."

Once we'd made friends, Pascal borrowed a machete and cut
sugarcane for me to chew on. With hard, frightening whacks he cut
the cane into popsicle lengths before replacing the machete beside
his father's hammock. The cane-sucking habit in Kilanga was no
doubt connected to the black stumps of teeth most everyone
showed off when they smiled at us, and Mother never lost an
opportunity to remark upon that connection. But Pascal had a fine
set of strong white teeth, so I decided to take my chances.

I invited Pascal into our kitchen house when Mother wasn't
there. We skulked about in the banana-smelling darkness, examining
the wall over the plank counter where Mother tacks up pictures she
tears out of magazines. They are company for her, I suppose, these
housewives, children, and handsome men from cigarette ads, of

which Father would disapprove if the Lord's path ever chanced to lead him through the kitchen, which isn't likely. Mother even has a photo of President Eisenhower in there. In the dimness the President's pale, bulbous head shines out like a lightbulb. Our substitute for electricity! But Pascal is always more interested in poking through the flour sacks, and he sometimes takes small handfuls of Carnation milk powder. I find that substance revolting, yet he eats it eagerly, as if it were candy.

In exchange for his first taste of powdered milk, Pascal showed me a tree we could climb to find a bird's nest. After we handled and examined the pink-skinned baby birds, he popped one of them in his mouth like a jujube. It seemed to please him a lot. He offered a baby bird to me, pantomiming that I should eat it. I understood perfectly well what he meant, but I refused. He did not seem disappointed to have to eat the whole brood himself.

On another afternoon Pascal showed me how to build a six-inch-tall house. Crouched in the shade of our guava, he planted upright twigs in the dirt. Then he built the twigs into walls with a sturdy basket weave of shredded bark all the way around. He spat in the dirt to make red mud, then patted this onto the walls until they were covered. Finally he used his teeth to square off the ends of palm fronds in a businesslike manner, for the roof. Finally he squatted back on his heels and looked over his work with an earnest, furrowed forehead. This small house of Pascal's, I realized, was identical in material and design to the house in which he lived. It only differed in size.

It struck me what a wide world of difference there was between our sort of games—"Mother May I?," "Hide and Seek"—and his: "Find Food," "Recognize Poisonwood," "Build a House." And here he was a boy no older than eight or nine. He had a younger sister who carried the family's baby everywhere she went and hacked weeds with her mother in the manioc field. I could see that the whole idea and business of Childhood was nothing guaranteed. It seemed to me, in fact, like something more or less invented by white people and stuck onto the front end of grown-up life like a frill on a dress. For the first time ever I felt a stirring of anger against my father for making me a white preacher's child from Georgia. This wasn't my fault. I bit my lip and labored on my own small house under the guava tree, but beside the perfect talents of Pascal, my own hands lumbered like pale flippers on a walrus out of its element. My embarrassment ran scarlet and deep, hidden under my clothes.

Ruth May Price

EVERY DAY MAMA SAID, You're going to crack your head wide open, but no sir. I broke my arm instead.

How I did it was spying on the African Communist Boy Scouts. Way up there in the tree I could see them but they couldn't see me. The tree had green alligator pears that taste like nothing much. Not a one of us but Mama will eat them, and the only reason is she can remember how they tasted back home from the Piggly Wiggly with salt and Hellman's mayonnaise. "Mayonnaise," I asked her. "What color was the jar?" But she didn't cry. Sometimes when I can't remember things from Georgia, she'll cry.

They looked like regular Congo Boy Scouts to me, marching, except they didn't have any shoes. The Belgium Army men all have shoes and guns and they come marching right straight through here sometimes, on their way to somewhere. Father said they are showing everybody Congolese, like Tata Undo, that Belgium is still calling the shots. But the other army is just boys that live around here. You can tell the difference. There aren't any white ones in charge, and they don't have all the same clothes. They've just got their shorts and barefooted or whatever they've got. One has got him a red Frenchie hat. Boy, I like that hat. The others have red hankies tied around their necks. Mama said they are *not* Boy Scouts, they are Jeune Mou-Pro. She says, "Ruth May, sugar, you don't have a speck of business with the Jeune Mou-Pro, so when you see them, why, you run on into the house." Mama does let us play with little children and boys, even if they are mostly naked, but not those ones in the red hankies. *Mbote ve!* That means no good. That is how I come to climb up the alligator pear tree when I saw them. For a long time I thought Mama was saying they were the Jimmy Crow, a name I knew from home.

In the morning we can't spy. My sisters have to sit and have their school, and I have to color and learn my letters. I don't like having school. Father says a girl can't go to college because they'll pour water in your shoes. Sometimes I can play with my pets instead of coloring, if I'm quiet. Here are my pets: Leon and the mongoose. Also the parrot. My father let the parrot go because we accidentally taught it to say bad words, but it didn't go plumb away. It goes and then it comes back because its wings aren't any count; it got too tamed and forgot how to fly away and eat by itself. I feed it sour limes from the *dima* tree to make it sneeze and wipe its bill off, one side and then the other side. *Mbote ve! Dima, dimba, dimbama.* I like to say all those words because they come out of your mouth and laugh. My sisters feel sorry for the parrot but I don't. I would have me a snake too if I could, because I'm not scared of them.

Nobody ever even gave me the mongoose. It came to the yard and looked at me. Every day it got closer and closer. One day the mongoose came in the house and then every day after that. It likes me the best. It won't tolerate anybody else. Leah said we had to name it Ricky Ticky Tabby but no sir, it's mine and I'm a-calling it Stuart Little. That is a mouse in a book. I don't have a snake because a mongoose wants to kill a snake. Stuart Little killed the one by the kitchen house and that was a good business, so now Mama lets it come on in the house. *Dimba* means *listen!* You listen here, Buster Brown! The snake by the kitchen house was a cobra that spits in your eyes. You go blind, and then it can just rare back and bite you any old time it feels like it.

We went and found the chameleon all on our own. Leah mostly found that one on her bed. Most animals are whatever color God made them and have to stay that way, but Leon is whatever dern color he wants to be. We take him in the house when Mama and Father are still at church and one time we put him on Mama's dress for an experiment and he turned flowered. If he gets out and runs away in the house, oh boy. Jeez old man. Then we can't find him. *Wenda mbote*—good-bye, fare ye well, and amen! So we keep him outside in a box that the comic books came in. If you poke him with a stick he turns black with sparkles and makes a noise. We do that to show him who's boss.

When I broke my arm it was the day Mr. Axelroot was supposed to come. Father said that was good timing by the grace a God. But when Mr. Axelroot found out we had to go to Stanleyville he turned around and took right off again up the river or something, nobody knew, and he'd be back tomorrow. Mama said, "That man." Father said, "What were you doing shimmying up that tree in the first place, Ruth May?" I said Leah was suppose to be watching me so it wasn't my fault. I said I was hiding from the Jimmy Crow boys.

"Oh, for Pete's sake," Mama said. "What were you doing out there at all when I told you to run inside whenever you see them coming?" She was afraid to tell Father because he might whip me, busted arm and all. She told him I was a lamb of God and it was a pure accident, so he didn't whip me. Not *yet*. Maybe when I'm all fixed, he will.

That arm hurt bad. I didn't cry, but I held it right still over my chest. Mama made me a sling out of the same bolt of cloth she brought over to make the bed sheets and baptizing dresses for the African girls. We haven't baptized any yet. Dunking them in the river, they won't have it, no sir, nothing doing. Crocodiles.

Mr. Axelroot did come back next day at noontime and smelled like when the fruit goes bad on you. Mama said it could wait one more day if we wanted to get there in one piece. She said, "Lucky it was just a broken bone and not a snakebite."

While we were waiting for Mr. Axelroot to sit in his airplane and get to feeling better, the Congolese ladies came on down to the airplane field with great big old bags of manioc on their heads and he gave them money. The ladies cried and yelled when he gave them the money. Father said that was because it was two cents on the dollar, but they don't even have regular dollars here. They use that pink money. Some of the ladies yelled hard at Mr. Axelroot and went away without giving him their stuff. Then we got in the plane and flew to Stanleyville: Mr. Axelroot, Father, and my broken arm. I was the first one of my sisters ever to break any bone but a toe. Mama wanted to go instead of him because I was a waste of Father's time. If she went I'd get to ride on her lap, so I said that to him, too, I was going to waste his time. But, no, then he decided after all he wanted to go walk on a city street in Stanleyville, so he went and Mama stayed. The back of the airplane was so full of bags I had to sit on them. Big scratchy brown bags with manioc and bananas and little cloth bags of something hard. I looked inside some of them: rocks. Sparkly things and dirty rocks. Mr. Axelroot told Father that food goes for the price a gold in Stanleyville, but it wasn't gold in the little cloth bags. No, sir, it was diamonds. I found that out and I can't tell how. Even Father doesn't know we rode in a airplane with diamonds. Mr. Axelroot said if I told, why then God would make Mama get sick and die. So I can't.

After I went to sleep and woke up again in the airplane Mr. Axelroot told us what all we could see from up there looking down: Hippos in the river. Elephants running around in the jungle, a whole bunch of them. A lion down by the water, eating. Its head moved up and down like our kitty in Atlanta. He told us there's little tiny Pygmy people down there too but we never saw any. Maybe too little.

I said to him, "Where is all the green mamba snakes?"

I know they live up in a tree so they can drop on you and kill you, and I wanted to see some. Mr. Axelroot said, "There's not a thing in this world hides as good as a green mamba snake. They're just the same color as what they lay up against," he said, "and they don't move a muscle. You could be right by one and not know it."

We landed nice as you please on the grass. It was bumpier up in the sky than down on the grass. The big huge house right there was the hospital and they had a lot of white people inside, and some other ones in white dresses. There were so many white people I forgot to count. I hadn't seen any but just us for a coon's age.

The doctor said, "What was a nice preacher's girl doing up a tree?" The doctor had yellow hair on his arms and a big face and sounded foreign. But he didn't give me a shot so I liked him all right.

Father said, "That is just what her mother and I wanted to know."

I said I didn't want anybody a-throwing me in a big pot and eating me, so I had to hide. The doctor smiled. Then I told him for real I was hiding from the Jimmy Crow, and the doctor didn't smile, he just looked at Father. Then he said to me, "Climbing trees is for boys and monkeys."

"We don't have boys in our family," I told him.

He laughed at that. He said, "Nor monkeys either, I should not think!"

He and Father talked about man things. The doctor was surprised about the Jimmy Crow boys being in our village. He didn't talk plain English like us; he said *I can not* instead of *I can't*, and *they are* and *did not* and such. *They have heard*, is what he asked Father. "They have heard of our Patrice Lumumba all the way down to Kilanga now?"

Father said, "Oh, we don't see too much of them. We hear rifle practice on occasion."

"Lord help us," said the doctor.

Father told him, "Why, the Lord *will* help us! We'll receive His divine mercy as his servants who bring succor."

The doctor frowned then. He said to forgive him but he did not agree. He called my father *Reverend*. He said, "Reverend, missionary work is a great bargain for Belgium but it is a hell of a way to deliver the social services."

He said that word: *hell*! I sucked in my breath and listened with my ears.

Father said: "Why, doctor, I am no civil servant. Some of us follow careers and some of us get called out. My work is to bring salvation into the darkness."

"Salvation my foot!" is what that doctor said. I do believe that man was a sinner, the way he sassed back at Father. We watched him mix up the white plaster and lay out strips. I hoped he and my father wouldn't get in a fight. Or, if they did, I hoped I could watch. I saw Father hit a man one time, who did not praise the Lord.

Without looking up from my arm, the doctor said, "We Belgians made slaves of them and cut off their hands in the rubber planta-tions. Now you Americans have them for a slave wage in the mines and let them cut off their own hands. And you, my friend, are stuck with the job of trying to make amens."

He was wrapping up my arm while he said all that about cutting off hands. He kept on wrapping the cool white strips around and around till it was all finished up and my arm inside like a hot dog in a bun. I was glad nobody wanted to cut off *my* hands. Because Jesus made me white, I reckon they wouldn't.

He told me, "That will bother you. We will take it off in six weeks."

"Okay," I said to his white coat sleeve. There was blood on it. Somebody else's.

But Father wasn't done with the doctor yet. He was hopping from one foot to the other and cried, "Up to *me* to make amens? I see no amens to make! The Belgians and American business brought civilization to the Congo! American aid will be the Congo's salvation. You'll see!"

The doctor held my white broken arm like a big bone in his two hands, feeling how my fingers bent. He raised his yellow eyebrows without looking up at Father, and said, "Now, Reverend, this civi-lization the Belgians and Americans brought, what would that be?"

Father said, "Why, the roads! Railroads . . ."

The doctor said, "Oh. I see." Then he bent down in his big white coat and looked at my face. He asked me, "Did your father bring you here by automobile? Or did you take the passenger railway?"

He was just being a smart aleck and Father and I didn't answer him. They don't have any cars in the Congo and he knew it.

He stood up then and clapped the white stuff off his hands, and I could see he was all done with my arm, even if Father wanted to argue till he went blue in the face. The doctor held the door open for us.

"*Reverend,*" he said.

"Sir?" asked my father.

"I do not like to contradict, but in seventy-five years the only roads the Belgians ever built are the ones they use to haul out diamonds and rubber. Between you and me, Reverend, I do not think the people here are looking for your kind of salvation. I think they are looking for Patrice Lumumba, the new soul of Africa."

"Africa has a million souls" is what Father told him. And Father ought to know, for he's out to save them all.

"Well, yes, indeed!" the doctor said. He looked out into the hallway and then closed the door with us still inside. He said in a lower voice, "And about half of them were right here in Stanleyville last week to cheer on their Tata Lumumba."

Father said, "Tata Lumumba, who from what I hear is a barefoot post office worker who's never even been to college."

"That is true, Reverend, but the man has such a way of moving a crowd he does not seem to need shoes. Last week he spoke for an hour on the nonviolent road to independence. The crowd loved it so much they rioted and killed twelve people."

The doctor turned his back on us then. He washed his hands in a bowl and wiped them on a towel like Mama after the dishes. Then he came back and looked hard at my arm for a minute, and then at Father. He told my father there were only eight Congolese men in all this land who have been to college. Not one single Congolese doctor or military officer, nothing, for the Belgians don't allow them to get an education. He said, "Reverend, if you are looking for Congo's new leaders, do not bother looking in a school hall. You might better look in prison—Mr. Lumumba landed himself there after the riots last week. By the time he is out I expect he will have a larger following than Jesus."

Hoo, boy! My father didn't like the doctor one bit after that. Saying anything is better than Jesus is a bad sin. Father looked up at the ceiling and out the window and tried not to hit anything until the doctor opened the door and time for us to go. The ceiling light was a clear glass bowl half full of something dark, like a coffee cup, only it was dead bugs. I know why. They like to come up to the light because it is so, so pretty like something they want, and then they get trapped in there.

I know how they would feel if you touched them. Like somebody's eyelashes right up against your fingers.

When we came home my sisters had to cut up my dinner every day and help me get dressed. It was the best thing that happened. I showed Leah where you could get into the alligator pear tree and she boosted me up. I could still climb just dandy with my other arm. I have to play with Leah the most because the others in my family have got something wrong with them or else they're too grown-up to play.

We had to wait up there in the tree. I told her, "Mr. Axelroot drinks red whiskey. He has it under the seat of his airplane. I rolled it out with my foot and then put it back."

I was the youngest, but I had something to tell.

You don't ever have to wait around for the Belgium Army. They always come at the same time. Right after lunch, when it isn't raining yet and all the women with their buckets and things have gone down to the river and the fields and the men are home sleeping. It's quiet. Then the army boys will come a-marching down the road saying a song in French. That white one knows who's boss and all the others have to yell back because they are the Tribes of Ham. But, boy oh boy, let me tell you, they all have shoes. They walk together hard in the road and then stop so fast the dust comes down on their shoes.

The Jimmy Crow boys are harder to see. They don't care for the Belgium Army, so they hide out. They come just every now and then and have meetings in a place back behind our chicken house. They squat down to listen to the main one that talks, and their legs and arms are so skinny you can tell just what shape a bone is. And no shoes, either. Just white scabby dust on the tops of their feet, and all of them with those dark black sores and scars. Every scar shows up good. Mama says their skin bears scars different from ours because their skin is a map of all the sorrows in their lives.

We were waiting to spy on them back there behind the chicken house when they came. Leah told me Mama says Mrs. Underdown says don't even look at them, if they come. They want to take over the whole country and throw out the whites.

I said, "I'd like to have me a red hat like that."

"Shhh, shut up," Leah said. But then she said, "Well, I would too. That's a good red hat." She said that because "Shut up" hurt my feelings.

The boys said, "Patrice Lumumba!"

I told Leah that means the new soul of Africa, and he's gone to jail and Jesus is real mad about it. I told her all that! I was the youngest one but I knew it. I lay so still against the tree branch I was just the same everything as the tree. I was like a green mamba snake. Poison. I could be right next to you and you wouldn't ever know it.

Rachel

WELL, HALLELUJAH and pass the ammunition. Company for dinner! And an eligible bachelor at that, without three wives or even one as far as I know. Anatole, the schoolteacher, is twenty-four years of age, with all his fingers still on, both eyes and both feet, and that is the local idea of a top-throb dreamboat. Well, naturally he is not in my color category, but even if I were a Congolese girl I'm afraid I'd have to say thanks but no thanks on Anatole. He has scars all over his face. Not accident scars, but thin little lines, the type that some of them here get done to them on purpose, like a tattoo. I tried not to stare but you end up thinking, How did somebody get all the cuts to line up so perfect like that? What did they use, a pizza-pie cutter or what? They were fine as a hair and perfectly straight, approximately a blue million of them, running from the middle of his nose to the sides of his face, like the ridges on a black corduroy skirt sewn on the bias, with the seam running right down the middle. It is not the kind of thing you see very much of here in our village, but Anatole is not from here. He is Congolese all right, but he has a different kind of eyes that slant a little bit like a Siamese, only more intellectual. We all had to make every effort not to stare. There he sat at our dinner table with his smooth haircut and a regular yellow button-down shirt and his intelligent brown eyes blinking very normal when he listened to you, but then, all those nerve-jangling scars. It gave him a mysterious air, like a putative from the law. I kept stealing glances at him across a plate of antelope meat and stale Potato Buds, which I guess just goes to show you how unaccustomed to the male species I have become.

Anatole speaks French and English both, and single-handedly runs the school all by himself. Six mornings a week, little noisy dirt-kicking crowds of boys from our village and the next one over come straggling in for their education. It's only the boys, and not all of them either, since most of the parents don't approve of learning French or the foreign element in general. But when those lucky few show up every morning, Anatole lines them up, littlest to biggest. If ever you happen to be out and about in our village at the crack of dawn, as I try not to be, you can watch them do it. Each boy stands with his hand on the shoulder of the taller boy ahead, creating a big long slope of arms. Leah drew a picture of them. Granted my sister is mentally disturbed. She titled it "The Inclined Plane of Males."

After the lineup Anatole marches them into the church and urges them, I guess, to wrestle with their numbers and their French congregations and what not. But they only take it so far, you see. If they haven't already lost interest by the time they are twelve or so, their education is over and out. It's more or less something like a law. Imagine: no school allowed after age twelve. (I wouldn't mind!) Mrs. Underdown told us the Belgians have always had the policy of steering the Congolese boys away from higher education. Girls too, I guess that goes without saying, because the girls around here, why, all they ever do is start having their own babies when they're about ten, and keep on having them till their boobies go flat as pancakes. Nobody has their eye on that all-important diploma, let me tell you. And yet here Anatole speaks French, English, Kikongo and whatever all he first started out with, plus knowing enough to be the one all-purpose schoolteacher. He must have been busy as a beaver during his fleeting school days.

Anatole was born up around near Stanleyville, but at a tender age with his mother being dead got sent to work on the rubber plantations near Coquilhatville, where more opportunities both good and bad present themselves—that was his way of putting it when he told us his personal life autography at dinner. He also spent some time at the diamond mines down south in Katanga, where he says one-quarter of all the world's diamonds come from. When he spoke of diamonds I naturally thought of Marilyn Monroe in her long gloves and pursey lips whispering "Diamonds Are a Girl's Best Friend." My best friend Dee Dee Baker and I have snuck off to see M.M. and Brigitte Bardot both at the matinee (Father would flat-out kill me if he knew), so you see I know a thing or two about diamonds. But when I looked at Anatole's wrinkled brown knuckles and pinkish palms, I pictured hands like those digging diamonds out of the Congo dirt and got to thinking, Gee, does Marilyn Monroe even know where they come from? Just picturing her in her satin gown and a Congolese diamond digger in the same universe gave me the weebie jeebies. So I didn't think about it anymore.

I inspected Anatole's special kind of face scarring instead. It is evidently considered beautifying in that region, or one of the places he's lived at any rate. Around here the people seem content to settle for whatever scars life whangs them with as a decoration. That plus the splectacular hairdos on the women, which, man alive, don't even get me started.

But Anatole not being from here, that explains why he doesn't have his mother and father and fourteen hundred cousins living with him like everybody else does. We'd already heard part of the story, that he was an orphan. The Underdowns took him on as a project because his family all got killed in some horrible way they love to hint at but never exactly tell. Back when they used to live here, they heard about Anatole from some other missionaries and saved him from the famous diamond mines and taught him to love Jesus and how to read and write. Then they installed him as the schoolteacher. Father says Anatole is "our only ally in all this," which is as clear as mud to me, but apparently Father's say-so was a good enough reason to invite him to dinner. At least it gave us something to look forward to besides these wonderful dead animals we get to eat. And it provided Mother something to get all franticky about. She declared she was at her wits' end to come up with a presentable meal. She'd cooked up some antelope meat and tried to make fried plantains that turned into something like black horse-hoof glue in the pan. She tried to make up for the food by using the white tablecloth and serving those pitiful black plantains in the bone-china platter with the forget-me-nots that she was so proud of—her one pretty thing in this big old mess we have to live in. And I will say she did her best to be the graceful hostess. Anyways Anatole gave her compliments right and left, which tells you right there he was either a polite young man or mentally cracked.

The small talk and compliments went on so long I was fixing to croak. My sisters gawked at the fascinating stranger and hung on his every syllabus of English, but as far as I was concerned it was just exactly like dinner with Father's prissy Bible-study groups back in Georgia, only with more repulsive food.

Then all of a sudden the fire hit the pan.

Anatole leaned forward and announced, "Our chief, Tata Ndu, is concerned about the moral decline of his village."

Father said, "Indeed he should be, because so few villagers are going to church."

"No, Reverend. Because so *many* villagers are going to church."

Well, that stupefied us all for a special moment in time. But Father leaned forward, fixing to rise to the challenge. Whenever he sees an argument coming, man oh man, does he get jazzed up.

"Brother Anatole, I fail to see how the church can mean anything but joy, for the few here who choose Christi-*an*-ity over *ignorance* and *darkness*!"

Anatole sighed. "I understand your difficulty, Reverend. Tata Ndu has asked me to explain this. His concern is with the important gods and ancestors of this village, who have always been honored in certain sacred ways. Tata Ndu worries that the people who go to your church are neglecting their duties."

"Neglecting their duties to false idolatry, you mean to say."

Anatole sighed again. "This may be difficult for you to understand. The people of your congregation are mostly what we call in Kikongo the *lenzuka*. People who have shamed themselves or had very bad luck or something like that. Tata Boanda, for example. He has had terrible luck with his wives. The first one can't get any proper children, and the second one has a baby now who keeps dying before birth and coming back into her womb, over and over. No one can help this family anymore. The Boandas were very careful to worship their personal gods at home, making the proper sacrifices of food and doing everything in order. But still their gods have abandoned them for some reason. This is what they feel. Their luck could not get any more bad, you see? So they are interested to try making sacrifices to your Jesus."

Father looked like he was choking on a bone. I thought: Is there a doctor in the house? But Anatole went right on merrily ahead, apparently unaware he was fixing to kill my father of a heart attack.

"Tata Ndu is happy for you to draw the bad-luck people away," he said. "So the village's spirit protectors will not notice them so much. But he worries you are trying to lure too many of the others into following corrupt ways. He fears a disaster will come if we anger the gods."

"*Corrupt*, did you say," Father stated, rather than asked, after locating where the cat had put his tongue.

"Yes, Reverend Price."

"Corrupt *ways*. Tata *Ndu* feels that bringing the Christian word to these people is leading them to corrupt *ways*."

"That is the best way I can think of to translate the message. Actually he said you are leading our villagers down into a hole, where they may fail to see the proper sun and become trapped like bugs on a rotten carcass."

Well, that did it! Father was going to keel plumb over. Call the ambulance. And yet, here was Anatole looking back at Father with his eyebrows raised very high, like "Do you understand plain English?" Not to mention my younger sisters, who were staring at Anatole like he was the Ripley's Believe It or Not Two-Headed Calf.

"Tata Ndu asked you to relay all that, did he?"

"Yes, he did."

"And do you agree that I am leading your fellow villagers to partake of the meat of a rotten *corpse*?"

Anatole paused. You could see him trying out different words in his head. Finally he said, "Reverend Price, do I not stand beside you in your church every Sunday, translating the words of the Bible and your sermons?"

My Father did not exactly say yes or no to that, though of course it was true. But that's Father, to a tee. He won't usually answer a question straight. He always acts like there's a trap somewhere and he's not about to get caught in it. Instead he asked, "And, Anatole, do you not now sit at my table, translating the words of Tata Ndu's bible of false idolatry and his sermon aimed at me in particular."

"Yes, sir, that is what I am doing."

Father laid his knife and fork crossways on his plate and took a breath, satisfied he'd gained the upper hand. Father specializes in the upper hand. "Brother Anatole, I pray every day for understanding and patience in leading Brother Ndu to our church," he said. "Perhaps I should pray for you as well."

This was Big Chief Ndu they were talking about, or "Mister Undo" as Ruth May calls him. And I don't mind saying he is a piece of work. It is hard to muster up the proper respect for a chief who wears glasses with no glass in them (he seems to think they raise his intelligence quotient), and the fur of a small animal clasped around his neck, a fashion trademark he shares with the elderly churchgoing ladies of Georgia, charmed I'm sure.

"If you are counting your enemies, you should not count me among them, sir," Anatole said. "And if you fear the rivals of your church, you should know there is another *nganga* here, another minister. People also put their trust in him."

Father loosened his tie and the collar of his short-sleeved Sunday shirt. "First of all, young man, I do not *fear* any man in Kilanga. I am a messenger of God's great good news for all mankind, and He has bestowed upon me a greater strength than the brute ox or the most stalwart among the heathen."

Anatole calmly blinked at that. I reckon he was wondering which one Father had him pegged for, brute ox or stalwart heathen.

"Second," Father went on, "I'll point out what you clearly must know, which is that Brother Ndu is not a minister of any kind. His business concerns the governing of human relations, not matters of the spirit. But you are quite right, there is another preacher aside from myself guiding my own right hand. The *Lord* is our *Shepherd*." Naturally Father had to give the impression he knew who, or what, Anatole was talking about, even if he didn't. What with him being the Father Knows Best of all times.

"Yes, yes, of course, the Lord is our Shepherd," Anatole said quickly, like he didn't believe it all that much and was just getting it out of the way. "But I am speaking of the *nganga* Tata Kuvudundu."

We all stared at the middle of the table like something dead with feet had just turned up there. Why, we *knew* Tata Kuvudundu. We'd seen him babbling and walking cockeyed down the road, leaning over so far you keep thinking he'll plumb fall over. He has six toes on one of his feet, and that's not even half the battle. Some days he sells aspirins in the market, all dignified like Dr. Kildare, yet other days he'll turn up with his body painted top to bottom (and I do mean bottom) in some kind of whitewash. We've also seen him squatting in his front yard surrounded by other old men, every one of them falling over from drinking palm wine. Father told us Tata Kuvudundu conducts the sin of false prophecy. Supposedly he and his grown-up sons tell fortunes by throwing chicken bones into a calabash bowl.

"Anatole, what do you mean by calling him a preacher?" Mother asked. "We kind of thought Tata Kuvudundu was the town drunk."

"No Mama Price, he is not. He is a respected *nganga,* a priest of the traditions, you might say. He is quite a good advisor to Tata Ndu."

"Advisor, *nothing,*" said Father, raising halfway up out of his chair and starting to get his Baptist voice. His red eyebrows flared above his scowling eyes, with the bad one starting to squint a little from the strain of it all. "He is a rare *nut*, is what he is. A *nut* of the type that never falls far from the *tree!* Where I come from, sir, that is what we call a *witch doctor.*"

Anatole took one of Mother's cloth napkins and blotted his face. Dots of perspiration were running into the little ridges along his nose. My sisters were still staring at him with all their might, and no wonder. We hadn't had any company since Mother vanished Mr. Axelroot from our table way last summer—merely because he spat and cursed; we didn't even know yet that he was a criminal element that would charge us for our own things. Since that time we hadn't heard word one of English at our dinner table from any mouth but a Price's. Six months is a long time for a family to tolerate itself without any outside distractions.

Anatole seemed to be getting ants in his pants but was still bound and determined to argue with Father. In spite of the seven warning signals of "You'll be sorry" written all over Father's face. Anatole said, "Tata Kuvudundu looks after many practical matters here. Men go especially to him when their wives are not getting children, or if they are adulterous." He glanced at me, of all things, as if I in particular were too young to know what that meant. Really.

Mother suddenly snapped out of it. "Help me out, girls," she said. "The dishwater is boiling away on the stove, I forgot all about it. You all clear the table and start washing up. Be careful and don't get burned."

To my surprise, my sisters practically ran from the table. They were curious, I'm sure, but the main consideration had to be Father. He was as flustrated as it gets and looked like he was fixing to throw a rod. I, however, didn't leave. I helped clear the dishes but then I sat back down. If anybody presumed I was too young for a conversation about adulters and not getting babies they had another think coming. Besides, this was the most exciting occasion that had happened to us since Ruth May fell out of a tree, which goes to show you how fascinating our life was. If big Daddy-O was going to blow his stack over a witch doctor, here's one cat that wasn't going to miss it.

Anatole told Father he ought not to think of Tata Kuvudundu as competition. He said barrenness and adultery were serious matters that probably ought to remain separate from Tata Jesus. But he assured us that many people in Kilanga remembered the missionary times, when Brother Fowles had gotten practically the whole town praying to Jesus, and it was their recollection that the gods hadn't been too angry over it, since no more bad things had happened in Kilanga than usual.

Well, that did it. *Remembered* the missionary times? This was a nerve shock even to me, to hear that the villagers thought Christianity was like some old picture show that was way out of date. What did that make Father then, Charlie Chaplin, waddling around duck-footed, waving his cane and talking without any sounds coming out?

Mother and I watched him, expecting the dreaded atomic blowup. Father actually did open and close his mouth like a silent-picture version of "What!" or "Waaa!" and his neck turned red. Then he got very still. You could hear Ruth May's creepy pet mongoose scurrying around under the table looking for somebody to drop something. Then Father's whole face changed and I knew he was going to use the special way of talking he frequently perpeturates on his family members, dogs that have peed in the house, and morons, with his words saying one thing that's fairly nice and his tone of voice saying another thing that is not. He told Anatole he respected and valued his help (meaning: I've had about enough of your lip, Buster Brown) but was disappointed by the villagers' childlike interpretations of God's plan (meaning: you are just as big of a dingwit as the rest of them). He said he would work on a sermon that would clear up all the misunderstandings. Then he announced that this conversation had come to an end, and Anatole could consider himself excused from the table and this house.

Which Anatole did, without delay.

"Well, that puts a whole new outlook on things, doesn't it?" Mother asked, in the very quiet silence that followed. I kept my head down and cleared off all the last things except the big blue-flowered platter in the middle of the table, which I couldn't reach without crossing into Father's atomic danger zone.

"I wonder what *outlook* you might think that to *be*," he said to Mother in that same special voice, for bad dogs and morons.

She brushed her hair out of her face and smiled at him as she reached across for the china platter. "Well, for one thing, sir, you and the good Lord better hope no lightning strikes around here in the next six months!"

"Orleanna, shut *up!*" he yelled, grabbing her arm hard and jerking the plate out of her hand. He raised it up over her head and slammed it down hard on the table, cracking it right in two. The smaller half flipped upside down as it broke, and lay there dribbling black plantain juice like blood onto the tablecloth. Mother stood helplessly, holding her hands out to the plate like she wished she could mend its hurt feelings.

"You were getting too fond of that plate. Don't you think I've noticed?"

She didn't answer him.

"I had hoped you might know better than to waste your devotion on the things of this world, but apparently I was mistaken. I am ashamed of you."

"You're right," she said quietly. "I *was* too fond of that plate."

He studied her. Father is not one to let you get away with simply apologizing. He asked her with a mean little smile, "Who were you showing off for here, with your tablecloth and your fancy plate?" He said the words in a sour way, as if they were well-known sins.

Mother merely stood there before him while all the sparkle drained out of her face.

"And your pitiful *cooking*, Orleanna? The way to a young Negro's heart is through his *stomach*—is that what you were counting on?"

Her light blue eyes had gone blank, like shallow pans of water. You could honestly not tell what she was thinking. I always watch his hands to see which way they're going to strike out. But Mother's shallow-water eyes stayed on his face, without really looking at it.

Finally he turned away from her and me both with his usual disgust. He went and sat at his desk, leaving us all in a silence even greater than before. I suppose he was working on the famous sermon he'd promised, which would clear up all misunderstandings. And since it's none other than Anatole himself who stands beside Father and translates the sermons into their language, I'm sure he figured Anatole would be the very first one of the childlike dog-pee dingwit congregation to be touched by God's pure light.

Adah Price

WALK TO LEARN. I and Path. Long one is Congo.
Congo is one long path and I learn to walk.

That is the name of my story, forward and backward. *Manene* is the word for path: *Manene enenam, amen.* On the Congo's one long *manene* Ada learns to walk, amen. One day she nearly does not come back. Like Daniel she enters the lions' den, but lacking Daniel's pure and unblemished soul, Ada is spiced with the flavors of vice that make for a tasty meal. Pure and unblemished souls must taste very bland, with an aftertaste of bitterness.

Tata Ndu reported the news of my demise. Tata Ndu is chief of Kilanga and everything past it in several directions. Behind his glasses and striking outfit he possesses an imposing bald forehead and the huge, triangular upper body of a comic-book bully. How would he even know about a person like me, the white little crooked girl as I was called? Yet he did. The day he visited my family I had been walking alone, making my way home on the forest path from the river. It was a surprising event for him to come to our house. He had never gone out of his way to see my father, only to avoid him, though he sometimes sent us messages through Anatole, his own sons, or other minor ambassadors. This day was different. He came because he had learned I was eaten by a lion.

Early that afternoon, Leah and I had been sent to bring back water. Sent together, the twin and the *niwt*, chained together always in life as in prelife. There was little choice, as Her Highness Rachel is above manual labor, and Ruth May beneath it so to speak, so

Leah and I were considered by our mother, by default, disposed for her errands. It is always the twin and the niwt she sends out to the *marché* on market day, to walk among all those frightening women and bring back fruit or a kettle or whatever thing she needs. She even sends us sometimes to bring back meat from the butcher *marché*, a place where Rachel will not set foot on account of the intestines and neatly stacked heads. We can look out our door and know when the butcher *marché* is open for business, if the big kapok tree down there is filled with black buzzards. This is the truth. We call them the Congolese billboard.

But above all else and every day, she would send us to get water. It was hard for me to carry the heavy pail with my one good hand, and I went too slowly. *Slow lee two went I.* My habit on that path was reciting sentences forward and back, for the concentration improved my walking. It helped me forget the tedium of moving only one way through the world, the way of the slow, slow body. So Leah took all the water and went ahead. As all ways.

The forest path was a live thing underfoot that went a little farther every day. For me, anyway, it did. First, it went only from one side of our yard to the other: what our mother could see and deem safe if she stood in the middle. At first we only heard stories about what happened to it on the north, after the forest closed down on it: a stream, a waterfall, clear pools for swimming. It went to a log bridge. It went to another village. It went to Léopoldville. It went to Cairo. Some of these stories were bound to be true, and some were not; to discover the line between, I decided to walk. I became determined to know a few steps more of that path every day. If we stayed long enough I would walk to Johannesburg and Egypt. My sisters all seemed determined to fly, or in Rachel's case, to ascend to heaven directly through a superior mind-set, but my way was slowly and surely to walk. What I do not have is *kakakaka*, the Kikongo word for hurrying up. But I find I can go a long way without *kakakaka*. Already I had gone as far as the pools and the log bridge on the north. And south, to clearings where women wearing babies in slings stoop together with digging sticks and sing songs (not hymns) and grow their manioc. Everyone knows those places. But without *kakakaka* I discover sights of my own: how the women working their field will stand up one after another, unwrap the *pagne* of bright cloth tied under their breasts, stretch it out wide before retying it. They resemble flocks of butterflies opening and closing their wings.

I have seen the little forest elephants that move in quiet bands, nudging the trees with their small, pinkish tusks. I have seen bands of Pygmies, too. When they smile they reveal teeth filed to sharp points, yet they are gentle, and unbelievably small. You can only believe they are men and women by their beards and breasts, and the grown-up way they move to protect their children. They always see you first, and grow still as tree trunks.

I discovered the *bidila dipapfumu*, the cemetery of witch doctors.

I discovered a bird with a black head and mahogany-colored tail as long as my arm, curved like a bow. In the *Field Guide to African Birds* left by our fowl-minded patron Brother Fowles, my bird is called the *paradise flycatcher*. In the notebook I keep in my pillowcase, in which I draw pictures of all things I know, I put a smile on the face of the paradise flycatcher and printed underneath, in my backward code for secrecy:

NEVAEH NI SEILF FO FOORP WEN .REHCTACYLF ESIDARAP

I also made a habit of following Methuselah as he made his way around our house in insecure spirals. He roosts right inside our latrine, which is near where his empty cage was thrown by the Reverend into the weeds. Its hulk rots there like a shipwreck. Methuselah, like me, is a cripple: the Wreck of Wild Africa. For all time since the arrival of Christ, he had lived on seventeen inches of a yardstick. Now he has a world. What can he possibly do with it? He has no muscle tone in his wings. They are atrophied, probably beyond hope of recovery. Where his pectoral muscles should be, he has a breast weighed down with the words of human beings: by words interred, free-as-a-bird absurd, unheard! Sometimes he flaps his wings as if he nearly remembers flight, as he did in the first jubilant terror of his release. But his independence was frozen in that moment. Now, after stretching his wings he retracts them again, stretches out his head, and waddles, making his tedious way up one branch and down another. Now Methuselah creeps each morning out of the little hole under the rafters of our latrine house, cocks his head, and casts one nervous eye upward as if in prayer: *Lord of the feathers, deliver me this day from the carnivores that could tear me breast from wishbone!* From there, I track his path. I set out small offerings of guava and avocado I have picked and broken open, exposing them to him as food. I do not think he would recognize these fruits wholly concealed in their own skins. After he learns to do that, it will be another whole step to make him see that fruit is not a thing he must rely on the hands of mankind for, but grows on trees. *Treason grows but for kind man.*

In following Methuselah on his slow forays through the forest, I discovered the boys and men practicing drills. This was not the Belgian Army, official conscripted protectors of white people, but a group of young men who held secret meetings in the woods behind our house. I learned that Anatole is more than a teacher of schoolboys and translator of sermons. *Ah Anatole, the lot an aha!* Anatole carried no gun in the clearing where I spied him, but he spoke to armed men who listened. Once he read aloud a letter about the Belgians setting a timetable for independence. Anatole said 1964. "*Mil neuf cent soixante quatre!*" The men threw back their heads at this and laughed ferociously. They cried out as if their skin had been torn.

I feared not, and grew accustomed to walking alone. Our mother did not think she allowed it, especially near dark. It was my secret. She never did realize that whenever she sent me anywhere with Leah, such as to the creek that day to carry water, it would mean coming back alone.

It was already late afternoon, and I passed through spotted light, then brighter clearings, with grass so tall it bent from both sides to form a tunnel overhead, then back under trees again. Leah long gone ahead of me with the water. But someone was behind, some one or some thing. I understood perfectly well that I was being followed. I cannot say I heard anything, but I knew. I wanted to think: Methuselah is playing a trick on me. Or the Pygmies. But I knew better. I paid attention to the small hairs rising on my nape. I did not feel afraid because it does no good in my case. I cannot run away on the muscular effects of adrenaline, but I could taste fear in the back of my throat and feel its despairing weight in my slack limbs. For some, I am told, this weighted-down helplessness comes in dreams. For me it is my life. In my life as Adah I must come to my own terms with the Predator.

I stopped, slowly turned, looked back. The movement behind me also stopped: a final swish in the tall grass by the path, like the swinging of a velvet curtain dropped. Each time I paused, this happened. Then I would wait in the still and growing darkness, till I could not wait anymore and had to walk on.

This is what it means to be very slow: every story you would like to tell has already ended before you can open your mouth. When I reached our house it was nighttime in another life.

Sunset at six o'clock means that life does go on after dark: reading by lamplight on the porch, our family's evening event. Leah had come home with the buckets of water, Mother had boiled it and set it out to cool while she worked on dinner, Rachel had dipped a cloth in it to drape across her forehead while she lay in the hammock examining her pores with the hand mirror. Ruth May had attempted to convince every family member in turn that she could lift a full water bucket by herself with her one remaining unbroken arm. I know all this without having been there. Somewhere in this subdued family din I was presumed to have been minding my own business for many hours. When I finally did return home it was as if, as usual, I had shown up late for my own life, and so I slipped into the hammock at the end of the porch and rested under the dark bougainvilleas.

A short while later Tata Ndu emerged out of darkness. He came up the steps to explain in his formal French that the tracks of a large lion, a solitary hunting male, had been spotted on the path from the river. Tata Ndu's eldest son had just come back from there and brought this report. He had seen the marks of the little girl who drags her right foot, and the lion tracks, very fresh, covering over her footprints. He found the signs of stalking, the sign of a pounce, and a smear of fresh blood trailing into the bush. And that is how they knew the little crooked white child, the little girl without *kakakaka*, had been eaten. *La petite blanche tordue a été mangée*. This was Tata Ndu's sad news. Yet he looked pleased. As a favor to my parents, a party of young men, including his sons, had gone in search of the body, or what might be left of it.

I found I could not breathe as I watched his face tell this story, and the faces of the others as they received the news. My sisters could not comprehend Tata Ndu's word salad of French and Kikongo, so were merely spellbound by the presence of a celebrity on the porch. I was the last thing on their minds, even Leah's. Leah who had left me to the lion's den in question. But my mother: Yes. No! She understood. She had hurried out to the porch from the cooking hut and still carried a large wooden paddle in her hand, which dripped steaming water onto the floor. Part of her hair fell in a wave across her face. The rest of her seemed unalive, like a pale wax model of my mother: the woman who could not fight fire with fire, even to save her children. Such affliction I saw on her face I briefly believed myself dead. I imagined the lion's eyes on me like the eyes of an evil man, and felt my own flesh being eaten. I became nothing.

Our Father rose and said in a commanding voice, "Let us all pray to the Lord for mercy and understanding."

Tata Ndu did not bow his head but raised it, not happily but proudly. Then I understood that he had won, and my father had lost. Tata Ndu came here personally to tell us that the gods of his village did not take kindly to the minister of corruption. As a small sign of Their displeasure, They ate his daughter alive.

It was very nearly impossible to make myself stand and come forward. But I did. Our Father stopped praying, for once. Tata Ndu drew back, narrowing his eyes. Perhaps it was not so much that he wanted me eaten, but that he did not like being wrong. He said no more than *mbote*—fare thee well. Then turned on his heel in a dignified way and left us to ourselves. He would not come back to our house again until much later, after many things had changed.

The next morning we heard the search party had found what the lion killed in my place: a yearling bushbuck. I wonder about its size and tenderness, whether the lion was greatly disappointed, and whether the bushbuck loved its life. I wonder that religion can live or die on the strength of a faint, stirring breeze. The scent trail shifts, causing the predator to miss the pounce. One god draws in the breath of life and rises; another god expires.

Leah

S OME PEOPLE WILL SEND a bread-and-butter note after you have
them over to dinner. Well, Anatole sent us a boy. He arrived at
our door with a written note stating that his name was Lekuyu but we
were kindly requested to call him Nelson. He was to be given his
meals, the privilege of sleeping in our chicken house (where a handful of wary hens had crept back home, after hiding from Mother's
killing spree for the picnic), and a basket of eggs to sell each week so
he could start saving up for a wife. In exchange, Nelson would chop
our firewood, boil up steaming pots of lumpy manioc, and bring us
fruit, greens, and bark potions collected from the forest. He concocted
a headache cure that Mother came to rely upon. He identified our
snakes according to the categories of death they liked to inflict, which
he acted out for us in action-packed dramas on the front porch. He
undertook other surprising tasks in our household, too, on his own
incentive. For example, one day he constructed a bamboo frame to
hold Rachel's hand mirror, so we could hang it up on the living-room
wall for better viewing. Subsequently Nelson began each day by
standing with his face three inches from the framed mirror and labo-
riously combing his scant hair in our living room, while smiling so
broadly we feared his molars would pop out. Other people also began
stepping into our house to avail themselves of our mirror in the same
way. Evidently, what we had hanging up on our wall was Kilanga's
only looking glass.

As he peers at his reflection, I catch myself studying Nelson: his
elbows darkened by use, his skin many tones of brown, like antique

mahogany furniture. Owing to his sugarcane habit, his stubby front teeth are all pretty much gone to the sweet hereafter. There's a disturbing, monkeylike glint of canines off to the sides when he grins. But still, when he smiles you know he really means it. He's cheerful and tidy and came to us with no possessions we could see other than an intact seat to his huge brown shorts, a red T-shirt he wears every day of his life, a leather belt, a pink plastic comb, a French grammar book, and a machete. Nelson travels light. He keeps his hair cut very close and has a perfectly round, pink scar on the back of his neck. Anatole chose Nelson to help us because, like Anatole, he's an orphan. Some years ago Nelson's entire family, including both parents, numerous older brothers, and a spanking newborn baby sister, drowned all together on a trip upriver when their boat overturned. The Congolese pirogues are made of a dense wood that sinks like pig iron when given half a chance. Since most Congolese can't swim, you'd think they would consider this a drawback to river travel, but evidently they don't. Merrily up the river and down they go, without a thought to capsizing. Nelson was left behind that fateful day by accident, he claims. He says his mother was so excited about showing off the baby to the upstream relatives he got jealous and hid out, and she plumb forgot to take him. Consequently Nelson places great stock in signs and superstitions. And now he had found himself at loose ends, having no family of his own to help support and being twelve years of age, finished with school.

Anatole wrote in his note that here was his best student and we would soon see why. We did. The day Nelson came to us he only spoke, "How are you, thank you please," for English, but after a few weeks he could say about anything that mattered, without turning it all on its head the way Mama Tataba used to. I would say Nelson is gifted. But I'll tell you what, gifted doesn't count for a hill of beans in the Congo, where even somebody as smart as Nelson isn't allowed to go to college, any more than us Price girls are. According to the Underdowns, the Belgians are bent on protecting against independent thought on native ground.

If that is so, I wonder about Anatole—how the Underdowns got away with putting him in as a schoolteacher, for instance. I have scenes in my mind sometimes where I ask him. When my sisters and I are lying down after lunch and my mind is idle, I think of these scenes. Anatole and I are walking on the path toward the river. There is some good reason we're doing this, either he's going to help me carry something home or maybe he invited me to discuss some point of the Scripture he's not totally clear on. And so there we are, and we talk. In my imaginary scene, Father has forgiven Anatole and encourages his friendship with our family. Anatole has a very understanding smile, with a slight gap between his perfect front teeth, and I imagine feeling so encouraged by that smile I even get up the nerve to ask him about his amazing face: how did they make every scar so perfectly straight? Did it hurt very much? And then he tells me about the rubber plantations. What were they like? I read in a book that they cut off the workers' hands if they hadn't collected enough rubber by the end of the day. The Belgian foremen would bring baskets full of brown hands back to the boss, piled up like a mess of fish. Could this be true of civilized white Christians?

In my imagination Anatole and I talk in English, though in real life he mostly speaks Kikongo to his schoolboys. His Kikongo accent is different from everyone else's—even I can hear that. He pulls his mouth into broad, exact shapes around his teeth as if he's forever worried about being misunderstood. I think Anatole helps out our family because he is an outsider here too, like us. He can sympathize with our predicament. And Father does seem grateful that he's still willing to translate the sermons, even after the two of them had words. Anatole could be my father's friend, if only he had a better grasp of the Scripture.

We were stumped as to why he was kind enough to send us Nelson, though. The first time Nelson fetched the water and boiled it by himself Mother was so grateful she sat down in a chair and cried. A prize pupil is a very large gift. My theory is it was because of two things Anatole saw in our house: one, plenty of books for a smart boy to read, even if he can't go to school anymore. And two, we needed the help about as badly as the children of Moses needed Moses. Somewhere around Thanksgiving, Mother had begun praying out loud in front of my father for the Lord to please deliver us out of here all in one piece. He did not care for her displays of faltering faith, and said so. It's true Ruth May gave us a bad scare, but he reminded Mother sensibly that a child can break an arm in Georgia or Kansas City or anywhere. And to tell the truth, if any of us was meant to do it, it was Ruth May. She tears through her life like she plans on living out the whole thing before she hits twenty.

And I hate to say it but Adah is just as ornery and bent on destruction, in her own slowpoke way. No one tells her to go off trailing through the jungle all alone. She could have stayed with me. The Lord is our Shepherd and the very least we sheep can do is keep up with the flock, by our own devices, I should think. Especially since we are practically grown-ups now, to hear others tell it. You always see twins dolled up together as kids, but you never see two grown women running around in identical outfits, holding hands. Are Adah and I expected to go on being twin sisters forever?

Nevertheless, we both had to do the Verse, Genesis 4, about Cain and Abel, after her so-called brush with the lion, and what with all that and the broken arm, Mother feared for our lives with fresh vigor. The rainy season had gotten heavier and the whole village was coming down with the *kakakaka*. We'd thought this just meant "hurry up." When Mama Mwanza told us all her children were getting it, we thought she meant they were getting restless or were finally scolded into doing their chores. But Nelson said, "No, no, Mama Price, *kakakaka!*" Evidently it's a disease where you have to go to the bathroom a thousand times a day. (He acted it out in a pantomime that made Ruth May laugh fiercely.) He said you go so many times you don't have anything left of your insides. Then the children sometimes will die. Well, Nelson says a lot of things. For example, if you run across two sticks in the shape of an X you have to hop over it backwards on your left foot. So we didn't know whether to believe him about the disease. But then, next thing we knew, the little house right down the road from us turned up with a funeral arch made of braided palm fronds and flowers and sad, sad faces in the yard. It wasn't a baby dead, but the mother of them all, who were left looking just that much more skinny and forlorn, as if the wind got knocked out of the family when the mama went. You do have to wonder what she died of, and if it's catching.

Well, that put Mother in a whole new frame of mind. Contagion, why, this was worse than snakes, since you couldn't see it coming! She dreamed up a hundred and one excuses for keeping us inside the house even when it wasn't raining. She invented "rest time," a period of endless inactivity stretching out after school and lunch, in which we were ordered to stay in our beds, under our mosquito-net canopies. Mother called it *siesta time*, which at first I mistook as *fiesta time*, a puzzlement to me since it was not at all festive. Ruth May usually fell asleep, open-mouthed in the heat, with her hair plastered down across her sweaty face like the poster child for fever. The rest of us just sweated like swine as we sprawled side by side in our metal-frame beds, separated by the ghostly walls of our mosquito nets, insulting each other out of a sense of general outrage and wishing we could get up. I had nothing to read but *The Bobbsey Twins in Eskimo Land*, a childish book with nothing whatsoever to hold my interest. I just envied those dumb Bobbseys for having a superior adventure to ours, in that cool, snowy place, where no one had to endure an enforced fiesta.

I missed my freedom. There were so many things I needed to keep up with in the village. Foremost among them, Eeben Axelroot. He was up to something. The last time Adah and I spied down there we heard the radio shrieking bloody murder, and for once we actually got to see him answer it. He rolled off his cot and muttered words I knew I could go to hell just for hearing. He knelt by the roaring footlocker and put a wire contraption against his head. He said, "Got it," many times over, and "As good as dead if they do, sir." Oh, mercy, I had to tear myself away!

And now I might never find out who or what was as good as dead, for it looked as if we were going to have to languish on our cots forever while the rain poured down. At least Rachel was useful, for once in her life. In desperate straits she can make us laugh, with her main talent being radio commercials oozed out in a fabulous fashion-model voice: "Medically tested Odo-ro-no, stops underarm odor and moisture at the source!" She'd toss her head then and throw her arms into the air, exposing her dark-stained underarms. She also did various hair products, swirling her white mane into a cow pie on top of her head, "For today's new look of luxury!" And she loved to remind us of Carnation instant nonfat dry milk ("New magic crystals dissolve instantly!"), which had become our mainstay food and did not dissolve instantly but clotted up like white blood in our glasses. We were all so sick of those crystallized lumps they choked us in our dreams.

Sooner or later she always ran out of commercials, though, like a toy winding down. Then all would go quiet and we'd return cheerlessly to our books. Our reading material was random and inappropriate, delivered to us in unlabeled cardboard boxes from Leopoldville. We suspected Mr. Axelroot of having better boxes that he took to luckier children elsewhere. Back in Bethlehem, we ourselves had organized book drives for the underprivileged, and now I pitied those children who got slogged with our dusty second-rate novels and outmoded home-carpentry manuals, and were expected to be grateful about it. When we get back home, I vow I shall give all my very best books to the underprivileged, once I have read them.

From the same nursery-school lot that brought the Bobbsey Twins I chose a Nancy Drew, out of pure boredom, feeling guilty and outraged to be reduced to that circumstance, as a young woman who menstruates and reads at the college level. Though I must confess, some of the Nancy Drews held my attention. One of them had a strange, secret-basement plot that led me astray, while I lay in bed trying to fall asleep, into long fantasies that felt sinful. I think maybe it is true that the idle mind is the Devil's workshop. I did have thoughts of the Devil at these times. I imagined Nancy descending a long iron staircase into the netherworld, and a man who waited for her at the bottom. Sometimes he was just a shadowy faceless man in a hat. Sometimes he had a gap-toothed smile and an elegant, scarred face. Other times he was that red Devil who lurks on the Underwood ham cans, self-satisfied and corrupt in his bow tie, mustache, and arrow-point tail. The first time I dreamed this scenario I can't really say whether I was still awake or had fallen into a feverish, colorful sleep. All I know is that suddenly I snapped out of it, surrounded by the sharp odor of my own sweat, and felt prickled and exquisitely wide awake below the waist. I knew this feeling was very wrong. Even so, I had more such dreams—and sometimes, I'm sure, I was still half awake when they began.

After a few weeks my fevers became more pronounced, and my mother realized that because I am large and active for my age she'd been underestimating my dosage of quinine. Those feelings below my waist, it turns out, were a side effect of malaria.

For Christmas Mother gave us all needlework things. We'd known not to expect much, and lest we forget, Father's Christmas-morning sermon was all about having grace in your heart, which displaces the lust for material things. But still. For a Christmas tree we had a palm frond stuck in a bucket of rocks. As we gathered around it and waited our turn to open our meager, constructive gifts, I stared at that pitiful frond decorated with white frangipani angels going brown around the edges, and decided the whole thing would have been better off ignored. Even when you've recently turned fifteen without a birthday cake, it's hard to be that mature about Christmas.

Mother announced that now we girls could use our idle time to build up our hope chests. I'd heard of this kind of thing before, without giving it a second thought. I'd seen those Mark Eden advertisements in the backs of comic books, which promised things embarrasing to look at, and so I assumed that building a hope chest was a question of exercising the muscles of the chest, to get busts. But no, that wasn't it at all. Mother meant the other kind of chest, like a steamer trunk, in which a girl was supposed to put everything she hoped she'd get to use one day after she got married. This was her rationale for all the embroidery floss, pinking shears, and so on that we toted (secretly or otherwise) across the Atlantic.

Now we were supposed to get enthusiastic about long-range marriage plans, while lying here in bed watching our shoes mildew. Rachel and Adah were assigned any number of hope-chest projects to work on, but the domestic arena was never my long suit, so I was to focus on a single, big project: a cross-stitch tablecloth. It's nothing but a thousand tiny x's to be made up in different colors of thread. The tablecloth has the pattern stamped straight on the linen in washable ink, like a paint-by-numbers picture. A monkey could do it, if he got bored enough. Certainly no talent is required for cross-stitch. The hopeful part, I guess, is that after you're done with it all, you'll find someone who'd want to marry you.

Personally I can't see it as likely. In the first place I am flat-chested, just plain too skinny. When Adah and I got moved up two grades, it just made things that much worse. We were preacher's daughters to begin with, and now we were *really* onions in the petunia patch, amongst all those ninth-grade girls with flirty eyes and foundation makeup and bosoms poking out the fronts of their mohair sweater sets. No boy ever looked at me except for homework help. And to tell the truth, I can't say that I care. Kissing looks like too much of somebody else's dental hygiene if you ask me. If you want to see stars—which is what Rachel claims it's all about—then why not just go climb up a tree in the dark? When I try to picture the future, I can't see myself as anything but a missionary or a teacher or a farmer, telling others how the Lord helps those that help themselves. Some kind of a life of piety, at any rate (which should guarantee that Adah's nowhere within a hundred miles); and I should like to spend as much time as I can out-doors, exulting in God's creation, and wear pants if at all possible.

I do sometimes picture myself with children, for why else am I keeping my notebook, with all the lessons of my childhood in Africa? Yet you can't say boo to your own children without a hus-band first. It does seem a dreadful obstacle.

My father says a girl who fails to marry is veering from God's plan—that's what he's got against college for Adah and me, besides the wasted expense—and I'm sure what he says is true. But without college, how will I learn anything of any account to teach others? And what red-blooded American boy will look twice at a Geography whiz with scabs on her knees, when he could have a Sweater Girl? I suppose I'll just have to wait and see. God must know his arithmetic. He'd plan it out well enough to plunk down a husband for every wife that He aims for to have one. If the Lord hasn't got a boyfriend lined up for me to marry, that's His business.

Rachel, on the other hand, has never had any doubts in this department. Once she got over the initial shock of no new record album by the Platters, no mohair twin set, nor any place to wear or dance to either one, she was thrilled by the notion of a hope chest, or pretended to be. Why, she'd throw herself belly down on her bed with her knees cocked and feet sticking up and her busy hands five inches in front of her eyes, plowing through her hope-chest projects in earnest. She seemed to think she needed to have it all finished up in the next week or so. Oh, she monogrammed guest towels and crocheted collars for her trousseau and I don't know what all. It was the only time she ever stopped rolling her eyes and flicking her hair, to settle down to a piece of honest work.

Adah and I dragged our sewing projects out to the porch so we could still keep an eye out for interesting goings-on in the world. Something had come between Adah and me for the worse, since the day she was supposed to have been followed by that lion, which the whole village was still talking about. They loved to point Adah out when they saw us, pantomiming a lion's roar, which didn't help us to put the affair behind us. But on the bright side, the event provided a great boost for Father's church. People seem to think that if Jesus could stop a lion from gobbling up a poor lame girl, he must be staying awake pretty good for the Christians—ha! Just when everybody was thinking their regular African gods were aggravated with us and fixing to teach us a lesson. The way they see it, it was kind of a wrestling match between the gods, with Jesus and Adah coming out on top. Father of course says this is superstitious and oversimplifying matters. But as luck would have it, he'd preached the parable of Daniel and the lions' den just a few days before, so naturally now they are knocking each other over to get to church on Sunday. And Adah is the cause. Father is pleased as punch with Adah, I don't care what he says—he put his arm around her shoulder in public! Which is not entirely fair.

But we still had to go on being each other's main company. Chained to the porch by Mother's instructions, like grumpy twin bears in captivity, we enviously watched Nelson as he went about his business, free to go back and forth to the village and contract the *kakakaka* any time he had a mind to. As he walked away we could see his round pink scar spying back at us through the trees like a small, laughing eye. We also watched Methuselah, who after four months of liberation still hung around our house mumbling. It was very strange to hear the voices of our own family members coming from the tree branches, as if we'd been transformed into flying spirits of a type preoccupied with peanuts, bananas, and common phrases of greeting. Sometimes at night he'd startle us, when we forgot he spent his lonely nights in the latrine. Believe me, it gives you a queer feeling to sit down in the dark to pee and hear a voice right behind you declare, "Sister, God is great!" But we felt sorry for him and took to leaving him pieces of fruit in there. We were careful to keep the latrine door shut and latched at night, so no mongoose or civet cat would find its way in and polish him off.

At first I wanted Methuselah to come back and live in his cage, until Father explained to me that this whole arrangement was wrong. We let Methuselah go because his captivity was an embarrassment to us. It made the parrot into a less noble creature than God intended. So I had to root for Methuselah to learn to be free. I don't know what Adah rooted for as we lay out there with our needlework, watching him waddle up and down the branches. I have to say she probably didn't care one way or the other, really, and was just fascinated to see what would happen next. Adah is that way. She feels no obligation to have good thoughts on behalf of her mortal soul in the hereafter, or even the here and now. She can simply watch life, without caring.

Certainly she wasn't putting in any effort on behalf of her future womanhood. Adah did weird, morbid things for her hope chest, black borders on cloth napkins and the like, which exhausted our mother. And Ruth May was exempt from hope chest, but was allowed to lie in a hammock with us and make cat's cradles out of yarn if she promised not to run off and break something.

I lolled on my back and worked on my tablecloth listlessly, to preserve my mother's fantasy that I'd be getting married one day, and after a while it began to draw me in. The cross-stitch itself was tedious, but the prospects were beautiful; Mother had the foresight to give me a botanical motif, knowing how I love green and growing things. Bunches of pansies and roses were meant to bloom in the four corners, all connected by a border of twining green vines. And in the very same way the Spirit long ago became manifest in the Body of Christ, the first cabbage rose began to materialize on my tablecloth. From there, I could envision the whole garden.

Still, the project seemed impossibly large. Rachel polished off a complete set of dinner napkins in the time it took me to fill in one pink rose. The humidity was so thick it dripped off our eyelashes, and in this damp atmosphere the first bouquet took so long that my metal embroidery hoops rusted in place.

The hope-chest program didn't last long as our main preoccupation. Rachel hoped too much and ran out of material, while the rest of us hoped too little and ran out of steam. Once in a great while I still do pull out my tablecloth and try to get reinspired. I've even prayed for God to make me more fit to be a wife. But the rusted embroidery hoops left an unsightly orange ring on the linen that may have damaged my prospects for good.

Ruth May

I TRIED TO SEE NELSON NAKED. I don't know why I wanted to. When he gets up in the morning first he washes his face out of a dingered-up bowl in the chicken house and puts on his pants and his shirt. He washes the back of his neck with the pink hole in it till his skin shines and water runs all down. Then he looks at his clothes real hard and says a hex before he puts them on. Brown pants, red T-shirt. That's all the clothes he has. Everybody here has just one clothes. My friends are the one with the blue pajama shirt, the one with the checkered pants with the legs rolled up, the one with shorts with big white pockets hanging out the bottom, and the one with the pinkish shirt down to his knees and no pants. The girls don't ever, ever wear pants. And the little babies don't wear a speck of clothes so they can just squat down and pee-pee ever-when they take a mind to.

The chicken house is made out of sticks. The wall has square little holes and I just wanted to see Nelson. I was bad. Sometimes I prayed for Baby Jesus to make me be good, but Baby Jesus didn't.

The chickens were setting on eggs. Good little mamas, we said, making us some more chickens. Their house was nothing but a shack. They tried to hide their nests in the bushes but Nelson and I found them. He said they were bad hens trying to steal their babies from us. I tried to scold them, but he said chickens don't understand English. He showed me how to sing to them: *Kuyiba diaki, kuyiba diaki, mbote ve! Mbote ve!* Then we took back all those eggs. I got to help Nelson in the morning when Rachel and them had school, if I promised Mama I wouldn't go near any other children. They are all sick. They have to go to the bathroom number two in the bushes and we might catch it.

We took the eggs in to Mama and she floated them in a bucket. Some sank on the bottom, and some floated on top like when you bob for apples. The sinkers are okay to eat and the floaters are the rotten ones. When you say, Last one in is a rotten egg! I reckon that means you're going to float. Nelson wanted those and Mama worried he'd get sick if he ate them but she said, "Oh, go ahead," and so he took them. But he didn't eat them. He hid them in a place. He said the witch doctor Tata Kuvudundu wanted those eggs for the dead people that needed to lie down. *Nganga* means witch doctor. Tata Kuvudundu is one because he has six toes on one of his feet. Nelson said Nganga Kuvudundu could make live people dead, and dead people come back alive. Nelson thinks Tata Kuvudundu is probably so important he could run the army, but he's too old. Maybe one of his sons instead. Nelson knows who Patrice Lumumba is, too, like me. He says some of them are saying to bury rocks in your garden right now, and after the white people are all dead, dig them up and those rocks will be turned into gold. Nelson said he didn't believe that. Nobody really believes it, he said, except the people that want to. I said, Why will all the white people be dead? Nelson didn't know.

There's all these extra people going to church now. Nelson says it's because the lion tried to eat up Adah, but Jesus turned her into a bushbuck right just at the last minute. Like in the Bible. And right when the lion's mouth bit down on the Adah that turned into a bushbuck, the real Adah disappeared from there and turned up okay on our porch.

Nelson says everybody's got their own little God here to protect them, special African ones that live in the little tiny thing they wear around their necks. A *gree-gree* is what you call it. It's like a little bottle, only made out of sticks and shells and things. Sometimes I think about all those little teeny Gods riding around on people's necks, a-hollering: Help! Let me out of here! Like the genie in the Laddin's lamp. You just rub it and say, Here, little God, you better watch out for me or you'll get eat up by the lion right along with me!

All the little Gods are mad at Jesus right now, and they'd like to hurt one of us if they could. If Jesus doesn't look out. I told Nelson that Jesus is way too big to ride around in a little *gree-gree*. He is big as a man, with long brown hair and sandals, size extra-large. Nelson says yes, everybody has figured out that He is a right good size. They've a lot of them started going to hear Father talk about Jesus and figure out what's what. But Nelson says they've got one foot in the door of the church and one foot out. If something bad happens to one of us, out they'll go.

After we found all the eggs in the bushes and took them, Baby Jesus made all the chickens be good and lay their eggs in the one big nest we made in the corner of the chicken house. Mama took a pencil and marked thirteen eggs with X. We kept those in the nest, and when the hens laid fresh ones, we took those for eating. Sometimes scrambled, sometimes hard-boiled. We don't ever eat the X-mark eggs, because they're a-going to turn into baby chickens. When they grow up they'll be our new laying hens, some of them. And the other ones will grow up to be fried chicken! The not-lucky ones. They'll get their necks chopped off and jump around squirting blood, ha ha ha, poor them. The chickens better get their own little *gree-grees* to wear on their necks, I reckon.

Every day I looked to see if the babies hatched out, and I was the first one to find them. They all hatched out but save for one, and it got squashed. It was flat against the mud wall behind the nest like a picture hanging up. Nelson lived in there with a dead baby chicken picture on the wall. I was sorry and didn't try to look at his peewee any more after that.

If it's dark outside and you see a snake, or even if you just want to talk about one, you can't say *snake*. You have to say *string*. You say, Remember that day we saw a little black string coming home from the picnic? If it's nighttime, that's how you talk. Nelson got so mad at me for saying *snake* when it was dark, because he says after the sun goes down a snake can hear you calling its name and it'll come a-running. Other animals too. They can hear real good in the dark, so watch out.

Nelson got mad at Leah, too, for keeping her a owl for a pet. The owl was a baby that couldn't fly right when we found it, so Leah made it a cage and fed it bugs and some meat. Its fur is white and sticks out all over. Leah named it a word in that language they have here: *Mvufu*. It means *owl*. But Leah's friend Pascal hates it, and Nelson hates it worse. Mama Mwanza hates it when she comes over scooting on her hands to trade us oranges for eggs. And Mama Boanda does. She's the one that wears the black skirt with the great big pink star across her bottom and a hairdo that looks like stars too, sticking up ever whichaways. The one that does people's hairdos is old Mama Lo, who's only just got the two teeth, one upstairs and one down, so she chews crossways. She hates our owl the most of all, and hollered at us for having it! Because her sister just died here awhile back. Everybody that ever sees our owl just plumb hates it. Nelson said take it out of the house or he wasn't coming in and that was that. Well, Mama made her take it outside, even though Leah pitched a fit because it was still yet just a baby. That's true, it was. It was getting feathers but mostly it still had white baby hair and was tame.

Nelson went and got Anatole, pulling on him by the hand like he was a note from home. Anatole said the Congo people don't like owls because an owl flies around at night and eats up the souls of dead people. And there's just way too many of them here lately, he said. Too many sick children for people to abide an owl hanging around and looking at them with his eyes still hungry. Even if the owl was just a baby himself. Maybe he'd want other babies for company.

Father said that was just all superstitions. So! Leah went and fetched the owl back and sashayed around the house with it sitting on her shoulder, saying Father was sticking up for her side of things. Uh-oh. He smacked her hard for the sin of pride, and made her do The Verse. She sat there holding the side of her neck while she wrote it out. When she put her hand down you could see the bruise just as plain. It looked like Father was holding his hand in front of the kerosene light and making a shadow on her. But he wasn't, he was in the other room a-reading in his Bible.

When she got done with her Verse, she went way down in the jungle to turn that baby owl loose, and we thought she never *would* come back. We were all scared half to death and sat up waiting for her, except Father. It was so quiet you could hear the second hand on Rachel's Timex going *sit-sit-sit*. The flames in the lantern went up and down and the shadows jiggled ever time you'd go to blink your eyes. It was way after dark by then. So whatever you were thinking might have got ahold of Leah out there, snake or leopard, you couldn't say anything out loud but *string* or *spotted cloth*. I said, "I hope a *string* didn't bite her!"

Father already went in his bedroom, way way earlier. He hollered finally for Mama to put us to bed and come on herself. He said our sister would be back, so we'd just as well go on about our business because she was just looking for the attention. He said not to pay her any mind or we'd get the same medicine. Then he said, "If an owl can eat up a soul outright, he is one step ahead of the Devil, for the Devil has to purchase them first, and I see he has made some purchases right here in my own household." Father was mad and wanted to get the subject off of Leah, since it was him that ran her off.

We didn't say boo to him, nor go to bed either. We just sat there. Mama stared out the open doorway with all her might, waiting on Leah to get home. The mosquitoes and big white moths came in the door and went out the windows. Some of them decided to take off their coats and stay awhile, so they flew in the kerosene lamp and got burned up. That is what happens to you if you're bad and don't go to heaven, you go and get burned up in the bad place instead. So that night our house was the bad place for the Congolese bugs. Ha ha.

Father is trying to teach everybody to love Jesus, but what with one thing and another around here, they don't. Some of them are scared of Jesus, and some aren't, but I don't think they love Him. Even the ones that go to church, they still worship the false-eye dolls and get married to each other time and again. Father gets right put out about it.

I'm scared of Jesus, too.

When she came back from the woods, we hooped and hollered and ran to the porch and just jumped up and down and pulled her inside by her shirttails. But uh-oh, there was Father in his dark bedroom doorway looking out. All you could see was his eyes. We didn't want to get the same medicine, so we just looked at Leah real hard with *I'm sorry for you* eyes and tried to get a nice message across. After we went to bed I reached over through the mosquito net and held her hand.

Mama didn't sleep in her room.

Mama says birds are going to be her death. I'd sooner say it was snakes. But I guess if a bird is going to eat up the dead children's souls, that is a worry. That is one more sound to listen for at night. One more thing you can't say out loud after dark.

Rachel

IN JANUARY the Underdowns showed up as a complete surprise from Leopoldville. They came in Mr. Axelroot's plane, when the most we were really expecting was Potato Buds and Spam. The Underdowns don't like to come out here in the boondoggles, so believe you me this was an occasion. They looked like they had nervous-tension headaches. Mother was upset because they're our bosses from the Mission League, and they'd caught her red-handed doing housework in her old black Capri pants with the knees worn through. She was a sight to behold there on the floor, scrubbing away, with her flyaway hair sticking out and dark bruise-colored circles under her eyes from all her worrying about us catching the kamikaze disease. What with the mongooses and lizards traipsing in and out of the house as they pleased, she had a lot more to be embarrassed about than just getting caught in her old clothes, it seems to me. But at least that horrible owl was gone. Thank goodness to that, even if Father did come down too hard on Leah about it. That was a bad scene. We were all tiptoeing around on the eggshells even more than usual, after that. But that owl stank of rotten meat so I do have to say, Good riddance.

But listen, why should we have to put on the Ritz for the Underdowns? They aren't even Baptists, I heard Father say; they just oversee the financial affairs for the Mission League since so many people have pulled out. They are Episcopotamians, and their real name is actually something foreign like On-tray-don. We just say *Underdown* because it's easier. To tell you the truth, the two of them are just a couple of the plainest Janes you ever saw, in their economical home haircuts and khaki trousers. The funny thing about Frank and Janna Underdown is that they look exactly alike except for the accessories: he has a mustache, she has little gold cross earrings and glasses on a chain. Mr. and Mrs. Potato Head.

They sat at our table sweating while Mother ran and squeezed the orangeade and served it. Even the glasses were dripping with sweat. Outside, the sky was getting its regular afternoon storm organized: wind whacking the palm leaves together, red dust ghosts flying up from the road, little kids running like bansheets for cover. Mother was too nervous to sit down with the company so she stood behind Father's chair, leaning on the windowsill, waiting for him to finish the newspaper they'd brought. All of them passed it around. Except Mr. Axelroot, the pilot, who probably wouldn't know what to do with a newspaper except wipe his you-know-what. Yes, he was there among our numbers too. He stood leaning in the back doorway and spitting until I thought I would croak. He stared right at me, undressing me mentally. I have said already my parents are entirely in the dark about certain things. I made faces at him and finally he went away.

While Father was reading the latest news, Mrs. Underdown tried to make friends with Mother by complaining about her houseboy in Leopoldville. "Honestly, Orleanna, he would steal anything except the children. And he would have those, too, if he thought he could sell them. If I try to lock things up, he slaps his hands over his heart as if I've accused him of murder. Even though I just caught him the night before with four of Frank's handkerchiefs and a kilo of sugar tucked into the front of his shirt. He always claims he has no idea how they got there."

"Well, my stars," Mother said, without seeming all that interested.

Mrs. Underdown stared at Mother, puzzled. "Your *stores*?" She always implies we have an accent, by repeating our words and expressions like little jokes. With her being somewhat of a foreigner herself, that's the pot calling the skillet black if you ask me.

For once, my sisters and I got excused from spending the whole livelong morning playing Ding Dong Schoolhouse with Mother. But we were curious about the Underdown visit and didn't really want to leave. We were so deprived of company, honestly. I lingered about the room checking my hairdo once or twice in the mirror and tidying up the desk, and finally ended up loitering out on the veranda with my sisters, close enough to the doorway so that we could keep tabs. We stared at the glasses of orangeade, wishing Mother had had the simple confederation to make enough for all of us, while we listened in and tried to get the picture of what had caused them to come out here. Even though I knew before it was over I would probably go bored out of my gourd.

Sure enough, when they'd finished passing around the newspaper article, they dropped the subject of the Underdowns' criminal-element houseboy and moved onto the subject of everything dull under the blue sky: new sheets, malaria pills, new Bibles for the school. That jazz.

I sashayed in and picked up the newspaper after Father had thrown it down on the floor. Well, why shouldn't I? It was written in red-blooded English, from New York, the United States of America. I read the page they'd folded back: "Soviet Plan Moves Forward in Congo." It said Khrushchev wanted to take over the Belgian Congo and deprive the innocent savages of becoming a free society, as part of his plan for world domination. Jeez Louise, if Khrushchev wants the Congo he can have it, if you ask me. The newspaper was from last December, anyway. If his big plan was going so well, seems like we would have seen hides or tails of the Russians by now. The article told how the Belgians are the unsung heroes, and when they come into a village they usually interrupt the cannibal natives in the middle of human sacrifice. Huh. If they came to our village that day they would have interrupted Mother in the middle of scrubbing the floor and about twelve little naked boys having a pee-pee contest across the road. I gave the newspaper to Adah, and Leah read it over her shoulder. They turned some pages and showed me a cartoon: big, fat, bald-headed Nikita Khrushchev in his Communist uniform was holding hands and dancing with a skinny cannibal native with big lips and a bone in his hair. Khrushchev was singing, "Bingo Bango Bongo, I don't want to leave the Congo!"

I stared out the window, wondering who wouldn't want to leave the Congo before you could say Jack Robinson if they had half a chance. The Underdowns and mother were just finishing up with the fascinating subject of quinine pills, and then it went quiet for, as they say, an uncomfortable silence. The Underdowns went "Ahem, ahem" and crossed their legs and got around to what appeared to be their big news: the Congo is going to have an election in May and declare their independence in June. As far as I am concerned you can chalk that one right up with malaria pills and Bibles for a tedulous topic, but Mother and Father seemed to take it as a shock. Mother's whole face dropped out of its socket. She looked like Claire Bloom in *Beauty and the Beast* when she finally gets a look at what she's going to have to marry. I kept waiting for Mother to snap back to her old Everything Is Just Fine attitude, but she stayed blanched out and kind of stopped breathing. She put her hand on her throat like she'd swallowed a shot of Mr. Clean, and that look scared me. I started paying attention.

"*This* June," Mother said.

"Belgium won't possibly accept the outcome of an election," Father said. Oh, well, naturally he already knew all about it. No matter what happens on God's green earth, Father acts like it's a movie he's already seen and we're just dumb for not knowing how it comes out. Leah, of course, was about to fall out of her hammock, hanging on his every word. Ever since Father smacked her over the owl, she's been trying twice as hard to win him back over.

"Belgium absolutely will, Nathan. This is the new official plan. King Baudouin invited eighty Congolese leaders to Brussels to chart a course for independence." So said Mr. Potato Head, who has no elocution in his voice whatsoever. I am positive he is foreign, or used to be.

"When?" Mother asked.

"Two weeks ago."

"And might we ask what happened to the *old* official plan?" Father said. He always has to say, "And might we ask?" Instead of just asking.

"Léopoldville and Stanleyville have been shut down with riots

and strikes, in case you haven't heard. The old official plan did not
go over so well."

"What about the threat of a Soviet takeover?" Mother wanted to
know.

"Frankly, I think Belgium is more concerned about the threat of
an *African* takeover," he said. Reverend Underdown, whose name is
Frank, says "Frankly" a lot, and he doesn't even see the humor. "The
Russians are a theoretical threat, whereas the Congolese are quite
actual and seem to mean business. We say in French, if your brother
is going to steal your hen, save your honor and give it to him first."

"So they would just hand over independence to the Congolese?"
Mother leaned forward over Father's head to speak. She looked like
Father's guardian angel with iron-poor tired blood. "Frank, what
leaders are you talking about, getting invited to Brussels? Who on
earth around here is eligible for a thing like that?"

"Tribal chiefs, heads of unions, and the like. They say it was a
pretty motley assembly. Joseph Kasavubu wavered between boy-
cotting and trying to run the show. Lumumba got out of jail just for
the occasion. They settled on a parliamentary system of government. Elections will be mid-May. Independence day, June thirtieth."

Methuselah had sidled up into the bougainvillea bush right
behind us, muttering, "Lubberlubberlubber." I swear it was like he
was trying to listen in on the conversation, too.

"Belgium has never been willing to *discuss* independence before,"
Father declared.

"That's true, Frank," Mother added. She had both hands on her
hair, pulling it back from her face like a skinned rabbit and fanning
her neck in the back. It wasn't at all becoming. "We discussed this
with the mission people in Atlanta before we ever decided to come.
They said the political advisors in Belgium had mapped out a plan
last year that would grant independence in, what was it, Nathan,
thirty years? Thirty years' time!"

Mother had raised her voice a little, and Mr. Potato Head looked
embarrassed. "I'm sorry to have to remind you that you were advised
not to come," he finally said.

"That's not exactly true," Mother said. She looked at Father, and Mrs. Potato Head looked at Father. Father stared at Mr. Potato Head, who didn't have the nerve to look him in the eye. The whole thing was out of this world.

Finally Mr. Potato Head dared to speak. "No offense intended," he said. "Your work here certainly has the blessings of the Mission League, Orleanna." He may have meant no offense but he pronounced my mother's name like a bad word. "And I would also say it has the admiration of many people who lack your family's . . . boldness." He looked at the button on his sleeve, probably sewn on upside-down or something by the handkerchief-stealing houseboy. Then he started turning his wet empty glass around and around on its damp ring on the table.

Everybody waited for what else Frank Underdown might have to say with no offense intended. Finally he allowed, "But you do know your mission here was not sanctioned." He glanced up at Mother, then back to his spinny-go-round glass.

"Well, whatever does that mean?"

"I think you know. You didn't get the language in-service or any of the ordinary kinds of training. I'm afraid the Mission League thinks of your stipend as an act of kindness on their part. I would not be too surprised to see the end of it now."

Well! Mother's hand hit the table, *bang!* "If you think my family is living in this moldy corner of hell for the fifty dollars a month!" she practically shouted at him. Man oh man, if the porch could have opened up and swallowed us all.

"Orleanna," Father said. (Dog peed on the carpet voice.)

"Well, Nathan, for heaven's sake. Can't you see you're being insulted?"

Usually Father doesn't have to look twice to see when he's being insulted. Usually he can see insults as big as a speck when they're hiding under a rock in the next county over. We all crossed our fingers.

"Now everyone simmer down," said Mr. Potato Head, trying for a fake friendly laugh. "Nobody is being insulted. We don't have any control over the decisions of the Mission League, you know that.

We are just humble administrators for the SBML and a lot of other organizations, who are all giving similar advice right now. We came here to talk with you personally, because we are deeply concerned about your witness for Christ and your precious children."

My mother, who had just said the word "hell," was about a million miles from her witness for Christ at the present time. I would say at the present time she looked ready to bean somebody with a baseball bat. She turned her back on the Underdowns. "Why in the world did they even let us come here, if it was dangerous?" she asked some birdy outside the window.

Father had not spoken up yet. My theory was he didn't know who to jump on first, the insulting Underdowns or his cussing wife, so he just stood there brewing like a coffeepot. Only with a coffeepot you know exactly what's going to come out of it.

"Now, please, Orleanna," Mr. Potato Head crooned. "This is not the fault of the Mission League. No one could have predicted the move to independence would come so suddenly."

She turned around and faced him. "Wasn't it somebody's darn business to predict it?"

"How could they?" he asked, opening his hands wide. "Last year when De Gaulle gave independence to all the French colonies, the Belgians insisted this had nothing to do with us! No one even took the ferry across to Brazzaville to watch the ceremony. The Belgians went on speaking of rule with a fatherly hand."

"A *fatherly hand*, is that what you call it!" She shook her head from side to side. "Using these people like slaves in your rubber plantations and your mines and I don't know what all? We've heard what goes on, Frank, do you think we're simpleminded? There's men right here in this village with tales to make your hair stand on end. One old fellow got his hand whacked off up at Coquilhatville, and ran away while he was still spurting blood!"

Father shot her a look.

"Well, honestly, Nathan. I talk to their wives." She looked at Mrs. Potato Head, who was keeping mum on the subject.

"We had no idea," Mother said quietly then, like she'd just figured the whole thing out. "Your King Baudouin is living off the fat of this land, is what he's doing, and leaving it up to penniless mission doctors and selfless men like my husband to take care of their every simple need. Is that how a father rules? Hell's bells! And he didn't expect trouble?"

She glanced back and forth between Mr. Underdown and Father like a nervous child herself, unsure which of the two men was entitled to give her a licking.

Mr. Underdown stared at Mother like he suddenly had no idea where she'd come from—like that houseboy that didn't know how the sugar got under his shirt. Man oh man, that made me nervous. Every grown-up in the room, including my mother, the Cussing Lady, and Mrs. Underdown, who kept rubbing her neck and craning her chin to the side, you could have mistaken for a mental psychiatry patient right then. Except for Father, and of course *he* is the one who is really mental.

The Reverend Underdown flung out his fist, and Mother flinched. But he wasn't aiming for her at all. It turns out he just meant for them all to admire his hand. "That is the relation of Belgium to her Congo," he said. "Look there! A strong hand, tightly clenched. No one could have predicted an uprising like this."

Mother walked straight out of the room, out the backdoor toward the kitchen. No one mentioned her absence. Then in a minute she came back, having just remembered, evidently, that she couldn't go hop on the Greyhound Bus to Atlanta.

"What's he really saying?" she asked Mrs. Underdown. "That there's going to be no transition at all? No interim period for—I don't know—a provisional government-in-training? Just wham, the Belgians are gone and the Congolese have to run everything on their own?"

Nobody answered, and I was scared Mother would start swearing about the King again, or crying. How embarrassing. But she didn't do either one. She pulled on her hair for a while and then tried out a new, improved Let's Get This All Straight voice. "Frank. Janna. Not a soul among these people has even gone to college or traveled abroad to study government. That's what Anatole tells us. And now you're saying they'll be left overnight to run every single school, every service, every government office? And the army? What about the *army*, Frank?"

Reverend Underdown shook his head. "I can't tell you *how*, Orleanna. I can only tell you what I know."

Home, home, home, home, I prayed. If the problem was big enough, we'd just have to go home. We could get on that plane tomorrow and fly right straight out of here, if only *he* would say so.

Father got up and came to stand in the doorway, facing out toward the porch. I shuddered, both hoping and dreading that he'd read my mind. But he wasn't looking at us girls. He just stared right past us, to make a point of turning his back on the present company of Underdowns and Mother. I slouched back into my hammock and attended to my cuticles while Father spoke to the great outdoors.

"Not a television set in this whole blessed country," he announced to the palm trees. "Radios, maybe *one* per hundred *thousand* residents. No telephones. Newspapers as scarce as hen's teeth, and a literacy rate made to match. They get their evening news by listening to their neighbors' drums."

That was all true. Almost every single night we could hear those drums from the next village over, which Nelson said was *talking* drums. But what in tarnation could you tell somebody with just a drum? It would have to be worse than that dip-dip-dop More Scold thing they use in the army.

Father said, "An *election*. Frank, I'm embarrassed for you. You're quaking in your boots over a fairy tale. Why, open your eyes, man. These people can't even read a simple slogan: Vote for Me! Down with Shapoopie! An *election!* Who out here would even know it happened?"

Nobody answered him. We girls never said a peep, of course, any more than the palm trees did, for we knew he was talking to Mother and the Underdowns. I knew just how they felt, getting one of Father's pop quizzes.

"Two *hundred* different languages," he said, "spoken inside the borders of a so-called country invented by Belgians in a parlor. You might as well put a fence around sheep, wolves, and chickens, and tell them to behave like brethren." He turned around, looking suddenly just like a preacher. "Frank, this is not a *nation*, it is the *Tower of Babel* and it *cannot* hold an election. If these people are to be united at all, they will come together as God's lambs in their simple love for Christ. Nothing else will move them forward. Not politics, not a desire for freedom—they don't have the temperament or the intellect for such things. I know you're trying to tell us what you've heard, but believe me, Frank, I *know* what I *see*."

Mrs. Potato Head spoke up for the first time since they'd drifted from the subject of malaria pills. "Orleanna, all we really came here for is to tell you to make your plans to leave. I know you were going to stay on till the fifteenth of June, but we have to send you home."

Boy, my heart did the cha-cha, hearing that. Home!

Well. If there's one solitary thing Father does not like it's being told what to do. "My contract expires in June," he announced to all concerned. "We will stay through July to help welcome the Reverend and Mrs. Minor when they come. I'm sure Christian charity will be forthcoming from America, regardless of any problems Belgium may have with its *fatherly hand*."

"Nathan, the Minors . . ." Frank started to say, but Father ran him right over and kept going.

"I've worked some miracles here, I don't mind telling you, and I've done it single-handedly. Outside help is of no concern to me. I can't risk losing precious ground by running away like a *coward* before we have made a proper transition!"

Transition *when*, is what I wanted to know. Another week? A month? July was practically half a year away!

"Frank, Janna," my mother said, in a voice that sounded scared. "For my own part," she said, and faltered. "For the girls, I'd like to . . ."

"You'd like to *what*, Orleanna." Father was still right out there in the doorway, so we could see his face. He looked like a mean boy fixing to smash puppies with a brick. "What is it you'd like to say, for your own part?" he asked.

Mrs. Underdown was shooting worried looks over at her husband like, "Oh, Lordy, what next?"

"Nathan, there may not be a transition," Mr. Underdown said nervously, saying Father's name the way you'd say a growling dog's name to calm it down. "The Minors have declined their contract, on our advice. It may be years before this mission resumes."

Father stared at the trees, giving no indication he'd heard his poor frightened wife, or any of this news. Father would sooner watch us all perish one by one than listen to anybody but himself. *Years* before they send someone else to this mission, I thought. *Years! Oh, please God make a tree fall on him and smash his skull! Let us leave right now!*

Mrs. Underdown pitched in helpfully, "We are making preparations to leave, ourselves."

"Oh, yes," her husband said. "Absolutely. We are packing to leave. We have called the Congo our home for many years, as you know, but the situation is very extreme. Nathan, perhaps you don't understand how serious this is. In all likelihood the embassy will evacuate from Léopoldville."

"I believe I understand perfectly well," Father said, turning around suddenly to face them. In his khakis and rolled-up white shirt sleeves he looked like a working man, but he raised up one hand above his head the way he does in church to pronounce the benediction.

"Only God knows when our relief may arrive. But God does know. And in His benevolent service we will stay."

Adah

So MUCH DEPENDS on a red wheelbarrow glazed with rain water standing beside the white chickens. That is one whole poem written by a doctor named William C. Williams. Chickens white beside standing water rain, with glazed wheelbarrow. Red on! Depends much. So?

I particularly like the name Williams C. William. He wrote the poem while he was waiting for a child to die. I should like to be a doctor poet, I think, if I happen to survive to adulthood. I never much imagined myself as a woman grown, anyway, and nowadays especially it seems a waste of imagination. But if I *were* a doctor poet, I would spend all day with people who could not run past me, and then I would go home and write whatever I liked about their insides.

We are all waiting now to see what will happen next. Waiting for a child to die is not an occasion for writing a poem here in Kilanga: it isn't a long enough wait. Every day, nearly, one more funeral. Pascal doesn't come anymore to play because his older brother died and Pascal is needed at home. Mama Mwanza without a leg to stand on lost her two smallest ones. It used to astonish us that everyone here has so many children: six or eight or nine. But now, suddenly, it seems no one has enough. They wrap up the little bodies in layers of cloth like a large goat cheese, and set it out in front of the house under a funeral arch woven from palm fronds and the howling sweet scent of frangipani flowers. All the mothers come walking on their knees. They shriek and wail a long, high song with quivering soft palates, like babies dying of hunger. Their tears run down and they stretch their hands out toward the dead child but never do they reach it. When they have finished trying, the men carry the body in a hammock slung between sticks. The women follow, still wailing and reaching out. Down the road past our house they go, into the forest. Our Father forbids us to watch. He doesn't seem to mind the corpses so much as the souls unsaved. In the grand tally Up Yonder, each one counts as a point against him.

According to my Baptist Sunday-school teachers, a child is denied entrance to heaven merely for being born in the Congo rather than, say, north Georgia, where she could attend church regularly. This was the sticking point in my own little lame march to salvation: admission to heaven is gained by the luck of the draw. At age five I raised my good left hand in Sunday school and used a month's ration of words to point out this problem to Miss Betty Nagy. Getting born within earshot of a preacher, I reasoned, is entirely up to chance. Would Our Lord be such a hit-or-miss kind of Saviour as that? Would he really condemn some children to eternal suffering just for the accident of a heathen birth, and reward others for a privilege they did nothing to earn? I waited for Leah and the other pupils to seize on this very obvious point of argument and jump in with their overflowing brace of words. To my dismay, they did not. Not even my own twin, who ought to know about unearned privilege. This was before Leah and I were gifted; I was still Dumb Adah. Slowpoke poison-oak running-joke Adah, subject to frequent thimble whacks on the head. Miss Betty sent me to the corner for the rest of the hour to pray for my own soul while kneeling on grains of uncooked rice. When I finally got up with sharp grains imbedded in my knees I found, to my surprise, that I no longer believed in God. The other children still did, apparently. As I limped back to my place, they turned their eyes away from my stippled sinner's knees. How could they not even question their state of grace? I lacked their confidence, alas. I had spent more time than the average child pondering unfortunate accidents of birth.

From that day I stopped parroting the words of *Oh, God! God's love!* and began to cant in my own backward tongue: *Evol's dog! Dog ho!*

Now I have found a language even more cynical than my own: in Kilanga the word *nzolo* is used in three different ways, at least. It means "most dearly beloved." Or it is a thick yellow grub highly prized for fish bait. Or it is a type of tiny potato that turns up in the market now and then, always sold in bunches that clump along the roots like knots on a string. And so we sing at the top of our lungs in church: "*Tata Nzolo!*" To whom are we calling?

I think it must be the god of small potatoes. That other Dearly Beloved who resides in north Georgia does not seem to be paying much attention to the babies here in Kilanga. They are all dying. Dying from *kakakaka*, the disease that turns the body to a small black pitcher, pitches it over, and pours out all its liquid insides. The heavy rains brought the disease down the streams and rivers. Everyone in this village knows more about hygiene than we do, we have lately discovered. While we were washing and swimming in the stream any old place, there were rules, it turns out: wash clothes downstream, where the forest creek runs into the crocodile river. Bathe in the middle. Draw water for drinking up above the village. In Kilanga these are matters of religious observance, they are baptism and communion. Even defecation is ruled by African gods, who command that we use only the bushes that Tata Kuvudundu has sanctified for those purposes—and believe you me, he chooses bushes far away from the drinking water. Our latrine was probably neutral territory, but on the points of bathing and washing we were unenlightened for the longest time. We have offended all the oldest divinities, in every thinkable way. "*Tata Nzolo!*" we sing, and I wonder what new, disgusting sins we commit each day, holding our heads high in sacred ignorance while our neighbors gasp, hand to mouth.

Nelson says it was our offenses that brought on this rainy season. Oh, it rains, it pours, Noah himself would be dismayed. This rainy season has shattered all the rules. When it came early and lasted so long and poured down so hard, the manioc hills melted and tubers rotted away from their vines, and finally the downpour brought us the *kakakaka*. After all, even when everyone defecates righteously, there are villages upstream from us. Downstream is always someone else's up. The last shall be first.

Now the thunderstorms have ended. The funerals are drying up as slowly as the puddles. Methuselah sits puny and still in his avocado tree with his eyes ticking back and forth, unprepared for a new season of overwhelming freedom. *Beto nki tutasala?* he mutters sometimes in Mama Tataba's ghost voice: What are we doing? It is a question anyone might ask. In the strange quiet our family doesn't know what to do.

Everyone else seems brain-dashed and busy at the same time, like dazed insects coming out after the storm. The women beat out their sisal mats and replant their fields while grieving for lost children. Anatole goes to our neighbors' houses, one by one, offering his condolences for our village's lost schoolboys. He is also, I have seen, preparing them for the election, and Independence. It is to be a kitchen election: since no one can read, every candidate is designated by a symbol. Wisely these men choose to represent themselves with useful things—knife, bottle, matches, cooking pot. Anatole has set out in front of the school a collection of big clay bowls and next to each one the knife, the bottle, or the matches. On election day every man in Kilanga is to throw in one pebble. The women tell their husbands constantly: the knife! The bottle! Don't forget what I'm telling you! The men, who get the privilege of voting, seem the least interested. The old ones say Independence is for the young, and perhaps this is true. The children seem most excited of all: they practice throwing pebbles into the bowls from across the yard. Anatole dumps these out at the end of each day. He sighs as the stones fall on the dirt in the shapes of new constellations. The make-believe votes of children. At the end of election day Tata Ndu's sons will put the pebbles in bags along with the proper symbol for each candidate—knife, bottle, or matches—and carry them by canoe all the way upriver to Banningville. Pebbles from all over Congo will travel up rivers that day. Indeed, the earth shall move. A dugout canoe seems such a fragile bird to carry that weight.

Toorlexa Nebee, Eeben Axelroot, is traveling also. He wastes no time. These days he makes as many trips as he can up the Kwilu River to wherever he goes in the south. Katanga and Kasai, his radio says. Where the mines are. He stops here every week just long enough to pay the women his nothing for their manioc and plantains, leaving them wailing like mourners at a funeral, flying away with whatever he can stuff into his sack, while he can. The Belgians and the Americans who run the rubber plantations and copper mines, I imagine, are using larger sacks.

The doctor poet in our village is the *nganga* Kuvudundu, I think. The rare nut, Our Father calls him, a thing, a seed to be cracked. The pot calls the kettle black. The *nganga* Kuvudundu is writing poems for us alone. So much depends on the white chicken bones in the calabash bowl left standing in a puddle of rain outside our door.

I saw him leave it there. I was looking out the window and he turned back just for a second, staring straight into my eyes. I saw a kindness there, and believe he means to protect us, really. Protect us from angry gods, and our own stupidity, by sending us away.

Bongo Bango Bingo. That is the story of Congo they are telling now in America: a tale of cannibals. I know about this kind of story—the lonely look down upon the hungry; the hungry look down upon the starving. The guilty blame the damaged. Those of doubtful righteousness speak of cannibals, the unquestionably vile, the sinners and the damned. It makes everyone feel much better. So, Khrushchev is said to be here dancing with the man-eating natives, teaching them to hate the Americans and the Belgians. It must be true, for how else would the poor Congolese know how to hate the Americans and the Belgians? After all, we have such white skin. We eat their food inside our large house, and throw out the bones. Bones that lie helter-skelter on the grass, from which to tell our fortunes. Why ever should the Congolese read our doom? After all, we have offered to feed their children to the crocodiles in order for them to know the Kingdom and the Power and the Glory.

All the eyes of America know what a Congolese looks like. Skin and bones dancing, lips upcurled like oyster shells, a no-count man with a femur in his hair.

The *nganga* Kuvudundu dressed in white with no bone in his hair is standing at the edge of our yard. He of eleven toes. He repeats the end of his own name over and over: the word *dundu*. *Dundu* is a kind of antelope. Or it is a small plant of the genus *Veronia*. Or a hill. Or a price you have to pay. So much depends on the tone of voice. One of these things is what our family has coming to us. Our Baptist ears from Georgia will never understand the difference.

Rachel

FATHER FLEW with Eeben Axelroot to Stanleyville for the same reason the bear went over the mountain, I guess. And all that he could see was the other side of the Congo. The other main reason for his trip was quinine pills, which we had just about run out of, how unfortunate. Quinine pills taste bad enough to give you a hair problem. I happen to know Ruth May doesn't even swallow hers all the time: once I saw her hide it behind her side teeth when she opened wide to show Mother it was down the hatch. Then she spat it out in her hand and stuck it on the wall behind her cot. Me, I swallow. All I need is to go back home with some dread disease. Sweet sixteen and never been kissed is bad enough, but to be Thyroid Mary on top of it? Oh, brother.

Father is mad at the Underdowns. Usually they send the basic necessities they think we will need every month (which believe you me is not much), but this time they just sent a letter: "Prepare your departure. We are sending a special Mission plane for your evacuation June 28. We are leaving Léopoldville the following week and have arranged for your family to accompany us as far as Belgium."

The end? And the Price family lived happily ever after? Not on your life. Father is all psyched up to stay here forever, I think. Mother tries to explain to him day in and day out about how he is putting his own children in jeopardy of their lives, but he won't even listen to his own wife, much less his mere eldest daughter. I screamed and kicked the furniture until one whole leg came off the table and threw a hissy fit they could probably hear all the way to

Egypt. Listen, what else can a girl do but try. Stay here? When everybody else gets to go home and do the bunny hop and drink Cokes? It is a sheer tapestry of justice.

Father returned from Stanleyville with his hair just about standing on end, he was so full of the daily news. They had their election, I guess, and the winner is a man named *Patrice*, if you can believe. Patrice Lumumba. Father said Lumumba's party won thirty-five of a hundredy-some-odd seats in the new parliament, mainly because of his natural animal magnetism. And also the large population of his hometown. It sounded kind of like student-council elections at Bethlehem High, where whoever has the biggest click of friends, they win. Not that a minister's daughter would ever have a chance, jeez-oh-man. No matter how much you flirt or carry on like a cool cat and roll up your skirt waistband on the bus, they still just think you're L–7. A square, in other words. Try to get a boyfriend under those conditions: believe you me, your chances are dull and void.

So Mr. *Patrice* will be the Prime Minister of the Congo now and it won't be the Belgian Congo anymore, it will be the Republic of Congo. And do you think anybody in this hip town we live in is actually going to notice? Oh, sure. They'll all have to go out and get their drivers' licenses changed. In the year two million that is, when they build a road to here and somebody gets a car.

Mother said, "Now is he the one they're saying is a Communist?"

Father said, "Not so's you'd notice." That is the one and only Mississippi expression he has ever picked up from Mother. We'll ask her something like "Did you iron my linen dress like I asked you to?" And she'll say, "Not so's you'd notice." Back home she could be a smart aleck sometimes, and how. When Father wasn't around, that is.

Father said he heard soon-to-be Prime Minister Lumumba talk on a radio in a barbershop in Stanleyville about neutral foreign policy and African Unity and all that jazz. He says now Patrice Lumumba and the other elected Congolese are trading chickens and eggs to set up a government that everybody in the parliament will go along with. But the problem is all of them still like their own tribes and their own chiefs the best. I can just picture the parliament room: a hundredy-some-odd Tata Ndus in pointy hats and no-glass glasses all flicking flies away with animal-tail magic wands in the sweltering heat, pretending to ignore each other. It will probably take them one hundred years just to decide which person gets to sit where. It's enough already. All I want is to go home, and start scrubbing the deep-seated impurities of the Congo out of my skin.

Ruth May

MAMA NEEDS her some Quick Energy. After Father went away with Leah on the plane, she went and got in her bed and won't get up.

It wasn't the Mr. Axelroot plane. He goes and comes whenever he feels like it. This was another airplane just as little but yellow this time. The driver had on a white shirt and Vitalis in his hair that you could smell. He smelled clean. He had Experimint gum and gave me a piece. He was a white man that talked French. Sometimes some of them do and I don't know why. We all put on our shoes and went down to see the airplane land. I have to wear white baby shoes even though I'm not a baby. When I am grown my mother will still have my shoes. She aims to turn them into brown shiny metal and keep them on the table in Georgia with my baby picture. She did it for all the others, even Adah and her one foot's no count; it curls up and makes the shoe wear out funny. Even that bad sideways-worn-out shoe Mama made into metal and saved, so she'll save mine.

Mama said the airplane was a special chart plane the Under-downs sent for us to get all our stuff that needed getting and fly on out of here. But Father wouldn't allow. Only he and Leah got on, and didn't take anything because they are coming back. Rachel sassed him straight to his face, and tried to climb right into the airplane with her things! He flung her back. She threw her stuff on the ground and said fine, then, she was going to go drown herself in the river, but we knew she wouldn't. Rachel wouldn't want to get that dirty.

Adah wasn't there either; she stayed home. Just me and Mama stood on the field to watch the plane fly away. But Mama wouldn't even jump up and wave bye. She just stood with her face getting smaller and smaller, and when you couldn't see the airplane anymore she went in the house and lay down on her bed. It was morning, not night. Not even nap time.

I told Rachel and Adah we needed some 7Up for Mama. Rachel does the radio advertisements from back home and that is one: "Bushed? Beat? Need ionizing? 7Up is the greatest discovery yet for getting new energy quick. In two to six minutes you'll feel like a new you."

But all day went by and it got dark and Mama still doesn't feel like a new Mama. Rachel won't talk to me about getting 7Up. She's sitting out on the porch looking at the hole in the sky where the airplane went away. And Adah doesn't talk anyway, because of how she is. Nelson got us our dinner, but he is sneaking around the house like somebody got in a fight and he's staying out of it. So it's real quiet. I tried to play but I didn't feel like it. I went in and picked up Mama's hand and it fell back down. Then I just crawled in the bed with her, and now that makes two of us that don't feel like getting up ever again.

Leah

My FATHER AND I have patched things up. He allowed me to accompany him to Leopoldville, where we got to see history in the making. We watched the Independence ceremonies from a giant rusty barge tied to the bank of the Congo River that was loaded with so many pushing, squirming people Mrs. Underdown said we'd probably all go down like the Titanic. It was such an important event King Baudouin of Belgium, himself, was going to be there. It was childish, I know, but I got very excited when she told me that. I suppose I was picturing someone in a crown and an ermine-trimmed scarlet robe, like Old King Cole. But the white men sitting up on the stage were all dressed alike, in white uniforms with belts, swords, shoulder fringe, and white flat-topped military hats. Not a single crown to be seen. As they waited their turn to speak, dark sweat stains blossomed under the arms of their uniforms. And when it was all over I couldn't even tell you which one had been the King.

The white men mostly spoke of the glorious days of the previous king of Belgium, King Léopold, who first made the Congo into what it is today. Mrs. Underdown reported this to me, in quick little bursts of translation while she squeezed my hand tightly, since it was mostly all in French. I didn't care for her holding my hand; I am as tall as she is and a good sight less of a scaredy-cat. But we could have gotten lost from one another in all those people, too. And Father wouldn't have held my hand for the world—he isn't like that. Mrs. Underdown called me a poor lost lamb. She couldn't believe it when Father and I showed up without the rest of them.

Her jaw dropped to her bosom. Later, when we were alone, she told me it was her opinion that Father was not in his right mind and should think of his poor children. I told her my father would know what was best in the sight of the Lord, and that we were privileged to serve. Why, that just flabbergasted her. She is a meek woman and I can't say that I respect her. They are leaving tomorrow to go to Belgium, and we're going back to Kilanga to hold the fort until another family can come. That is Father's plan. Reverend Underdown is pretending not to be mad at us.

After the King and the other white men spoke, they inaugurated Patrice Lumumba as the new Prime Minister. I could tell exactly which one he was. He was a thin, distinguished man who wore real eyeglasses and a small, pointed beard. When he stood up to speak, everyone's mouth shut. In the sudden quiet we could hear the great Congo River lapping up its banks. Even the birds seemed taken aback. Patrice Lumumba raised his left hand up and seemed to grow ten feet tall, right there and then. His eyes shone bright white with dark centers. His smile was a triangle, upcurved on the sides and reaching a point below, like his beard. I could see his face very clearly, even though we were far away.

"Ladies and gentlemen of the Congo," he said, "who have fought for the independence won today, I salute you!"

The quiet crowd broke open with cheers and cheers. *"Je vous salue! Je vous salue encore!"*

Patrice Lumumba asked us to keep this day, June 30, 1960, in our hearts forever and tell our children of its meaning. Everyone on the raft and the crowded banks would do what he said, I knew. Even me, if I ever get to have any children. Whenever he paused to take a breath, the people screamed and waved their arms.

First he talked about our equal partner, Belgium. Then he said other things that made Mrs. Underdown nervous. "Our lot was eighty years of colonial rule," she translated, and then she stopped. She let go my hand, wiped it on her slacks, and grabbed me again.

"What all's he saying?" I asked her. I didn't want to miss word one of Patrice Lumumba. As he spoke his eyes seemed to be on fire.

I have seen preachers at revival meetings speak like that, with voices rising in such a way that heaven and anger get mingled together. The people cheered more and more.

"He's saying we despoiled their land and used the Negroes for slaves, just as long as we could get away with it," she said.

"We did that?"

"Well. The Belgians in general. He's very mad about all the nice things they said earlier about King Léopold. Who *was* a bad egg, I'll admit that."

"Oh," I said. I narrowed my eyes to a hard focus on Patrice Lumumba and tried to understand his words. I was jealous of Adah, who picked up languages easier than she could tie her own shoes. I wished I'd studied harder.

"We have known *les maisons magnifiques* for the whites in the cities, and the falling-down houses for the Negroes." Oh, I understood that all right. He was right, I'd seen it myself when we went to the Underdowns'. Leopoldville is a nice little town of dandy houses with porches and flowery yards on nice paved streets for the whites, and surrounding it, for miles and miles, nothing but dusty run-down shacks for the Congolese. They make their homes out of sticks or tin or anything in the world they can find. Father said that is the Belgians' doing and Americans would never stand for this kind of unequal treatment. He says after Independence the Americans will send foreign aid to help them make better houses. The Underdowns' house has soft red Persian rugs, chairs with matching ottomans, even a radio. She had a real china tea set on the dark wooden sideboard. Last night I watched her pack up all the fragile cups, moaning about what she'd have to leave and who'd get it. For dinner the houseboy brought us one thing after another until I thought I'd burst: real meat, orange cheeses wrapped in red wax, canned yellow asparagus. After a hundred white meals of *fufu*, bread, Potato Buds and Carnation milk, it was too much taste and color for me. I chewed and swallowed slowly, feeling sick. After dinner, why, chocolate cookies from France! The Underdowns' two sons, big crew-cut boys shifting around in grown men's bodies, grabbed handfuls of cookies with their big hands and bolted from the table. I took only one and couldn't get my mouth to eat it, though I wanted to badly. The Underdowns' skinny houseboy sweated in his ironed white apron while he hurried to bring us more things. I thought about the kilo of sugar he'd tried to stash under his shirt. With so much else around, why wouldn't Mrs. Underdown just go ahead and give it to him? Was she actually going to take all her sugar back to Belgium?

Tomorrow she'll be gone, and I'll still be here, I thought to myself as we stood on our barge fastened to the bank of the Congo, watching history. A rat ran under the bare feet of some people standing near us, but no one paid any attention. They just cheered. Patrice Lumumba had stopped speaking for a moment to take off his glasses and mop his forehead with a white handkerchief. He wasn't sweating in his dark suit the way the white men had stained their white uniforms, but his face gleamed.

"Tell me what he's saying," I pleaded with Mrs. Underdown. "I've only gone as far as the past perfect tense in my French book."

Mrs. Underdown relented after a while and told me certain sentences. Much of the rest of it began to come to me in bursts of understanding, as if Patrice Lumumba were speaking in tongues and my ears had been blessed by the same stroke of grace. "My brothers," he said, "*Mes frères*, we have suffered the colonial oppression in body and heart, and we say to you, all of that is finished. Together we are going to make a place for justice and peace, prosperity and grandeur. We are going to show the world what the *homme noir* can do when he works for freedom. We are going to make the Congo, for all of Africa, the heart of light."

I thought I would go deaf from the roaring.

Adah

E MULP DER ENO. So much depends on the single red feather I saw when I stepped out of the latrine.

It is early morning now, rooster-pink sky smoky air morning. Long shadows scissoring the road from here to anywhere. Independence Day. June thirtieth.

Does anyone here know about the new freedom? These women squatting, knees wide apart in their long wrapped skirts, throwing handfuls of peppers and small potatoes into hissing pans over cook-fires? These children defecating earnestly or weakly, according to their destiny, in the bushes? One red feather for celebration. No one yet has seen it but me.

When Miss Dickinson says, "Hope is the thing with feathers," I always think of something round—a ball from one of the games I will never play—stuck all around like a clove-orange sachet with red feathers. I have pictured it many times–*Hope!*—wondering how I would catch such a thing one-handed, if it did come floating down to me from the sky. Now I find it has fallen already, and a piece of it is here beside our latrine, one red plume. In celebration I stooped down to pick it up.

Down in the damp grass I saw the red shaft of another one, and I reached for it. Following the trail I found first the red and then the gray: clusters of long wing feathers still attached to gristle and skin, splayed like fingers. Downy pale breast feathers in tufted mounds. Methuselah.

At last it is Independence Day, for Methuselah and the Congo. O

Lord of the feathers, deliver me this day. After a lifetime caged away from flight and truth, comes freedom. After long seasons of slow preparation for an innocent death, the world is theirs at last. *From the carnivores that would tear me, breast from wishbone.*

Set upon by the civet cat, the spy, the eye, the hunger of a superior need, Methuselah is free of his captivity at last. This is what he leaves to the world: gray and scarlet feathers strewn over the damp grass. Only this and nothing more, the tell-tale heart, tale of the carnivore. None of what he was taught in the house of the master. Only feathers, without the ball of Hope inside. Feathers at last at last and no words at all.

Book Three

THE JUDGES

*And ye shall make no league with the
inhabitants of this land;
ye shall throw down their altars . . .*

*They shall be as thorns in your sides,
and their gods shall be a snare unto you.*

JUDGES 2:2–3

Orleanna Price

SANDERLING ISLAND, GEORGIA

LISTEN, LITTLE BEAST. Judge me as you will, but first listen. I am your mother. What happened to us could have happened anywhere, to any mother. I'm not the first woman on earth to have seen her daughters possessed. For time and eternity there have been fathers like Nathan who simply can see no way to have a daughter but to own her like a plot of land. To work her, plow her under, rain down a dreadful poison upon her. Miraculously, it causes these girls to grow. They elongate on the pale slender stalks of their longing, like sunflowers with heavy heads. You can shield them with your body and soul, trying to absorb that awful rain, but they'll still move toward him. Without cease, they'll bend to his light.

Oh, a wife may revile such a man with every silent curse she knows. But she can't throw stones. A stone would fly straight through him and strike the child made in his image, clipping out an eye or a tongue or an outstretched hand. It's no use. There are no weapons for this fight. There are countless laws of man and of nature, and none of these is on your side. Your arms go weak in their sockets, your heart comes up empty. You understand that the thing you love more than this world grew from a devil's seed. It was you who let him plant it.

The day does come, finally, when a daughter can walk away from a man such as that—if she's lucky. His own ferocity turns over inside her and she turns away hard, never to speak to him again. Instead she'll begin talking to *you*, her mother, demanding with a world of indignation: *How could you let him? Why?*

There are so many answers. All of them are faultless, and none good enough.

What did I have? No money, that's for sure. No influence, no friends I could call upon in that place, no way to overrule the powers that governed our lives. This is not a new story: I was an inferior force.

There was another thing too, awful to admit. I'd come to believe that God was on his side. Does this make me seem lunatic? But I did believe it; I must have. I feared him more than it's possible to fear a mere man. Feared Him, loved Him, served Him, clamped my hands over my ears to stop His words that rang in my head even when He was far away, or sleeping. In the depths of my sleepless nights I would turn to the Bible for comfort, only to find myself regaled yet again. *Unto the woman God said: I will greatly multiply thy sorrow and thy conception, in sorrow thou shalt bring forth children; and thy desire shall be to thy husband, and he shall rule over thee.*

Oh, mercy. If it catches you in the wrong frame of mind, the King James Bible can make you want to drink poison in no uncertain terms.

My downfall was not predicted. I didn't grow up looking for ravishment or rescue, either one. My childhood was a happy one in its own bedraggled way. My mother died when I was quite young, and certainly a motherless girl will come up wanting in some respects, but in my opinion she has a freedom unknown to other daughters. For every womanly fact of life she doesn't get told, a star of possibility still winks for her on the horizon.

Jackson, Mississippi, in the Great Depression wasn't so different from the Congo thirty years later, except that in Jackson we knew of *some* that had plenty and I guess that did make us restless from time to time. In Kilanga, people knew nothing of things they might have had—a Frigidaire? a washer-dryer combination? Really, they'd sooner imagine a tree that could pull up its feet and go bake bread. It didn't occur to them to feel sorry for themselves. Except when children died—then they wept and howled. Anyone can recognize the raging injustice *there*. But otherwise I believe they were satisfied with their lot.

And so it was for me, as a child in the Depression, with that same practical innocence. So long as I was surrounded only with what I knew, that's what life had to offer and I took it. As a noticeably pretty child, and later on, a striking girl, I had my own small way in the world. My father, Bud Wharton, was an eye doctor. We lived on the outskirts of Jackson proper, in a scrubby settlement called Pearl. Dad saw patients in the back room of the house, which had metal cabinets for his nested lenses that tinkled like glass wind chimes when you opened and shut the drawers. Up front, we ran a store. We had to, because in hard times everyone's eyes get better or at least good enough. In the store we sold fresh produce my cousins brought in from their truck farm, and also dry goods and a little ammunition. We squeaked by. We all lived upstairs. At one time there were eleven altogether, cousins from Noxubee County, uncles who came and went with the picking season, and my old Aunt Tess. She was a mother to me if I needed one. What Aunt Tess loved to say was: "Sugar, it's no parade but you'll get down the street one way or another, so you'd just as well throw your shoulders back and pick up your pace." And that was more or less what we all believed in.

I don't think Dad ever forgave me, later on, for becoming a Free Will Baptist. He failed to see why anyone would need more bluster and testimony about God's Plan than what he found, for example, within the fine-veined world of an eyeball. That, and a good chicken dinner on Sundays. Dad drank and cursed some but not in any way that mattered. He taught me to cook, and otherwise let me run wild with my cousins. On the outskirts of Pearl lay a wilderness. There we discovered pitcher-plant bogs where we'd hike up our dresses, sink on our knees in the rich black muck, and stare carnivory right in the lips, feeding spiders to the pitcher plants. This was what I worshiped and adored as a child: miracles of a passionate nature. Later on, we discovered kissing boys. Then tent revivals.

It was some combination of all those things that ran me up against Nathan Price. I was seventeen, bursting utterly with happiness. Arm in arm we girls marched forward in our thin cotton dresses with all eyes upon us. Tossing our hair, down the aisle we went between the rows of folding chairs borrowed from the funeral home, right straight to the front of the crowded tent for the Lord's roll call. We threw ourselves at Jesus with our unsaved bosoms heaving. We had already given a chance to all the other red-necked hooligans in Pearl by then, and were looking for someone who better deserved us. Well, why not Jesus? We were only in it for the short run anyhow—we assumed He would be gone by the end of the week, the same as all others.

But when the tent folded up, I found I had Nathan Price in my life instead, a handsome young red-haired preacher who fell upon my unclaimed soul like a dog on a bone. He was more sure of himself than I'd thought it possible for a young man to be, but I resisted him. His seriousness dismayed me. He could be jolly with old ladies in crepe de chine dresses, patting their hunched backs, but with me he could not let go the subject of heaven except to relieve it occasionally with his thoughts on hell.

Our courtship crept up on me, mainly because I didn't recognize that's what it was. I thought he was just bound and determined to save me. He'd park himself on our dusty front-porch steps, fold his suit jacket neatly on the glider, roll up his sleeves, and read to me from the Psalms and Deuteronomy while I shelled beans. *How say ye to my soul, Flee as a bird to your mountain?* The words were mysterious and beautiful, so I let him stay. My prior experience with young men was to hear them swear "Christ almighty in the craphouse!" at any dress with too many buttons. Now here was one from whose mouth came, *The words of the Lord are pure words: as silver tried in a furnace of earth, purified seven times;* and *He maketh me to lie down in green pastures.* Oh, I wanted those green pastures. I could taste the pale green sweetness of the blade of wheat, stripped and sucked between my teeth. I wanted to lie down with those words and rise up speaking a new language. So I let him stay.

As a young and ambitious revival preacher, his circuit was supposed to divide him equally between Rankin, Simpson, and Copiah counties, but I'll tell you what: more souls got saved in Pearl that summer than the Lord probably knew what to do with. Nathan hardly missed a Sunday chicken dinner at our house. Aunt Tess finally said, "You're a-feeding him anyways, child, why not go on and marry him if that's what he's after."

I suppose I'll never know if that was what he was after. But when I told him Aunt Tess was more or less needing an answer, before committing more chickens to the project, the idea of marriage suited him well enough so that he owned it as his. I hardly had time to think about my own answer—why, it was taken to be a foregone conclusion. And even if anyone had been waiting for my opinion, I wouldn't have known how to form one. I'd never known any married person up close. What did I know of matrimony? From where I stood, it looked like a world of flattering attention, and what's more, a chance to cross the county line.

We married in September and spent our honeymoon picking cotton for the war effort. In '39 and '40 there had been such talk of war, the boys were getting called up just to make a show of being ready for anything, I suppose. But Nathan had always been exempted, as an indispensible worker—not for the Lord, but for King Cotton. He did farm labor between revivals, and in the autumn of '41 it was our first enterprise as newlyweds to bend our backs together in the dusty fields. When the rough cotton pokes were filled, our hands clawed raw and our hair and shoulders tufted with white, we believed we'd done our part. Never did we dream that shortly the bombs would fall on a faraway harbor whose name struck a chill across our own small, landlocked Pearl.

By the end of that infamous week, half the men in all this world were pledged to a single war, Nathan included. He was drafted. At Fort Sill, his captain made note of Nathan's faith and vouched that he'd serve as a hospital cleric or chaplain, decently removed from enemy lines. I let out my breath: now I could truly say I loved the Lord! But then, without any explanation, Nathan found himself in Paris, Texas, training for the infantry. I was allowed to spend two weeks with him there on the wind-swept plain, mostly waiting in the strange vacancy of a cold apartment, trying to compose cordial things to say to the other wives. What flotsam and jetsam we were, women of all accents and prospects washed up there boiling grits or pasta, whatever we knew as comfort, united by our effort not to think about our husbands' hands learning to cradle a gun. At night I cradled his head on my lap and read him the Scriptures: *The Lord is my rock and my fortress . . . the horn of my salvation . . . so shall I be saved from mine enemies.* When he left, I went home to Pearl.

He wasn't even gone three months. He was trucked, shipped, and shuttled on the Asiatic Fleet, and finally encamped under palm trees on the Philippine shore, to make his stand for General MacArthur. His company fought their way into Luzon, facing nothing worse than mosquitoes and jungle to begin with, but on their second night were roused from sleep by artillery. Nathan was struck in the head with a shell fragment. He ran for cover, dazed, and spent the night in a bamboo pig shed. He had suffered a concussion but gradually regained consciousness through the dawn and staggered about half-blinded into the open, with no more sense of direction than an insect rushing at flame. By pure luck, just before nightfall, he was spotted on the beach and picked up by a PT boat. From a hospital bunker in Corregidor Island he wrote me a cheerful V-mail letter about his salvation by the grace of God and a Jap hog manger. He couldn't tell his location, of course, but promised me he was miraculously mostly intact, and coming home soon!

That was the last I would ever hear from the man I'd married— one who could laugh (even about sleeping in a manger), call me his "honey lamb," and trust in the miracle of good fortune. I can still picture the young soldier who wrote that letter while propped up in bed, smiling through his eyepatch and bandages, showing the nurses a photo of his pretty bride with Delta cotton poking out of her hair. Enjoying, as it turned out, the last happy hours of his life. He hadn't yet learned what happened to the rest of his company. In a few days the news would begin to reach Corregidor. Through the tunnels of that island fortress came wind of a horror too great to speak aloud—a whispered litany that would take years to be fully disclosed to the world, and especially to me. It would permanently curl one soldier's heart like a piece of hard shoe leather.

When the shelling began that night, as Nathan was hit and stumbled unseen through the darkness into a pig shed, the company received orders to move quickly to the Bataan Peninsula, where they could hide in the jungle, regroup, then march back to retake Manila. It was an error of a commander's overconfidence, small in history, large in the lives of those men. They were trapped on the peninsula, starving and terrified, and finally rounded up at bayonet point to be marched north through tepid rice paddies and blazing heat, marched through exhaustion and sickness and beyond it, marched from their feet to their hands and knees, emaciated, hallucinating from thirst and racked with malaria, toward a prison camp which few of them ever reached, and fewer survived. Nathan's company died, to the man, on the Death March from Bataan.

Private Price was evacuated from Corregidor just a few weeks before MacArthur himself abandoned that post, with his famous promise to return. But he would not be back, so far as those boys in Bataan were concerned, and neither would the soldier boy I'd married. He came home with a crescent-shaped scar on his temple, seriously weakened vision in his left eye, and a suspicion of his own cowardice from which he could never recover. His first words to me were to speak of how fiercely he felt the eye of God upon him. He pulled away from my kiss and my teasing touch, demanding, "Can't you understand the Lord is watching us?"

I still tried to tell him we were lucky. I believed the war had made only the smallest possible dent in our plans. Nathan was changed, I could see, but he only seemed more devout, and it was hard to name the ruin in that. At last I'd get to cross the state lines I'd dreamed of, traveling as a minister's wife.

Lord have mercy, that I did—Mississippi, Alabama, Georgia. We crossed lines in sand drawn through palmetto scrub, lines down the middle of highways, soup-kitchen lines, lines of worry, souls lined up awaiting the burning tongue of salvation. Nathan aimed to scorch a path as wide as Sherman's. With no money and no time to settle, we moved to a different ramshackle rental cottage or boardinghouse every season until I was so pregnant with Rachel that our nomad state seemed disreputable. One night we simply chose Bethlehem, Georgia, off a map. By good luck or Providence our station wagon made it that far, and Bethlehem turned out to be an open market for Evangelical Baptists. I tried to laugh about it, for here we were: man and swollen wife and no more room at the inn.

Nathan did not laugh at that hopeful comparison. In fact, it brought his hand down against me for the first time. I recall that I was sitting on the edge of a chair in our still-unpacked kitchen, holding my huge body together with both hands as we listened to the radio. A man had been reading a long war story, as they did then: a firsthand account of a prison camp and a dreadful march, where exhausted men struggled hopelessly, fell behind, and perished in brief orange bursts of pistol fire in the darkness. I was only half listening, until Nathan brought me to attention.

"Not a one of those men will ever see a son born to carry on his name. And you dare to gloat before Christ himself about your undeserved blessing."

Until that night I'd never known the details of where Nathan had been, nor the full measure of what he was still escaping.

He was profoundly embarrassed by my pregnancies. To his way of thinking they were unearned blessings, and furthermore each one drew God's attention anew to my having a vagina and his having a penis and the fact we'd laid them near enough together to conceive a child. But, God knows, it was never so casual as that. Nathan was made feverish by sex, and trembled afterward, praying aloud and blaming me for my wantonness. If his guilt made him a tyrant before men, it made him like a child before his God. Not a helpless or pleading child, but a petulant one, the type of tough boy who's known too little love and is quick to blame others for his mistakes. The type who grows up determined to show them all what he can do. He meant personally to save more souls than had perished on the road from Bataan, I think, and all other paths ever walked by the blight of mankind.

And where was I, the girl or woman called Orleanna, as we traveled those roads and crossed the lines again and again? Swallowed by Nathan's mission, body and soul. Occupied as if by a foreign power. I still appeared to be myself from the outside, I'm sure, just as he still looked like the same boy who'd gone off to war. But now every cell of me was married to Nathan's plan. His magnificent *will*. This is how conquest occurs: one plan is always larger than the other. I tried hard to do what I believed a wife ought, things like washing white shirts and black socks separately in rooming-house sinks. Making meal after meal of fried corn mush. The towns where we preached were stripped bare of young men, with it still being wartime, and this fanned the fires of Nathan's private torture. When he looked out over those soldierless congregations, he must have seen ghosts, marching north. For my part, I merely watched young, deprived female bosoms panting before my handsome husband, soldier of the Lord. (I longed to shout: Go ahead and try him, girls, I am too tired!) Or else I was home waiting for him, drinking four glasses of water before he arrived so I could watch him eat whatever there was without my stomach growling. When I was carrying the twins I had such desperate cravings I sometimes went out at night on my hands and knees and secretly ate dirt from the garden. Three babies in less than two lonely years I had. I cannot believe any woman on earth has ever made more babies out of less coition.

Three babies were too much, and I sensed it deep in my body. When the third one was born she could not turn her head to the side or even properly suckle. That was Adah. I'd cried for days when I learned I was carrying twins, and now I lay awake nights wondering whether my despair had poisoned her. Already Nathan's obsession with guilt and God's reproof was infecting me. Adah was what God sent me, either as punishment or reward. The world has its opinion on that, and I have mine. The doctors gave her little hope, though one of the nurses was kind. She told me formula was the very best thing, a modern miracle, but we couldn't afford it for two. So I ended up suckling greedy Leah at my breast and giving Adah the expensive bottles, both at the same time; with twins you learn how to do everything backhanded. Not only twins, mind you, but also a tow-headed toddler, whose skin seemed too thin, for she wailed at the slightest discomfort. Rachel screamed every single time she wet her diaper, and set the other two off like alarm bells. She also screamed excessively over teething. Adah howled from frustration, and Leah cried over nightmares. For six years, from age nineteen until I turned twenty-five, I did not sleep uninterrupted through a single night. There it is. And you wonder why I didn't rise up and revolt against Nathan? I felt lucky to get my shoes on the right feet, that's why. I moved forward only, thinking each morning anew that we were leaving the worst behind.

Nathan believed one thing above all else: that the Lord notices righteousness, and rewards it. My husband would accept no other possibility. So if we suffered in our little house on the peanut plain of Bethlehem, it was proof that one of us had committed a failure of virtue. I understood the failure to be mine. Nathan resented my attractiveness, as if slender hips and large blue eyes were things I'd selected intentionally to draw attention to myself. The eyes of God were watching, he gave me to know. If I stood still for a moment in the backyard between hanging up sheets to notice the damp grass tingling under my bare feet, His eyes observed my idleness. God heard whenever I let slip one of my father's curse words, and He watched me take my bath, daring me to enjoy the warm water. I could scarcely blow my nose without feeling watched. As if to compensate for all this watching, Nathan habitually overlooked me. If I complained about our life, he would chew his dinner while looking tactfully away, as one might ignore a child who has deliberately broken her dolls and then whines she has nothing to play with. To save my sanity, I learned to pad around hardship in soft slippers and try to remark on its good points.

If there was still some part of a beautiful heathen girl in me, a girl drawn to admiration like a moth to moonlight, and if her heart still pounded on Georgia nights when the peeper frogs called out from roadside ditches, she was too dumbfounded to speak up for herself. Once or twice while Nathan was away on a revival I may have locked the doors and breathed into my own mouth in the mirror, putting on red lipstick to do the housework. But rarely. I encountered my own spirit less and less. By the time Ruth May was born, we'd moved into the parsonage on Hale Street and Nathan was in full possession of the country once known as Orleanna Wharton. I accepted the Lord as my personal Saviour, for He finally brought me a Maytag washer. I rested in this peace and called it happiness. Because in those days, you see, that's how a life like mine was known.

It took me a long time to understand the awful price I'd paid, and that even God has to admit the worth of freedom. *How say ye to my soul, Flee as a bird to your mountain?* By then, I was lodged in the heart of darkness, so thoroughly bent to the shape of marriage I could hardly see any other way to stand. Like Methuselah I cowered beside my cage, and though my soul hankered after the mountain, I found, like Methuselah, I had no wings.

This is *why*, little beast. I'd lost my wings. Don't ask me how I gained them back—the story is too unbearable. I trusted too long in false reassurances, believing as we all want to do when men speak of the national interest, that it's also ours. In the end, my lot was cast with the Congo. Poor Congo, barefoot bride of men who took her jewels and promised the Kingdom.

The Things We Didn't Know

KILANGA, SEPTEMBER 1960

Leah

FOR THE SECOND TIME, we flew from Leopoldville over the jungle and down into that tiny cleared spot that was called Kilanga. This time it was just Father and me in the airplane, plus Mr. Axelroot, and twenty pounds of dry goods and canned whole prunes the Underdowns couldn't take with them when they fled the Congo. But this second bumpy touchdown didn't have the same impact as our first arrival. Instead of excitement, I felt a throb of dread. Not a single soul was standing at the edge of the field to greet us—no villagers, not even Mother or my sisters. This much is for sure, nobody was pounding on drums or stewing up a goat for us. As Father and I crossed the lonely field and made for our house I couldn't help but think about that earlier night and the welcome feast, all the tastes and sounds of it. How strange and paltry it seemed at the time, and now, looking back, what an abundance of good protein had been sacrificed in our honor. A shameful abundance, really. My stomach growled. I silently pledged to the Lord that I would express true gratitude for such a feast, if ever one should happen again. Rachel's opinion of goat meat notwithstanding, we could sure use a good old feast, because how else were we going to eat now? You can only get so far in this life on canned whole prunes.

On account of Independence I'd been thinking more about money than ever before in my life, aside from story problems for sixth-grade math. Fifty dollars a month in Belgian francs might not sound like much, but in Kilanga it had made us richer than anybody. Now we are to get by on zero dollars a month in Belgian francs, and it doesn't take long to figure out that story problem.

Sure enough, within a few weeks of Father's and my empty-handed return, the women figured out we had no money, and stopped coming to our door to sell us the meat or fish their husbands had killed. It was a gradual understanding, of course. At first they were just confused by our lowered circumstances. We spelled out our position as best we could: *fyata*, no money! This was the truth. Every franc we'd saved up had gone to Eeben Axelroot, because Father had to bribe him flat-out to fly the two of us back from Leopoldville. Yet our neighbors in Kilanga seemed to think: Could this really be, a white person *fyata*? They would remain in our doorway for the longest time just staring us up and down, while their baskets of plenty loomed silently on their heads. I suppose they must have thought our wealth was infinite. Nelson explained again and again, with Rachel and Adah and me looking over his shoulder, that it was Independence now and our family didn't get paid extra for being white Christians. Well, the women made lots of sympathetic noises upon hearing *that*. They bounced their babies on their hips and said, *Á bu*, well then, *ayi*, the Independence. But they still didn't believe it, quite. Had we looked *everywhere*, they wanted to know? Perhaps there is still a little money stashed under those strange, tall beds, or inside our cabinet boxes? And the little boys still attacked us like good-natured bandits whenever we went outside—*cadeau, cadeau!*—demanding powdered milk or a pair of pants, insisting that we still had a whole slew of these things stashed away at home.

Mama Mwanza from next door was the only one who felt sorry for us. She made her way over on the palms of her hands to give us some oranges, Independence or not. We told her we didn't have a thing to give her back, but she just waved up at us with the heels of both her hands. *Á bu*, no matter! Her little boys were good at finding oranges, she said, and she still had a *bákala mpandi* at her house—a good strong man. He was going to set his big fish traps later in the week, and if the catch was good, he would let her bring us some fish. Whenever you have plenty of something, you have to share it with the *fyata*, she said. (And Mama Mwanza is not even

Christian!) Really you know things are bad when a woman without any legs and who recently lost two of her own kids feels sorry for *you*.

Mother was taking life hard. The last we knew, when Father and I took off on the plane for Leopoldville, she was still trying to rise to the occasion; but in the short time we were away she'd stopped rising and gone downhill. Now she tended to walk bewildered around the house in her nightgown, scuffed brown loafers, no socks, and an unbuttoned pink blouse, spending both nights and days only halfway dressed for either one. A lot of the time she spent curled up on the bed with Ruth May. Ruth May didn't want to eat and said she couldn't stand up right because she was sweating too much. The truth is, neither one of them was taking a healthy interest.

Nelson told me confidentially that Mother and Ruth May had *kibáazu*, which means that someone had put a curse on them. Furthermore he claimed he knew who it was, and that sooner or later the *kibáazu* would get around to all the females in our house. I thought of the chicken bones in a calabash bowl left on our doorstep by Tata Kuvudundu some weeks back, which had given me the creeps. I explained to Nelson that his voodoo was absolutely nonsense. We don't believe in an evil god that could be persuaded to put a curse on somebody.

"No?" he asked. "Your god, he didn't put a curse on Tata Chobé?" This was on a sweltering afternoon as Nelson and I chopped firewood to carry into the kitchen house. It was endless work to feed our cast-iron stove just for boiling the water, let alone cooking.

"Tata Chobé?" I was wary of this conversation but curious to know how well he'd learned the teachings of the Bible. Through the very large holes in his red T-shirt I watched the strings of muscle tense up in Nelson's back for one hard second as he raised his machete and split the deep purple heart of a small log. Nelson used his machete for everything under the sun, from splitting kindling to shaving (not that he had a real need at age thirteen) to cleaning the stove. He kept it extremely sharp and clean.

He stood to catch his breath. He laid the machete carefully on the ground and threw his arms in wide circles to loosen them out. "Your god put a *kibáazu* on Tata Chobé. He gave him the pox and the itches and killed all his seven children under one roof."

"Oh, *Job*," I said. "Why, that wasn't a curse, Nelson. God was testing his faith."

"*Á bu*," Nelson said, meaning more or less, "Okay, fine." After he'd taken up his weapon again and split three or four more purpleheart logs he said, "Somebody is testing faith for your mother and your little sister. The next one he will be testing is the Termite."

Mvúla—a pale white termite that comes out after a rain—is what people here call Rachel, because she's so pallid. Their opinion is that she gets that way from staying indoors too much and being terrified of life in general. Rachel doesn't think much of termites, needless to say, and insists that the word has some other, higher meaning. I am generally called *Leba*, a much nicer word that means *fig tree*. At first we thought they couldn't say "Leah" but it turns out they can say it perfectly well and are being nice to avoid it, because *Léa* is the Kikongo word for *nothing much*.

I repeated to Nelson that, however he might interpret the parable of Job, our family doesn't believe in witch-doctor *ngangas* and evil-eye fetishes and the *nkisis* and *gree-grees* people wear around their necks, to ward off curses and the like. "I'm sorry, Nelson," I told him, "but we just don't worship those gods." To make our position perfectly clear I added, "*Baka veh*." This means, "We don't pay for that," which is how you say that you don't believe.

Nelson gently stacked wood into my outstretched arms. "*Á bu*," he said sorrowfully. I had no choice but to look closely into Nelson's sweat-glazed face as he arranged the wood in my awkward embrace—our work brought us that close together. I could see that he seemed truly sad for us. He clicked his tongue the way Mama Tataba used to, and told me, "Leba, the gods you do not pay are the ones that can curse you best."

Adah

WONK TON O DEW.

The things we do not know, independently and in unison as a family, would fill two separate baskets, each with a large hole in the bottom.

Muntu is the Congolese word for *man*. Or *people*. But it means more than that. Here in the Congo I am pleased to announce there is no special difference between living people, dead people, children not yet born, and gods—these are all *muntu*. So says Nelson. All other things are *kintu*: animals, stones, bottles. A place or a time is *hantu*, and a quality of being is *kuntu*: beautiful, hideous, or lame, for example. All these things have in common the stem word *ntu*. "All that is being here, *ntu*," says Nelson with a shrug, as if this is not so difficult to understand. And it would be simple, except that "being here" is not the same as "existing." He explains the difference this way: the principles of *ntu* are asleep, until they are touched by *nommo*. *Nommo* is the force that makes things live as what they are: man or tree or animal. *Nommo* means *word*. The rabbit has the life it has—not a rat life or mongoose life—because it is named *rabbit*, *mvundla*. A child is not alive, claims Nelson, until it is named. I told him this helped explain a mystery for me. My sister and I are identical twins, so how is it that from one single seed we have two such different lives? Now I know. Because I am named *Adah* and she is named *Leah*.

Nommo, I wrote down on the notebook I had opened out for us at our big table. *Nommo ommon NoMmo*, I wrote, wishing to learn this word forward and backward. Theoretically I was in the process of showing Nelson, at his urging, how to write a letter (ignoring the fact he would have no way to mail it). He enjoys my silent tutelage and asks for it often. But Nelson as a pupil is apt to turn teacher himself at the least provocation. And he seems to think his chatter improves our conversation, since I only write things on paper.

"*NOMMO MVULA* IS MY SISTER RACHEL?" I queried.

He nodded.

Ruth May, then, is *Nommo Bandu*, and Leah is *Nommo Leba*. And where does *Nommo* come from?

He pointed to his mouth. *Nommo* comes from the mouth, like water vapor, he said: a song, a poem, a scream, a prayer, a name, all these are *nommo*. Water itself is *nommo*, of the most important kind, it turns out. Water is the word of the ancestors given to us or withheld, depending on how well we treat them. The word of the ancestors is pulled into trees and men, Nelson explained, and this allows them to stand and live as *muntu*.

A TREE IS ALSO MUNTU? I wrote. Quickly I drew stick man and stick tree side by side, to clarify. Our conversations are often mostly pictures and gestures. "A *tree* is a type of person?"

"Of course," Nelson said. "Just look at them. They both have roots and a head."

Nelson was puzzled by my failure to understand such a simple thing.

Then he asked, "You and your sister Leba, how do you mean you came from the same seed?"

Twins, I wrote. He didn't recognize the word. I drew two identical girls side by side, which he found even more baffling, given that Leah and I—the beauty and the beast—were the twins under consideration. So then, since no one was around to watch us and Nelson seems incapable of embarrassment, I brought forth a shameless pantomime of a mother giving birth to one baby, then—oh my!—another. *Twins*.

His eyes grew wide. "*Báza!*"

I nodded, thinking he was not the first to be amazed by this news about Leah and me. But it must have been more than that, because he leaped away from me with such haste that he knocked over his chair.

"*Báza?*" he repeated, pointing at me. He delicately touched my forehead and recoiled, as if my skin might burn him.

I scribbled with some defensiveness: *You never saw twins?*

He shook his head with conviction. "Any woman who has *báza* should take the two babies to the forest after they are born and leave them there. She takes them fast, right away. That is very very *very* necessary."

Why?

"The ancestors and gods," he stammered. "*All* gods. What god would not be furious at a mother who kept such babies? I think the whole village would be flooded or mostly everyone would die, if a mother kept her *báza.*"

I looked around the room, saw no immediate evidence of catastrophe, and shrugged. I turned the page on our lesson in business correspondence, and began to work on an elaborate pencil drawing of Noah's ark. After a while Nelson righted his chair and sat down approximately four feet away from me. He leaned very far over to try to peer at my picture.

THIS IS NOT ABOUT TWINS, I wrote across the top. Or who knows, maybe it is, I thought. All those paired-up bunnies and elephants.

"What happened to your village when your mother did not take you to the forest?"

I considered the year of my birth, and wrote: *WE WON THE WAR.* Then I proceeded to draw the outline of an exceptionally elegant giraffe. But Nelson glowered, still waiting for evidence that my birth had not brought down a plague upon my house. *NO FLOODS. NO EPIDEMICS,* I wrote. *ALL IS WELL IN USA, WHERE MOTHERS KEEP THEIR BÁZA EVERY DAY.*

Nelson stared at me with such pure, annoyed skepticism I was tempted to doubt my own word. Hadn't there been, say, a rash of hurricanes in the months after Leah and I were born? A bad winter nationwide for the flu? Who knew. I shrugged, and drew a second giraffe with a dramatic, Z-shaped crook to its neck. The *benduka* giraffe.

Nelson was not going to let me off. Clearly my twinhood was a danger to society. "Tata Jesus, what does he say?"

TOO MUCH, AS A RULE.

"What does he say to do when a woman has . . ." he hesitated over even saying the word in English.

I shrugged, but Nelson kept pushing me on this point. He would not believe that the Jesus Bible, with its absolutely prodigious abundance of words, gave no specific instructions to mothers of newborn twins. Finally I wrote: *JESUS SAYS TO KEEP THEM, I GUESS.*

Nelson became agitated again. "So you see, both wives of Tata Boanda go to the Jesus Church! And the Mama Lakanga! All these women and their friends and husbands! They think they will have twins again, and Tata Jesus will not make them leave the babies in the forest."

This was fascinating news, and I queried him on the particulars. According to Nelson's accounting, nearly half my father's congregation were relatives of dead twins. It is an interesting precept on which to found a ministry: The First Evangelical Baptist Church of the Twin-Prone. I also learned from Nelson that we are hosting seven lepers every Sunday, plus two men who have done the thing that is permanently unforgiven by local gods—that is, to have accidentally killed a clansman or child. We seem to be the Church for the Lost of Cause, which is probably not so far afield from what Jesus himself was operating in his time.

This should not have been a great surprise. Anatole had already tried to explain to us the societal function of our church, during that fateful dinner that ended in a shattered plate. But the Reverend feels he is doing such a ripping job of clarifying all fine points of the Scripture to the heathen, he cannot imagine that he is still merely serving the purpose of cleaning up the streets, as it were.

Removing troublesome elements from the main ceremonial life of Kilanga. The Reverend failed to notice that every churchgoing family whose children were struck hard with the *kakakaka* quietly removed themselves back to ancestor worship, while a few of the heathen families that were hard hit quietly came and tried out Christianity. While it makes perfect sense to me, this pragmatic view of religion escapes the Reverend utterly. Each time a new convert limps through the door on a Sunday morning, he will boast over dinner that he is "really calling them home now, buddy. Finally attracting the attention of some of the local big shots."

And so he continues ministering to the lepers and outcasts. By pure mistake, his implementation is sometimes more pure than his intentions. But mostly it is the other way around. Mostly he shouts, "Praise be!" while the back of his hand knocks you flat.

How did he come to pass, this *nommo* Nathan Price? I do wonder. In the beginning was the word, the war, the way of all flesh. The mother, the Father, the son who was not, the daughters who were too many. The twins who brought down the house, indeed. In the beginning was the word the herd the blurred the turd the debts incurred the theatrical absurd. Our Father has a bone to pick with this world, and oh, he picks it like a sore. Picks it with the Word. His punishment is the Word, and his deficiencies are failures of words— as when he grows impatient with translation and strikes out precariously on his own, telling parables in his wildly half-baked Kikongo. It is a dangerous thing, I now understand, to make mistakes with *nommo* in the Congo. If you assign the wrong names to things, you could make a chicken speak like a man. Make a machete rise up and dance.

We his daughters and wife are not innocent either. The players in his theater. We Prices are altogether thought to be peculiarly well-intentioned, and inane. I know this. Nelson would never come out and say as much. But he has always told me, when I ask, the words we get wrong. I can gather the rest. It is a special kind of person who will draw together a congregation, stand up before them with a proud, clear voice, and say words wrong, week after week.

Bandika, for example: to kill someone. If you spit it out too quickly, as the Reverend does, it means to pinch back a plant or deflower a virgin. What a surprise it must be to the Congolese to hear that brave David, who intended to smite the mighty Goliath, was actually jumping around pinching back plants, or worse.

Then there is *batiza,* Our Father's fixed passion. *Batiza* pronounced with the tongue curled just so means "baptism." Otherwise, it means "to terrify." Nelson spent part of an afternoon demonstrating to me *that* fine linguistic difference while we scraped chicken manure from the nest boxes. No one has yet explained it to the Reverend. He is not of a mind to receive certain news. Perhaps he should clean more chicken houses.

Ruth May

SOMETIMES YOU JUST WANT to lay on down and look at the whole world sideways. Mama and I do. It feels nice. If I put my head on her, the sideways world moves up and down. She goes: *hhh-huh. hhh-huh*. She's soft on her tummy and the bosoms part. When Father and Leah went away on the airplane we just needed to lay on down awhile.

Sometimes I tell her: Mommy Mommy. I just say that. Father isn't listening so I can say it. Her real name is Mother and Misrus Price but her secret name to me is Mommy Mommy. He went away on the airplane and I said, "Mama, I hope he never comes back." We cried then.

But I was sad and wanted Leah to come back because she'll pick me up and carry me piggyback sometimes, when she's not hollowing at me for being a pest. Everybody is nice sometimes and Baby Jesus says to love everybody no matter how you really do feel. Baby Jesus knows what I said about wishing Father would never come back anymore, and Father is the preacher. So God and them love him the best.

I dreamed I climbed away up to the top of the alligator pear tree and was a-looking down at all of them, the teeny little children with crooked cowboy legs and their big eyes looking up and the teeniest wrapped-up babies with little hands and faces that are just as fair till they get older and turn black, for it takes a spell I guess before God notices they are the Tribes of Ham. And the dirt-color houses all just the same as the dirt they're sitting on. Mama says not a thing in the whole village that won't melt in a good hard rain. And I could see Mommy Mommy, the top of her. I could see everything she was thinking, like Jesus does. She was thinking about animals.

Sometimes when you wake up you can't tell if it was dreaming or real.

Adah

GOD WORKS, as is very well known, in mysterious ways. There is just nothing you can name that He won't do, now and then. Oh, He will send down so much rain that all his little people are drinking from one another's sewers and dying of the *kakakaka*. Then he will organize a drought to scorch out the yam and manioc fields, so whoever did not die of fever will double over from hunger. What next, you might ask? Why, a mystery, that's what!

After the Independence cut off our stipend and all contacts with the larger world, it seems God's plan called for Mother and Ruth May to fall sick nigh unto death. They grew flushed and spotted and thick-tongued and tired and slow-moving near unto the lower limit of what is generally thought to constitute a living human body.

The Reverend seemed unconcerned about this. He forged ahead with his mission work, leaving his three older girls in charge of hearth and home for days on end while he sallied out to visit the unsaved, or to meet with Anatole about imposing Bible classes upon boys of tender years. Oh, that Bible, where every ass with a jawbone gets his day! (Anatole evidently was not keen on the plan.) Often the Reverend simply went out and walked along the river for hours, alone, trying out his sermons on the lilies of the field—who understand him about as well as his congregation and frankly are better listeners. All in all, being God's sole and abandoned emissary to Kilanga was keeping Our Father very busy. If we plagued him with our worries about Mother, he merely snapped that she would heed God's call soon enough, and get herself up and around. At night we overheard strange, tearful arguments, in which Mother spoke in a quiet, slurred, slow-motion voice, like a phonograph record on the wrong speed, outlining the possibilities for our family's demise. In a small fraction of the time it took her to form her plea, Our Father irritably countered that the Lord operates in mysterious ways. As if she did not know.

Serious delirious imperious weary us deleterious ways.

Our neighbors seemed fairly indifferent to our reduced circumstances, as they were occupied with their own. Leah's friend Pascal was the only one who still came around occasionally, wanting Leah to come out and scout the bush for adventures with him. While we labored over changing beds or washing up dishes, Pascal would wait outside, teasing for our attention by shouting the handful of American phrases Leah had taught him: *"Man-oh-man! Crazy!"* It used to make us laugh, but now we cringed for having trained him in insolence.

Our childhood had passed over into history overnight. The transition was unnoticed by anyone but ourselves.

The matter of giving us each day our daily bread was clearly up to us girls to figure out, and the sheer work of it exhausted me. I often felt like taking to bed myself. My sisters were similarly affected: Rachel became hollow-eyed and careworn, sometimes combing her hair only once per day. Leah slowed from a run to a walk. We had not understood what our mother had gone through to get square meals on the table for the past year. Father still didn't, as he thought nothing of leaving it in the charge of a cripple, a beauty queen, and a tomboy who approaches housework like a cat taking a bath. What a family unit we do make.

Sometimes in the middle of the night Leah would sit bolt upright in her bed, wanting to talk. I think she was frightened, but she frequently brought up her vexation with Mama Mwanza, who had spoken so matter-of-factly about having a strong husband at home. It troubled Leah that people thought our household deficient, not because our mother was parked at death's door, but because we lacked a *bákala mpandi*—a strong man—to oversee us.

"Father doesn't hunt or fish because he has a higher calling," Leah argued from her cot, as if I might not have thought of this. "Can't they see he works hard at his own profession?"

Had I felt like entering the discussion, I would have pointed out that to Mama Mwanza his *profession* probably resembles the game of "Mother May I?," consisting of very long strings of nonsense words in a row.

It took less than a month for our household to fall into chaos. We had to endure Father's escalating rage, when he returned home to find dinner no farther along than an unresolved argument over whether there *are* or *are not* worms in the flour, or any flour at all. After his displeasure had reached a certain point, the three of us rubbed our bruises and called ourselves to a womanly sort of meeting. At the great wooden table where we had spent many a tedious hour studying algebra and the Holy Roman Empire, we now sat down to take stock.

"First of all, we have to keep boiling the water, no matter what," announced Rachel, our elder. "Write that down, Adah. If we don't boil our water for thirty full minutes we'll get plebiscites and what not."

Duly noted.

"Second of all, we have to figure out what to eat."

On the pantry shelves in the kitchen house we still had some flour, sugar, Carnation milk powder, tea, five cans of sardines, and the Underdown prunes; I recorded all this in a column in my notebook. Wrote it, for the benefit of my sisters, left to right. Leah added to the list: mangoes, guavas, pineapples, and avocados, all of which came and went in mysterious seasons (not unlike the Lord's ways) but at least did grow in our yard, free of charge. Bananas were so abundant around the village people stole them off each other's trees in broad daylight. When Mama Mwanza's children cut down a bunch from the Nguzas' big garden, Mama Nguza picked up the ones they'd dropped and brought them over later. Thus emboldened, Leah and I cut down a bunch the size of Ruth May from behind Eeben Axelroot's outhouse, while he was inside. Fruit, then, was one thing we could have without money. Oranges we had always bought at the *marché*, as they grew deep in the jungle and were difficult to find, but Leah claimed to know where to look. She appointed herself in charge of fruit gathering, not surprisingly, this being the category of housework that takes place farthest from a house. She pledged to collect palm nuts also, even though these taste to us exactly like candle wax, however much the Congolese children seem to prize them. Still, I wrote "Palm nuts" in my book, to prolong the list. The point of our exercise was to convince ourselves that the wolf was not actually at the back door but perhaps merely salivating at the edge of our yard.

Resting up between crucial observations, Rachel was studying the tails of her hair very closely for split ends. She resembled a cross-eyed rabbit. At the mention of palm nuts she whined, "But, you *all*, on a diet of just fruit we could plumb die or even get diarrhea."

"Well, what else is free?" Leah asked.

"The chickens, of course," Rachel said. "We can kill those."

We couldn't kill them all, Leah explained, because then we'd have no eggs for omelets—one of the few things we knew how to cook. But if we let some of the hens brood, to increase our flock, we might get away with frying a rooster once a month or so. My sisters put me in charge of all chicken decisions, thinking me the least likely to act on a rash impulse that would cause regrets later. The rash-impulse portion of my brain was destroyed at birth. We did not discuss who would be in charge of killing the unfortunate roosters. In earlier times our mother did that, with a flourish. Back when she was a happier woman, she used to claim Father married her for the way she wrung a rooster's neck. Our mother used to have mystery under her skin, and we paid not the slightest attention.

Next, Leah raised the difficult issue of Nelson: nearly half our eggs went to him for his pay. We discussed whether we needed Nelson more, or the eggs. There was not much now for him to cook. But he did haul our water and cut wood, and he elucidated for us the many daily mysteries of Kilanga. As I was not good at hauling water or cutting wood, I could not personally argue for a life without Nelson. My sisters, I think, had separate fears of their own. In secret ballot we voted unanimously to keep him.

"And I will bake the bread. Mother will show me how," Rachel announced, as if that finally solved all our troubles.

Mother had wandered unnoticed into our meeting and was standing at the front window, looking out. She coughed, and we all three turned to regard her: Orleanna Price, former baker of our bread. Really she did not look like someone who could teach you how to button your shirt on straight. It's a disturbing thing, after a decade of being told to tuck in shirttails and walk like a lady, to see your own mother unkempt. Feeling our silent disapproval, she turned to look at us. Her eyes had the plain blue look of a rainless sky. Empty.

"It's okay, Mama," Leah said. "You can go on and lie back down if you want to." Leah had not called her "Mama" since we cut our first molars. Mama *née* Orleanna came over and kissed us on the tops of our heads, then shuffled back to her deathbed.

Leah turned to Rachel and hissed, "You priss, you couldn't even sift the flour!"

"Oh, the girl genius speaks," Rachel said. "And may I ask why not?" I chewed on my pencil and witnessed the proceedings.

"No special reason," Leah said, scratching her shaggy pixie haircut behind the ear. "I'm sure you won't mind sticking your hand down in the flour bag with all those weevils and maggots in there."

"There's not *always* maggots in the flour."

"No, you're right. Sometimes the tarantulas eat them."

I laughed out loud. Rachel got up and left the table.

Having broken my silence in Leah's favor, though, I felt I had to scold her for the sake of balance. "IF WE DO NOT ALL HANG TOGETHER . . ." I wrote on my pad.

"I know. We'll all hang separately. But Rachel needs to get off her high horse, too. She's never lifted a finger around here and now all of a sudden she's the Little Red Hen?"

True enough. Having Rachel in charge was very much as if Mrs.

Donna Reed from television suddenly showed up to be your mother. It had to be an act. Soon she would take off her apron and turn into someone who didn't give a hoot about your general welfare.

Poor tyrannical Rachel keeps trying to build a big-sister career upon a slim sixteen-month seniority, insisting that we respect her as our elder. But Leah and I have not thought of her in that way since the second grade, when we passed her up in the school spelling bee. Her downfall was the ridiculously easy word *scheme*.

Leah

After three weeks of the doldrums I made Ruth May get out of bed. Just like that, I said, "Ruth May, honey, get up. Let's go poke around outside awhile." There wasn't much to be done about Mother, but I've spent a lot of time in charge of Ruth May and I think I should know by now what's good for her. She needed something to boss around. Our pets had mostly escaped by then, or been eaten up, as in the case of Methuselah, but the Congo still offered a wealth of God's creatures to entertain us. I took Ruth May outside to get some sunshine on her. But she slumped wherever I put her, with no gumption in her at all. She acted like a monkey-sock doll that has been run through the machine.

"Where do you think Stuart Little's gone to?" I asked her. I used that name just to please her, practically admitting it was *her* mongoose. She hadn't captured it or taken any special care beyond naming it after an incorrect storybook animal, namely a mouse. But I couldn't deny it followed her around.

"He ran off. I don't care, either."

"Look-a-here, Ruth May. Ant lions."

In the long, strange drought we were having in place of last year's rainy season, soft dust had spread across our yard in broad white patches. It was pocked all over with little funnel-shaped snares, where the ant lions lay buried at the bottom, waiting for some poor insect to stumble into the trap and get devoured. We had never actually seen the ant lions themselves, only their wicked handiwork. To amuse Ruth May I'd told her they looked like lions with six legs and were huge, as big as her left hand. I don't really know what they look like, but given how things grow in the Congo, that size seemed possible. Back before she got sick, Ruth May thought she could lie on her belly and sing to lure them out: "Wicked bug, wicked bug, come out of your hole!" shouted in singsong for whole afternoons at a time, even though it never worked. Ruth May's foremost personality trait was stick-to-it-iveness. But now when I suggested it, she merely turned her head to the side and laid it down in the dust.

"I'm too hot to sing. They never come out anyway."

I was determined to rile her up someway. If I couldn't find any spark left in Ruth May, I was afraid I might panic, or cry.

"Hey, watch this," I said. I found a column of ants running up a tree trunk and picked a couple out of the lineup. Bad luck for those poor ants, singled out while minding their own business amongst their brethren. Even an ant's just got its own one life to live, and I did consider this briefly as I crouched down and dropped a partly squashed ant into an ant lion's trap. They used to feed Christians to the lions, and now Adah uses that phrase ironically, referring to how I supposedly left her to be eaten up on the path. But Adah is no more Christian than an ant.

We squatted over the hole and waited. The ant struggled in the soft, sandy trap until a pair of pincers suddenly reached up and grabbed it, thrashed up a little dust, and pulled it under. Gone, just like that.

"Don't do any more of them, Leah," Ruth May said. "The ant wasn't bad."

I felt embarrassed, being told insect morals by my baby sister. Usually cruelty inspired Ruth May no end, and I was just desperate to help her get her spirits back.

"Well, even wicked bugs have to eat," I pointed out. "Everything has to eat something." Even lions, I suppose.

I picked up Ruth May and dusted off her cheek. "Sit in the swing and I'll comb out your pigtails," I said. I'd been carrying the comb around in my back pocket for days, meaning to get to Ruth

May's hair. "After I get your braids fixed up I'll push you awhile in the swing. Okay?"

Ruth May didn't seem to have strong feelings one way or another. I sat her in the swing, which Nelson had helped us hang with a huge, oily rope he found on the riverbank. The seat was an old rectangular palm-oil drum. All the kids in the village used our swing. I beat some dust off the comb and began to tease out the yellow mass of knots her hair had turned into. I could hardly do it without hurting her, yet she hardly whined, which I took as a bad sign.

Out of the corner of my eye I saw Anatole half hidden in the cane thicket at the edge of our yard. He wasn't cutting cane, since he doesn't chew it—I think he's a little vain of his strong white teeth with the handsome little gap in the center. But he was standing there watching us anyway, and I flushed red to think he might have seen me feeding the ant lions. It seemed very childish. In the light of day, almost everything we did in Kilanga seemed childish. Even Father's walking the riverbank talking to himself, and our mother drifting around half dressed. Combing out Ruth May's hair at least seemed motherly and practical, so I concentrated on that. In spite of myself I pictured a father with shiny black arms pulling fish from the river and a mother with dark, heavy breasts pounding manioc in a wooden trough. Then out of habit I fired off the Repentance Psalm: *Have mercy upon me, O God, according unto the multitude of thy tender mercies.* But I was unsure which commandment my thoughts had broken—Honor thy father and mother, or not coveting thy neighbor's parents, or even something more vague about being true to your own race and kind.

Anatole started toward us. I waved and called to him, "*Mbote*, Anatole!"

"*Mbote, Béene-béene*," he said. He has special names for each of my sisters and me, not the hurtful ones other people use, like Termite and *Benduka*, for Adah, which means Crooked Walker. Anatole wouldn't tell us what his names meant. He tousled Ruth May's head and shook my hand in the Congolese way, with his left hand clasping his right forearm. Father said this tradition was to show they aren't hiding any weapon.

"What's the news, sir?" I asked Anatole. This is what Father always said to him. In spite of how badly that first dinner had gone, Father relied greatly on Anatole and even looked forward to his visits, somewhat nervously, I think. Anatole always surprised us by knowing important news from the outside world—or from outside Kilanga, at least. We weren't sure where he got his information, but it generally turned out to be true.

"A lot of news," he said. "But first I have brought you a pig in a sack."

I loved hearing Anatole speak English. His pronunciation sounded British and elegant, with "first" coming out as "fest," and "brought" more like "brrote." But it sounded Congolese in the way it rolled out with equal weight on every syllable—*a pig in a sack*—as if no single word wanted to take over the whole sentence.

"A poke," I said. "Mother says that: Never buy a pig in a poke. I guess a poke is a sack."

"Well, at any rate it's not a pig, and you don't have to buy it. If you guess what it is, then you may have it for your dinner." On a string slung over his shoulder he had a brown cloth sack, which he handed to me. I closed my eyes and assessed its weight, bouncing it up and down a little. It was the size of a chicken but too heavy to be a bird. I held the bag up and examined the rounded bulge at its bottom. It had little points, possibly elbows.

"*Umvundla!*" I cried, jumping up and down like a child. This was jungle rabbit. Nelson could make a rabbit stew with *mangwansi* beans and mangoes that even Rachel couldn't help eating, it was that good.

I'd guessed right: Anatole smiled his thrilling white smile. I can scarcely even remember how he first looked to us, when we were shocked by the scars across his face. Now I could only see Anatole the man, square-shouldered and narrow-hipped in his white shirt and black trousers, Anatole with his ready smile and lively walk. A man who was kind to us. His face has many other interesting features besides the scars, such as almond-shaped eyes and a finely pointed chin. I hadn't realized how much I liked him.

"Did you kill it yourself?"

He held up both hands. "I would like to say yes, so you would think your friend Anatole is a good hunter. But, alas. A new pupil brought it this morning to pay for his schooling."

I looked in the sack. There it was with its small, furry head curled unnaturally backward due to a broken neck. It had been trapped, not shot. I clasped the sack to my chest and looked up at Anatole sideways. "Would you really have taken it back if I hadn't guessed right?"

He smiled. "I would have given you a lot of chances to guess right."

"Well! Is that the kind of leniency you show your boys on their math and French in school? They must never learn anything!"

"Oh, no, miss! I crack their naughty heads with a stick and send them home in disgrace." We both laughed. I knew better.

"Please come for dinner tonight, Anatole. With this rabbit we'll have too much to eat." In fact this lonely rabbit would make a small stew and we would still be hungry while we washed the dishes afterward—a feeling we were trying to get used to. But that was how people said thank you in Kilanga. I'd learned a few manners at least.

"Perhaps I will," he said.

"We'll make a stew," I promised.

"*Mangwansi* beans are high in the *marché*," he pointed out. "Because of the drought. All the gardens are drying up."

"I happen to know who has some: Mama Nguza. She makes her kids haul water up from the creek to pour on her garden. Haven't you seen it? It's sensational."

"No, I have not seen this *sensation*. I will have to make better friends with Tata Nguza."

"I don't know about him. He sure doesn't talk to me. *Nobody* talks to me, Anatole."

"Poor Béene."

"It's true! I don't have a single solitary friend here but Nelson and Pascal, two little boys! And you. All the girls my age have their own babies and are too busy. And the men act like I'm a snake fixing to bite them."

He shook his head, laughing.

"They do *so*, Anatole. Yesterday I was sitting in the weeds watching Tata Mwanza make fish traps, and when I stood up and asked him to show me how, he ran away and jumped in the water! I swear it!"

"Béene, you were naughty. Tata Mwanza could not be seen talking to a young woman, you know that. It would be a scandal."

"Hmmph," I said. Why was it scandalous for me to converse with any man in Kilanga old enough to have a whole seat in his pants, *except* for Anatole? But I didn't ask. I didn't want to jinx our friendship.

"What I do happen to know," I said, being maybe a tiny bit coy, "is that a civet cat got all of the Nguzas' hens last Sunday. So Mama Nguza will be in a mood to trade *mangwansi* beans for eggs, don't you think?"

Anatole smiled enormously. "Clever girl."

I smiled, too, but didn't know what else to say after that. I felt embarrassed and returned to combing out Ruth May's hair.

"She appears to be a very glum little girl today," Anatole said.

"She's been sick in bed for weeks. Mother has too. Didn't you notice when you came by the other day how she was standing out on the porch just staring into space? Father says they'll both be all right, but . . ." I shrugged. "It wouldn't be the sleeping sickness, do you think?"

"I think no. Now is not the season for tsetse flies. There is hardly any sleeping sickness at all in Kilanga right now."

"Well, that's good, because what I've heard about sleeping sickness is you die of it," I said, still combing, feeling like someone who's been hypnotized into that one single motion. Sleeping in her braids for sweaty days and nights on end had creased Ruth May's dark blond hair into shining waves like water. Anatole stared at it as I combed it down her back. His smile got lost somewhere in that quiet minute.

"There is news, Béene, since you asked for it. I'm afraid it is not very good. I came to talk to your father."

"He's not here. I can tell him whatever it is, though."

I wondered if Anatole would consider me a sufficient messenger. I'd noticed Congolese men didn't treat even their own wives and daughters as if they were very sensible or important. Though as far as I could see the wives and daughters did just about all the work.

But Anatole apparently felt I could be spoken to. "Do you know where Katanga Province is?"

"In the south," I said. "Where all the diamond mines are." I'd overheard talk of it when Mr. Axelroot flew Father and me back from Leopoldville. Evidently Mr. Axelroot went there often. So I was guessing, but I guessed with my father's trademark confidence.

"Diamonds, yes," Anatole said. "Also cobalt and copper and zinc. Everything my country has that your country wants."

This made me feel edgy. "Did we do something bad?"

"Not *you*, Béene."

Not me, not *me!* My heart rejoiced at that, though I couldn't say why.

"But, yes, there is a bad business going on," he said. "Do you know the name Moise Tshombe?"

I might have heard it, but wasn't sure. I started to nod, but then admitted, "No." I decided right then to stop pretending I knew more than I did. I would be myself, Leah Price, eager to learn all there is to know. Watching my father, I've seen how you can't learn anything when you're trying to look like the smartest person in the room.

"Moise Tshombe is leader of the Lunda tribe. For all practical purpose he is leader of Katanga Province. And since a few days ago, leader of his own nation of Katanga. He declared it separate from the Republic of Congo."

"*What?* Why?"

"Now he can make his own business with the Belgians and Americans, you see. With all his minerals. Some of your country-men have given a lot of encouragement to his decision."

"Why can't they just make their deals with Lumumba? He's the one that got elected. They ought to know that."

"They know. But Lumumba is not eager to give away the store. His loyalty is with his countrymen. He believes in a unified Congo for the Congolese, and he knows that every Katanga diamond from the south can pay a teacher's salary in Leopoldville, or feed a village of Warega children in the north."

I felt both embarrassed and confused. "Why would the businessmen take Congo's diamonds away? And what are Americans doing down there anyhow? I thought the Congo belonged to Belgium. I mean before."

Anatole frowned. "The Congo is the Congo's and ever has been."

"Well, I know that. But—"

"Open your eyes, Béene. Look at your neighbors. Did they ever belong to Belgium?" He pointed across our yard and through the trees toward Mama Mwanza's house.

I'd said a stupid thing, and felt terrible. I looked, as he commanded: Mama Mwanza with her disfigured legs and her small, noble head both wrapped in bright yellow calico. In the hard-packed dirt she sat as if planted there, in front of a little fire that licked at her dented cooking can. She leaned back on her hands and raised her face to the sky, shouting her bidding, and a chorus of halfhearted answers came back from her boys inside the mud-thatch house. Near the open doorway, the two older daughters stood pounding manioc in the tall wooden mortar. As one girl raised her pounding club the other girl's went down into the narrow hole—up and down, a perfect, even rhythm like the pumping of pistons. I'd watched them time and again, attracted so to that dance of straight backs and muscled black arms. I envied these daughters, who worked together in such perfect synchrony. It's what Adah and I might have felt, if we hadn't gotten all snared in the ropes of guilt and unfair advantage. Now our whole family was at odds, it seemed: Mother against Father, Rachel against both of them, Adah against the world, Ruth May pulling helplessly at anyone who came near, and me trying my best to stay on Father's side.

We were tangled in such knots of resentment we hardly understood them.

"Two of her children died in the epidemic," I said.

"I know."

Of course he knew. Our village was small, and Anatole knew every child by name. "It's a terrible shame," I offered, inadequately.

He merely agreed, "*E-é.*"

"Children should never have to die."

"No. But if they never did, children would not be so precious."

"Anatole! Would you say that if your own children died?"

"Of course not. But it is true, nevertheless. Also if everyone lived to be old, then old age would not be such a treasure."

"But everybody wants to live a long time. It's only fair."

"Fair to want, *e-é.* But not fair to get. Just think how it would be if all the great-grandparents still were walking around. The village would be crowded with cross old people arguing over who has the most ungrateful sons and aching bones, and always eating up the food before the children could get to the table."

"It sounds like a church social back in Georgia," I said.

Anatole laughed.

Mama Mwanza shouted again and clapped her hands, bringing a reluctant son out of the house, dragging the flat, pinkish soles of his feet. Then I laughed, too, just because people young and old are more or less the same everywhere. I let myself breathe out, feeling less like one of Anatole's schoolboys taking a scolding.

"Do you see *that*, Béene? That is Congo. Not minerals and glittering rocks with no hearts, these things that are traded behind our backs. The Congo is us."

"I know."

"Who owns it, do you suppose?"

I did not hazard a guess.

"I am sorry to say, those men making their agreements in Katanga just now are accustomed to getting what they want."

I drew the edge of the comb slowly down the center of Ruth May's head, making a careful part. Father had said the slums outside

Leopoldville would be set right by American aid, after Independence. Maybe I was foolish to believe him. There were shanties just
as poor in Georgia, on the edge of Atlanta, where black and white
divided, and that was smack in the middle of America.

"Can you just *do* that, what they did down there? Announce your
own country?" I asked.

"Prime Minister Lumumba says no, absolutely not. He has asked
the United Nations to bring an army to restore unity."

"Is there going to be a war?"

"There is already a kind of war, I think. Moise Tshombe has Belgians and mercenary soldiers working for him. I don't think they
will leave without a fight. And Katanga is not the only place where
they are throwing stones. There is a different war in Matadi,
Thysville, Boende, Leopoldville. People are very angry at the Europeans. They are even hurting women and little children."

"What are they so mad at the white people for?"

Anatole sighed. "Those are big cities. Where the boa and the hen
curl up together, there is only trouble. People have seen too much
of the Europeans and all the things they had. They imagined after
Independence life would immediately become fair."

"Can't they be patient?"

"Could *you* be? If your belly was empty and you saw whole baskets of bread on the other side of a window, would you continue
waiting patiently, Béene? Or would you throw a rock?"

My belly *is* empty, I thought of telling Anatole. "I don't know," I
confessed. I thought of the Underdowns' home in Leopoldville
with its Persian rugs and silver tea service and chocolate cookies,
surrounded by miles of tin shanties and hunger. Perhaps there were
boys stomping barefoot through that house right now, ransacking
the near-empty pantry and setting fire to the curtains in a kitchen
that still smelled of Mrs. Underdown's disinfectant soap. I couldn't
say who was wrong or right. I did see what Anatole meant about
the snakes and hens too close together in a place like that: you
could trace the belly scales of hate, and come up howling. I glanced
nervously at our own house, with no rugs or tea service, but how

much did that matter? Would Jesus protect us? When He looked in our hearts to weigh our worth, would he find love for our Congolese neighbors, or disdain?

"Well, it's the job of the United Nations to keep the peace," I said. "When will they come?"

"That is what everybody would like to know. If they won't come, the Prime Minister has threatened to ask Mr. Khrushchev for help."

"*Khrushchev*," I said, trying to cover my shock. "The *Communists* would help the Congo?"

"Oh, yes, I think they would." Anatole eyed me strangely. "Béene, do you know what a Communist is?"

"I know they do not fear the Lord, and they think everybody should have the same . . ." I found I couldn't complete my own sentence.

"The same kind of house, more or less," Anatole finished for me. "That is about right."

"Well, I want the United Nations to come right away, and fix it up so everything's fair, this minute!"

Anatole laughed at me. "I think you are a very impatient girl, eager to grow up into an impatient woman."

I blushed.

"Don't worry about Mr. Khrushchev. When Lumumba says he might get help from Russia, it is, what do you call this? *Il trompe son monde*, like the hen who puffs up her feathers like so, very big, to show the snake she is too big to eat."

"A bluff," I said, delighted. "Lumumba's bluffing."

"A bluff, exactly. I think Lumumba wants to be neutral, more than anything. More than he loves his very own life. He doesn't want to give away our wealth, but he most especially does not want your country for an enemy."

"He has a hard job," I said.

"I can think of no person in all the world right now with a harder job."

"Mr. Axelroot doesn't think much of him," I confessed. "He says Patrice Lumumba is trouble in a borrowed suit."

Anatole leaned close to my ear. "Do you want to know a secret? I think Mr. Axelroot is trouble in his own stinking hat."

Oh, I laughed to hear that.

We stood awhile longer watching Mama Mwanza argue good-naturedly with her lazy son and take several broad swipes at him with her big cooking spoon. He jumped back, making exaggerated shouts. His sisters scolded him, too, laughing. I realized that Mama Mwanza had an extraordinarily pretty face, with wide-set eyes, a solemn mouth, and a high, rounded forehead under her kerchief. Her husband had taken no other wife, even after her terrible accident and the loss of their two youngest children. Their family had seen so much of hardship, yet it still seemed easy for them to laugh with each other. I envied them with an intensity near to love, and near to rage.

I told Anatole: "I saw Patrice Lumumba. Did you know that? In Leopoldville my father and I got to watch him give his inaugural speech."

"*Did* you?" Anatole seemed impressed. "Well, then, you can make up your own mind. What did you think of our Prime Minister?"

It took me a moment's pause to discover what I thought. Finally I said, "I didn't understand everything. But he made me want to believe in every word. Even the ones I wasn't sure of."

"You understood well enough, then."

"Anatole, is Katanga close to here?"

He flipped his finger against my cheek. "Don't worry, Béene. No one will be shooting at you. Go and cook your rabbit. I'll come back when I can smell *umvundla* stew from my desk in the school-house. *Sala mbote!*"

"*Wenda mbote!*" I clasped my forearm and shook his hand.

I called to his back as he walked away, "Thank you, Anatole." I wasn't just thanking him for the rabbit but also for telling me things. For the way he said, "Not *you*, Béene," and "You understood well enough."

He turned and walked backwards for a few bouncing steps. "Don't forget to tell your father: Katanga has seceded."

"I won't possibly forget."

I returned to Ruth May's braids, but was very conscious of Anatole's broad shoulders and narrow waist, the triangle of white shirt moving away from us as he walked purposefully down the dirt road back to the village. I wish the people back home reading magazine stories about dancing cannibals could see something as ordinary as Anatole's clean white shirt and kind eyes, or Mama Mwanza with her children. If the word "Congo" makes people think of that big-lipped cannibal man in the cartoon, why, they're just wrong about everything here from top to bottom. But how could you ever set them right? Since the day we arrived, Mother has nagged us to write letters home to our classmates at Bethlehem High, and not one of us has done it yet. We're still wondering, Where do you start? "This morning I got up . . ." I'd begin, but no, "This morning I pulled back the mosquito netting that's tucked in tight around our beds because mosquitoes here give you malaria, a disease that runs in your blood which nearly everyone has anyway but they don't go to the doctor for it because there are worse things like sleeping sickness or the *kakakaka* or that someone has put a *kibáazu* on them, and anyway there's really no doctor nor money to pay one, so people just hope for the good luck of getting old because then they'll be treasured, and meanwhile they go on with their business because they have children they love and songs to sing while they work, and . . ."

And you wouldn't even get as far as breakfast before running out of paper. You'd have to explain the words, and then the words for the words.

Ruth May remained listless while I explored my thoughts and finished up her braids. I knew I ought to have bathed her and washed her hair before combing it out, but the idea of lugging the big tub out and heating a dozen teakettles of water so she wouldn't get chilled—it was more than a day's work, and now I had *mangwansi* beans to worry about and the skinning of a rabbit. That is surely childhood's end, when you look at a thing like a rabbit needing skinned and have to say: "Nobody else is going to do this." So no bath for Ruth May that day. I merely pushed her awhile in the swing as I'd promised, and she did kick her feet a little. Maybe it made her happy, I can't say. I hope it did. Anatole's words had pushed things around inside of me. It's true that sickness and death make children more precious. I used to threaten Ruth May's life so carelessly just to make her behave. Now I had to face the possibility that we really could lose her, and my heart felt like a soft, damaged place in my chest, like a bruise on a peach.

She flew forward and back and I watched her shadow in the white dust under the swing. Each time she reached the top of her arc beneath the sun, her shadow legs were transformed into the thin, curved legs of an antelope, with small rounded hooves at the bottom instead of feet. I was transfixed and horrified by the image of my sister with antelope legs. I knew it was only shadow and the angle of the sun, but still it's frightening when things you love appear suddenly changed from what you have always known.

Ruth May

ALL THOSE BLACK FACES in the black night a-looking at me. They want me to come play. But you can't say the words out loud at night. Mother May I? No you may not! Mama says no. Mama is here breathing. When we're both asleep I hear her talk and that's what she says: no no no no. But the lizards run away up the walls with the rest of her words, and I can't hear.

Sometimes I wake up and: nobody. Outside there's sunshine so I know it's broad day, but everybody is gone and I'm sweating too much and can't talk about it. Other times it is dark, and Mama and Father are saying secrets. Mama begs Father. She says they went after the white girls up in Stanleyville. They went in their houses and took everything they wanted to, the food and the radio batteries and all. And they made the missionaries stand naked on top of the roof without any clothes on, and then they shot two of them. Everybody is talking about it and Mama heard. In Stanleyville is where the doctor put a cast on my arm. Did he have to go on the roof of the hospital without any clothes? I never can stop thinking about the doctor with no clothes on. The lizards run away up the walls and take all the words I want to say. But Father says what the Bible says: The meek shall inherit. He started to put his hand on Mama and she pushed him away. *Hearken therefore unto the supplications of thy servant, that thine eyes may be open toward this house night and day.*

Night and day and night and day. Jesus is looking right in the windows no matter what. He can see through the roof. He can see inside our heads, where we think the bad things. I tried not to think of the doctor with no clothes on with all of them up on the roof but he had that yellow hair on his arms. Rachel screamed and thrashed her white hair and sassed back at Father bad: "Who cares who cares who cares! Who is even going to know the difference if we scoot out of here and go back home where it's safe?" Father yelled, "*God will know the difference!*" And Rachel fell down hard before I even heard the sound of the wall and his hand. "*God despises a coward who runs while others stand and suffer.*"

Where will we be safe? When Mama raises her eyes up to him they are so cold there isn't even any Mama home inside there, and she says, "Nathan Price, the meek shall inherit. You wait and see."

I know the meek shall inherit and the last shall be first, but the Tribes of Ham were last. Now will they be first? I don't know.

In our family, Mama comes last. Adah is next to last because her one whole side is bad, and then comes Mama last of all, because something in her is even worse hurt than what Adah's got.

Nelson told me how to find a safe place. One time I woke up and there he was: Nelson.

Oh, is he mad because I tried to see him naked, I don't know. My mouth couldn't say any words. But there he was by the bed, and Mama gone from beside me.

He put his hand over my mouth, stooping down and nobody else there. Nobody else. Shhh, he said and put his hand. I thought he was going to hurt me, but instead he was my friend. Shhh, he said, and took his hand off my mouth and gave me a present. *Á bu,* Bandu. Take this!

Bandu is my name. *Nommo Bandu!* It means the littlest one on the bottom. And it means the reason for everything. Nelson told me that.

What is it? I said, but not any words came out of my mouth. I looked inside my two hands, where he put it, and there was a tiny box like what matches come in. A matchbox. The matchbox had a picture of a lion on the outside and I thought there would be a tiny little lion inside to be my pet, like the mean ones that eat the ants only nicer. Stuart Lion. But no. Nelson opened it up and took out something, I couldn't tell what. It looked like a piece of chicken bone with gristle and string all on it and sticky and something black. What was it, something that died? I was scared and started fixing to cry.

Nelson said, Don't be scared. He said, this has been in the magic fire. You call this *nkisi*. He made me touch it and it didn't burn me. Look, he said. He held it right up to my eye. There was a tiny hole in the side and a tiny peg that fit in the hole, tied with string. Put your spirit inside here, he said, here quick, blow in this hole. He opened up the peg and I blew in the little hole and quick he said my name *Nommo Bandu Nommo Bandu Nommo Bandu!* and shut up the hole with the little peg and Now you are safe. He said now if anything happens to me, if I start fixing to die or something, hold on to this tight and *bambula!* Ruth May will disappear.

How do you know? But Nelson knows everything about dead people. His mama and father and brothers and baby sister are all dead on the bottom of the river.

I don't want to disappear, I said.

But he said, Only if you are going to die. He said this way I won't die, I will just disappear for a second and then I'll turn up some-place else, where it's safe. Instead of dead I'll be safe. But first I have to think of that place every day, so my spirit will know where to run away to, when it's time. *You have to think of your safe place every day.* Nelson's face was bigger than a candle right in my face and I could hear the good way he smelled. That soap he uses for washing up and his clothes. All those smells were so loud in my ears. Nelson is my friend that showed me how to sing to the chickens. *Bidumuka* is the magic name of a chicken. Nobody else knows that, not even Leah or Father.

Nelson said, Don't forget!

I put the matchbox with the lion picture on it, and the magic burned bones inside, I put it under my pillow. *Nkisi.* Sometimes I wake up and it is still there. If they come and try to make me go up on the roof naked I will just disappear, and turn up some whole other place. But first I have to think of where I will go. I can feel the box in my hand. My pillow is wet and the tiny little box is soft but I know what is inside. Secret. There is the window, and it's daytime now and people in the other room talking and they don't know I have a secret. But Nelson has gone somewhere and his mama dead; I wonder where and I can't remember the song we sang to the chickens.

Leah

RUTH MAY'S SICKNESS stayed with her, but Mother began pulling herself together. Seeing the two of them curled in the same bed, one slowly emerging and the other losing ground, put me back onto familiar, unpleasant thoughts of Adah and me in the womb. I have prayed a thousand times for God to tell me: Did I do that to Adah? If I showed her more kindness now, could I be forgiven for making her a cripple? But a debt of that size seems so impossible to pay back it is a dread thing even to start on.

Mother used her own reserves, without stealing the life out of Ruth May or anyone else. She seemed to draw strength right out of the muggy air. Sometimes I saw her sit on the side of the bed for a while before getting up, drawing in deep breaths through thin, pursed lips. She had her good and bad phases, but finally stopped sleepwalking once and for all. It happened rather suddenly one day, after Rachel burned up an egg omelet. She burned two in a row, to be exact—she had the fire in the stove stoked up way too high. The only way to get a slow heat for baking bread or cooking a tender thing like an omelet is to build up a big fire first with good, stout wood and then cook while the coals die slowly down. Rachel could never get the hang of that. She was trying to start the fire and cook all at once, which will never get you anywhere. You can't keep a new fire low; it must grow or die. Nelson taught me that.

But Nelson had gone to get water before dark so Rachel was trying to cook all alone. It was her day in charge of dinner and she had failed to think ahead. Now I could hear her screaming vile things out there in the kitchen house. I went out to investigate and let her know we were hungry.

"I'll hungry *you*," she yelled. "Can't you see I've only got two hands?"

I could. She was using both of them to gouge at the burned skillet with a wooden spatula of Nelson's making. Her hair had come down from its French knot and stuck all over her face, and her good blouse was smeared with black ash. She looked like Cinderella in reverse, stepped out from her life at the ball for a day of misery among the ashes.

"You've built the fire up way too hot," I told her.

"Go to hell, Leah, just go straight, directly to hell."

"I'm just trying to help. Look, see how the metal's glowing red hot on top? When it gets like that you just have to wait and let it cool off. Then you can try again."

Rachel blew out her breath hard. "Oh, whatever would I do without my child-progeny sister to tell me what to do."

"Prodigy," I corrected.

"Shut *up*, damn it! I wish you'd just shut up forever like your Goddamn deaf-mute genius twin!" She whirled around and threw the spatula, not missing my head by all that wide a margin. It banged loudly on the back door of the main house. I was shocked, not so much by her language but by the strength of that pitch. Usually Rachel threw underhanded and was no threat at all.

"Oh, P.S., Leah, there's no more eggs," she added with satisfaction. "For your information."

"Well, we have to eat something. I guess we'll just eat the burnt ones."

"This! Oh I'm sure. I'd rather die than have to serve this to Father." She made a horrible face at the pan and gave it a vicious shake. "*This* adventure in fine dining looks like it's been drug through hell backwards."

Rachel looked up at me and clapped her left hand over her mouth. I turned around. There was Mother in the doorway behind me, holding up the spatula.

"Rachel," Mother said. "I believe you dropped this."

We stood frozen before the altar of a red-hot cookstove. Rachel took the spatula without a word.

"Rachel, sugar, let me tell you something. I understand you're miserable. But I'm afraid this is your penance for sixteen years of pulling up your nose at my cooking. I want to see you bring that mess in here and serve it up to your father and all the rest of us, including yourself. And I want to see you clean your own plate, without one word. Tomorrow I'll start teaching you how to cook."

Mother kept her promise. She'd gotten up changed from her month in bed. For one thing, she was now inclined to say whatever was on her mind right in front of God and everybody. Even Father. She didn't speak to him directly; it was more like she was talking straight to God, or the air, or the lizards who'd paused halfway up the walls, and if Father should overhear her, that was his nickel. She declared she was taking us out of here as soon as she found the way to do it. She had even asked Eeben Axelroot flat out if he would take us. Not at the moment, was his reply, since he'd probably get shot down over Leopoldville with a planeload of white ladies, and he didn't want to make that kind of headlines. But on another day he came back smiling sideways and confided to Mama that every man has his price. From the looks of Mama, she means to pay it.

I was shocked and frightened to see her flout Father's authority, but truthfully, I could feel something similar moving around in my own heart. For the first time in my life I doubted his judgment. He'd made us stay here, when everybody from Nelson to the King of Belgium was saying white missionaries ought to go home. For us to be here now, each day, was Father's decision and his alone. Yet he wasn't providing for us, but only lashing out at us more and more. He wasn't able to protect Mother and Ruth May from getting sick. If it's all up to him to decide our fate, shouldn't protection be part of the bargain?

I *wanted* to believe in him. We had much more of the Lord's work to do here, that was plain. And what better time to do it, Father had told me reasonably on the plane coming back from Leopoldville, than in the festive atmosphere of Independence, when all Congolese are free to learn from us and make their own choices? Father believes they will choose the Lord's infinite love, and *us*, of course, as we are God's special delegation to Kilanga. He says we're being brave and righteous. Bravery and righteousness—those are two things that cannot go unrewarded in the sight of the Lord. Father never doubts it, and I can see that for him it's true. He's lived all his days by the laws of Christ, standing up tall and starting to preach in tent revivals when he was hardly older than I am now, and for all that time people flocked to his word and his wisdom. He was brave in the war, I'm sure, for he won a Purple Heart. For Father, the Kingdom of the Lord is an uncomplicated place, where tall, handsome boys fight on the side that always wins. I suppose it resembles Killdeer, Mississippi, where Father grew up, and played the position of quarterback in high school. In that kind of a place it is even all right for people to knock into each other hard every once in a while, in a sportsmanlike way, leaving a few bruises in the service of the final score.

But where is the place for girls in that Kingdom? The rules don't quite apply to us, nor protect us either. What do a girl's bravery and righteousness count for, unless she is also *pretty*? Just try being the smartest and most Christian seventh-grade girl in Bethlehem, Georgia. Your classmates will smirk and call you a square. Call you worse, if you're Adah.

All my life I've tried to set my shoes squarely into his footprints, believing if only I stayed close enough to him those same clean, simple laws would rule my life as well. That the Lord would see my goodness and fill me with light. Yet with each passing day I find myself farther away. There's a great holy war going on in my father's mind, in which we're meant to duck and run and obey orders and fight for all the right things, but I can't always make out the orders or even tell which side I am on exactly. I'm not even allowed to carry a gun. I'm a girl. He has no inkling.

If his decision to keep us here in the Congo wasn't right, then what else might he be wrong about? It has opened up in my heart a sickening world of doubts and possibilities, where before I had only faith in my father and love for the Lord. Without that rock of certainty underfoot, the Congo is a fearsome place to have to sink or swim.

Rachel

I WAS IN THE KITCHEN HOUSE slaving over a hot stove when everybody came running by. All the raggedy little children with the mothers right behind them, all hollering *"Tata Bidibidi! Tata Bidibidi!"* That means Mr. Bird, according to Leah, who ran right out to join them. If Mr. Bird—whosoever that might be—was going to put in an appearance, Leah sure wasn't going to miss it. They were saying he'd come up the river in some kind of old boat and was down there unloading his family and what not.

Being the new Chef Boy-ar-dee of the Price family, I had no time for fun and games. The only way I'd ever find out what was up in Kilanga, nowadays, was if it passed by the door of our kitchen house.

Well, turns out I didn't have to wait long, for they made straight for our doorstep! What to our wondering eyes should appear out there on the porch but a white man, very old and skinny, wearing a denim shirt so old you could practically see through it and a little wooden cross hanging on a leather string around his neck, the way the Congolese wear their evil-eye fetishes. He had a white beard and twinkly blue eyes, and all in all gave the impression of what Santa Claus would look like if he'd converted to Christian and gone without a good meal since last Christmas. When I got out to the porch he was already shaking hands with Mother and introducing his wife, a tall Congolese woman, and their children, who were variable in age and color but mostly were hiding behind the long colorful skirts of Mrs. Bird. Mother was confused, but she always has the good manners to be hospitalizing even to perfect strangers, so she asked them in and told me to run squeeze some orange juice. So back to the kitchen for Rachel the slave!

By the time I got back with a big dripping jar of orange juice and flopped down in a chair to rest, I'd already missed everything. I couldn't say what or who they were, but yet here was Mother yakking it up with them like old home week. They sat in our living-room chairs asking about people in the village like they knew their way around. "Mama Mwanza, och, how is she? Mama Lo is still doing coiffure and pressing palm oil? Bless her heart, she must be a hundred and ten, and she never married at all—that just goes to show you. Now Mama Tataba, where is she? Ah, but Anatole! We had better go see him at once." That kind of thing. Reverend Santa seemed like a kindly old man. The way he talked sounded part Yankee, part foreign, like one of those friendly Irish policemen in the old movies: "Och, mind you!"

Ruth May, who'd been up out of bed for a few days and seemed to be on the mend, was so enraptured with him she sat with her head practically leaning up against his worn-out trousers. The old man rested a hand on Ruth May's head and listened very closely to everything Mother said, nodding thoughtfully in a way that was quite complimentary. His wife was approximately a hundred years younger than him and attractive in her own way, and was mostly quiet. But she could speak English perfectly. They asked how things were going down at the church. Father was out somewhere looking for trouble as usual, and we hardly knew how to answer that question ourselves. Mother said, "Well, it's difficult. Nathan's very frustrated. It's all so clear to him that the words of Jesus will bring grace to their lives. But people here have such different priorities from what we're used to."

"They are very religious people, you know," the old man said. "For all that."

"How do you mean?" Mother asked.

"Everything they do is with one eye to the spirit. When they plant their yams and manioc, they're praying. When they harvest, they're praying. Even when they conceive their children, I think they're praying."

Mother seemed very interested. But Leah crossed her arms and asked, "Do you mean praying to their own pagan gods?"

Reverend Santa smiled at Leah. "What do you imagine our God thinks of this little corner of His creation: the flowering trees in the forest, the birds, the drenching downpours, the heat of the sun—do you know what I'm talking about?"

"Oh, yes," Leah said, straight-A pupil as always.

"And do you think God is pleased with these things?"

"Oh, I think He *glories* in them!" she hastened to say. "I think he must be prouder of the Congo than just about any place He ever made."

"I think so, too," he said. "I think the Congolese have a world of God's grace in their lives, along with a dose of hardship that can kill a person entirely. I happen to think they already knew how to make a joyful noise unto the Lord a long time ago."

Leah leaned back in her chair, probably wondering what Father would say to that. As if we didn't know. He'd say the Irish and them are well known to be Catholic papists and worshipers of the false idols. The business about the flowers and little birdies just clinches the deal.

"Have you heard the songs they sing here in Kilanga?" he asked. "They're very worshipful. It's a grand way to begin a church service, singing a Congolese hymn to the rainfall on the seed yams. It's quite easy to move from there to the parable of the mustard seed. Many parts of the Bible make good sense here, if only you change a few words." He laughed. "And a lot of whole chapters, sure, you just have to throw away."

"Well, it's every bit God's word, isn't it?" Leah said.

"God's word, brought to you by a crew of romantic idealists in a harsh desert culture eons ago, followed by a chain of translators two thousand years long."

Leah stared at him.

"Darling, did you think God wrote it all down in the English of King James himself?"

"No, I guess not."

"Think of all the duties that were perfectly obvious to Paul or Matthew in that old Arabian desert that are pure nonsense to us now. All that foot washing, for example. Was it really for God's glory, or just to keep the sand out of the house?"

Leah sat narrow-eyed in her chair, for once stumped for the correct answer.

"Oh, and the *camel*. Was it a *camel* that could pass through the eye of a needle more easily than a rich man? Or a coarse piece of yarn? The Hebrew words are the same, but which one did they mean? If it's a camel, the rich man might as well not even try. But if it's the yarn, he might well succeed with a lot of effort, you see?" He leaned forward toward Leah with his hands on his knees. "Och, I shouldn't be messing about with your thinking this way, with your father out in the garden. But I'll tell you a secret. When I want to take God at his word exactly, I take a peep out the window at His Creation. Because *that,* darling, He makes fresh for us every day, without a lot of dubious middle managers."

Leah didn't commit herself one way or the other. "The flowers and birds and all, you mean to say that's your Gospel."

"Ah, you're thinking I'm a crazy old pagan for sure." Old Tata Bird laughed heartily, fingering the cross around his neck (another warning sign of Catholic papism), and he didn't sound repentant.

"No, I understand," Mother said thoughtfully. She appeared to understand him so well she'd like to adopt him and have his mixed-race family move right in.

"You'll have to forgive me. I've been here so long, I've come to love the people here and their ways of thinking."

That goes without saying, I thought. Given his marital situation.

"Well, you must be famished!" Mother said suddenly, jumping up out of her chair. "Stay for dinner, at least. Nathan should be home soon. Do you actually live on that little boat?"

"We do, in fact. It's a good home base for doing our work—a little collecting, a little nature study, a little ministry, a little public health and dispensing of the quinine. Our older children stay in

Léopoldville most of the year for their schooling, but they've come with us on a little holiday to visit the relatives." He glanced at his wife, who smiled.

She explained quietly, "Tata Fowells is especially interested in the birds. He has classified many kinds in this region that were never known before by the Europeans."

Tata Fo-wells? Where had I heard that name before? I was racking my brain, while Mother and the Mrs. began an oh-so-polite argument about whether the family would stay for dinner. Mother apparently forgot we didn't have one decent thing fit to eat, and little did that family know what they were in for if they stayed. Tata Fowells, I kept turning that over. Meanwhile Adah pulled her chair up next to him and opened one of the old musty bird books she'd found in this house, which she adores to carry around.

"Och," he cried happily, "I'd forgotten these books entirely. How wonderful you're putting them to use. But you have to know, I've many better ones down on the boat."

Adah looked like she would just love to run down there and read them all backwards right this minute. She was pointing out different pictures of long-tail squawk jays and what not, and he was so bubbling over with information that he probably failed to notice Adah can't talk.

Oh! I suddenly thought to myself: Brother Fowles! That Brother Fowles! The minister who had this mission before us and got kicked out for consorting with the natives too much. Well, I should say so! Now everything fell into place. But it was too late for me to say anything, having missed the introductions on account of being the maidservant. I just sat there, while Adah got bird lessons and Leah cajoled the shy little Fowles children to come in off the porch and sit on the floor with her and Ruth May and read comic books with them.

Then suddenly the room went dark, for Father was at the door. We all froze, except for Brother Fowles, who jumped up and held out his hand to Father with the left hand clasping his forearm, secret handshake of the Congolese.

"Brother Price, at last," he said. "I've held you in my prayers, and now I've had the blessing of meeting your lovely family. I am Brother Fowles, your predecessor in this mission. My wife, Celine. Our children."

Father didn't offer his hand. He was studying that big Catholic-looking cross around the neck, and probably thinking over all we'd heard about Brother Fowles going off the deep end, plus every curse word ever uttered by the parrot. Finally he did shake hands, but in a cool way, American style. "What brings you back here?"

"Ah, we were passing this way! We do most of our work down-river near the Kwa, but my wife's parents are at Ganda. We thought we might look in on you and our other friends in Kilanga. Sure, we should pay our respects to Tata Ndu."

You could see Father's skin crawl when he heard the name of his archenemy, the chief. Spoken in a Yank accent, to boot. But Father played the cool cat, not admitting what a miserable failure he had been so far at the Christianizing trade. "We're just fine and dandy, thank you. And what work is it you do now?" He emphasized the *now*, as if to say, We know very well you got kicked out of preaching the *Gospel*.

"I rejoice in the work of the Lord," said Brother Fowles. "I was just telling your wife, I do a little ministering. I study and classify the fauna. I observe a great deal, and probably offer very little salvation in the long run."

"That is a pity," Father declared. "Salvation is the way, the truth, and the light. For whosoever shall call upon the name of the Lord shall be saved. And how then shall they believe in him of whom they have not heard? and how shall they hear without a preacher? . . . As it is written, 'How beautiful are the feet of them that preach the gospel of peace, and bring glad tidings of good things!'"

"'Glad tidings of good things,' that is precious work indeed," said Brother Fowles. "Romans, chapter ten, verse fifteen."

Wow. This Yank knew his Bible. Father took a little step backwards on that one.

"Certainly I do my best," Father said quickly, to cover his shock.

"I take to heart the blessed words, 'Believe on the Lord Jesus Christ, and thou shalt be saved, and thy house. And they spake unto him the word of the Lord, and to all that were in his house.'"

Brother Fowles nodded carefully. "Paul and Silas to their jailer, yes, after the angels so considerately set them free with an earthquake. The Acts of the Apostles, chapter sixteen, is it? I've always been a little perplexed by the next verse, 'And he took them the same hour of the night, and washed their stripes.'"

"The American Translation might clear that up for you. It says, 'washed their wounds.'" Father sounded like the know-it-all kid in class you just want to strangulate.

"It does, yes," replied Brother Fowles, slowly. "And yet I wonder, who translated this? During my years here in the Congo I've heard so many errors of translation, even quite comical ones. So you'll forgive me if I'm skeptical, Brother Price. Sometimes I ask myself: what if those stripes are not wounds at all, but something else? He was a prison guard; maybe he wore a striped shirt, like a referee. Did Paul and Silas do his *laundry* for him, as an act of humility? Or perhaps the meaning is more metaphorical: Did Paul and Silas reconcile the man's doubts? Did they listen to his divided way of feeling about this new religion they were springing upon him all of a sudden?"

The little girl sitting on the floor with Ruth May said something in their language. Ruth May whispered, "Donald Duck and Snow White, they got married."

Father stepped over the children and pulled up a chair, which he sat in backwards as he loves to do whenever he has a good Christian argument. He crossed his arms over the chair back and smirked his disapproval at Brother Fowles. "Sir, I offer you my condolences. Personally I've never been troubled by any such difficulties with interpreting God's word."

"Indeed, I see that," Brother Fowles said. "But I assure you it is no trouble to me. It can be quite a grand way to pass an afternoon, really. Take for example your Romans, chapter ten. Let's go back to that. The American Translation, if you prefer. A little farther on we find this promise: 'If the first handful of dough is consecrated, the whole mass is, and if the root of a tree is consecrated, so are its branches. If some of the branches have been broken off, and you who were only a wild olive shoot have been grafted in, and made to share the richness of the olive's root, you must not look down upon the branches. Remember that you do not support the root; the root supports you.'"

Father kind of sat there blinking, what with all the roots and shoots.

But old Santa's eyes just twinkled; he was having a ball. "Brother Price," he said, "don't you sometimes think about this, as you share the food of your Congolese brethren and gladden your heart with their songs? Do you get the notion *we* are the branch that's grafted on here, sharing in the richness of these African roots?"

Father replied, "You might look to verse twenty-eight there, sir. 'From the point of view of the good news they are treated as enemies of God.'"

"Sure, and it continues: 'but from the point of view of God's choice, they are dear to him because of their forefathers.'"

"Don't be a fool, man!" Father cried. "That verse refers to the children of Israel."

"Maybe so. But the image of the olive tree is a nice one, don't you think?"

Father just squinted at him, like here was one tree he'd like to make into firewood.

Brother Fowles didn't get the least bit steamed up, however. He said, "I'm a plain fool for the nature images in the Bible, Brother Price. That fond of it. I find it all so handy here, among these people who have such an intelligence and the great feeling for the living world around them. They're very humble in their debts to nature. Do you know the hymn of the rain for the seed yams, Brother Price?"

"Hymns to their pagan gods and false idols? I'm afraid I haven't got the time for dabbling in that kind of thing."

"Well, you're that busy I'm sure. But it's interesting, just the same. In keeping with what you were quoting there in your Romans, chapter twelve. You remember the third verse, do you not?"

Father answered with his teeth showing: "For I say, through the grace given unto me, to every man that is among you, not to think of himself more highly than he ought . . ."

". . . For as we have many members in one body, and all members have not the same office, so we, being many, are one body in Christ . . ."

"In *Christ!*" Father shouted, as if to say, "Bingo!"

"And every one, members one of another," Brother Fowles went on to quote. "Having then gifts that differ according to the grace that is given to us, whether prophecy, or ministry, or he that teacheth. He that giveth, let him do it with simplicity . . . He that sheweth mercy, with cheerfulness. Let love be without dissimulation. Be kindly affectioned to one another with brotherly love."

"Chapter twelve. Verse ten. Thank you, *sir.*" Father was plainly ready to call a halt to this battle of the Bible verses. I'd bet he'd like to of given Brother Fowles The Verse to copy out for punishment. But then the old man would just stand there and rattle it off from memory with a few extra images of nature thrown in for free.

Father suddenly remembered he needed to stomp off and do some very important thing or another, and to make a long story short, they didn't stay for dinner. They got the picture that they weren't welcome in our house or the whole village probably, in Father's humble opinion. And they were the type that seemed like they'd rather sit down and eat their own shoes before they'd put you out in any way. They told us they planned to spend the afternoon visiting a few old friends, but that they needed to be on up the river before nightfall.

We about had to tie ourselves to the chairs to keep from tagging after them. We were so curious about what they'd be saying to Tata Ndu and them. Jeepers! All this time we've been more or less thinking we were the one and only white people who ever set foot here. And all along, our neighbors had this whole friendship with Brother Fowles they'd just kept mum about. You always think you know more about their kind than they know about yours, which just goes to show you.

They came back before sundown and invited us to come see their boat before they shoved off, so Mother and my sisters and I trooped down to the riverbank. Brother Fowles had some more books he wanted to give Adah. That's not the half of it, either. Mrs. Fowles kept bringing out more presents to give Mother: canned goods, milk powder, coffee, sugar, quinine pills, fruit cocktail, and so many other things it seemed like they really *were* Mr. and Mrs. Santa Claus, after all. And yet their boat was hardly more than a little floating shack with a bright green tin roof. Inside, it had all the comforts, though: books, chairs, a gas stove, you name it. Their kids ran around and flopped on the chairs and played with stuff, giving no indication they thought it peculiar to reside on a body of water.

"Oh my stars, oh goodness, you're too kind," Mother kept saying, as Celine brought out one thing after another and put it into our hands. "Oh, I can't thank you enough."

I was of a mind to slip them a note, like a captivated spy girl in the movies: "*Help! Get me out of here!*" But that loaded-down little boat of theirs already looked like it was fixing to sink if you looked at it wrong. All the canned goods they gave us probably helped them stay afloat.

Mother was also taking stock of things. She asked, "How do you manage to stay so well supplied?"

"We have so many friends," Celine said. "The Methodist Mission gets us milk powder and vitamins to distribute in the villages along the river. The tins of food and quinine pills come from the ABFMS."

"We're terribly interdenominational," said Brother Fowles, laughing. "I even get a little stipend from the National Geographic Society."

"The ABFMS?" Mother queried.

"American Baptist Foreign Mission Service," he said. "They have a hospital mission up the Wamba River, have you not heard of it? That little outfit has done a world of good in the ways of guinea-worm cure, literacy, and human kindness. They've put old King Léopold's ghost to shame, I would say. If such a thing is possible. It's run by the wisest minister you'll ever meet, a man named Wesley Green, and his wife, Jane."

Brother Fowles added as an afterthought, "No offense to your husband, of course."

"But *we're* Baptists," Mother said, sounding hurt. "And the Mission League cut off our stipend right before Independence!"

Mr. Fowles thought this over before offering, tactfully, "For certain, Mrs. Price, there are Christians and then there are Christians."

"How far away is this mission? Do you get there on your boat?" Mother was eying the boat, the canned goods, and perhaps the whole of our future.

But both Brother and Mrs. Fowles laughed at that, shaking their heads like Mother had asked if they take their boat to the moon frequently to fetch green cheese.

"We can't take this old bucket more than fifty miles down the Kwilu," he explained. "You run into the rapids. But the good road from Léopoldville crosses the Wamba and reaches this river at Kikwit. Sometimes Brother Green comes up in his boat, hitches a ride on a truck and meets us at Kikwit. Or we go to the airfield at Masi Manimba to meet our packages. By the grace of God, we always seem to get whatever it is we really need to have."

"We rely very much on our friends," Celine added.

"Ah, yes," her husband agreed. "And that means to get one good connection made, you have to understand the Kituba, the Lingala, the Bembe, Kunyi, Vili, Ndingi, and the bleeding talking drums."

Celine laughed and said yes, that was true. The rest of us felt like fish out of water as usual. If Ruth May had been feeling up to snuff she'd have already climbed aboard and started jabbering with the Fowles children in probably all those languages plus French and Siamese. Which makes you wonder, are they really speaking real words, or do little kids just start out naturally understanding each other before the prime of life sets in? But Ruth May was not up to snuff, so she was being quiet, hanging on to Mother's hand.

"They asked us to leave," Mother said. "In no uncertain terms. Really I think we should have, but it was Nathan's decision to stay."

"Sure there was quite a rush for the gate, after Independence," Brother Fowles agreed. "People left for a million reasons: common sense, lunacy, faintness of heart. And the rest of us stayed, for the very same reasons. Except for faintness of heart. No one can accuse us of that, can they, Mrs. Price?"

"Well . . ." Mother said uncertainly. I guess she hated to admit that if it was up to her we'd be hightailing it out of here like rabbits. Me too, and I don't care who calls me yellow. *Please help*, I tried to say to Mrs. Fowles just with my eyes. *Get us out of here! Send a bigger boat!*

Finally Mother just sighed and said, "We hate to see you go." I'm sure my sisters all agreed with that. Here we'd been feeling like the very last people on earth of the kind that use the English language and can openers, and once that little boat went put-put-put up the river we'd feel that way again.

"You could stay in Kilanga awhile," Leah offered, though she didn't tell them they could stay with *us*. And she didn't say, You'd have some explaining to do to Father, who thinks you're a bunch of backsliders. She didn't have to. Those words were unspoken by all present.

"You're very kind," Celine said. "We need to go to my mother's family. Their village is starting a soybean farm. We'll be back this way after the end of the rainy season, and we will be sure to visit you again."

Which, of course, could be any time from next July to the twelfth of never, as far as we knew. We just stood there getting more and more heartbroken as they gathered things up and counted their kids.

"I don't mean to impose on you," Mother said, "but Ruth May, my little one here—she's had a high fever for more than a month. She seems to be getting the best of it now, but I've been so worried. Is there a doctor *anywhere* we could get to easily?"

Celine stepped over the side of the boat and put a hand on Ruth May's head, then stooped down and looked in her eyes. "It could be malaria. Could be typhus. Not sleeping sickness, I don't think. Let me get you something that might help."

As she disappeared back into the boat, Brother Fowles confided to Mother in a low voice, "I wish we could do more for you. But the mission planes aren't flying at all and the roads are anyone's guess. Everything is at sixes and sevens. We'll try to get word over to Brother Green about your little one, but there's no saying what he could do, just now." He looked at Ruth May, who seemed to have no inkling they were discussing the fate of her life. He asked carefully, "Do you think it's a matter of great urgency?"

Mother bit her fingernail and studied Ruth May. "Brother Fowles, I have no earthly notion. I am a housewife from Georgia."

Just then Celine appeared with a small glass bottle of pink capsules. "Antibiotics," she said. "If it's typhus or cholera or any number of other things, these may help. If it's malaria or sleeping sickness, I'm afraid they won't. In any case we will pray for your Ruth."

"Have you spoken with Tata Ndu?" Brother Fowles put in. "He is a man of surprising resources."

"I'm afraid Nathan and Tata Ndu have locked horns. I'm not sure he would give us the time of day."

"You might be surprised," he said.

They really were leaving, but Mother seemed just plain desperate to keep the conversation going. She asked Brother Fowles while he wound up some ropes and things on the deck, "Were you really on such good terms with Tata Ndu?"

He looked up, a little surprised. "I respect him, if that's what you mean."

"But as a Christian. Did you really get anywhere with him?"

Brother Fowles stood up and scratched his head, making his white hair stand on end. The longer you watched that man doing things, the younger he looked. Finally he said, "As a Christian, I respect his judgments. He guides his village fairly, all things considered. We never could see eye to eye on the business of having four wives. . . ."

"He has more than that *now*," Leah tattled.

"Aha. So you see, I was not a great influence in that department," he said. "But each of those wives has profited from the teachings of Jesus, I can tell you. Tata Ndu and I spent many afternoons with a calabash of palm wine between us, debating the merits of treating a wife kindly. In my six years here I saw the practice of wife beating fall into great disfavor. Secret little altars to Tata Jesus appeared in most every kitchen, as a result."

Leah tossed him the tie rope and helped him push the boat out of the shallow mud into deeper water. She just slogged right in up to her knees, blue jeans and all, without the slightest regard. Adah was clutching her new books about the ornithoptery of butterflies to her bosom, while Ruth May waved and called out weakly, "*Wenda mbote! Wenda mbote!*"

"Do you feel what you did was enough?" Mother asked Brother Fowles, as if it hadn't sunk in that we'd already said good-bye here and this conversation was over-and-out.

Brother Fowles stood on the deck facing back, looking Mother over like he just didn't know what to do about her. He shrugged finally. "We're branches grafted on this good tree, Mrs. Price. The great root of Africa sustains us. I wish you wisdom and God's mercy."

"Thank you kindly," she said.

They were pretty far out on the water when he perked up suddenly and shouted, "Oh, the parrot! Methuselah! How is he?"

We looked at each other, reluctant to end the visit on what you might call a sour note. It was Ruth May who hollered out in her puny little voice, "Bird heaven! He's went to bird heaven, Mr. Fowles!"

"Ha! Best place for him, the little bastard!" cried Brother Fowles, which shocked the pants off us naturally.

Meanwhile, every child in the village had gathered around and was jumping in the mud of the riverbank. They'd all gotten presents too, I could see: packets of milk powder and such. But they were yelling so happily it seemed like they loved Brother Fowles for more reasons than just powdered milk. Like kids who only ever get socks for Christmas, but still believe with all their hearts in Santa.

Mother alone didn't wave. She stood ankle-deep in the mud, like it was her job to bear witness as their boat shrank down to a speck on the shimmering water, and she didn't move from her post till they were long out of sight.

Adah

To market to market to buy a fat pig! Pigfat a buy! To market to market! But wherever you might look, no pigs now. Hardly even a dog worth the trouble and stove wood. Goats and sheep, none. Half-hour after daybreak the buzzards rise from the leafless billboard tree and flap away like the sound of old black satin dresses beat together. Meat market closed for the duration of this drought, no rain and still no rain. In the way of herbivores, nothing left here to kill.

July had brought us only the strange apparition of the family Fowles, and in its aftermath, the conviction in all our separate minds that their visit could only have been a dream. All minds except Father's, that is, who frequently takes the name of Brother Fowles in vain, feeling certain now that all the stones in his path were laid by this deluded purveyor of Christian malpractice.

And August brought us no pleasant dreams at all. Ruth May's condition pitched suddenly into decline, as inexplicably as it had earlier improved. Against all hope and Mrs. Fowles's antibiotics faithfully delivered, the fever rose and rose. Ruth May fell back into bed with her hair plastered to her head in a dark sweat. Mother prayed to the small glass god with pink capsules in its belly.

The second half of August also brought us a special five-day Kilanga week, beginning and ending on market day, which did not contain a Sunday but left Sundays standing on either side of it like parentheses. That particular combination stands as one chance in seven, by the way. It should occur on average seven times per year, separated by intervals just slightly longer than that endured by Noah on his putative ark.

Was this blue-moon event special to our neighbors? Did they notice? I have no idea. Such was our fellowship with our fellow man in Kilanga. But in our household it passed as a bizarre somber holiday, for on each of those five days the village chief of Kilanga, Tata Ndu, came to our house. *Udn Atat.* He sent his sons ahead of him shouting and waving ceremonially preserved animal parts to announce his eminence.

On each occasion he brought a gift: first, fresh antelope meat wrapped in a bloody fold of cloth (how hungrily we swooned at the sight of that blood!). Day two: a neat spherical basket with a tight-fitting lid, filled with *mangwansi* beans. Third, a live grouse with its legs tied together; fourth, the soft, tanned pelt of an ant bear. And on the last day, a small carving of a pregnant woman made of pink ivory. Our Father eyed that little pink woman and became inspired to strike up a conversation with Tata Ndu on the subject of false idols. But up until day five—and ever afterward, on the whole—Our Father was delighted with this new attention from the chief. The Reverend cockadoodled about the house, did he. "Our Christian charity has come back to us sevenfold," he declared, taking liberty with mathematics, gleefully slapping the thighs of his khaki pants. "Hot dog! Orleanna, didn't I tell you Ndu would be on our side in the end?"

"Oh, is it the end now, Nathan?" Mother asked. She was silent on the subject of Tata Ndu as a houseguest. We ate the meat all right and were glad to have it, but the trinkets she sequestered in her bedroom, out of sight. We were curious to inspect and handle these intriguing objects, especially the little pink madonna, but Mother felt we should not show excessive interest. In spite of Brother Fowles's vouching for his character, Mother suspected these gifts from the chief were not without strings attached. And she was right, it turned out. Though it took us a month of Sundays to catch on.

At first we were simply flattered and astonished: *Udn Atat* walking right through the front door of our very house, standing a moment before the shrine of Rachel's hand mirror-mirror on the wall, then settling himself into our single good chair with arms. Enthroned there under his hat, he observed our household through his un-glasses and swished the animal-tail fly swatter that denoted his station in life. Whenever he took off his strange peaked hat, he revealed himself as a large, powerful man. His dark half-dome forehead and gravely receding hairline emphasized a broad face, broad chest and shoulders, and enormously muscular arms. He pulled his colorful drape up under his armpits and crossed his arms over the front of his chest as a man only does when proud of his physique. Our Mother was not impressed. But she mustered manners enough to make orange juice, of which the chief was fond.

Our Father, who now made a point of being home to receive Tata Ndu, would pull up one of the other chairs, sit backward with his arms draped over the back, and talk Scripture. Tata Ndu would attempt to sway the conversation back around to village talk, or to the vague gossip we had all been hearing about the riots in Matadi and Stanleyville. But mainly he regaled Our Father with flattering observations, such as: "Tata Price, you have *trop de jolies filles*—too many pretty daughters," or less pleasant but more truthful remarks such as: "You have much need of food, *n'est-ce pas?*" For his esoteric amusement he commanded the *jolies filles* (and we obliged) to line up in front of him in order of height. The tallest being Rachel, at five feet six inches and the full benefit of Miss America posture; the shortest being myself, two inches lesser than my twin on account of crookedness. (Ruth May, being delirious and prone, was exempt from the lineup.) Tata Ndu clucked his tongue and said we were all very thin. This caused Rachel to quiver with pride and stroll about the house preceded by her pelvis in the manner of a high-fashion model. She tended to show off excessively during these visits, rushing to help Mother out in ways she would not have dreamed of without an audience.

"Tata Ndu," Mother hinted, "our youngest is burning up with fever. You're a man of such importance I hope by coming here you aren't exposing yourself to some dreadful contagion." This was the nearest she could come to asking outright for help.

Tata Ndu's attention then lapsed for a number of days, during which time we went to church, swallowed our weekly malaria pill, killed another hen from our dwindling flock, and stole turns sneaking into our parents' bedroom to examinine the small carved woman's genitalia. Then, after two Sundays had passed, he returned. This time his gifts were more personal: a *pagne* of beautifully dyed cloth, a carved wooden bracelet, and a small jar of a smelly waxy substance, whose purpose we declined to speculate on or discuss with Tata Ndu. Mother accepted these gifts with both hands, as is the custom here, and put them away without a word.

Nelson, as usual, was the one who finally took pity upon our benighted stupidity and told us what was up: *kukwela*. Tata Ndu wanted a wife.

"A *wife*," Mother said, staring at Nelson in the kitchen house exactly as I had seen her stare at the cobra that once turned up in there. I wondered whether she might actually grab a stick and whack Nelson behind the head, as she'd done to the snake.

"Yes, Mama Price," he said tiredly, without a trace of apology. Nelson was used to our overreactions to what he felt were ordinary things, such as cobras in the kitchen. But his voice had a particularly authoritative ring when he said it, for he had his head stuck in the oven. Mother knelt beside him, helping to steady the heavy ash can while Nelson cleaned the ashes out of the cookstove. They both had their backs to the door, and did not know I was there.

"One of the girls, you mean," Mother said. She pulled on the nape of Nelson's T-shirt, extracting him from the stove so she might speak to him face to face. "You're saying Tata Ndu wants to marry one of my daughters."

"Yes."

"But, Nelson, he already *has* six or seven wives! Good Lord."

"Yes. Tata Ndu is very rich. He heard about Tata Price having no money now for food. He can see your children are thin and sick. But he knows it is not the way of Tata Price to take help from the Congolese. So he can bargain man to man. He can help your family by paying Tata Price some ivory and five or six goats and maybe a little bit of cash to take the *Mvúla* out of his house. Tata Ndu is a good chief, Mama Price."

"He wants Rachel!"

"The Termite is the one he wants to buy, Mama Price. All those goats, *and* you won't have to feed her anymore."

"Oh, Nelson. Can you even imagine?"

Nelson squatted on his heels, his ashy eyelids blinking earnestly as he inspected Mother's face.

Surprisingly, she started to laugh. Then, more surprisingly, Nelson began to laugh, too. He threw open his near-toothless mouth and howled alongside Mother, both of them with their hands on their thighs. I expect they were picturing Rachel wrapped in a *pagne* trying to pound manioc.

Mother wiped her eyes. "Why on earth do you suppose he'd pick Rachel?" From her voice I could tell she was not smiling, even after all that laughter.

"He says the *Mvúla's* strange color would cheer up his other wives."

"What?"

"Her color." He rubbed at his own black forearm and then held up two ashy fingers, as if demonstrating how the ink in Rachel's sad case had all come off. "She doesn't have any proper skin, you know," Nelson said, as if this were something anyone could say of a woman's daughter without offending her. Then he leaned forward and ducked his head and shoulders far back into the stove for the rest of the ashes. He did not speak again until he emerged from the depths.

"People say maybe she was born too soon, before she got finished cooking. Is that true?" He looked at Mother's belly inquiringly.

She just stared at him. "What do you mean, her color would cheer up his other wives?"

He looked at Mother in patient wonder, waiting for more of a question.

"Well, I just don't understand. You make it sound like she's an *accessory* he needs to go with his outfit."

Nelson paused for a long time to wipe the ash from his face and puzzle over the metaphor of accessories and outfits. I stepped into the kitchen house to get a banana, knowing there would likely be nothing more to overhear. My mother and Nelson had reached the limits of mutual understanding.

Leah

HERE WAS OUR PROBLEM: Tata Ndu would be very offended if Father turned down his generous offer to marry Rachel. And it wasn't just Tata Ndu involved. Whatever we might think of this imposing man in his pointed hat, he is a figurehead who represents the will of Kilanga. I believe this is why Brother Fowles said we should respect him, or at least pay attention, no matter how out-of-whack the chief might seem. He's not just speaking for himself. Every few weeks Tata Ndu has meetings with his sous-chiefs, who have their own meetings with all the families. So by the time Tata Ndu gets around to saying something, you can be pretty sure the whole village is talking to you.

Anatole has been explaining to me the native system of government. He says the business of throwing pebbles into bowls with the most pebbles winning an election—that was *Belgium's* idea of fair play, but to people here it was peculiar. To the Congolese (including Anatole himself, he confessed) it seems odd that if one man gets fifty votes and the other gets forty-nine, the first one wins altogether and the second one plumb loses. That means almost half the people will be unhappy, and according to Anatole, in a village that's left halfway unhappy you haven't heard the end of it. There is sure to be trouble somewhere down the line.

The way it seems to work here is that you need one hundred percent. It takes a good while to get there. They talk and make deals and argue until they are pretty much all in agreement on what ought to be done, and then Tata Ndu makes sure it happens that way. If he does a good job, one of his sons will be chief after he dies.

If he does a bad job, the women will chase Tata Ndu out of town with big sticks and Kilanga will try out a new chief. So Tata Ndu is the voice of the people. And that voice was now telling us we'd be less of a burden to ourselves and others if we let him buy Rachel off our hands for some goats. It kind of put us on the spot.

Rachel went into a frenzy, and for once in my life I couldn't blame her. I was very glad he hadn't picked me. Mother crossed her heart to Rachel that we weren't going to sell her, but reassurances of this kind are not the words you're prepared to hear coming out of your mother's mouth. The very thought of being married to Tata Ndu seemed to contaminate Rachel's frame of mind, so that every ten minutes or so she'd stop whatever she was doing and scream with disgust. She demanded to Father's face that we go home this instant before she had to bear one more day of humiliation. Father disciplined her with The Verse that ends on honoring thy father and mother, and no sooner had she finished it than Father smote her with it again! We'd run out of blank paper so she had to write out the hundred verses in a very tiny hand on the backs of old letters and envelopes left from when we were still getting mail. Adah and I took pity and secretly helped her some. We didn't even charge her ten cents a verse, as we used to back home. For if we did, how would she pay?

We couldn't refuse visits from the chief, no matter how we felt. But Rachel began to behave very oddly whenever he came to the house. Frankly, she was odd when he didn't, too. She wore too many clothes at once, covering herself entirely and even wearing her raincoat indoors, as hot and dry as it was. She also did strange things with her hair. With Rachel, that is a deep-seated sign of trouble. There was nervous tension in our household, believe you me.

Ever since Independence we'd heard stories of violence between blacks and whites. Yet if we looked out our own window, here's what we'd see: Mama Nguza and Mama Mwanza chatting in the road and two little boys stepping sideways trying to pee on each other. Everybody still poor as church mice, yet more or less content. The Independence seemed to have passed over our village, just as the plague did on that long ago night in Egypt, sparing those who had the right symbol marked over their doorsills. Still, we didn't know what the symbol was, or how we were spared. We barely knew what was going on in the first place, and now, if things had changed, we didn't know what to believe or how to act. There was an unspoken feeling of danger, which we couldn't discuss but felt we should be attending to at all times. Mother had little tolerance for Rachel's tantrums. She told Rachel to straighten up because right now she had her hands full with Ruth May sick.

Ruth May was now getting rashes all over her back and was hot to the touch. Mother gave her cool sponge baths every hour or so. She spent most nights curled up at the foot of my parents' iron double bed. Mother decided we should move Ruth May's cot out into the main room so she could be with us in the daytime, where we could keep a closer eye. Rachel and I helped move it, while Adah rolled up the bedding. Our cots were made of iron pipes welded together, about as heavy as you'd think a bed could be. First we had to pull down all the mosquito netting from the frame. Then with a grand heave-ho we shoved the bed away from the wall. What we saw on the wall behind it made us stare.

"What *are* those?" Rachel asked.

"Buttons?" I guessed, for they were perfectly round and white. I was thinking of our hope-chest projects. Whatever this was, it had been Ruth May's project for a very long time.

"Her malaria pills," Mother said, and she was right. There must have been a hundred of them, all partly melted and stuck in long crooked rows behind where the bed had been.

Mother stood looking at them for a good long while. Then she left, and came back with a table knife. Carefully she pried the pills off the plaster wall, one by one, into her cupped hand. There were sixty-one. Adah kept count, and wrote that number down. Exactly how many weeks we'd been in the Congo.

Rachel

MAN ALIVE, I am all steamed up with no place to go. When Tata Ndu comes to our house, jeez oh man. I can't even stand to look at him looking at me. I revert my eyes. Sometimes I do unlady-like things like scratch myself and pretend I'm retarded. But I suppose he'd be just as happy to add a retarded wife to his collection; maybe he doesn't have one yet. Jeepers. The very fact my parents even let him in the door! I refuse to give Father the pleasure of a reply when he talks to me. Mother either, if I can help it. Ruth May is all she cares about: poor Ruth May this and Ruth May that! Well, jeez, maybe she is sick, but it's no easy street for me either, being here and taking this guff. My family is thinking of everything but my personal safety. The instant we get back to Georgia I am filing for an adoption.

And if that wasn't already the living end, now my knight in shin-ing armor has arrived: Mr. Stinkpot Axelroot. He just showed up in the yard one day, right when Tata Ndu was coming up the steps in his stupid hat and his no-glass glasses, and the two of them had a word of exchange. After that Tata Ndu only stayed about ten min-utes and then left. I was just getting going on my retarded-daughter presentation. Too bad!

Well, it turns out Father and Mr. Axelroot hatched up a plan to get me out of marrying Tata Ndu without hurting the whole vil-lage's feelings. They're setting it up to look like I was already promised in marriage to Eeben Axelroot! I about croaked. Mother says don't let it get me down, it is only for appearance's sake. But that means now *he* comes around the house all the time, too, and I have to act engaged! *And,* naturally, we have to act like it out on the front porch so everybody can see. Sit out there and watch the grass dry up, is my social life at this point in time. Don't let it get me down? Man, oh man! I always wanted to be the belle of the ball, but, jeepers, is this ever the wrong ball.

The very first time we were alone for ten seconds on the porch, believe it or not, Axelroot tried to get fresh. He put his arm on the back of my chair. I slapped him hard like Elizabeth Taylor in the *Hot Tin Roof* and I guess that showed him a thing or two. But then he *laughed,* if you can believe. Well! I reminded him this entire engagement was a lot of bunk and don't you forget it. "Mr. Axelroot," I said, "I will commiserate your presence on this porch with me but only as a public service to keep the peace in this village. And furthermore, it would help if you took a bath once every year or two." I'm willing to be a philanderist for peace, but a lady can only go so far where perspiration odor is concerned. I kept thinking of Brigitte Bardot and all those soldiers.

So he behaves pretty well now. I just call him Axelroot. He calls me Princess, which really is maybe too much polish for the jalopy, but he means it in the right way, I think. He can be halfway decent if he tries. He actually did start taking baths and leaving his horrible hat at home, praise the Lord. Mother hates him as much as ever, and I guess I do too, but what am I supposed to do? I talk to him. As long as you're sitting out there pretending to be engaged to somebody, you might as well pass the time. And his company does keep the children away. They don't care for Axelroot. He smacks them. Well, all right, he shouldn't, I know that! But at least I don't have to be surrounded with little brats jumping up and pulling on my hair all the livelong day. Normally they clamber around me until I feel like Gulliver among the Lepidopterans.

My unspoken plan is that, if I can butter him up enough, maybe he'll change his mind and fly us out of here. Mother already secretly offered him her wedding ring plus a thousand dollars, which supposedly we'd dig up after we got back to Georgia without Father or any visible means of self-support. Axelroot said, "Cash only, ladies," he doesn't take credit. But maybe he'll take pity!

So I pass the time by telling him stories from home: the kids I knew back at Bethlehem High and things we used to do. It makes me homesick. But, oh boy, if those fast cheerleaders who teased me for being a preacher's kid could see me now, practically engaged to an *older man!* He has been around the block, let me tell you, being born in South Africa and spending his youth here and there, partly even in Texas, from what I gather. His accent sounds normal. And he makes up these cockalamie stories to stand my hair on end about being a flying fighter. How he has shot very influential men in cold blood and dropped fire bombs from the air that can burn up a whole field of crops in ten seconds flat. He's not just an errand boy flying missionaries around, no, sir! That's only his cover, or so he informed me. He claims he's actually a very important figure in the Congo at this moment of history. Sometimes he rattles off all these names of people I can never keep straight: CIA Deputy Chief, Congo Station Chief. He has code names for everybody. Big Shot is the Deputy Chief, and the Station Chief he calls Devil One. Oh, it's all a game I'm sure. A man of his age might seem too old to be playing Zorro, but then consider the source.

I asked him, "If you're such an important figure in the Congo, how come all we've seen you do is pay too-cheap prices for people's stuff to sell in the city and come back with our powdered milk and comic books from Leopoldville?"

He says he hasn't been at liberty to discuss his real work, but now he has U.S. protection and he can tell me a thing or two, so long as I keep it under my hat. Well, natch, even if it were true—who would I tell? An innocent teenager in the middle of God's green hell with no telephone, and not on speaking terms with her parents? Although Father hasn't noticed I'm not talking to him, as far as I can tell. Mother has, though. Sometimes she tries to get chummy and ask me a lot of personal questions. She's hoping to find out, Who is the real Rachel Price?

But I won't tell her. I prefer to remain anomalous.

Ruth May

A T NIGHT the lizards run up the walls and upside down over the bed looking down at me. They stick up there with their toes. Mice, too. They can talk to me. They said Tata Undo wants to marry Rachel. She did her hope chest already, so she can. But Tata Undo is a Congolese. Can they marry us? I don't know. But I'd sure like to see Rachel in the white dress; she'll be pretty. Then they said she was going to marry Mr. Axelroot instead, but he is mean. Sometimes I dream it is Father she's marrying and I get mixed up and sad. Because then: where is Mama?

The lizards make a sound like a bird at night. In the dreams that I get to watch I can catch the lizards and they're my pets. They stay right in my hand and don't run off. When I wake up I don't have them anymore and I'm sad. So I don't wake up if I don't have to.

I was in the dark in Mama's room but now I'm out here. It's bright and everybody talks and talks. I can't say what I aim to. I miss my lizards at night, is what I want to say. They won't come out in the bright and it hurts my eyes too. Mama puts the cold wet rag all over and then my eyes feel better, but she doesn't look right. She's all big, and everybody is.

Circus mission. That's what they said. Tata Undo keeps on coming over. He is orange sometimes, his clothes. Black skin and an orange dress. It looks pretty. He told Father Rachel would have to have the circus mission where they cut her so she wouldn't want to run around with people's husbands. I can't hear him when he talks French but Father told Mama about it at night. The circus mission.

He said they do it to all the girls here. Father said, Can't you see how much work we must do? They are leading these female children like lambs to the slaughter. Mama said, Since when did he start to care about protecting young ladies. She said her first job was to take care of her own and if he was any kind of a father he would do the same.

Father said he was doing what he could and at least Mr. Axelroot was a better bargain. Mama had a conniption fit and ripped a sheet in two. She doesn't like either one of them but they still have to come because Tata Undo is the chief of everything, and Mr. Axelroot is a bargain. But everybody keeps on having a conniption fit. Rachel especially.

Mama found the pills I stuck on the wall. They came out of my mouth. I couldn't help it. They tasted too bad and they stick on the wall better after they go in your mouth. Mama got them all off with a knife and put them in a white teacup. I saw where she put it, on the shelf with the Bayer aspirins we ran out of. Rachel said, What are we going to do with those? and Mama said, Take them of course, Ruth May will have to and all the rest of us when we run out. But I don't want to, they make me sick. Rachel said she won't either. She got disgusted and said, Ye gads, like ABC gum, already been chewed. Rachel gets disgusted a right smart lot of the time. Mother said, Fine if you want to get sick like Ruth May go on ahead, make your own bed and then lie in it. So that's what happened to me. I made my own bed and now I'm sick. I thought I was just too hot but she told Rachel I'm sick bad. Mama and Father talk about it sometimes and he says The Good Lord and she says A Doctor. They don't agree with each other and I'm the reason.

I went to the doctor before in Stanleyville two times, when I broke my arm and when it was fixed. My cast got dirty. He cut it off with the biggest scissors that didn't hurt. But now we can't go because they are having big fights and making all the white people go naked in Stanleyville. They killed some. When we went up there the first time I saw those little dirty diamonds in a sack in the back of the airplane. Mr. Axelroot didn't like to catch me spying on his stuff. While we were waiting for Father to come back from the bar-bershop Mr. Axelroot put his hands on me hard. He said, You tell anybody you saw diamonds in those bags your Mama and Daddy both will get sick and die. I didn't know what the diamonds were till he said that. I didn't tell. So I got sick instead of Mama and Daddy both. Mr. Axelroot still lives down at his shack and when he comes up here he looks at me to see if I told. He can see right inside like Jesus. He comes to our house and says he heard what all's going on with Tata Undo wanting to get married to Rachel. All the people around here know about that. Father says white people have to stick together now so we have to be Mr. Axelroot's friend. But I don't want to. When we were waiting in the airplane, he put his hands on me hard.

I broke my arm because I was spying and Mama told me not to. This time I got sick because Baby Jesus can see ever what I do and I wasn't good. I tore up some of Adah's pictures and I lied to Mama four times and I tried to see Nelson naked. And hit Leah on the leg with a stick and saw Mr. Axelroot's diamonds. That is a lot of bad things. If I die I will disappear and I know where I'll come back. I'll be right up there in the tree, same color, same everything. I will look down on you. But you won't see me.

Rachel

SEVENTEEN! I am now one score and seven years old. Or so I thought, until Leah informed me that means *twenty*-seven. If God really aims to punish you, you'll know it when He sends you not one but *two* sisters who are younger than you but already have memorized the entire dictionary. I just thank heavens that only one of them talks.

Not that I actually got a speck of attention on my birthday. Two birthdays now I have had in the Congo, and I thought the first one was the worst there could be. Last year on my birthday Mother at least did cry, and showed me the Angel Dream cake-mix box she brought over all the way from the Bethlehem Piggly Wiggly to help ease the burden of spending my tender teen years in a foreign land. I felt put out because I didn't get any nice presents: no sweater set, no phonograph records—oh, I thought that day was the lowest a girl can go.

Boy oh boy. Never did I dream I'd be spending *another* birthday here, another August 20 in the exact same clothes and underwear as last year, all grown shabby, except for the Bobbie girdle I quit wearing right off the bat, this horrid sticky jungle being no place for Junior Figure Control. And now on top of everything, a birthday passed by with hardly anybody even noticing. "Oh, it's August twentieth today, isn't it?" I asked several times out loud, looking at my watch like there was something I needed to do. Adah, on account of keeping her backwards diary, is the only one that keeps a close track of what day it is. Her and Father, of course, who has his little church calendar for all his important appointments, in case he ever gets any. Leah just ignored me, sitting herself right down at Father's desk to work on her teacher's-pet arithmetic program. Leah thinks she is all high and mighty ever since Anatole asked her to help teach some lessons at the school. Really, what a thing to get all jazzed up about. It is only math, the dullest bore in the entire world, and he only lets her teach the very littlest kids anyway. I wouldn't do it even if Anatole paid me in greenback American dollars. I'd probably get highway hypnosis, watching the snot run down all those little snotroads from their noses to their lips.

So I asked Adah rather loudly, "Say, isn't today's date the twentieth of August?" She nodded that it was, and I looked around me in amazement, for there was my very own family, setting the breakfast table and making lesson plans and what not as if this were simply the next day after yesterday and not even anything as special as Thursdays back home in Bethlehem, which was always the day we had to set out the trash.

Mother did finally remember, as it happened. After breakfast she gave me a pair of her own earrings and a matching bracelet I had admired. It's only cut glass, but a very pretty shade of green that happens to set off my hair and eyes. And since it was about the only jewelry I'd seen in an entire year, it could have been diamonds—I was that depraved. Anyway it was nice to have some small token. She'd wrapped it up in a piece of cloth and written on a card made from Adah's notebook paper: *For my beautiful firstborn child, all grown up.* Sometimes Mother really does try. I gave her a kiss and thanked her. But then she had to go back to giving Ruth May her sponge baths, so that was the whole show. Ruth May's fever shot up to a hundred and five, Adah got stung on the foot by a scorpion spider and had to soak it in cold water, and a mongoose got in the chicken house and ate some eggs, all on the same day: *my birthday!* And all of them just to detract attention away from me. Except, I guess, the mongoose.

Adah

"TATA JESUS IS BÄNGALA!" declares the Reverend every Sunday at the end of his sermon. More and more, mistrusting his interpreters, he tries to speak in Kikongo. He throws back his head and shouts these words to the sky, while his lambs sit scratching themselves in wonder. *Bangala* means something precious and dear. But the way he pronounces it, it means the poisonwood tree. Praise the Lord, hallelujah, my friends! for Jesus will make you itch like nobody's business.

And while Our Father was preaching the gospel of poisonwood, his own daughter Ruth May rose from the dead. Our Father did not particularly notice. Perhaps he is unimpressed because he assumed all along this would happen. His confidence in the Lord is exceptional. *Dog ho! Evol's dog!* The Lord, however, may or may not be aware that our mother assisted this miracle by forcing Ruth May to eat the same pills twice.

Sllip emas. There is no stepping in the same river twice. So say the Greek philosophers, and the crocodiles make sure. Ruth May is not the same Ruth May she was. Yam Htur. None of us is the same: Lehcar, Hael, Hada. Annaelro. Only Nahtan remains essentially himself, the same man however you look at him. The others of us have two sides. We go to bed ourselves and like poor Dr. Jekyll we wake up changed. Our mother, the recent agoraphobe, who kept us pumpkin-shelled indoors through all the months of rain and epidemic and Independence, has now turned on her protector: she eyes our house suspiciously, accuses it of being "cobwebby" and "strangling us with the heat." She speaks of it as a thing with will and motive. Every afternoon she has us put on our coolest dresses and run away from our malignant house. Down the forest path we march, single file, to the stream for a picnic. When we run off and she thinks we cannot see her she sways in the clearing, gently, like a tree blown by wind. Despite the risk of hookworm, she removes her shoes.

And now rejoice, oh, ye faithful, for Ruth May has risen, but she has the naked stare of a zombie and has lost interest in being first or best at anything. Nelson will not go near her. This is his theory: the owl we held as a temporary captive memorized our floor plan so it could find its way back through a window and consume her soul.

My other sisters, in different ways, have become stricken with strange behavior regarding men. Rachel is hysterical and engaged. The engagement is feigned, but that does not keep her from spending hours at a time playing "Mirror Mirror on the Wall" in her new green glass earrings, then throwing tantrums of protest against her upcoming marriage.

And Leah, the tonier twin. Leah has come down with a devout interest in the French and Kikongo languages—specifically, in learning them from Anatole. In the mornings she teaches arithmetic to his younger pupils, and afterward spends many hours at his bright-white shirtsleeve conjugating the self-same reflexive verbs— *l'homme se noie*—which a year ago she declared pointless. Apparently reflexive verbs gain a new importance for certain girls at the age of fifteen. She is also being instructed in the art of bow hunting. Anatole gave her as a gift a small, highly functional bow and a quiver of arrows with red tail feathers—like the "Hope" in Miss Dickinson's poem, and like the quite hopelessly dead Methuselah, our former parrot. Anatole, with his very own knife, slipped these gifts for Leah out of a branch of greenheart wood.

Here is my palindrome poem on the subject: *Eros, eyesore.*

Nelson, however, is cheered. He views Leah's bow and arrows as a positive development in our household after so many other discouraging ones, such as the death, for all practical purposes, of Ruth

May. Nelson has taken it upon himself to supervise Leah's military education. He makes targets of leaves, and pins them to the trunk of the great mango at the edge of our yard. The targets grow smaller each day. They began with a giant elephant-ear leaf, like a big triangular apron flapping in the breeze, which was nearly impossible to miss. One at a time Leah sent her wobbling arrows through the slashed green margin. But she has worked her way steadily down, until she now aims at the round, shiny, thumb-sized leaflet of a guava. Nelson shows her how to stand, close one eye, and whack her arrow trembling into the heart of a leaf. She is a frighteningly good shot.

My hunt-goddess twin and I are now more distant kin than ever, I suppose, except in this one regard: she is beginning to be looked upon in our village as bizarre. At the least, direly unfeminine. If anything, I am now considered the more normal one. I am the *bënduka,* the single word that describes me precisely: someone who is bent sideways and walks slowly. But for my twin who now teaches school and murders tree trunks I have heard various words applied by our neighbors, none with much fondness. The favored word, *bákala,* covers quite a lot of ground, including a hot pepper, a bumpy sort of potato, and the male sexual organ.

Leah does not care. She claims that since Anatole gave her the bow, and since it was Anatole who requisitioned her to teach school, she must not be breaking any social customs. She fails to see that Anatole is breaking rules for her, and this will have consequences. Like an oblivious Hester Prynne she carries her letter, the green capital D of her bow slung over her shoulder. D for Dramatic, or Diana of the Hunt, or Devil Take Your Social Customs. Off with her bow to market she goes and even to church, although on Sundays she must leave the arrows behind. Even our mother, who is not on the best of terms with Jesus just now, still draws the line at marching into His house toting ammunition.

Leah

ANATOLE'S FACE IN PROFILE, with his down-slanted eye and high forehead, looks like a Pharaoh or a god in an Egyptian painting. His eyes are the darkest brown imaginable. Even the whites are not white, but a pale cream color. Sometimes we sit at the table under the trees outside the schoolhouse after the boys are finished with their school day. I study my French and try not to bother him too much while he prepares the next day's lessons. Anatole's eyes rarely stray from his books, and I'll admit I find myself thinking of excuses to interrupt his concentration. There are too many things I want to know. I want to know why he's letting me teach in the school now, for instance. Is it because of Independence, or because of me? I want to ask him if all the stories we're hearing are true: Matadi, Thysville, Stanleyville. A can trader passing through Kilanga on his way to Kikwit gave us terrifying reports of the slaughter in Stanleyville. He said Congolese boys wearing crowns of leaves around their heads were invulnerable to Belgian bullets, which passed through them and lodged in the walls behind them. He said he'd seen this with his own eyes. Anatole was standing right there but seemed to ignore the tales. Instead, he carefully examined and then purchased a pair of spectacles from the can trader. The spectacles have good lenses that magnify things: when I try them on, even French words look large and easy to read. They make Anatole look more intelligent, though somewhat less Egyptian.

Most of all I want to ask Anatole this one unaskable question: Does he hate me for being white?

Instead I asked, "Why do Nkondo and Gabriel hate me?"

Anatole gave me a surprised look over the horn rims and genuine lenses of his new glasses. "Nkondo and Gabriel, more than the others?" he said, slowly bringing his focus onto the present conversation, and me. "How can you tell?"

I blew air out through my lips like an exasperated horse. "Nkondo and Gabriel more than the others because they play their chairs like drums and drown me out when I try to explain long division."

"They are naughty boys, then."

Anatole and I both knew this was not exactly the case. Drumming on chairs might have been of no special consequence in a Bethlehem school where little boys acted up whenever they took a mind. But these boys' families were scraping together extra food or cash for their sons to go to school, and no one ever forgot it. Going to school was a big decision. Anatole's students were as earnest as the grave. Only when I tried to teach math, while Anatole was working with the older students, did they raise pandemonium.

"Okay, you're right. They *all* hate me," I whined. "I guess I'm not a good teacher."

"You are a fine teacher. That isn't the problem."

"What *is* the problem?"

"Understand, first, you are a girl. These boys are not accustomed to obeying their own grandmothers. If long division is really so important to a young man's success in the world, how could a pretty girl know about it? This is what they are thinking. And understand, second, you are white."

What did he mean, *pretty girl*? "White," I repeated. "Then they don't think white people know about long division, either?"

"Secretly, most of them believe white people know how to turn the sun on and off and make the river flow backward. But officially, no. What they hear from their fathers these days is that now Independence is here and white people should not be in Congo telling us what to do."

"They also think America and Belgium should give them a lot of money, I happen to know. Enough for everybody to have a radio or a car or something. Nelson told me that."

"Yes, that is number three. They think you represent a greedy nation."

I closed the book on French verbs for the day. "Anatole, that doesn't make a bit of sense. They don't want us to be friends, and they don't respect us, and in Leopoldville they're ransacking white people's houses. *But* they want America to give them money."

"Which part does not make sense to you?"

"All of it."

"Béene, think," he said patiently, as if I were one of his school-boys stumped on an easy problem. "When one of the fishermen, let's say Tata Boanda, has good luck on the river and comes home with his boat loaded with fish, what does he do?"

"That doesn't happen very often."

"No, but you have seen it happen. What does he do?"

"He sings at the top of his lungs and everybody comes and he gives it all away."

"Even to his enemies?"

"I guess. Yeah. I know Tata Boanda doesn't like Tata Zinsana very much, and he gives Tata Zinsana's wives the most."

"All right. To me that makes sense. When someone has much more than he can use, it's very reasonable to expect he will not keep it all himself."

"But Tata Boanda *has* to give it away, because fish won't keep. If you don't get rid of it, it's just going to rot and stink to high heaven."

Anatole smiled and pointed his finger at my nose. "That is just how a Congolese person thinks about money."

"But if you keep on giving away every bit of extra you have, you're never going to be rich."

"That is probably true."

"And *everybody* wants to be rich."

"Is that so?"

"Sure. Nelson wants to save up for a wife. You probably do, too." For some reason I couldn't look at him when I said that. "Tata Ndu is so rich he has *six* wives, and everybody envies him."

"Tata Ndu has a very hard job. He needs a lot of wives. But don't be so sure everyone envies him. I myself do not want his job." Anatole laughed. "*Or* his wives."

"But don't you want lots of money?"

"Béene, I spent many years working for the Belgians in the rubber plantation at Coquilhatville, and I saw rich men there. They were always unhappy and had very few children."

"They probably would have been even more unhappy if they'd been poor," I argued.

He laughed. "You might be right. Nevertheless, I did not learn to envy the rich man."

"But you need *some* money," I persisted. I do realize Jesus lived the life of poverty, but that was another place and time. A harsh desert culture, as Brother Fowles had said. "You need enough to pay for food and doctors and all."

"All right then, *some* money," he agreed. "One automobile and a radio for every village. Your country could give us that much, *e-é*?"

"Probably. I don't think it would really make a dent. Back in Georgia everybody we knew had an automobile."

"*Á bu*, don't tell stories. That is not possible."

"Well, not everybody. I don't mean babies and children. But every single family."

"Not possible."

"Yes, it is! Some families even have two!"

"What is the purpose of so many automobiles at the same time?"

"Well, because everybody has someplace to go every day. To work or to the store or something."

"And why is nobody walking?"

"It's not like here, Anatole. Everything's farther apart. People live in big towns and cities. Bigger cities than Leopoldville, even."

"Béene, you are lying to me. If everyone lived in a city they could never grow enough food."

"Oh, they do that out in the country. In big, big fields. Peanuts and soybeans and corn, all that. The farmers grow it, then they put it on big trucks and take it all to the city, where people buy it from the store."

"From the market."

"No, it isn't a bit like the market. It's a great big house kind of thing, with bright lights and all these shelves inside. It's open every day, and just one person sells all the different things."

"One farmer has so many things?"

"No, not a farmer. A storekeeper buys it all from the farmers, and sells it to the city people."

"And so you don't even know whose fields this food came from? That sounds terrible. It could be poisoned!"

"It's not bad, really. It works out."

"How can there be enough food, Béene? If everyone lives in a city?"

"There just is. Things are different from here."

"What is so different?"

"Everything," I said, intending to go on, but my tongue only licked the backs of my teeth, tasting the word *everything*. I stared at the edge of the clearing behind us, where the jungle closed us out with its great green wall of trees, bird calls, animals breathing, all as permanent as a heartbeat we heard in our sleep. Surrounding us was a thick, wet, living stand of trees and tall grasses stretching all the way across Congo. And we were nothing but little mice squirming through it in our dark little pathways. In Congo, it seems the land owns the people. How could I explain to Anatole about soybean fields where men sat in huge tractors like kings on thrones, taming the soil from one horizon to the other? It seemed like a memory trick or a bluegreen dream: impossible.

"At home," I said, "we don't have the jungle."

"Then what is it you have?"

"Big fields, like a manioc garden as wide and long as the Kwilu. There used to be trees, I guess, but people cut them down."

"And they did not grow back?"

"Our trees aren't so vivacious as yours are. It's taken Father and me the longest time just to figure out how things grow here. Remember when we first came and cleared out a patch for our garden? Now you can't even see where it was. Everything grew like

Topsy, and then died. The dirt turned into dead, red slop like rotten meat. Then vines grew all over it. We thought we were going to teach people here how to have crops like we have back home."

He laughed. "Manioc fields as long and wide as the Kwilu."

"You don't believe me, but it's true! You can't picture it because here, I guess, if you cut down enough jungle to plant fields that big, the rain would just turn it into a river of mud."

"And then the drought would bake it."

"Yes! And if you ever did get any crops, the roads would be washed out so you'd never get your stuff into town anyway."

He clucked his tongue. "You must find the Congo a very unco-operative place."

"You just can't imagine how different it is from what we're used to. At home we have cities and cars and things because nature is organized a whole different way."

He listened with his head cocked to the side. "And still your father came here determined to plant his American garden in the Congo."

"My father thinks the Congo is just lagging behind and he can help bring it up to snuff. Which is crazy. It's like he's trying to put rubber tires on a horse."

Anatole raised his eyebrows. I don't suppose he's ever seen a horse. They can't live in the Congo because of tsetse flies. I tried to think of some other work animal for my parable, but the Congo has none. Not even cows. The point I was trying to make was so true there was not even a good way to say it.

"On a goat," I said finally. "Wheels on a goat. Or on a chicken, or a wife. My father's idea of what will make things work better doesn't fit anything here."

"*Áyi*, Béene. That poor goat of your father's is a very unhappy animal."

And his wife! I thought. But I couldn't help picturing a goat with big tires stuck in the mud, and it made me giggle. Then I felt stupid. I could never tell if Anatole respected me or just thought I was an amusing child.

"I oughtn't to laugh at my father," I said.

"No," he said, touching his lips and rolling his eyes upward.

"I shouldn't! It's a sin." Sin, sin, I felt drenched and sick of it. "I used to pray to God to make me just like him. Smart and righteous and adequate to His will," I confessed. "Now I don't even know what to wish for. I wish I were more like everybody else."

He leaned forward and looked into my eyes. His finger moved from his lips toward my face and hovered, waiting for a place to plant its blessing. "Béene, if you were more like everybody else, you would not be so *béene-béene.*"

"I wish you'd tell me what that means, *béene-béene.* Don't I have a right to know my own name?"

His hand dropped to the table. "I will tell you someday."

If I never learned my French conjugations from Anatole, at least I would try to learn patience.

"Can I ask you something else?"

He considered this request, his left hand still holding his place in his book. "Yes."

"Why do you translate the sermons for my father? I know what you think of our mission here."

"Do you?"

"Well, I think I do. You came to dinner that time and explained how Tata Ndu doesn't like so many people following Christian ways, instead of the old ways. I guess you probably think that, too, that the old ways were better. You don't care for the way the Belgians did the elections, and I don't think you're even so sure about girls teaching school."

"Béene, the Belgians did not come to me and ask, Anatole Ngemba, how shall we make the election? They merely said, 'Kilanga, here are your votes. You may cast them in this calabash bowl or that calabash bowl, or toss them all in the river.' My job was to explain that choice."

"Well, but still. I don't think you're very keen on what my father aims to accomplish here."

"I don't entirely know what he aims to accomplish here. Do you?"

"Tell the stories of Jesus, and God's love. Bring them all to the Lord."

"And if no one translated his sermons, how would he tell those stories?"

"That's a good question. I guess he'd keep trying in French and Kikongo, but he gets those mixed up pretty bad. People probably never would get it straight what he was doing here exactly."

"I think you are right. They might like your father more, if they couldn't understand him, or they might like him less. It's hard to say. But if they understand his words, they can make up their own minds."

I looked long and hard at Anatole. "You respect my father, then."

"What I respect is what I have seen. Nothing can stay the same, when somebody new walks into your house bringing gifts. Let's say he has brought you a cooking pot. You already had a cooking pot you liked well enough, but maybe this new one is bigger. You'll be very pleased, and gloat about it by giving the old one to your sister. Or maybe the new pot has a hole in the bottom. In that case you will thank your visitor very much, and when he is gone you'll put it in the yard for feeding fish scales to the chickens."

"So you're just being polite. You don't believe in Jesus Christ at all."

He clicked his tongue. "What I believe in is not so important. I am a teacher. Do I believe in the multiplication tables? Do I believe in *la langue française*, with its extra letters hanging onto every word like lazy children? No matter. People need to know what they are choosing. I've watched many white men come into our house, always bringing things we never saw before. Maybe scissors or medicine or a motor for a boat. Maybe books. Maybe a plan for digging up diamonds or growing rubber. Maybe stories about Jesus. Some of these things seem very handy, and some turn out to be not so handy. It is important to distinguish."

"And if you didn't translate the Bible stories, then people might sign up to be Christian for the wrong reasons. They'd figure our God gave us scissors and malaria pills so He's the way to go."

He smiled at me sideways. "This word *béene-béene*, you want to know what it means, then?"

"Yes!"

"It means, as true as the truth can be."

I felt a tingling blush in my cheeks, and the embarrassment made me blush more. I tried to think of something to say, but couldn't. My eyes returned to French sentences I found I couldn't translate.

"Anatole," I said finally, "if you could have anything in the world, what would you want?"

Without hesitation he said, "To see a map of the whole world at once."

"Really? You never have?"

"Not all of it at once. I can't work out whether it's a triangle, a circle, or a square."

"It's round," I said, astonished. How could he not know? He'd gone to plantation schools and served in the houses of men who had shelves full of books. He spoke better English than Rachel. Yet he didn't know the true shape of the world. "Not a circle, but like this," I said, cupping my hands. "Round like a ball. Really you've never seen a globe?"

"I heard about a globe. A map on a ball. I wasn't sure I under-stood it correctly because I couldn't see how it would fit on a ball. Have you seen one?"

"Anatole, I *have* one. In America lots of people have them."

He laughed. "For what? To help them decide where to drive the automobile?"

"I'm not joking. They're in schoolrooms and everywhere. I've spent so much time staring at globes I could probably *make* one."

He gave me a doubting look.

"I could. I mean it. You bring me a nice clean calabash and I'll make you a globe of your own."

"I would like that very much," he said, speaking to me now as a grown-up friend, not a child. For the first time ever, I felt certain of it.

"You know what, I shouldn't be teaching math. I should teach geography. I could tell your boys about the oceans and cities and all the wonders of the world!"

He smiled sadly. "Béene, they would not believe you."

Rachel

THE DAY AFTER MY BIRTHDAY, Axelroot came over and we went for a walk. I more or less knew to expect him. His routine was to fly out to his mystery destination on Thursdays, come back Mondays, and come to our house on Tuesdays. So I'd put on my tulip-tailored poison-green suit, which has now officially faded to poison drab and lost two of its buttons. For the first half of last year I prayed for a full-length mirror, and the second half I praised the Lord we didn't have one. Still, who cares if my suit wasn't perfect. It wasn't a date, just a make-believe date for appearances. I planned to walk with him around the village, and not a speck farther. I swore to Mother I would not set foot into the forest with him or anywhere out of sight. She says she doesn't trust him as far as she could throw him, and believe you me from the look in her eye I think she could throw him pretty far. But he is polite and has cleaned up his style. Standing in the doorway waiting for me in his regulation Sanforized wash-and-wear khakis and pilot sunglasses, why, he very nearly almost looked handsome. If you could ignore the telltale signs that he is a certified creep.

So we strolled out into the unbearable heat of August twenty-first, Nineteen-thousand-and-sixty. Bugs buzzed so loud it hurt your ears, and tiny red birds perched on the ends of long grass stalks beside the road, all swaying this way and that. Outside our village the elephant grass grows so tall it meets above the road to make a shady tunnel. Sometimes you can start thinking the Congo is almost pretty. *Almost*. And then, don't look now but a four-inch-long cockroach or something will scurry across the path in front of you. That is exactly what happened next, and Axelroot kind of jumped on it and smashed it. I couldn't bear to look. The sound was bad enough, honestly. A cross between crackle and squish. But I suppose it was a civilrous gesture on his part.

"Well, I do have to say, it's nice to be protected for a change," I said. "Around my house if a giant cockroach turns up someone will either tame it for a pet or cook it for dinner."

"You have an unusual family."

"*And how*!" I said. "That is about the politest way you could put it."

"I've been meaning to ask," he said. "What happened to your sister?"

"Which one? As far as I can tell they all three got dropped on their heads when they were babies."

He laughed. "The one that limps," he said. "Adah."

"Oh, her. Hemiplegia. Half her brain got wrecked some way before she was born so the other half had to take over, and it makes her do certain things backwards." I am used to having to give the scientific explanation for Adah.

"I see," he said. "Are you aware that she spies on me?"

"She spies on everybody. Don't take it personally. Staring at somebody without making a peep is her idea of a conversation."

We strolled past Mama Mwanza's and a bunch of other houses where mostly old men were sitting on buckets without a single tooth in their heads. We were also graced by the presence of little children running around totally naked except for a string of beads around their bellies. I ask you, why bother? They all ran out to the road to see how close they could get to us before they had to scream and run away. That is the favorite game. The women were all down at the manioc fields because it was still the end of the morning.

Axelroot took out a pack of Lucky Strikes from his shirt pocket and shook it sideways toward me. I laughed and started to remind him that I'm not old enough, but then realized, my gosh, I was *seventeen years old*. I could smoke if I wanted to—why ever not? Even some Baptists smoke on appropriate occasions. I took one.

"Thanks. You know I turned seventeen yesterday," I told him, resting the cigarette lightly on my lips and pausing in the shade of a palm tree so he could light it for me.

"Congratulations," he said, muffled through the cigarette he put in his own mouth. "I'd have taken you for older."

That made me tingle, but not half as much as what happened next. Right there in the middle of the road he took the cigarette out of my mouth and put it in his, then struck a match on his thumbnail and lit the two of them together, exactly like Humphrey Bogart. Then, ever so gently, he put the lit cigarette back in my lips. It seemed almost like we had kissed. Chills ran down my back, but I couldn't tell for sure if it was thrill chills or the creeps. Sometimes it is very hard to know the difference. I tried out holding the filter tip between my two fingers like the girls in magazine ads. So far so good with smoking, I thought. Then I drew in a breath, puckered my lips and puffed it out, and almost instantly I felt dizzy. I coughed a time or two, and Axelroot laughed.

"I haven't smoked for a while," I said. "*You* know. It's hard for us to get things now."

"I can get you all the American cigarettes you want. Just say the word."

"Well, I wouldn't actually say anything about it to my parents. They're not big smokers." But it dawned on me to wonder, How in the world would he get American cigarettes in a country where you can't even buy toilet paper? "You know a lot of men in high places, don't you?"

He laughed. "Princess, you don't know the half of it."

"I'm sure I don't," I said.

A bunch of the younger men were up on top of the church-schoolhouse patching the roof with palm leaves. Father must have organized this barnstorming party, I thought, and then I panicked: Oh Lordy! Here I was right out in broad daylight refreshing my taste with a Lucky Strike. But a quick glance around told me Father was nowhere to be seen, thank goodness. Just a bunch of men singing and blabbing in the Congo language and fixing a roof, that's all it was.

Why fix the roof now? That was a good question. Last year

around the time of my birthday it was pouring down rain every single afternoon, come heck or high river, but this summer, not a drop yet. Just the bugs screeching in the crackly dry grass and the air getting heavier and heavier on these muggy waiting-for-it days. The mugginess just made everybody itch for something, I think.

Just then a large group of women passed us coming back from their manioc field. Huge bundles of giant brown roots tied together with rope were balanced on their heads. The women moved slowly and gracefully, putting one foot ahead of the other, and with their thin bodies all draped in colorful *pagnes* and their heads held so straight and high—honestly, though it is strange to say, they looked like fashion models. Maybe it has just been too long since I've seen a fashion magazine. But some of them here I guess are very pretty in their way. Axelroot seemed to think so. He gave them a little salute to the tip of his hat, which he probably forgot he wasn't wearing. "*Mbote a-akento akwa Kilanga. Bënzika kooko.*"

Every single one of them looked away from us, toward the ground. It was very strange.

"What in the world did you say to them?" I asked after they'd passed by.

"Hey there, ladies of Kilanga. Why don't you cut me some slack for a change. That's more or less what I said."

"Well, sir, they sure didn't, did they?"

He laughed. "They just don't want any trouble with jealous husbands."

This is what I mean about Axelroot: you can't for one minute let yourself forget he is a creep. Right there in front of me, his supposed fiancée, flirting with the entire female contribution of Kilanga. And the bit about jealous husbands, I'm *sure*. As far as we could see nobody in Kilanga liked Axelroot one iota—man or woman. Mother and Father had commented on this. The women seemed to despise him especially. Whenever he tried to make deals with them to fly their manioc and bananas to Stanleyville, I had personally seen them spit on his shoes.

"No great loss, believe me," he said. "I prefer *a-akento akwa* Elisabethville."

"And what is so special about women from Elisabethville?"

He tipped back his head, smiled, and blew smoke into the muggy sky. Today it *really* looked like it might rain at last, and felt like it too. The air felt like somebody's hot breath all over your body, even under your clothes.

"Experience," he said.

Well, I knew I had better change the train of *this* conversation. I took a nonchalant puff on my cigarette without breathing in very much. I still felt dizzy. "Where *is* Elisabethville, anyway?"

"Down south, Katanga Province. The new nation of Katanga, I should say. Did you know Katanga has seceded from the Congo?"

I sighed, feeling light-headed. "I'm just happy to know somebody has succeeded in something. Is that where you go on your trips?"

"Sometimes," he said. "From now on, more than sometimes."

"Oh, really. You have new orders from the commando, I suppose."

"You have no idea," he said again. I was getting a little tired of hearing how I had no idea. Honestly, did he think I was a child?

"I'm sure I don't," I said. We'd gotten to the edge of the village, past the chief's house, where we were supposed to make a point of Tata Ndu seeing us together, which we both forgot about. Now we were out where there were no more huts and the tall elephant grass started to get tangled up with the edge of the jungle. I'd sworn I wouldn't go past the end of the village, but it's a woman's provocative to change her mind. Axelroot just kept walking, and suddenly I didn't care what happened next. I kept walking too. Maybe it was the cigarettes: I felt very rash. I would get him to fly us out of here by hook or by crook, is what I was thinking deep in my heart. It was cooler in the forest anyway, and very quiet. When you listened there were only bird sounds with silence in between, and those two sounds put together somehow seemed even quieter than no sound at all. It was very shadowy and nearly dark, even though it was the middle of the day. Axelroot stopped and put out his cigarette with his boot. He took mine from me, cupped my chin in his hand, and started to kiss me. Oh, lordy! My first kiss, and I didn't even get a chance to get ready for it. I didn't and I did want him to do it.

Mostly I did. He tasted like tobacco and salt and the whole experience was very wet. Finally I pushed him away.

"That's enough of *that*," I said. "If we do anything, we should do it where people will see us, you know."

"Well, well." He was smiling, and ran the back of his hand along the side of my face. "I'd expect more modesty from a preacher's daughter."

"I'll show you preacher's daughter. Go to hell, Axelroot!" I turned around and started walking fast back toward the village. He caught up to me and put his arm on my shoulder to slow me back down to a stroll.

"Mustn't let Tata Ndu see us having a lovers' quarrel," he said, leaning down into my face. I tossed my head so my hair flew right in his nosy mug. We were still in the forest anyways, nowhere near Tata Ndu's house or anybody else's.

"Come on," he coaxed. "Give me a smile. One pretty smile and I'll tell you the biggest damn secret in Africa."

"Oh, I'm *sure*," I said. But I was curious. I glanced at him. "So what's the secret? Does my family get to go home?"

He laughed. "You still think you're the epicenter of a continent, don't you, Princess?"

"Don't be ridiculous," I said. I would have to ask Leah if an *episender* sent out good things or bad. If a man you are supposedly engaged to calls you one, you ought to know.

He'd slowed me down till we were walking at an absolute snail's pace. It made me nervous. But he was going to tell me his secret if I just waited. I could tell he was itching to, so I didn't ask. I know a thing or two about men. Finally, here it came. "Somebody's going to die," he announced.

"Well, big surprise," I said. "Somebody dies around here about every ten and a half seconds." But of course I wondered: *Who*? I felt a little scared but still didn't ask. We kept walking, step by step. I had to. He still had his arm around me.

"Somebody that matters," he said.

"Everybody matters," I informed him. "In the eyes of our Lord

Jesus Christ they do. Even the sparrows that fall out of their little nest and what not."

He positively snorted at that. "Princess, you have much to learn. Alive, nobody matters much in the long run. But dead, some men matter more than others."

I was sick of his guessing game. "All right then, *who*?"

He put his mouth so close to my ear I could feel his lips on my hair. He whispered, "*Lumumba.*"

"Patrice Lumumba, the *President*?" I asked out loud, startled. "Or whatever he is? The one they elected?"

"As good as dead," he said in a quiet, so-what voice that chilled my blood.

"Do you mean to tell me he's sick or something?"

"I mean his number is up. He's going to get it."

"And how would you happen to know that?"

"I would happen to know that," he said, mocking me, "because I'm in a position to know. Take my word for it, sister. Yesterday Big Shot sent a cable to Devil One with orders to replace the new Congolese government by force. I intercepted the news in code on my radio. My own orders will be coming before the end of the week, I guarantee you."

Now *that* was so much bunk I am sure, because nobody in our village has a radio. But I let him go on talking in his little riddles if that was what buttered his toast. He said Devil One was supposed to get his so-called operatives to convince the army men to go against Lumumba. Supposedly this Devil One person was going to get one million dollars from the United States to pay soldiers to do that, go against the very person they all just elected. A million dollars! When we couldn't even get fifty measly greenbacks a month for our bread and board. That was a likely story. I almost felt sorry for Axelroot, wanting so bad to impress me into kissing him again that he'd make up ridiculous stories. I may be a preacher's daughter, but I know a thing or two. And one of them is, when men want to kiss you they act like they are just on the brink of doing something that's going to change the whole wide world.

Adah

*PRESENTIMENT—is that long Shadow—on the Lawn—
  Indicative that Suns go down—
The Notice to the startled Grass
That Darkness—is about to pass—*

Pity the poor dumb startled grass, I do. *Ssap ot tuoba.* I am fond of Miss Emily Dickinson: *No snikcidy lime*, a contrary name with a delicious sourgreen taste. Reading her secrets and polite small cruelties of her heart, I believe she *enjoyed* taking the dumb grass by surprise, in her poem. Cumbered in her body, dressed in black, hunched over her secret notebook with window blinds shut against the happy careless people outside, she makes small scratching sounds with her pen, covering with nightfall all creatures that really should know what to expect by now, but don't. She liked herself best in darkness, as do I.

In darkness when all cats are equally black, I move as gracefully as anyone. *Bënduka* is the bent-sideways girl who walks slowly, but *bënduka* is also the name of a fast-flying bird, the swallow with curved wings who darts crookedly quick through trees near the river. This bird I can follow. I am the smooth, elegant black cat who slips from the house as a liquid shadow after dark. Night is the time for seeing without being seen. With my own narrow shadow for a boat I navigate the streams of moonlight that run between shadow islands in the date-palm grove. Bats pierce the night with bell voices like knives. *Bats stab!* And owls call out to the *bikinda*, spirits of the dead. The owls, only hungry like everyone else, looking for souls to eat.

In the long perishing of children from *kakakaka* I saw the air change color: it was blue with *biläla*, the wailing for the dead. It came inside our house, where our mother stopped up her ears and her mouth. *Bí la ye bandu! Bí la ye bandu!* Why why why, they sang, the mothers who staggered down our road behind small tightly wrapped corpses, mothers crazy-walking on their knees, with mouths open wide like a hole ripped in mosquito netting. That mouth hole! Jagged torn place in their spirits that lets the small flying agonies pass in and out. Mothers with eyes squeezed shut, dark cheek muscles tied in knots, heads thrashing from side to side as they passed. All this we saw from our windows. Two times I saw more. The Reverend forbade us to observe any ritual over which he was not asked to preside, but twice, at night, I slipped out to spy on the funerals. Inside a grove of trees the mothers threw themselves on mounds of dirt that covered their children. Crawled on their hands and knees, tried to eat the dirt from the graves. Other women had to pull them away. The owls croon and croon, and the air must be thick with the spirits of children dead.

Months have passed since then, and the Reverend has spoken with every mother who lost children. Some are pregnant again. He reports to his family after a long day's work: these women don't wish to speak of the dead. They will not say their children's names. He has tried to explain how baptism—the *batiza*—would have changed everything. But the mothers tell him no, no, they had already tied the *nkisi* around the child's neck or wrist, a fetish from the Nganga Kuvudundu to ward off evil. They were good mothers and did not neglect this protection, they tell the Reverend. Someone else just had a stronger evil. Our Father tries to make them understand the *batiza* is no fetish but a contract with Jesus Christ. If baptized, the children would be in heaven now.

And the mothers look at him slant-eyed. If my daughter were in *heaven* could she still watch the baby while I work in my manioc? Could she carry water for me? Would a son in *heaven* have wives to take care of me when I am old?

Our Father takes their ironical and self-interested tone to indicate a lack of genuine grief. His scientific conclusion: the Congolese do not become attached to their children as we Americans do. Oh, a man of the world is Our Father. He is writing a learned article on this subject for the Baptist scholars back home.

Outside the house of Toorlexa Nebee I peer through the window, reep I, yps a ma I, in darkness one small dark left eye at the glass. Banana leaves cover the dirty glass like papery window blinds leaving long narrow triangles for my eye. Toorlexa Nebee caught me near his latrine one afternoon, *loitering* he said, as if that stinking place were a coveted shelter and myself a supplicant to his excrement, and now he believes he has frightened me off for good. For good and evil. Now I go only at night when all is plainer: plain-lit shapes inside, his face and radio ringed with bright devil halos in kerosene-lantern light. The radio a live mass of wire oozing from his trunk, a seething congregation of snakes. He speaks through the snakes and he speaks unutterable things. Names in code. Some I understand: Eugor, I-W, W-I Rogue. A form of name that belongs to some form of a man. Between two leaves I finally saw W. I. Rogue. He came in the airplane at dusk and stayed until morning, hidden in the house of Toorlexa. The two men drank whiskey from bottles and filled the room with a stratified lake of cigarette smoke in the flame-white light of night. They pronounced a litany of names to the mass of snakes. Other names they spoke aloud to each other.

Always they say: as good as dead. Patrice Lumumba. The voice on the radio said it many times. But the name the two men spoke out loud to each other was The President. Not Lumumba. President: Eisenhower, We Like Ike. Eki Ekil Ew. The King of America wants a tall, thin man in the Congo to be dead. Too many pebbles cast for the bottle. The bottle must be broken.

My knees plunged, a rush of hot blood made me fall. A faintness of the body is my familiar, but not the sudden, evil faint of a body infected by horrible surprise. By this secret: the smiling bald man with the grandfather face has another face. It can speak through snakes and order that a president far away, after all those pebbles were carried upriver in precious canoes that did not tip over, this President Lumumba shall be killed.

I crept to my bed and wrote what I had seen and heard, then wrote the ending backward. Stared at the words in my notebook, my captive poem: *Redrum sekil oh weki ekil ew.*

By morning it had lost the power to shock. Really, in daylight, where is the surprise of this? How is it different from Grandfather God sending the African children to hell for being born too far from a Baptist Church? I should like to stand up in Sunday school now and ask: May Africa talk back? Might those pagan babies send *us* to hell for living too far from a jungle? Because we have not tasted the sacrament of palm nuts? Or. Might the tall, thin man rise up and declare: We don't like Ike. So sorry, but Ike should perhaps be killed now with a poisoned arrow. Oh, the magazines would have something to say about that all right. What sort of man would wish to murder the president of another land? None but a barbarian. A man with a bone in his hair.

I want to see no more but go back anyway, called back one-track jet-black Ada, damn mad Ada. Ada who swears to wear black and scratch out dreadful poems. Ha! I want to make the shadow pass over all the clean, startled faces, all those who believe in president grandfathers. Starting with Leah.

Called back among the banana leaves that do not speak in the silent night, I listen. Joe from Paris coming, the radio says. Joe from Paris has made a poison that will seem to be a Congolese disease, a mere African death for Lumumba. W. I. Rogue says they will put it in his toothpaste. Toorlexa laughs and laughs, for here they do not use toothbrushes. They chew the *muteete* grass to clean their teeth. Toorlexa grows angry then. He has lived here ten years and knows more, he says. He should be running the show, he says. And I wonder, what is the show?

Through triangles between quiet banana leaves I saw flame-haloed faces laugh at the promise of death everlasting. Presentiment that long shadow passes over, and we are the startled grass.

Leah

T HIS AWFUL NIGHT is the worst we've ever known: the *nsongonya*.
They came on us like a nightmare. Nelson bang-bang-banging
on the back door got tangled up with my sleep, so that, even after I was
awake, the next hours had the unsteady presence of a dream. Before I
even knew where I was, I found myself pulled along by somebody's
hand in the dark and a horrible fiery sting sloshing up my calves. We
were wading through very hot water, I thought, but it couldn't be
water, so I tried to ask the name of the burning liquid that had flooded
our house—no, for we were already outside—that had flooded the
whole world?

"Nsongonya," they kept shouting, "*Les fourmis! Un corps d'armée!*"

Ants. We were walking on, surrounded, enclosed, enveloped,
being eaten by *ants*. Every surface was covered and boiling, and the
path like black flowing lava in the moonlight. Dark, bulbous tree
trunks seethed and bulged. The grass had become a field of dark
daggers standing upright, churning and crumpling in on themselves. We walked on ants and ran on them, releasing their vinegary
smell to the weird, quiet night. Hardly anyone spoke. We just ran as
fast as we could alongside our neighbors. Adults carried babies and
goats; children carried pots of food and dogs and younger brothers
and sisters, the whole village of Kilanga. I thought of Mama
Mwanza: would her sluggish sons carry her? Crowded together we
moved down the road like a rushing stream, ran till we reached the
river, and there we stopped. All of us shifting from foot to foot, slapping, some people moaning in pain but only the babies shrieking

and wailing out loud. Strong men sloshed in slow motion through waist-deep water, dragging their boats, while the rest of us waited our turn to get in someone's canoe.

"Béene, where is your family?"

I jumped. The person beside me was Anatole.

"I don't know. I don't really know where anybody is, I just ran." I was still waking up and it struck me now with force that I should have been looking out for my family. I'd thought to worry about Mama Mwanza but not my own crippled twin. A moan rose out of me: "Oh, God!"

"What is it?"

"I don't know where they are. Oh, dear God. Adah will get eaten alive. Adah and Ruth May."

His hand touched mine in the dark. "I'll find them. Stay here until I come back for you."

He spoke softly to someone next to me, then disappeared. It seemed impossible to stand still where the ground was black with ants, but there was nowhere else to go. *How could I leave Adah behind again?* Once in the womb, once to the lion, and now like Simon Peter I had denied her for the third time. I looked for her, or Mother or anyone, but only saw other mothers running into the water with small, sobbing children, trying to splash and rub their arms and legs and faces clean of ants. A few old people had waded out neck-deep. Far out in the river I could see the half-white, half-black head of balding old Mama Lalaba, who must have decided crocodiles were preferable to death by *nsongonya*. The rest of us waited in the shallows, where the water's slick shine was veiled with a dark lace of floating ants. *Father forgive me according unto the multitude of thy mercies. I have done everything so wrong, and now there will be no escape for any of us.* An enormous moon trembled on the dark face of the Kwilu River. I stared hard at the ballooning pink reflection, believing this might be the last thing I would look upon before my eyes were chewed out of my skull. Though I didn't deserve it, I wanted to rise to heaven remembering something of beauty from the Congo.

Rachel

I THOUGHT I HAD DIED and gone to hell. But it's worse than that—I'm *alive* in hell.

While everybody was running from the house, I cast around in a frenzy trying to think what to save. It was so dark I could hardly see, but I had a very clear presence of mind. I only had time to save one precious thing. Something from home. Not my clothes, there wasn't time, and not the Bible—it didn't seem worth saving at that moment, so help me God. It had to be my mirror. Mother was screaming us out the door with the very force of her lungs, but I turned around and shoved straight past her and went back, knowing what I had to do. I grabbed my mirror. Simply broke the frame Nelson had made for it and tore it right down from the wall. Then I ran as fast as my legs would carry me.

Out in the road it was a melee of shoving, strangers touching and shoving at me. The night of ten thousand smells. The bugs were all over me, eating my skin, starting at my ankles and crawling up under my pajamas till they would end up only God knows where. Father was somewhere nearby, because I could hear him yelling about Moses and the Egyptians and the river running with blood and what not. I clasped my mirror to my chest so it wouldn't get lost or broken.

We were running for the river. At first I didn't know why or where, but it didn't matter. You couldn't go anywhere else because the crowd just forced you along. It caused me to recall something I'd read once: if ever you're in a crowded theater and there's a fire, you should stick out your elbows and raise up your feet. *How to Sur-*

vive 101 Calamities was the name of the book, which covered what to do in any dire situation—falling elevators, train wrecks, theater fires exetera. And thank goodness I'd read it because now I was in a jam and knew just what to do! I stuck my elbows very hard into the ribs of the people who were crushing in around me, and kind of wedged myself in. Then I just more or less picked up my feet and it worked like a charm. Instead of getting trampled I simply floated like a stick in a river, carried along on everyone else's power.

But as soon as we reached the river my world came crashing down. The rush came to a standstill, yet the ants were still swarming everywhere. The minute I stood up on the riverbank I got covered with them again, positively crawling. I couldn't bear it another second and wished I would die. They were in my hair. Never in my innocent childhood did I prepare for being in the Congo one dark night with ants tearing at my scalp. I might as well be cooked in a cannibal pot. My life has come to this.

It took me a moment to realize people were climbing into boats and escaping! I screamed to be put in a boat, but they all ignored me. No matter how hard I screamed. Father was over yonder trying to get people to pray for salvation, and no one listening to him either. Then I spotted Mama Mwanza being carried on her husband's back toward the boats. They went right past me! She did deserve help, poor thing, but I personally have a delicate constitution.

I waded out after her and tried to get into their family's boat. All the Mwanza children were still clambering in, and since I am their neighbor I thought surely they would want me with them, but I was suddenly thrown back by someone's arm across my face. Slam bang, thank you very much! I was thrown right into the mud. Before I even realized what had happened, my precious mirror had slipped from my hand and cracked against the side of the boat. I scooped it up quickly from the river's edge, but as I stood up the pieces slid apart and fell like knives into the mud. I stood watching in shock as the boat sloshed away from the shore. They left me. And my mirror, strewn all around, reflecting moonlight in crazy shapes. Just left me flat, in the middle of all that bad luck and broken sky.

Ruth May

EVERYBODY WAS WHOOPING and hollowing and I kicked my legs to get down but I couldn't because Mama had a hold of me so tight it was hurting my arm. *Hush, little baby! Hush!* She was running along, so it kind of bounced when she said it. She used to sing me: *Hush, little baby! Mama's going to buy you a looking glass!*

She was going to buy me every single thing, even if it all got broke or turned out wrong.

When we got down there where everybody was she put me over her shoulder and stepped in the boat sideways with somebody's hands holding me up and the boat was wobbly. We sat down. She made me get down. It hurt, the little ants were biting us all over bad and it burned. That time Leah fed one to the ant lion, Jesus saw that. Now his friends are all coming back to eat us up.

Then we saw Adah. Mama reached out to her and started to cry and talk loud, like crying-talking, and then somebody else had a hold of me. It was somebody Congolese and not even Mama anymore, so I cried too. Who will buy me a looking glass that gets broke and a mockingbird that won't sing? I kicked and kicked but he wouldn't put me down. I heard babies crying and women crying and I couldn't turn my head around to see. I was going away from Mama is all I knew.

Nelson says to think of a good place to go, so when it comes time to die I won't, I'll disappear and go to that place. He said think of that place every day and night so my spirit will know the way. But I hadn't been. I knew where was safe, but after I got better I forgot to think about it anymore. But when Mama ran down the road with me I saw everybody was going to die. The whole world a-crying and yelling bad. So much noise. I put my fingers in my ears and tried to think of the safest place.

I know what it is: it's a green mamba snake away up in the tree. You don't have to be afraid of them anymore because you are one. They lie so still on the tree branch; they are the same everything as the tree. You could be right next to one and not even know. It's so quiet there. That's just exactly what I want to go and be, when I have to disappear. Your eyes will be little and round but you are so far up there you can look down and see the whole world, Mama and everybody. The tribes of Ham, Shem, and Japheth all together. Finally you are the highest one of all.

Adah

L IVE WAS *I ere I saw evil.*
  Now I am on the other side of that night and can tell the story, so perhaps I am still alive, though I feel no sign of it. And perhaps it was not evil I saw but merely the way of all hearts when fear has stripped off the husk of kind pretensions. Is it evil to look at your child, then heft something else in your arms and turn away?

Nod, nab, abandon.

Mother, I can read you backward and forward.

Live was I ere I saw evil.

I should have been devoured in my bed, for all I seem to be worth. In one moment alive, and in the next *left behind.* Tugged from our beds by something or someone, the ruckus, banging and shouting outside, my sisters leaped up screaming and were gone. I could not make a sound for the ants at my throat. I dragged myself out to moonlight and found a nightmare vision of dark red, boiling ground. Nothing stood still, no man or beast, not even the grass that writhed beneath the shadow, dark and ravenous. Not even the startled grass.

Only my mother stood still. There she was, planted before me in the path, rising on thin legs out of the rootless devouring earth. In her arms, crosswise like a load of kindling, Ruth May.

I spoke out loud, the only time: help me.

"Your father . . ." she said. "I think he must have gone on ahead with Rachel. I wish he'd waited, honey, he'd carry you but Rachel was . . . I don't know how she'll get through this. Leah will, Leah can take care of herself."

She can you can't you can't!

I spoke again: Please.

She studied me for a moment, weighing my life. Then nodded, shifted the load in her arms, turned away.

"Come on!" she commanded over her shoulder. I tried to stay close behind her, but even under the weight of Ruth May she was sinuous and quick in the crowd. My heels were nipped from behind by other feet. Stepped on, though I felt it vaguely, already numb from the burning ants. I knew when I went down. Someone's bare foot was on my calf and then my back, and I was being trampled. A crush of feet on my chest. I rolled over again and again, covering my head with my arms. I found my way to my elbows and raised myself up, grabbing with my strong left hand at legs that dragged me forward. Ants on my earlobes, my tongue, my eyelids. I heard myself crying out loud—such a strange noise, as if it came from my hair and fingernails, and again and again I came up. Once I looked for my mother and saw her, far ahead. I followed, bent on my own rhythm. Curved into the permanent song of my body: *left . . . behind.*

I did not know who it was that lifted me over the crowd and set me down into the canoe with my mother. I had to turn quickly to see him as he retreated. It was Anatole. We crossed the river together, mother and daughter, facing each other, low in the boat's quiet center. She tried to hold my hands but could not. For the breadth of a river we stared without speaking.

That night I could still wonder why she did not help me. *Live was I ere I saw evil.* Now I do not wonder at all. That night marks my life's dark center, the moment when growing up ended and the long downward slope toward death began. The wonder to me now is that *I* thought myself worth saving. But I did. *I did, oho, did I!* I reached out and clung for life with my good left hand like a claw, grasping at moving legs to raise myself from the dirt. Desperate to save myself in a river of people saving themselves. And if they chanced to look down and see me struggling underneath them, they saw that even the crooked girl believed her own life was precious. That is what it means to be a beast in the kingdom.

Leah

SUDDENLY THEN I was pushed from behind and pulled by other hands into a boat and we were on the water, crossing to safety. Anatole clambered in behind me. I was stunned to see he had Ruth May over his shoulder, like a fresh-killed antelope.

"Is she okay?"

"She is sleeping, I think. Twenty seconds ago she was screaming. Your mother and Adah have gone ahead with Tata Boanda," he said.

"Praise God. Adah's all right?"

"Adah is safe. Rachel is a demon. And your father is giving a sermon about Pharaoh's army and the plagues. Everyone is all right."

I squatted low with my chin on my knees and watched my bare feet change slowly from dark auburn, to speckled, to white as the ants dispersed and forayed out into the bottom of the canoe. I could hardly feel the pain now—the feet I gazed at seemed to be someone else's. I gripped both sides of the boat, suddenly fearing I might vomit or pass out. When I could hold my head up again, I asked Anatole quietly, "Do you think this is the hand of God?"

He didn't answer. Ruth May whimpered in her sleep. I waited so long for his answer I finally decided he hadn't heard me.

And then he simply said, "No."

"Then why?"

"The world can always give you reasons. No rain, not enough for the ants to eat. Something like that. *Nsongonya* are always moving anyway, it is their nature. Whether God cares or not." He sounded bitter against God. Bitter with reason. The night felt like a dream rushing past me too fast, like a stream in flood, and in this uncontrollable dream Anatole was the one person who cared enough to help me. God didn't. I tried to see through the thick darkness that clung to the river, searching out the opposite shore.

"God hates us," I said.

"Don't blame God for what ants have to do. We all get hungry. Congolese people are not so different from Congolese ants."

"They have to swarm over a village and eat other people alive?"

"When they are pushed down long enough they will rise up. If they bite you, they are trying to fix things in the only way they know."

The boat was crammed with people, but in the dark I couldn't recognize their hunched backs. Anatole and I were speaking English, and it seemed no one else was there.

"What does that mean? That you think it's right to hurt people?"

"You know me as a man. I don't have to tell you what I am."

What I knew was that Anatole had helped us in more ways than my family could even keep track of. My sister was now sleeping on his shoulder.

"But you believe in what they're doing to the whites, even if you won't do it yourself. You're saying you're a revolutionary like the *Jeune Mou Pro*."

The dark, strong arms of a stranger paddled us forward while I shuddered with cold dread. It occurred to me that I feared Anatole's anger more than anything.

"Things are not so simple as you think," he finally said, sounding neither angry nor especially kind. "This is not a time to explain the history of Congolese revolutionary movements."

"Adah says President Eisenhower has sent orders to kill Lumumba," I confessed suddenly. After holding in this rank mouthful of words for many days, I spilled them out into our ant-infested boat. "She heard it on Axelroot's radio. She says he's a mercenary killer working for the Americans."

I waited for Anatole to make any response at all to this—but he didn't. A coldness like water swelled inside my stomach. It couldn't possibly be true, yet Adah has always had the power to know things I don't. She showed me the conversation between Axelroot and another man, written down in her journal. Since then I've had no clear view of safety. Where is the easy land of ice-cream cones and new Keds sneakers and *We Like Ike*, the country where I thought I knew the rules. Where is the place I can go home to?

"Is it true, Anatole?"

The water moved under us and away, a cold, rhythmic rush.

"I told you, this is not a time to talk."

"I don't care! We're all going to die anyway, so I'll talk if I please."

If he was even still listening, he must have considered me a tedious child. But I had so much fright in me I couldn't stop it from coming out. I longed for him to shush me, just tell me to be still and that I was good.

"I want to be righteous, Anatole. To know right from wrong, that's all. I want to live the right way and be redeemed." I was trembling so hard I feared my bones might break.

No word.

I shouted to make him hear. "Don't you believe me? When I walk through the valley of the shadow the Lord is supposed to be with me, and he's not! Do you see him here in this boat?"

The man or large woman whose back I'd been leaning against shifted slightly, then settled lower. I vowed not to speak another word.

But Anatole said suddenly, "Don't expect God's protection in places beyond God's dominion. It will only make you feel punished. I'm warning you. When things go badly, you will blame yourself."

"What are you telling me?"

"I am telling you what I'm telling you. Don't try to make life a mathematics problem with yourself in the center and everything coming out equal. When you are good, bad things can still happen. And if you are bad, you can still be lucky."

I could see what he thought: that my faith in justice was childish, no more useful here than tires on a horse. I felt the breath of God grow cold on my skin. "We never should have come here," I said. "We're just fools that have gotten by so far on dumb luck. That's what you think, isn't it?"

"I will not answer that."

"Then you mean no. We shouldn't have come."

"No, you shouldn't. But you are here, so yes, you should be here. There are more words in the world than no and yes."

"You're the only one here who'll even talk to us, Anatole! Nobody else cares about us, Anatole!"

"Tata Boanda is carrying your mother and sister in his boat. Tata Lekulu is rowing his boat with leaves stuffed in his ears while your father lectures him on loving the Lord. Nevertheless, Tata Lekulu is carrying him to safety. Did you know, Mama Mwanza sometimes puts eggs from her own chickens under your hens when you aren't looking? How can you say no one cares about you?"

"Mama Mwanza does that? How do you know?"

He didn't say. I was stupid not to have figured it out. Nelson sometimes found oranges and manioc and even meat in our kitchen house when nothing was there the night before. I suppose we believed so hard in God's providence that we just accepted miracles in our favor.

"You shouldn't have come here, Béene, but you are here and nobody in Kilanga wants you to starve. They understand that white people make very troublesome ghosts."

I pictured myself a ghost: bones and teeth. Rachel a ghost with long white hair; Adah a silent, staring ghost. Ruth May a tree-climbing ghost, the squeeze of a small hand on your arm. My father was not a ghost; he was God with his back turned, hands clasped behind him and fierce eyes on the clouds. God had turned his back and was walking away.

Quietly I began to cry, and everything inside me came out through my eyes. "Anatole, Anatole," I whispered. "I'm scared to death of what's happening and nobody here will talk to me. You're the only one." I repeated his name because it took the place of prayer. Anatole's name anchored me to the earth, the water, the skin that held me in like a jar of water. I was a ghost in a jar. "I love you, Anatole."

"Leah! Don't ever say that again."

I never will.

We arrived at the opposite shore. Someone's rescued hen fluttered up to the bow of our boat and strutted placidly along the gunwale, its delicate wattles shaking as it plucked up ants. For the first time that night, I thought of our poor chickens shut up for the night in their coop. I pictured their bones laid clean and white in a pile on top of the eggs.

Two days later, when the rebel army of tiny soldiers had passed through Kilanga and we could go home again, that is exactly how we found our hens. I was surprised that their dislocated skeletons looked just the way I'd imagined them. This is what I must have learned, the night God turned his back on me: how to foretell the future in chicken bones.

Book Four

BEL AND
THE SERPENT

Do you not think that Bel is a living God?
Do you not see how much he eats and
drinks every day?

BEL AND THE SERPENT, 1:6

Orleanna Price

SANDERLING ISLAND

T HE STING OF A FLY, the Congolese say, can launch the end of the world. How simply things begin.

Maybe it was just a chance meeting. A Belgian and an American, let's say, two old friends with a hunger in common, a hand in the diamond business. A fly buzzes and lights. They swat it away and step into the Belgian's meticulously polished office in Elisabethville. They're careful to ask after each other's families and profits, and to speak of how they are living in a time of great change, great opportunity. A map of the Congo lies on the mahogany table between them. While they talk of labor and foreign currency their hunger moves apart from the gentlemanly conversation with a will of its own, licking at the edges of the map on the table, dividing it between them. They take turns leaning forward to point out their moves with shrewd congeniality, playing it like a chess match, the kind of game that allows civilized men to play at make-believe murder. Between moves they tip their heads back, swirl blood-colored brandy in glass globes and watch it crawl down the curved glass in liquid veins. Languidly they bring their map to order. Who will be the kings, the rooks, and bishops rising up to strike at a distance? Which sacrificial pawns will be swept aside? African names roll apart like the heads of dried flowers crushed idly between thumb and forefinger—Ngoma, Mukenge, Mulele, Kasavubu, Lumumba. They crumble to dust on the carpet.

Behind the gentlemen's barbered heads, dark mahogany planks stand at attention. The paneling of this office once breathed the humid air of a Congolese forest, gave shelter to life, felt the scales of snake belly on its branches. Now the planks hold their breath, with their backs to the wall. So do the mounted heads of rhinoceros and cheetah, evidence of the Belgian's skill as a sport hunter. Cut down, they are now mute spies in the house built by foreigners. Outside the window palm fronds rattle in a rising wind. An automobile creeps past. Leaves of unraveling newspaper blow into the rank water that runs in an open ditch; the newspaper wheels along the street, scattering its sheets onto the water, where they float as translucent squares of lace. No one can say whether it's good news or bad. A woman strides alongside the ditch under her basket of roasted corn. When the Belgian rises to close the window, the scent of all this reaches him: the storm, the ditch, the woman with the corn. He shuts the window and returns to the world of his own making. The curtains are damask. The carpet is Turkish. The clock on the table is German, old but still accurate. The heads on the wall observe with eyes of imported glass. The perfect timepiece ticks, and in that small space between seconds the fancy has turned to fact.

Given time, legions of men are drawn into the game, both ebony and ivory: the Congo's CIA station chief, the National Security Council, even the President of the United States. And a young Congolese man named Joseph Mobutu, who'd walked barefoot into a newspaper office to complain about the food he was getting in the army. A Belgian newspaperman there recognized wit and raw avarice—a useful combination in any game. He took this young Mobutu under his wing and taught him to navigate the airy heights where foreigners dwell. A rook who would be king. And the piece that will fall? Patrice Lumumba, a postal worker elected to head his nation. The Belgians and Americans agree, Lumumba is difficult. Altogether too exciting to the Congolese, and disinclined to let White control the board, preferring the counsel and company of Black.

The players move swiftly and in secret. Each broad turn sweeps across rivers, forests, continents, and oceans, witnessed only by foreign glass eyes and once-mighty native trees cut away from their roots.

I've surmised this scene, assembled it piece by piece over many years from the things I read, when it all began to come out. I try to imagine these men and their game, for it helps place my own regrettable acts on a broader field, where they seem smaller. What trivial thing was I doing while they divided the map beneath my feet? Who was the woman walking by with the roasted corn? Might she have been some distant kin of someone I haggled with on market days? How is it that neither of us knew the ways of the world for so long?

Fifteen years after Independence, in 1975, a group of Senators called the Church Committee took it upon themselves to look into the secret operations that had been brought to bear on the Congo. The world rocked with surprise. The Church Committee found notes from secret meetings of the National Security Council and President Eisenhower. In their locked room, these men had put their heads together and proclaimed Patrice Lumumba a danger to the safety of the world. The same Patrice Lumumba, mind you, who washed his face each morning from a dented tin bowl, relieved himself in a carefully chosen bush, and went out to seek the faces of his nation. Imagine if he could have heard those words—dangerous to the safety of the world!—from a roomful of white men who held in their manicured hands the disposition of armies and atomic bombs, the power to extinguish every life on earth. Would Lumumba have screamed like a cheetah? Or merely taken off his glasses, wiped them with his handkerchief, shaken his head, and smiled?

On a day late in August, 1960, a Mr. Allen Dulles, who was in charge of the CIA, sent a telegram to his Congolese station chief suggesting that he replace the Congolese government at his earliest convenience. The station chief, Mr. Lawrence Devlin, was instructed to take as bold an action as he could keep secret: a coup would be all right. There would be money forthcoming to pay soldiers for that purpose. But assassination might be less costly. A gang of men quick with guns and unfettered by conscience were at his disposal. Also, to cover all bases, a scientist named Dr. Gottlieb was hired to make a poison that would produce such a dreadful disease (the good doctor later testified in the hearings), if it didn't kill Lumumba outright it would leave him so disfigured that he couldn't possibly be a leader of men.

On the same August day, this is all I knew: the pain in my household seemed plenty large enough to fill the whole world. Ruth May was slipping away into her fever. And it was Rachel's seventeenth birthday. I was wrapping up green glass earrings in tissue paper, hoping to make some small peace with my eldest child, while I tried to sponge the fire out of my youngest. And President Eisenhower was right then sending his orders to take over the Congo. Imagine that. His household was the world, and he'd finished making up his mind about things. He'd given Lumumba a chance, he felt. The Congo had been independent for fifty-one days.

Mr. Devlin and his friends sat down with the ambitious young Mobutu, who'd been promoted to colonel. On September 10, they provided one million dollars in UN money for the purpose of buying loyalty, and the State Department completed its plans for a coup that would put Mobutu in charge of the entire army. All the ducks were lined up. On September 14, the army took control of the momentarily independent Republic of Congo, and Lumumba was put under house arrest in Léopoldville, surrounded by Mobutu's freshly purchased soldiers.

Throughout those days, while we scratched and haggled for our daily bread, I had a photograph of President Eisenhower for company in my kitchen house. I'd cut it out of a magazine and nailed it over the plank counter where I kneaded the bread. It was so much a part of my life I remember every detail of him: the clear-rimmed glasses and spotted tie, the broad smile, the grandfatherly bald head like a warm, bright light bulb. He looked so trustworthy and kind. A beacon from home, reminding me of our purpose.

On November 27, very early in the day, probably while I was stoking our woodstove for breakfast, Lumumba escaped. He was secretly helped along by a net of supporters stretching wide across the Congo, from Léopoldville to our own village and far beyond. Of course, no one spoke to me about it. We'd only heard faint rumors that Lumumba was in trouble. Frankly, we were more interested in the news that heavy rain was falling to the west of us and might soon reach our own parched village. The rain provided the Prime Minister's cover, as it turned out. Léopoldville had been drenched the previous night. I can imagine the silk texture of that cool air, the smell of Congolese earth curling its toes under a thatch of dead grass. In the dense fog, the nervous red glow of a guard's cigarette as he sits dreaming, cursing the cold but probably rejoicing in the rain—most likely he'd be the son of farmers. But in any case, alone now, at the front gate of Lumumba's prison house in Léopoldville. The tires of a station wagon hiss to a stop in the darkness. The guard sits up, touches his uniform, sees the station wagon is full of women. A carload of household employees from the night shift on their way home to the shantytown margins of the city. The boy puts on an attitude of impatience: he's much too busy with matters of state to be bothered by maids and a chauffeur. He flicks his thumb and forefinger, motioning for the station wagon to pass.

Behind the backseat, pressed against the white-stockinged knees of the maids, the Prime Minister crouches under a blanket.

A Peugeot and a Fiat are waiting down the street to file in behind the station wagon. All three cars head east, out of the city. After they've crossed the Kwango River by ferryboat, the Prime Minister rises from the backseat, stretches his long, narrow frame, and joins his wife, Pauline, and small son, Roland, in a car belonging to the Guinean embassy. It proceeds alone, east toward Stanleyville, where loyal crowds wait to hail their chief, believing with all their hearts that he'll restore their dreams of a free Congo.

But the roads are terrible. The same delicious mud that's salvation to manioc is the Waterloo of an automobile. They inch forward through the night, until dawn, when Lumumba's party is halted by a flat tire. He paces on the flattened grass by the ditch, remaining remarkably clean, while the driver labors to change the tire. But the effort stirs the black, wet road to a mire, and when he starts up the car again, it won't move. Lumumba kneels in the mud to add the force of his own shoulder to the back bumper. It's no use; they're hopelessly bogged down. They'll have to wait for help. Still exuberant with freedom, they remain confident. Two of Lumumba's former cabinet members are behind them, coming from Léopoldville in another car.

But there has been bad luck. Those two men have reached the Kwango River and are gesturing helplessly at an astonished fisherman. They want him to go wake the ferryman. The ferry squats low in the water at the opposite shore, where it left off Lumumba's party the night before. These fugitive dignitaries are both from the Batetela tribe and learned French in mission schools, but have no inkling of how to talk to the Kwango tribesmen who fish the rivers east of Léopoldville. It never mattered before; prior to Independence, hardly anyone gave a thought to the large idea of a geographical Congo. But now, on the morning of November 28, it means everything. The river is not so wide. They can plainly see the ferry, and point to it. But the fisherman stares at these men's city suits, their clean hands, and their mouths, which exaggerate incomprehensible syllables. He can see they're desperate. He offers fish.

This is how things go.

Lumumba's party waited most of the day, until they were found and rescued by a regional commissioner, who took them to Bulungu. There they paused, since Lumumba's wife and son were hungry and needed to eat. While he waited in the shade of a tree, brushing dried mud from his trousers, the Prime Minister was recognized by a villager and pulled into what quickly became an excited crowd. He gave an impromptu speech about the unquenchable African thirst for liberty. Somewhere deep in that crowd was a South African mercenary pilot who owned a radio. Very shortly, the CIA station chief knew Lumumba was free. All across the Congo on invisible radio waves flew the code words: *The Rabbit has escaped.*

The army recaptured Lumumba less than fifty miles from our village. People flocked to the roads, banging with sticks and fetishes on the hoods of the army convoy that took him away. The event was reported quickly with drums, across our province and beyond, and some of our neighbors even ran there on foot to try to help their captured leader. But in the midst of all that thunder, all that news assaulting our ears, we heard not a word. Lumumba was taken to

Thysville prison, then flown to Katanga Province, and finally beaten so savagely they couldn't return the body to his widow without international embarrassment.

Pauline and her children grieved, but having no body to bury properly is a terrible thing for a Congolese family. A body unmourned can't rest. It flies around at night. Pauline went to bed those nights begging her husband not to gnaw with his beak at the living. That's what I believe, anyway. I think she would have pled with him not to steal the souls of those who would take his place. Despite her prayers, the Congo was left in the hands of soulless, empty men.

Fifteen years after it all happened, I sat by my radio in Atlanta listening to Senator Church and the special committee hearings on the Congo. I dug my nails into my palms till I'd pierced my own flesh. Where had I been? Somewhere else entirely? Of the coup, in August, I'm sure we'd understood nothing. From the next five months of Lumumba's imprisonment, escape, and recapture, I recall—what? The hardships of washing and cooking in a drought. A humiliating event in the church, and rising contentions in the village. Ruth May's illness, of course. And a shocking scrap with Leah, who wanted to go hunting with the men. I was occupied so entirely by each day, I felt detached from anything so large as a month or a year. History didn't cross my mind. Now it does. Now I know, whatever your burdens, to hold yourself apart from the lot of more powerful men is an illusion. On that awful day in January 1961, Lumumba paid with a life and so did I. On the wings of an owl the fallen Congo came to haunt even our little family, we messengers of goodwill adrift on a sea of mistaken intentions.

Strange to say, when it came I felt as if I'd been waiting for it my whole married life. Waiting for that ax to fall so I could walk away with no forgiveness in my heart. Maybe the tragedy began on the day of my wedding, then. Or even earlier, when I first laid eyes on Nathan at the tent revival. A chance meeting of strangers, and the end of the world unfolds. Who can say where it starts? I've spent too many years backing over that muddy road: If only I hadn't let the children out of my sight that morning. If I hadn't let Nathan take us to Kilanga in the first place. If the Baptists hadn't taken upon themselves the religious conversion of the Congolese. What if the Americans, and the Belgians before them, hadn't tasted blood and money in Africa? If the world of white men had never touched the Congo at all?

Oh, it's a fine and useless enterprise, trying to fix destiny. That trail leads straight back to the time before we ever lived, and into that deep well it's easy to cast curses like stones on our ancestors. But that's nothing more than cursing ourselves and all that made us. Had I not married a preacher named Nathan Price, my particular children would never have seen the light of this world. I walked through the valley of my fate, is all, and learned to love what I could lose.

You can curse the dead or pray for them, but don't expect them to do a thing for you. They're far too interested in watching us, to see what in heaven's name we will do next.

What We Lost

KILANGA, JANUARY 17, 1961

Leah

YOU CAN'T JUST POINT to the one most terrible thing and wonder why it happened. This has been a whole terrible time, from the beginning of the drought that left so many without food, and then the night of the ants, to now, the worst tragedy of all. Each bad thing causes something worse. As Anatole says, if you look hard enough you can always see reasons, but you'll go crazy if you think it's all punishment for your sins. I see that plainly when I look at my parents. God doesn't need to punish us. He just grants us a long enough life to punish ourselves.

Looking back over the months that led to this day, it seems the collapse of things started in October, with the vote in church. We should have been good sports and lit out of the Congo right then. How could Father not have seen his mistake? The congregation of his very own church interrupted the sermon to hold an election on whether or not to accept Jesus Christ as the personal Saviour of Kilanga.

It was hot that day, in a season so dry our tongues went to sleep tasting dust and woke up numb. Our favorite swimming holes in the creek, which should have been swirling with fast brown water this time of year, were nothing but dry cradles of white stones. Women had to draw drinking water straight from the river, while they clucked their tongues and told stories of women fallen to crocodiles in other dry years, which were never as dry as this one. The manioc fields were flat: dead. Fruit trees barren. Yellow leaves were falling everywhere, littering the ground like a carpet rolled out for the approaching footsteps of the end of time. The great old kapoks and baobabs that shaded our village ached and groaned in their branches. They seemed more like old people than plants.

We'd heard rumors of rain in the river valleys west of us, and those tales aroused the deepest thirst you can imagine—the thirst of dying crops and animals. The dead grass on the distant hills was a yellowish red, not orange but a drier color: orange-white, like the haze in the air. Monkeys gathered in the high, bare branches at sunset, whimpering to one another as they searched the sky. Anything living that could abandon its home, some of our neighbors included, had migrated westward, in the direction from which we heard drums every night. Tata Kuvudundu cast his bone predictions, and nearly every girl in the village had danced with a chicken held to her head, to bring down rain. People did what they could. Church attendance rose and fell; Jesus may have sounded like a helpful sort of God in the beginning, but He was not bearing out.

That Sunday morning Tata Ndu himself sat on the front bench. Tata Ndu rarely darkened the door of the church, so this was clearly a sign, though who could say whether a good or bad one. He didn't appear to be paying much heed to the sermon. Nobody was, since it didn't have to do with rain. A month earlier when thunderstorms seemed imminent, Father had counseled his congregation to repent their sins and the Lord would reward them with rain. But in spite of all this repentance the rain hadn't come, and now he told us he refused to be party to the superstitions. This morning he was preaching on Bel in the temple, from the Apocrypha. Father has always stood firm on the Apocrypha, though most other preachers look down on him for it. They claim those books to be the work of fear-mongers who tagged them on to the Old Testament just to scare people. Yet Father always says, if the Lord can't inspire you to leave off sinning any other way, why then, it's His business to scare the dickens out of you.

Bel and the Serpent wasn't so frightening, as it mainly featured the quick wits of Daniel. This time Daniel was out to prove to the Babylonians that they were worshiping false idols, but even I was having trouble paying attention. Lately I'd rarely felt touched by Father's enthusiasm, and never by God.

"Now the Babylonians had an *idol* they called *Bel*," he declared, his voice the only clear thing in the haze that hung over us. People fanned themselves.

"Every day they bestowed upon the statue of Bel twelve bushels of flour, forty sheep, and fifty gallons of wine."

Anatole translated this, substituting *fufu*, goats, and palm wine. A few people fanned themselves faster, thinking of all that food going to just one hungry god. But most had dozed off.

"The people *revered* the statue of Bel and went every day to *worship* it, but *Daniel* worshiped the Lord our *Saviour*. And the King said to him, 'Why don't you worship Bel?' Why, Daniel replied, 'I do not *revere* false idols but the *living* God, who is *chief* of all mankind.' And the Babylonians said"—here my father dropped his voice to a more conversational tone—"'Can't you see Bel is a living God? Don't you see how much he eats and drinks every day?'

"Daniel laughed and told them, 'Don't be fooled! That is only a statue made of clay and bronze.'"

Father paused, and waited for Anatole to catch up.

I personally like Bel and the temple; it's a good story, but with all the delays for translation it was going too slowly to hold people's interest. It's a private-eye story, really. That's how I'd tell it, if it were up to me: Daniel knew very well that the King's high priests were sneaking in at night and taking all that food. So Daniel set up a trick. After everyone left their offerings in the temple, he went in and spread fireplace ashes all over the floor. That night the priests snuck in as usual through a secret stairway under the altar. But they didn't notice the ashes, so they left their footprints all over the floor of the temple. They were having a big old party every night, compliments of their pal Bel. But with the ashes on the floor, Daniel caught them red-handed.

Father was poised to go on with the story when suddenly Tata Ndu stood right straight up, cutting him off in the middle of hammering home his message. We all stared. Tata Ndu held up his hand

and declared in his deep, big-man's voice, giving each syllable the exact same size and weight: "Now it is time for the people to have an election."

"What?" I said out loud.

But Father, who's accustomed to knowing everything before it happens, took this right in stride. He replied patiently, "Well, now, that's good. Elections are a fine and civilized thing. In America we hold elections every four years to decide on new leaders." He waited while Anatole translated that. Maybe Father was dropping the hint that it was time for the villagers to reconsider the whole proposition of Tata Ndu.

Tata Ndu replied with equal patience, "*Á yi bandu,* if you do not mind, Tata Price, we will make our election now. *Ici, maintenant.*" He spoke in a careful combination of languages that was understood by everyone present. This was some kind of a joke, I thought. Ordinarily Tata Ndu had no more use for our style of elections than Anatole did.

"With all due *respect,*" my father said, "this is not the time or the place for that kind of business. Why don't you sit down now, and announce your plans after I've finished with the sermon? Church is not the place to vote anyone in or out of public office."

"Church is the place for it," said Tata Ndu. "*Ici, maintenant,* we are making a vote for Jesus Christ in the office of personal God, Kilanga village."

Father did not move for several seconds.

Tata Ndu looked at him quizzically. "Forgive me, I wonder if I have paralyzed you?"

Father found his voice at last. "You have not."

"*Á bu,* we will begin. *Beto tutakwe kusala.*" There was a sudden colorful bustle through the church as women in their bright *pagnes* began to move about. I felt a chill run down my spine. This had been planned in advance. The women shook pebbles out of cal-abash bowls into the folds of their skirts and moved between the benches, firmly placing one pebble into each outstretched hand. This time women and children were also getting to vote, apparently. Tata Mwanza's father came forward to set up the clay voting bowls in front of the altar. One of the voting bowls was for Jesus, the other was against. The emblems were a cross and a bottle of *nsamba*, new palm wine. Anyone ought to know that was not a fair match.

Father tried to interrupt the proceedings by loudly explaining that Jesus is exempt from popular elections. But people were excited, having just recently gotten the hang of the democratic process. The citizens of Kilanga were ready to cast their stones. They shuffled up to the altar in single file, just exactly as if they were finally coming forward to be saved. And Father stepped up to meet them as if he also believed this was the heavenly roll call. But the line of people just divided around him like water around a boulder in the creek, and went on ahead to make their votes. The effect of it wasn't very dignified, so Father retreated back to his pulpit made of wired-together palm fronds and raised up one hand, intending I guess to pronounce the benediction. But the voting was all over with before he could really get a word in sideways. Tata Ndu's assistant chiefs began counting the pebbles right away. They arranged them in clusters of five in a line on the floor, one side matched up against the other, for all to see.

"*C'est juste,*" Tata Ndu said while they counted. "We can all see with our own eyes it was fair."

My father's face was red. "This is *blasphemy!*" He spread his hands wide as if casting out demons only he could see, and shouted, "There is nothing fair here!"

Tata Ndu turned directly to Father and spoke to him in surprisingly careful English, rolling his r's, placing every syllable like a stone in a hand. "Tata Price, white men have brought us many programs to improve our thinking," he said. "The program of Jesus and the program of elections. You say these things are good. You cannot say now they are *not* good."

A shouting match broke out in the church, mostly in agreement with Tata Ndu. Almost exactly at the same time, two men yelled, "*Ku nianga, ngeye uyele kutala!*"

Anatole, who'd sat down in his chair a little distance from the pulpit, leaned over and said quietly to Father, "They say you thatched your roof and now you must not run out of your house if it rains."

Father ignored this parable. "Matters of the spirit are not decided at the marketplace," he shouted sternly. Anatole translated.

"*Á bu, kwe?* Where, then?" asked Tata Nguza, standing up boldly. In his opinion, he said, a white man who has never even killed a bushbuck for his family was not the expert on which god can protect our village.

When Anatole translated that one, Father looked taken aback. Where we come from, it's hard to see the connection.

Father spoke slowly, as if to a half-wit, "Elections are good, and Christianity is good. Both are good." We in his family recognized the danger in his extremely calm speech, and the rising color creeping toward his hairline. "You are right. In America we honor both these traditions. But we make our decisions about them in different houses."

"Then you may do so in America," said Tata Ndu. "I will not say you are unwise. But in Kilanga we can use the same house for many things."

Father blew up. "Man, you understand *nothing*! You are applying the logic of children in a display of childish ignorance." He slammed his fist down on the pulpit, which caused all the dried-up palm fronds to shift suddenly sideways and begin falling forward, one at a time. Father kicked them angrily out of the way and strode toward Tata Ndu, but stopped a few feet short of his mark. Tata Ndu is much heavier than my father, with very large arms, and at that moment seemed more imposing in general.

Father pointed his finger like a gun at Tata Ndu, then swung it around to accuse the whole congregation. "You haven't even learned to run your own pitiful country! Your children are dying of a hundred different diseases! You don't have a pot to piss in! And you're presuming you can take or leave the benevolence of our Lord Jesus Christ!"

If anyone had been near enough to get punched right then, my father would have displayed un-Christian behavior. It was hard to believe I'd ever wanted to be near to him myself. If I had a prayer left in me, it was that this red-faced man shaking with rage would never lay a hand on me again.

Tata Ndu seemed calm and unsurprised by anything that had happened. "*Á*, Tata Price," he said, in his deep, sighing voice. "You believe we are *mwana,* your children, who knew nothing until you came here. Tata Price, I am an old man who learned from other old men. I could tell you the name of the great chief who instructed my father, and all the ones before him, but you would have to know how to sit down and listen. There are one hundred twenty-two. Since the time of our *mankulu* we have made our laws without help from white men."

He turned toward the congregation with the air of a preacher himself. Nobody was snoozing now, either. "Our way was to share a fire until it burned down, *ayi*? To speak to each other until every person was satisfied. Younger men listened to older men. Now the *Beelezi* tell us the vote of a young, careless man counts the same as the vote of an elder."

In the hazy heat Tata Ndu paused to take off his hat, turn it carefully in his hands, then replace it above the high dome of his forehead. No one breathed. "White men tell us: *Vote, bantu!* They tell us: You do not all have to agree, *ce n'est pas nécessaire!* If two men vote yes and one says no, the matter is finished. *Á bu*, even a child can see how that will end. It takes three stones in the fire to hold up the pot. Take one away, leave the other two, and what? The pot will spill into the fire."

We all understood Tata Ndu's parable. His glasses and tall hat did not seem ridiculous. They seemed like the clothes of a chief.

"But that is the white man's law, *n'est-ce pas?*" he asked. "Two stones are enough. *Il nous faut seulement la majorité.*"

It's true, that was what we believed: the majority rules. How could we argue? I looked down at my fist, which still clutched my pebble. I hadn't voted, nor Mother either. How could we, with Father staring right at us? The only one of us who'd had the nerve was Ruth May, who marched right up and voted for Jesus so hard her pebble struck the cross and bounced. But I guess we all made our choices, one way or the other.

Tata Ndu turned to Father and spoke almost kindly. "Jesus is a white man, so he will understand the law of *la majorité*, Tata Price. *Wenda mbote.*"

Jesus Christ lost, eleven to fifty-six.

Rachel

M AYBE I SHOULDN'T SAY SO but it's true: Leah is the cause of all our problems. It goes back to when she and Father commenced World War Three at our house. What a crazy mixed-up scene. Leah would rare up and talk back to Father straight to his face, and then, boy oh boy. The rest of us would duck and cover like you have to do whenever they drop the A-bomb. Leah always had the uppermost respect for Father, but after the hullabaloo in church where they voted Father out, she just plumb stopped being polite.

How it started was her declaring she was going hunting with her little bow and arrow. My sister, little Miss The-Lord-Is-My-Shepherd, now thinks she is Robin Hood. I am surprised she hasn't tried to shoot an apple off my head, *if* we had an apple that is. There is not a speck of food anywhere. The ants ate everything people had stored up, which was not much to begin with because of the drought. It clouds up every morning and gets muggy for an hour, but then the sun beats down and dries up everything. Market day looks like you just came out of your fallout shelter after the bomb attack: nobody there but a few old guys with car parts and knives and cookpots, hoping to trade for food. Lots of luck, Charlie! We're only still scraping by with what Mrs. Fowles gave us off their boat, plus some eggs, because thank goodness Mama Mwanza brought us over two laying hens after the ants ate up ours. She lets her chickens just run here, there, and everywhere, so they escaped their fateful death by flapping up into the treetops. I happen to think Axelroot could get us some food too, if he tried, but he has been making himself scarce for months now, supposedly because he's on some top-secret mission. It's enough to drive you crazy. He said he'd bring me cigarettes and Hershey's chocolate when he came back, and I was very thrilled at the time, I'm sure, but, jeez, oh man. Right now I'd settle for a good old-fashioned loaf of Wonder Bread.

Well, the next thing we knew, Tata Ndu announced the whole village has to go on a big hunt, and *that* will save us. All of us together! It is quite involved. The plan, as Nelson explained it, is they start a fire in a huge circle around the big hill behind the village. That hill is mostly tall dead grass, not jungle, so it would burn up in a flash. The women are supposed to wave palm leaves and chase the flames in toward the middle until all the trapped animals inside get completely nerve-racked and jump out through the fire. That is the cue for the men to shoot them. Kids and old folks get the wonderful job of walking along behind and picking up all of God's creatures that got burnt to a crisp. Nelson says every person in the village is to be there, required precipitation.

Well, fine, I can go walk through a burnt field and get covered with soot from head to toe. I gave up long ago trying to pass the white-glove test. But Leah's little plan is to go with the men right up front and shoot things with her bow and arrow. Her new best friend, Anatole, seems to encourage it. When they held the meeting about it, he kept remarking how she is a very good shot, and if we're dying of hunger why should we care who shoots the antelope as long as it gets killed? And Nelson jumped right in to agree with Anatole, saying we should be glad for every arrow that shoots straight, even if it comes from a girl. Honestly. Nelson is just proud of being the one that taught her to shoot. And Leah is just primarily a show-off.

Tata Ndu and the older men were all against, at the meeting. Tata Kuvudundu especially. He sat with his lips pursed until whenever it came around again for his turn to talk. Then he'd stand up in his white wraparound robe and tell whole entire stories about horrid things that happened in the olden days: poison water coming out of the ground, elephants going berserk, exetera, whenever people didn't listen to him and insisted on doing things not the normal way. Then they'd all say, "Oh, yeah, I remember." The old men all nodded a lot, sitting up straight with their elbows close to their sides, hands on their laps, and feet flat on the ground a little bit pigeon-toed. The younger men leaned back on their stools with their knees wide apart, taking up all the room they needed, and were quick to yell out what was on their minds. Mostly it was in French and such, but Adah took things down in English in her notebook and held it where I could read it. So for once she made herself useful as well as a bump on a log.

Naturally Father had his own addenda for the meeting. When he got his one chance to speak, he tried to turn the whole hunt around into a kind of new, improved prayer meeting with animal shooting at the end. Which nobody listened to, because they were all jazzed up about a girl wanting to hunt with the men. I'm sure Father resented his own daughter being such a distraction. It's just lucky for Father he never had any sons. He might have been forced to respect them.

In the end it came down to Tata Ndu, Tata Kuvudundu, and Anatole doing the talking. Tata Ndu in his orange-and-white-striped cloth wrapped across his chest. He gave the impression, "I am the chief and don't you forget it," and of course Tata Kuvudundu is the voodoo witch doctor and you don't forget that either, what with him having six toes and going cross-eyed in the middle of a sentence just for the scary effect. But Anatole is the schoolteacher, after all, and a lot of the boys that now at the ripe age of nineteen or so have wives and families formerly learned their two-plus-two from him in the first place. They still call him *Monsieur* Anatole, instead of the usual "Tata," because he was their schoolmaster. So it got to be divided down the lines of young against old, with Anatole persuading a lot of the younger men. And in our village, believe you me, people die for the slightest provocation so there are not that many old people still hanging around.

Leah had to sit in the front of the room all night long without saying a peep. She kept looking at Anatole, but after a while you couldn't tell really if he was on her side. He stopped mentioning what a good shot she was and moved on to the subject of whether you should kill a rat for its skin or kill a rat for being a rat. Whatever that may mean. Tata Ndu said if it runs in a rat's skin it is a rat. Then they all got to yelling about foreigners, the army takeover, and somebody thrown in prison which if you ask me is at least a more favorable subject than rats.

At the end it got turned into another showdown: were we going to keep talking about this all night, or have a vote? Anatole was very against the voting. He said this was a matter to be discussed and agreed on properly, because even if Kilanga ran one white family out of town, there were a million more whites in the world and if you couldn't learn to tell a good rat from a bad one, you'd soon be living with both in your house. *And*, he said, don't be surprised when your own daughter or wife wants to shoot a bow and arrow behind your back. Well, everybody laughed at that, but I failed to see the humor. Was he calling us rats?

Tata Ndu had had just about enough. He marched up and plunked down two big clay voting bowls in front of Leah. It kind of made people mad when he did it. You could see them siding with Anatole, that it needed more talk. But, no, time's up. As for Leah, she looked like a chicken fixing to get thrown in the stewpot. But was I supposed to feel sorry for her? She asked for it! With all her attention-getting mechanisms. Some of the men still seemed to think the whole thing was funny, so maybe they thought she'd shoot an arrow through her foot, for all I know. But when it came time to walk up and cast their votes, fifty-one stones went in the bowl with Leah's bow-and-arrow by it. Forty-five for the one with the cookpot.

Man alive, Tata Kuvudundu was not one bit happy then. He stood up and hollered that we'd turned over the natural way of things and boy, would we be sorry. He made a very big point of looking at Anatole when he said that, but he also seemed put out with Tata Ndu for the voting activity, which got backfired on him. Tata Ndu didn't say much, but he frowned so hard his big bald forehead wrinkled up like the bread dough when you punch it down. He held his big muscle-man arms across his chest, and even though he was an elderly man of fifty or so, he looked like he could still beat the pants off anybody in the room.

"The animals are listening to us tonight!" Tata Kuvudundu yelled out and kind of started singing with his eyes closed. Then he stopped. It got real quiet and he looked very slowly around the room. "The leopards will walk upright like men on our paths. The snakes will come out of the ground and seek our houses instead of hiding in their own. *Bwe?* You did this. You decided the old ways are no good. Don't blame the animals, it was your decision. You want to change everything, and now, *kuleka?* Do you expect to sleep?"

Nobody said a word, they just looked scared. Tata Ndu sat with his head thrown back and his eyes just little slits, watching.

"No one will sleep!" Tata Kuvudundu suddenly shrieked, leaping up and waving his arms in the air.

Everybody else kind of jumped at that, but Leah sat stock-still. Like I said, showing off. She didn't even blink. Then we all got up and left and she followed us out, and no one in our family said boo to each other all the way home. When we got to the door Father stopped, blocking the way. Oh, brother. We were going to have to stand out there on the porch and hear the moral of the story.

"Leah," he said, "who is the master of this house?"

She stood with her chin down, not answering. Finally she said, "You are," in a voice as little as an ant.

"I'm sorry, I didn't hear you?"

"You are!" she screamed at him.

Mother and I jumped, but Father merely replied in a normal voice, "What occurred this evening may be of some consequence to the village, but it's of no consequence to you. God has ordained that you honor thy father and submit thyself to the rules of his house."

Leah didn't even move. Her chin was still tilted down, but her eyes were straight on him like nobody's business. "So," she said quietly, "you agree with Tata Ndu and the witch doctor."

Father sucked in his breath. "They agree with *me*. It's nonsense for you to hunt with the men. You're only causing trouble, and I forbid it."

Leah slung her bow over her shoulder. "I'm going with the men and that's final." Marched off the porch, right out into the dead of night, where supposedly the animals were wide awake and walking around like human beings. Mother and Adah and I stood there with our traps hanging open. You could have knocked us over with a feather.

Father went crazy. We'd always wondered what would happen if we flat-out disobeyed him. Now we were fixing to see. He lit out after her with his wide leather belt already coming out of his pants as he stomped through the dirt. But by the time he got to the edge of the yard she was gone. She'd vamoosed into the tall grass, and off she was headed for the jungle, where it was plain to see he'd never find her. Leah can climb trees like a chimpanzee, when nobody's even chasing her.

Instead of coming back, he acted like he'd just decided to stroll out there for the sake of thrashing the trees with his belt, and man alive, he did. We heard him for an hour. We peeked out the window and saw he'd cut down a whole stand of sugar cane by lashing it with his belt. We started to get scared about what he'd do when he finally came in, for there was really no telling. Our doors didn't lock, but Mother came in our room with us and helped us push the beds around so the door was blocked. We went to bed early, with metal pot lids and knives and things from the kitchen to protect ourselves with, because we couldn't think of anything else. It was like the armor they had in the nights of old. Ruth May put an aluminum saucepan on her head and slid two comic books down the seat of her jeans in case of a whipping. Mother slept in Leah's bed. Or lay there quiet, rather, for really none of us slept a wink. Leah came in the window before dawn and whispered to Mother awhile, but I don't think she slept either.

Half the village was in the same boat with us, even though I guess for different reasons. After the way Tata Kuvudundu carried on at the meeting and gave off the evil eye, nobody could sleep. According to Nelson that was the one and only topic of conversation. They said their animals were looking at them. People killed the last few they had—goats, chickens, or dogs. You could smell the blood everywhere. They put the animals' heads in front of their houses in calabash bowls, to keep away the *kibaazu,* they said.

Well, why were they dumb enough to vote for Leah anyway, is what I asked Nelson. If they knew it was going to get Tata Kuvudundu so riled up? Nelson said some of them that voted for her were put out with Tata Ndu, and some were put out with Father, so everybody ended up getting what they didn't want, and now had to go along with it. Nobody even cares that much one way or another about Leah, is what Nelson said. Oh, well, I told him. That is what we call Democracy.

Strange to say, at our house the next morning it was suddenly peace on earth. Father acted like nothing much had happened. He had cuts and poisonwood boils on his arms from all his thrashing in the bushes, but yet he just drank his tea at breakfast without a word and then put some poultice on his arms and went out on the porch to read his Bible. We wondered: Is he looking for the world's longest The Verse to give Leah on the subject of impudence? Is he looking up what Jesus might have to say about preachers that murder their own daughters? Or maybe he'd decided he couldn't win this fight, so he was going to pretend it never happened and Leah was beneath his notice. With Father, life's just one surprise after another.

Leah did at least have the brains to make herself scarce. She stayed either at Anatole's school or out in the woods having a bow-and-arrow contest with Nelson to see who could shoot a bug off a branch. That was the kind of thing she usually did. But there was plenty of nervous tension left in our household, believe you me. Ruth May peed in her pants just because Father coughed out on the porch. And guess who had to be the one to get her cleaned up: me. I did not appreciate what we were being put through, all because of Leah.

That evening was the night before the hunt, with Leah still keeping her distance. But her pal Anatole found an evil sign outside his hut. So we were told by Nelson. Mother had sent him over to the school to take Leah some boiled eggs for dinner, and he came running back to tell us Anatole was over there looking like he'd seen a ghost. Nelson wouldn't say what the evil sign was, just that it was a dreaded *kibaazu* sign of a bad curse put on Anatole. We kind of thought he might have made the whole thing up. Nelson could be dramatic.

Well, no, sir. Next morning bright and early, Anatole found a green mamba snake curled up by his cot, and it was just by the grace of God he didn't get bit on the leg and die on the spot. Good luck, or a miracle, one. They said he usually always gets out of bed before daybreak and goes out for his constitutional and would have stepped right on it, but that morning for some reason he woke up too early and decided to light his lamp and read in bed awhile before getting up, and that's when he saw it. He thought someone had thrown a rope inside his house for another evil sign, but then it moved! No more signs; this was the true evil thing! The story went buzzing around the village quicker even than if we'd had telephones. People were running around because it was the big day and they had to get ready, but this gave them something extra to think about, and boy oh boy, they did. I don't care if they were followers of God almighty or the things that bump you in the night, they were praying to it now, believe you me. Thanking their lucky stars that what happened to Anatole hadn't happened to them.

Adah

BETO NKI TUTASALA means: What are we doing? Doing, we are what? *Alas atuti knot eb.* Alas. The night before the hunt there was no sleep at all. *Eye on sleep peels no eye!* We thought we were looking, but could not see what was before us. Leopards walked upright on the paths and snakes moved quietly from their holes. The S on the floor was not for sleep.

People are *bantu*; the singular is *muntu*. *Muntu* does not mean exactly the same as *person*, though, because it describes a living person, a dead one, or someone not yet born. *Muntu* persists through all those conditions unchanged. The Bantu speak of "self" as a vision residing inside, peering out through the eyeholes of the body, waiting for whatever happens next. Using the body as a mask, *muntu* watches and waits without fear, because *muntu* itself cannot die. The transition from spirit to body and back to spirit again is merely a venture. It is a ride on the power of *nommo*, the force of a name to call oneself. *Nommo* rains from a cloud, rises in the vapor from a human mouth: a song, a scream, a prayer. A drum gives *nommo* in Congo, where drums have language. A dance gives *nommo* where bodies are not separate from the will that inhabits them. In that other long-ago place, America, I was a failed combination of too-weak body and overstrong will. But in Congo I am those things perfectly united: *Adah*.

The night before the hunt, while no one slept, every *muntu* in Kilanga danced and sang: drums, lips, bodies. In song they named the animals that would become our feast and salvation in the morning. And they named the things they feared: Snake. Hunger. Leopards that walk upright on the paths like men. These are the *nommo,* they chanted, these bodies living and dancing and joining together with slick, black other bodies, all beating the thing with feathers: beating out the dear, dear hope, a chance to go on living. But *muntu* did not care if the bodies lived or died on the morrow. *Muntu* peered out through the eyeholes, watching closely to see what would happen next.

Before first light we all came together at the edge of the village, not down by the river, where Our Father would have gathered us, but away from there, on the side toward the hill, where our salvation lay. We made our march into the field of elephant grass, tramped upon the big hill rising. Grass as tall as living men, and taller, but dry and white as a dead woman's hair. With sticks the men laid the tall grass down. They beat it in unison as if beating down grass were a dance, grunting softly in a long, low rhythm that ran back to us from the head of the file. Men with bows and arrows, men with spears, even a few with guns were up ahead of us. Their chant was the only sound in the cool morning haze. Children and women followed, carrying the largest baskets their arms were able to circle. Mine hung on a strap over my shoulder because my arms do not circle well. Behind us came the oldest women, carrying smoldering torches, greenheart poles wrapped in palm-oil-soaked rags. High up they held their torches, bruising the air overhead with the smoke of our procession. The sun hung low on the river, seeming reluctant to enter this strange day. Then it rose redly into the purpled sky, resembling a black eye.

At a signal given by Tata Ndu our single file divided and curved outward to either side of the hill. A solemn wishbone of eager, hungry people—that is how we might have appeared to the *muntu* dead and unborn who watched from above. In half an hour the fronts of the two lines met, and we hungry wishbone people of Kilanga completed our circle around the hill. A shout fluttered up. The fire starters laid down their torches. Younger women opened their *pagnes* and ran forward, fanning the flames like moths dancing before a candle.

Our circle was so large the shouts we heard from the other side seemed to come from another country. Soon all sound was swallowed by the fire. It did not roar but grumbled, cracked, shushed, sucking the air from our throats and all speech with it. The flame rose and licked the grass and we all moved forward, chasing the line of brightness ahead of us. Chasing flames that passed hungrily over the startled grass, leaving nothing of life behind. Nothing but hot, black, bare ground and delicate white filaments of ash, which stirred and crumbled under the trample of bare feet. Now the men rushed ahead with bows cocked, impatient for the circle to shrink toward its center. Smaller and smaller the circle ungrew, with all the former life of a broad grassy plain trapped inside. The animals all caught up in this dance together, mice and men. Men who pushed and pranced, appearing to us as dark stick puppets before the wall of fire. The old people and children came along slowly behind. We were like odd ruined flagpoles, bent double, with our bright clothes flapping. Slow scavengers. We fanned out across the hissing black field, picking up charred insects. Most common were the crisp *nguka* caterpillars, favorite snack of Anatole's schoolboys, which resembled small twigs and were impossible to see until I learned to sense their particular gray curve. We picked them up by the basketful until they filled my mind's eye so completely I knew I would see them in my sleep. Easier to find were the *dikonko*, edible locusts and crickets, whose plump abdomens were shrunk translucent like balloons half-filled with water. Caterpillars one after another I laid on my tongue, their char crisp bristle taste a sweet momentary salve to a body aching for protein. Hunger of the body is altogether different from the shallow, daily hunger of the belly. Those who have known this kind of hunger cannot entirely love, ever again, those who have not.

The fire moved faster than we did, we the young and elderly shepherdesses of dead insects. Sometimes I stood up straight to let the blood run from my head to the numb slabs of muscle at the backs of my thighs. Mother held on tight to the hand of Ruth May, her chosen child, but also stayed near me. Since the terrible night of the ants, Mother had been creeping her remorse in flat-footed circles around me without ever speaking of it, wearing her guilt like the swollen breasts of a nursing mother. So far I had refused to suckle and give her relief, but I kept close by. I had no choice, since she and Ruth May and I were thrown together by caste, set apart from Leah the Huntress. By choice, we also stayed far from Rachel and Father. Their noisy presences, of two different kinds, embarrassed us in this field of earnest, quiet work. Sometimes I set a hand above my eyes and looked for Leah, but did not see her. Instead I watched Ruth May crunch thoughtfully on a caterpillar. Soiled and subdued, she looked like a small malnourished relative of my previous sister. The faraway look of her eyes must have been the *muntu* of Ruth May, chained to this briefly belligerent child through forelife, life, and afterlife, peering out through her sockets.

The fire ran ahead at times, and sometimes flagged, as if growing tired like the rest of us. The heat was unspeakable. I imagined the taste of water.

As the ring burned smaller we suddenly caught sight of its other side, the red-orange tongues and black ash closing in. The looming shapes of animals bunched up inside: antelopes, bushbucks, broad-headed warthogs with warthog children running behind them. A troop of baboons ran with arched tails flying as they zigzagged, not yet understanding their entrapment. Thousands of insects beat the air to a pulpy soup of animal panic. Birds hit the wall of fire and lit like bottle rockets. When it seemed there was no more air, no more hope, the animals began to run out through the fire into the open, where spears and arrows waited. The antelopes did not leap gracefully as I imagined they would; they wheeled like spooked horses around the inside of the circle, then suddenly veered out as if by accident or blindness. Seeing their companions shot in the neck with arrows, they heeled in panic, sometimes turning back to the flames but mostly running straight on, straight toward people and death. A small spotted antelope fell down very near me and presented me with the strange, singular gift of its death. I watched its heaving sides slowly come to rest, as if it had finally caught its breath. Dark blood leaked from its delicate black mouth onto the charred ground.

For every animal struck down, there rose an equal and opposite cry of human jubilation. Our hungry wishbone cracked and ran slick with marrow. Women knelt with their knives to skin the meat, even before the hooves stopped beating the ground in panic. Of the large animals who came through the fire—bushbuck, warthog, antelope—few escaped. Others would not come out and so they burned: small flame-feathered birds, the churning insects, and a few female baboons who had managed against all odds to carry their pregnancies through the drought. With their bellies underslung with precious clinging babies, they loped behind the heavy-maned males, who would try to save themselves, but on reaching the curtain of flame where the others passed through, they drew up short. Crouched low. Understanding no choice but to burn with their children.

The curtain of heat divided the will to survive from survival itself. I could have fallen trembling on the ground but stood and watched instead, watched Kilanga's children shout and dance each time they found the scorched, angular bodies of a mother baboon and baby seared together. On account of these deaths, Kilanga's gleeful children would live through another season. The *bantu* who watched from above would have seen a black festival of life and death indistinguishable one from the other against the black-scorched ground.

As that day would turn out, my sister Rachel became (briefly) a vegetarian. My sisters Ruth May and Leah: forager and hunter. I became something else. On the day of the hunt I came to know in the slick center of my bones this one thing: all animals kill to survive, and we are animals. The lion kills the baboon; the baboon kills fat grasshoppers. The elephant tears up living trees, dragging their precious roots from the dirt they love. The hungry antelope's shadow passes over the startled grass. And we, even if we had no meat or even grass to gnaw, still boil our water to kill the invisible creatures that would like to kill us first. And swallow quinine pills. The death of something living is the price of our own survival, and we pay it again and again. We have no choice. It is the one solemn promise every life on earth is born and bound to keep.

Leah

I KILLED MY FIRST GAME, a beautiful tawny beast with curved horns and a black diagonal stripe across his flank: a young male impala. He was completely bewildered by the fire, too young to have any good strategy for danger, but old enough to need to put on a show. He ran pell-mell, snorting like a playground bully till he was one of the last of his kind left inside the circle. I knew he'd soon come through. The way his hooves tore at the ground was so desperate, and his family already gone. I crouched near Nelson, watching. Nelson had taken down two bushbucks, one after the other, and signaled to me that he was going to claim his arrows. The impala he was leaving to me. I followed it with my eye as Nelson had taught me to do, looking for the path of its hopes. Suddenly I saw exactly where it would break through the fire. He would come straight toward me and veer to my right, where his mother had gone. Even a playground bully will want his mother in the bitter end. I held my breath to stop my arms from trembling. I had the hunger and thirst of a famine all to myself, smoke in my burning eyes, and no strength left. I prayed to Jesus to help me, then to any other god who would listen. Help me keep my left arm straight and my right pulled back and my arrow tight against the gutstring ready to sing and fly. One, he came and dodged . . . two, he came closer . . . three, he broke his gait, paused . . . *four!*

He leaped sideways away from me, all four legs drawn together in midair for half a second, and then he ran on. Only when I saw the spray of brown blood did I understand I'd hit him. My own heart plunged and burst against my ears. *I have killed an animal larger than myself!* I screamed as if struck by an arrow myself. Before I realized my legs had moved me I was chasing the impala down the path of his hopes—the forest he could see at the end of the long, charred valley, where he would find his mother and safety. But he crumpled, slowed and fell down. I stood over him, breathing fast. It took me a minute to understand what I saw: two arrows in his flank. Neither one of them fletched red, as my arrows were. And Tata Ndu's oldest son Gbenye shouting at me to get away, go on away, "*Á, baki!*" Meaning that I was a thief.

But then Nelson was beside me, waving my arrow. "*This arrow killed that impala,*" he shouted at Gbenye. "It passed through the neck. Look at yours. Two little pricks in his flank. He never even felt them before he died."

Gbenye's lip curled. "How would a woman's arrow kill a yearling impala?"

"By making a hole in his neck, Gbenye. Your arrows went for the tail like a dog after his bitch. Where was your aim, nkento?"

Gbenye raised his fist, and I was sure he would kill Nelson for that insult. But he flung his finger toward me instead, and shook it as if he were ridding himself of blood or slime. Commanded me to skin the impala and bring the meat down to the village. Then turned and walked away from us.

Nelson drew his knife and knelt to help me with the tedious work of cutting through the tendons and peeling back the pelt. I felt mixed up, grateful, and sick at heart.

Nelson had ridiculed Gbenye's aim by calling him *nkento*. A woman.

Rachel

IF YOU EVEN THINK you can picture how awful it was, you are wrong. Lambs to the slaughter. We were, or the animals were, I don't even know who I feel sorry for the most. It was the most despicable day of my life. I stood on that burnt-up field with the taste of ashes in my mouth, ashes in my eyes, on my hair and my dress, all stained and tarnished. I stood and prayed to the Lord Jesus if he was listening to take me home to Georgia, where I could sit down in a White Castle and order a hamburger without having to see its eyes roll back in its head and the blood come spurting out of its corpse.

Oh, they cheered to see it. I have not seen so much cheering since a homecoming game. Everybody jumped for joy. Me too at first, for I was thinking, Hooray, a halfway decent meal at last. If I eat one more egg omelet I think I'll turn over easy and cluck. But by the end of the day everybody was smeared with blood like creepy, happy ghouls, and I couldn't bear to be one of them myself. Everything changed. The villagers transformed into brutish creatures before my very eyes, with their hungry mouths gaping wide. My own sister Leah got down on her knees and eagerly skinned a poor little antelope, starting out by slitting its belly and peeling back the skin over its back with horrible ripping sounds. She and Nelson hunkered down side by side, using a knife and even their teeth to do it. Both of them were so covered with ashes they looked like the pot and the kettle, each one blacker than the other. When they finished with the thing, it lay there limp on the ground all shiny blue and red, covered with a slick white film. It looked like our old hound dog Babe, except all made of gristle and blood. Its bare dead eyes gaped out of its head, pleading for mercy. I bent over and threw up on my PF Flyers. Lord Jesus. I couldn't help it.

I went straight back down the burned-up hill and marched all the way home, without even telling Mother I was leaving. I am seventeen years old, after all, not a child, and I alone will decide the fate of my life. The rest of them were all going to the stupid town square, with the plan I'm sure being to whoop and holler about our good fortune and divide up all the dead loot.

Not me. I latched myself up tight in our kitchen house, tore off my filthy clothes and threw them into the stove. I heated the big kettle of water and poured it into the galvanized tub and sat in it like a scalded potato, alone in this world, just crying. Mother's picture of President Eisenhower looked down at me from the wall, and I crossed my arms over my naked chest for shame, crying even harder. I felt my red skin was going to scald plumb off, and then I'd look just like that poor antelope. They wouldn't be able to tell me from any other skinned carcass they drug home that day. Fine with me if I died right along with the rest of the poor animals. Who would care anyway? While the water cooled down I sat there looking up at the President. His round white head was so friendly and kind, I cried like a baby because I wanted him for a father instead of my own parents. I wanted to live under the safe protection of somebody who wore decent clothes, bought meat from the grocery store like the Good Lord intended, and cared about others.

I vowed that if I lived through this ordeal, I would not touch a single one of those animals they trapped and killed out there on the hillside like innocent children. That's all they were—the baboons and warthogs and antelopes scared crazy by the fire. And the people no different from animals: Leah and all those men licking their lips, already tasting roasted meat in the smoke of the fire. And poor little Ruth May picking up burnt grubworms and putting them straight in her mouth because her own parents can't keep her fed. All of them out there in the hot sun that day were just dumb animals cursed with the mark of ash on their brow. That's all. Poor dumb animals running for their lives.

Leah

IT SHOULD HAVE BEEN the most glorious day in our village, but instead it all came crashing down. Fifty years from now if I'm still living I will look back on that one afternoon, and the morning that followed. Even then I swear I'll know it for what it was: the most terrible day of our lives.

After the hunt ended there was supposed to be a celebration, but before the old men could drag their drums out under the tree and get the dancing started, it had already turned into a melee of screaming and fighting. Men we had known as kindly, generous fathers suddenly became strangers with clenched fists and wide eyes, shouting into each other's faces. Ruth May burst into tears and hid in Mother's skirt. I don't think she ever understood what happened. Not ever.

I know I played a part. I do understand that. But so much had already gone wrong before I joined in. From the time we first set foot in Kilanga things were going wrong, though we couldn't see it. Even the glorious Independence was not going to be good for everyone, as they'd promised that day on the riverbank, when Lumumba and the Belgians raised up their different promises and the white King lurked somewhere in disguise. There were going to be winners and losers. Now there are wars in the south, killings in the north, rumors that foreigners took over the army and want to murder Lumumba. On the day of the hunt a war was already roaring toward us, whites against blacks. We were all swept up in a greediness we couldn't stop.

My argument with Gbenye over the impala, which really I killed, became a shouting match between people who'd voted for me and those who'd voted against. Some changed sides, mostly turning against me because of Tata Kuvudundu's warnings. The terrible things he promised were already starting to happen. Eyes watched us from the trees as we dragged our burden of meat down to the village, piled it up, and gathered around in a hungry knot. Gbenye was the first to move, pulling my antelope off the pile and holding it proudly in the air. Tata Ndu took it from him, raised his machete, and with one hard blow sliced off a hindquarter. This he picked up and threw toward me. It hit the ground with a thump in front of me, throwing blood on my socks. In the perfect absence of any human sound, the locusts in the leaves above us roared in my ears.

I knew what I ought to do: pick it up in both hands and give it to Mama Mwanza. I should turn the other cheek. But the sin of pride took hold of me with a fierce grip. I picked up the whole bleeding leg and threw it at Gbenye, hitting him square across the back as he gloated to his friends. He staggered forward and one of his friends laughed.

Tata Ndu turned to me, his eyes ferocious under his huge furrowed brow. He flung his hand toward us in disgust. "Tata Price has refused his family's share of meat," he announced in Kikongo. "*Á bu mpya.* Who's next?"

He glared at each silent face in turn.

"Anatole!" he declared at last. "*Anatole báana bansisila áù á-aana!*" Anatole the orphan without descendants!—the bitterest insult that could be borne by a Congolese man. "For you this will be plenty," pronounced Tata Ndu, pointing at the same skimpy hindquarter in the dirt. Only hours ago it had been the strong hind leg of an antelope boy. Now it lay naked at our feet, covered with filth. It looked more like a curse than a gift.

Anatole answered in his polite schoolteacher's voice. "*Excusez-moi, Tata Ndu, mais non. Ça, c'est de compte à demi de la famille Price. La grande bête là, c'est la mienne.*" In his two hands, by himself, Anatole the orphan without descendants began to drag away one of the large bushbucks he'd shot on the hill. It wasn't right for Tata Ndu to insult Anatole, who hadn't really taken my side but only argued for people to think for themselves. Now I was terrified that he'd be driven away from associating with our family at all.

Tata Boanda stepped forward to help Anatole, I saw with relief. But then Tata Boanda pulled away abruptly and began to shout, and I understood he was claiming Anatole's bushbuck for himself. The elder Mama Boanda ran forward screaming and struck Anatole in the face. He let go, stumbling backward. I ran to steady him but was rammed from behind by old one-armed Tata Kili, who could not get past me fast enough in his hurry to claim his own stake. Behind him came the two Mama Kilis, determined to oversee his claim and raise it. Tata Ndu spoke again but was drowned out by the wave of our neighbors that rolled forward, parting and closing around him.

And so it came to pass that the normal, happy event of dividing food after a hunt became a war of insults and rage and starving bellies. There should have been more than enough for every family. But as we circled to receive our share of providence, the fat flanks of the magnificent beasts we'd stalked on the hill shrank to parched sinew, the gristle of drought-starved carcasses. Abundance disappeared before our eyes. Where there was plenty, we suddenly saw not enough. Even little children slapped their friends and stole caterpillars from each other's baskets. Sons shouted at their fathers. Women declared elections and voted against their husbands. The elderly men whose voices hardly rose above a whisper, because they were so used to being listened to, were silenced completely in the ruckus. Tata Kuvudundu looked bedraggled and angry. His white robe was utterly blackened with ash. He raised his hands and once again swore his prophecy that the animals and all of nature were rising up against us.

We tried to ignore his strange remarks, but we all did hear him. In some corner of our hearts we all drew back, knowing he was right. The dead beasts in our hands seemed to be cursing and mocking us for having killed them. In the end we all crept home with our meat, feeling hunted ourselves. What was surely the oldest celebration of all, the sharing of plenty, had fallen to ruin in our hands.

Rachel

B Y NIGHTFALL my sisters and parents came home and everything had gone crazy. Nothing went the way I expected.

I had gotten out of my bath, dressed in clean clothes, towel-dried my hair, and was sitting quietly in the front room prepared to announce to my family that I was a vegetarian. I understood full well what this meant: from now on I would have to exist on bananas and have poor nutrition. I knew Mother would have strong opinions about where I'd wind up, with curved legs and weak bones like the poor Congolese children. But I shan't care, not even if my hair falls out. At seventeen I have my rights, and besides, I'd made my own secret plan. As soon as Eeben Axelroot came back I was determined to use my feminine wilds to my own advantage. No matter what it took, I would get him to take me away from here in his airplane. "My fiancé, Mr. Axelroot, and I are planning on returning to America," I would tell them, "where it's a free country and you can get anything to eat that you want."

But this is not the conversation that happened. When they came home, everybody was having a conniption about a big giant fight in the village over who got whose share of their horrid meat. They went on talking and remarking about it while Mother built a fire in the stove and put in their antelope leg to roast, and mashed some plantains. It did smell so good. You could hear it all sizzling and crispy and juicy, and I have to confess when dinnertime came I did eat a few small bites, but only because I was positively weak with hunger. And I got to thinking about my hair falling out. But! If there had been a grocery store within one hundred miles, believe me, I would have walked there on my own reconnaisance for some cuisine that didn't still have feet attached to it.

At dinner the ruckus of our household was still going on, with Leah still saying over and over how she shot a whole antelope herself and it was not fair that our family didn't get it. Father informed her that God showed no mercy upon those who flouted their elders, and that he, Reverend Price, had washed his hands of her moral education. He said this in just the plainest everyday voice, as if discussing that the dog had gotten into the garbage again. He stated that Leah was a shameful and inadequate vessel for God's will, and that was why he would no longer even stoop to punishing her when she needed it.

Leah spoke back to him in a calm voice as if she too were discussing whatever had gotten into the garbage and it certainly wasn't *her*. She said, "Is that your point of view, Father? How interesting that you think so," and so forth. Which was fine and dandy for her, I guess, if she wasn't going to get punished for it! Lucky duck. Ruth May and Adah and I stayed out of it, us still being adequate vessels for a good licking, the last we'd heard. Even though someone could have pointed out to Father that at least *somebody* finally brought home some bacon at our house. Someone could have remarked that it is Leah who wears the pants in our family, which is true. Mother took sides against Father without saying so, in the noisy way she stacked the plates.

Then suddenly from one second to the next they were all transposed on Nelson, who came running into the house afraid for his life. It was something about a snake. He'd seen the evil sign outside our chicken house. Well, that was hardly a surprise because for the last few days people had been finding snakes everyplace. Inside the house, for instance, inside a bean basket with the lid on tight. Places where you wouldn't think it was natural for a snake to be. Everybody was so afraid, Nelson said, you could see Afraid walking around on its own two feet. When he saw the evil sign it sent him singing like a canary, because our chicken house is where he sleeps.

He was positive he was doomed, and there was just no reasoning with him. Mother did try, but he wouldn't listen. He said he'd been just fixing to go to bed when he heard a sound and went outside to look. When he stepped out the door, two shadows in the shape of an X fell across his path. Lately he's been tying the chicken-house door shut with a rope when he turns in for the night, but now it was plain to see no rope was going to be strong enough. Nelson was not going to sleep in our chicken house for all the teeth in China.

Well, any two straight things can make a shadow of an X is what Mother told him, which is true, especially with a wild imagination coming into play. Probably some clown is just trying to scare him and needs a good poke in the puss. But Nelson said this was not just ordinary shadows. He said it was the dreaming of snakes.

Father announced this was the unfortunate effect of believing in false idols and he washed his hands of the affair. He was washing his hands left and right that evening. Mother didn't necessarily agree with him, but I could see she didn't want us going anywhere near that chicken house to investigate. Father quoted a Bible verse about the only thing we had to fear was fear itself. He told Mother if she let Nelson sleep in our house that night she'd be playing directly into the hands of the idol worshipers, and if she wanted to count herself as one of them she could take her children and go seek shelter among them. Then he turned to us and declared it was high time for us to go to bed and put the light out on laughable Congolese superstitions.

But Nelson slunk out of the house in such a terrified state we couldn't find anything to laugh about, that is for sure. Even Anatole had been telling us to be extra careful right now, and Anatole, I must admit, has his head firmly attached to his shoulders. We tried to get ready for bed, but all we could hear was Nelson outside whimpering to be allowed to come in, and we became scared out of our minds. Even Leah did. We did not believe in voodoo spirits, and informed each other of that fact till we were blue in the face. But still there was some dark thing out there watching us from the forest and coiling up under people's beds at night, and whether you call it fear or the dreaming of snakes or false idolatry or what—it's still *something*. It doesn't care what prayers we say at bedtime, or whether we admit we believe in it. Does *it* believe in *us*, that's the question.

We lay in our beds listening to Nelson's steady, high-pitched begging. Sticky-toed lizards ran sideways along the walls. The moon made shadows on our mosquito netting. Nelson pleaded, "*Bäkala mputu Nelson, bäkala mputu*," over and over like a poor starving dog that's been whining so long it doesn't know how to stop. We heard Father's bedsprings groan suddenly, then Father at the window yelling for him to shut up. Leah rolled over and put her pillow on her head. I felt sick to my stomach. We all did. Father's hatefulness and Mother's silent fright were infecting our minds.

"This is wrong," Leah said finally. "I'm going to help him. Who has the guts to come with me?"

The thought of going out there gave me the willies. But if the others went, I wasn't going to stay in here with the shadows and lizards, either. I think our house gave me the worst willies of all. That house was the whole problem, because it had our family in it. I was long past the point of feeling safe huddling under my parents' wings. Maybe when we first came to Congo I did, because we were all just hardly more than children then. But now everything has changed; being American doesn't matter and nobody gives us any special credit. Now we're all in this stewpot together, black or white regardless. And certainly we're not children. Leah says in Congo there's only two ages of people: babies that have to be carried, and people that stand up and fend for themselves. No in-between phase. No such thing as childhood. Sometimes I think she's right.

After a while she said again, "I'm going out there to help Nelson, and Father can go straight to hell."

Whether we said so or not, the rest of us certainly agreed upon where Father could go straight to.

Surprisingly, Adah sat up and started to pull on her jeans. That was her way of saying, "I'm in." So I felt around on the floor for my penny loafers. Leah pulled Ruth May's shirt on over her head and stuck her tennis shoes on her feet. As quiet as mice, we crept outside through the window.

What we decided to do was to set a trap, like Daniel in the temple. This was Leah's inspiration. Nelson raked a pan of cold ashes out of the stove, and together we strewed them all around the hard-pan-dirt yard outside the chicken house. Inside it, too. We worked by candlelight. Nelson kept a lookout to make sure no one saw us. But Ruth May was careless, and the rest of us were also, to some extent, and made tracks over each other's tracks. Then our two chickens got disturbed by our lights, since they'd come from a different way of life over at Mama Mwanza's and weren't used to living in our chicken house yet, so they ran around making chicken tracks on top of everything. We had to sweep it all up and start over. The second time we were much more careful. We made Ruth May stand in one spot, and chased the chickens back into the nest box to roost. They looked down at us with their stupid little eyes and made soft noises into their feathers to calm themselves down.

When it was all done, we made Nelson promise to hide out the night at Anatole's and come back before daybreak. Leah ran halfway there with him, because he was scared, and came back by herself. We all tiptoed inside to our beds, leaving the ashes perfect behind us like newly fallen snow. If anyone or anything set foot in our chicken house—if it had feet, that is—we would catch the culprit red-handed.

Adah

THERE ARE SEVEN WAYS for a foot to touch the ground, each with its own particular power. Did he know how it would come to us in the end? Should I have known? For I had watched him, long before. Watched him dancing, foot to ground, watched him throw the bones. In the clearing behind our house is where he made his trouble. With his machete he cut off the heads of two small living dogs and pressed their noses to the ground, reciting promises. Against him, quietly, I unlocked my voice and sang in the forest. I sang against him my most perfect backward-forward hymns, because I have no other powers of my own.

> Lived a tune, rare nut, a devil,
>> Lived a devil!
>> Lived a devil!
> Wets dab noses on bad stew,
>> Evil deed live!
>> Evil deed live!
> Sun! opus! rat! See stars upon us,
>> Eye, level eye!
>> Eye, level eye!
> Warn rotten Ada, net torn raw:
>> Eye did peep did eye.

On the morning after we spread the ashes, we woke before sunrise. Wondering what we might have caught in our trap, we lay still and wide-eyed in our beds until Nelson's face appeared at our open window. Then, while our parents still slept, we tiptoed out of the house. Nelson with a pole twice as tall as himself waited for us. In the company of nothing but our fear itself, we went to the chicken house.

Strange to say, if you do not stamp yourself with the words *exhilarated* or *terrified*, those two things feel exactly the same in a body. Creeping past our parents' bedroom and out the door, our bodies felt as they did on Christmas Past and all the Easter mornings of the world, when Christ is risen and our mother has hidden a tribe of sugared marshmallow bunnies in the startled grass of a parsonage lawn in Bethlehem, Georgia. Ruth May marvel-eyed with a hand cupped over her mouth, I have willed myself to forget, forget, forget, and not forget, for those eyes will see through anything, even my dreams. Ruth May with the eyes of an Easter morning.

As Nelson knew it would be, it was there inside the chicken house. He stopped us in the doorway, and we froze behind his outstretched arm until we saw it too in the far corner, in the nest box, curled tightly around our two precious hens and all their eggs. Two poor, ruffle-feathered mothers without a breath between them, bound to their stillborn future. Nest, eggs, and hens were all one package, wrapped in a vivid, slender twine of brilliant green. It was so pretty, so elaborately basket-woven among hen and egg, we did not at first understand what we saw. A tisket, a tasket, a gift. Nelson raised his long pole and shoved hard, hitting the wall above the nest so dust rained down on the dark, quiet hens. The green vine shifted suddenly, every part at once moving up, down, or sideways. Stopped, then moved forward one more inch through the path of its knot. A small blunt head emerged and swiveled to face us. Very slowly it split itself wide, showing the bright blue inside of its mouth, two bare fangs. A tongue, delicately licking the air.

Suddenly it flew at the pole, striking twice, then flung itself from the nest box and shot past us out the door into the bright morning, gone.

Without breathing we stared at the place where the snake had been until our eyes caught up and we could all witness our memory of what had passed before us. Green mamba, mistress of camouflage, agility, aggressiveness, and speed. *L'ingéniosité diabolique de la nature a atteint avec ce serpent le plus haut degré de perfection*, the experts claim in the library book of snakes: In this serpent the diabolic genius of nature has attained the highest degree of perfection. What had passed before us was a basket of death, exploded. A gift meant for Nelson. Three of us, then, breathed. Together. Dropped our eyes to the white-ash floor.

A foot had marked that floor in all the seven ways of a dance. Footprints fanned out in tight circles. *Evil deed live.* Not the paws of a leopard walking upright, turned against men by irreverence. Not the belly slither of angry snakes coming up from the sheltered ground of their own accord to punish us. Only a man, one man and no other, who brought the snake in a basket or carried it stunned or charmed like a gift in his own two hands. Only one single dancer with six toes on his left foot.

Leah

I ONLY REMEMBER hearing a gulp and a sob and a scream all at once, the strangest cry, like a baby taking its first breath. We couldn't tell where it came from, but strangely enough, we all looked up at the treetops. A nervous wind stirred the branches, but nothing more. Only silence fell down.

It's a very odd thing to recall, that we all looked up. Not one of us looked at Ruth May. I can't say that Ruth May was even there with us, in that instant. Just for the moment it was as if she'd disappeared, and her voice was thrown into the trees. Then she returned to us, but all that was left of her was an awful silence. The voiceless empty skin of my baby sister sitting quietly on the ground, hugging herself.

"Ruth May, honey, it's all right," I said. "The bad snake is gone." I knelt down beside her, gently taking hold of her shoulder. "Don't be scared. It's gone."

Nelson knelt too, putting his face close to hers. He opened his mouth to speak, to reassure her, I imagine, for he loved Ruth May. I know this. I've seen how he sings to her and protects her. But the terrible silence took hold of Nelson, too, and no words came. His eyes grew wide as we all watched her face change to a pale blue mask pulled down from her hairline to her swollen lips. No eyes. What I mean is that no one we recognized was looking out through her eyes.

"Ruth May, what is it? What! *What did you see?*" In my panic I shook her hard, and I think I must have screamed those words at her. I can't change what I did: I shook her too hard, and screamed at her. Maybe that was the last she knew of her sister Leah.

Nelson shoved me away. He'd come to life again suddenly and spoke so fast in Kikongo I couldn't think how to understand. He tore her blouse open, just ripped it, and put his face against her chest. Then drew back in horror. As we watched in dismay I remember thinking I should pay attention to where the buttons fell, so I could help her sew them back on later. Buttons are so precious here. The strangest things I thought of, so ridiculous. Because I couldn't look at what was in front of me.

"Midiki!" he screamed at me. I waited for the word to pierce my dumb, thick brain and begin to mean something. "Milk," he was shouting. "Get milk. Of a goat, a dog, any kind, to draw out the poison. Get Mama Nguza," he said, "she will know what to do, she saved her son from a green mamba once. *Kakakaka*, go!"

But I found I couldn't move. I felt hot and breathless and stung, like an antelope struck with an arrow. I could only stare at Ruth May's bare left shoulder, where two red puncture wounds stood out like red beads on her flesh. Two dots an inch apart, as small and tidy as punctuation marks at the end of a sentence none of us could read. The sentence would have started somewhere just above her heart.

Adah

BECAUSE I COULD NOT STOP FOR DEATH—*He kindly stopped for me.*
I was not present at Ruth May's birth but I have seen it now, because I saw each step of it played out in reverse at the end of her life. The closing parenthesis, at the end of the palindrome that was Ruth May. Her final gulp of air as hungry as a baby's first breath. That last howling scream, exactly like the first, and then at the end a fixed, steadfast moving backward out of this world. After the howl, wide-eyed silence without breath. Her bluish face creased with a pressure closing in, the near proximity of the other-than-life that crowds down around the edges of living. Her eyes closed up tightly, and her swollen lips clamped shut. Her spine curved, and her limbs drew in more and more tightly until she seemed impossibly small. While we watched without comprehension, she moved away to where none of us wanted to follow. Ruth May shrank back through the narrow passage between this brief fabric of light and all the rest of what there is for us: the long waiting. Now she will wait the rest of the time. It will be exactly as long as the time that passed before she was born.

Because I could not stop for death he kindly stopped for me, or paused at least to strike a glancing blow with his sky-blue mouth as he passed. A lightning that cannot strike twice, our lesson learned in the hateful speed of light. A bite at light at Ruth a truth a sky-blue presentiment and oh how dear we are to ourselves when it comes, it comes, that long, long shadow in the grass.

Rachel

THERE'S A STRANGE MOMENT IN TIME, after something horrible happens, when you know it's true but you haven't told anyone yet. Of all things, that is what I remember most. It was so quiet. And I thought: Now we have to go in and tell Mother. That Ruth May is, oh, sweet Jesus. Ruth May is gone. We had to tell our parents, and they were still in bed, asleep.

I didn't cry at first, and then, I don't know why, but I fell apart when I thought of Mother in bed sleeping. Mother's dark hair would be all askew on the pillow and her face sweet and quiet. Her whole body just not knowing yet. Her body that had carried and given birth to Ruth May last of all. Mother asleep in her nightgown, still believing she had four living daughters. Now we were going to put one foot in front of the other, walk to the back door, go in the house, stand beside our parents' bed, wake up Mother, say to her the words *Ruth May*, say the word *dead*. Tell her, *Mother wake up!*

The whole world would change then, and nothing would ever be all right again. Not for our family. All the other people in the whole wide world might go on about their business, but for us it would never be normal again.

I couldn't move. None of us could. We looked at each other because we knew someone should go but I think we all had the same strange idea that if we stood there without moving forever and ever, we could keep our family the way it was. We would not wake up from this nightmare to find out it was someone's real life, and for once that someone wasn't just a poor unlucky nobody in a shack you could forget about. It was *our* life, the only one we were going to have. The only Ruth May.

Until that moment I'd always believed I could still go home and pretend the Congo never happened. The misery, the hunt, the ants, the embarrassments of all we saw and endured—those were just stories I would tell someday with a laugh and a toss of my hair, when Africa was faraway and make-believe like the people in history books. The tragedies that happened to Africans were not mine. We were different, not just because we were white and had our vaccinations, but because we were simply a much, much luckier kind of person. I would get back home to Bethlehem, Georgia, and be exactly the same Rachel as before. I'd grow up to be a carefree American wife, with nice things and a sensible way of life and three grown sisters to share my ideals and talk to on the phone from time to time. This is what I believed. I'd never planned on being someone different. Never imagined I would be a girl they'd duck their eyes from and whisper about as tragic, for having suffered such a loss.

I think Leah and Adah also believed these things, in their own different ways, and that is why none of us moved. We thought we could freeze time for just one more minute, and one more after that. That if none of us confessed it, we could hold back the curse that was going to be our history.

Leah

MOTHER DID NOT RANT or tear her hair. She behaved as if someone else had already told her, before we got there.

Silently she dressed, tied back her hair, and set herself to a succession of chores, beginning with tearing down the mosquito netting from all of our beds. We were afraid to ask what she was doing. We didn't know whether she wanted us all to get malaria now, for punishment, or if she had simply lost her mind. So we stood out of her way and watched. All of us, even Father. For once he had no words to instruct our minds and improve our souls, no parable that would turn Ruth May's death by snakebite into a lesson on the Glory of God. My Father, whose strong hands always seized whatever came along and molded it to his will, seemed unable to grasp what had happened.

"She wasn't baptized yet," he said.

I looked up when he said this, startled by such a pathetically inadequate observation. Was that really what mattered to him right now—the condition of Ruth May's soul? Mother ignored him, but I studied his face in the bright morning light. His blue eyes with their left-sided squint, weakened by the war, had a vacant look. His large reddish ears repelled me. My father was a simple, ugly man.

It's true that she wasn't baptized. If any one of us had cared about that, we could lay the blame on Father. He'd maintained that Ruth May was still too young to take the responsibility of accepting Christ, but in truth I think he was holding her back for the sake of pageantry. He was going to baptize his own child along with all of

Kilanga's, on that great day down at the river when his dream finally came true. It would lend an appearance of sincerity to the occasion.

Now he seemed narrow-witted and without particular dreams. I couldn't stand to look at him standing in the doorway, his body hanging from its frame with nothing but its own useless hands for company. And all he could think to say to his wife was "This can't be."

It couldn't be, but it was, and Mother alone among us seemed to realize that. With a dark scarf over her hair and the sleeves of her stained white blouse rolled up, she did her work as deliberately as the sun or moon, a heavenly body tracking its course through our house. Her tasks moved her continually away from us—her senseless shadows, a husband and living daughters. With determined efficiency she gathered up everything she would need from one room before she moved to the next, in the way I remember her doing when we were all much younger and needed her more.

She went out to the kitchen house, fired the stove, warmed a pan of water, then carried it back into the house and set it on the big dining table where Nelson had laid the body on a bedsheet. Mother bathed Ruth May with a washcloth as if she were a baby. I stood with my back to the wall, remembering too much of another time, as I watched her rub carefully under the chin and in the folds at the backs of the elbows and knees. In our house in Bethlehem I used to stand outside the bathroom door, where I could see the two of them in the mirror. Mother singing soft questions and kissing her answers into the tiny, outstretched palms. Adah and I were nine then, too old to be jealous of a baby, but still I had to wonder if she had ever loved me that much. With twins, she could only have loved each of us by half. And Adah was the one who required more of her.

A honeycreeper sang from the bushes outside the window. It seemed impossible that an ordinary, bright day should be proceeding outside our house. Mother spread a small, soft hand onto hers and washed the fingers one at a time. She cradled and lifted the head to rinse it, taking care not to get the soapy water in Ruth May's eyes. As she dried the limp blond hair with a towel, she leaned in close, inhaling the scent of my sister's scalp. I felt invisible. By the force of my mother's desire to conduct this ritual in private, she had caused me to disappear. Still, I couldn't leave the room. After she dried and wrapped her baby in a towel she hummed quietly while combing out the tangles and plaiting the damp hair. Then she began to cut our mosquito netting into long sheets and stitch the layers together. At last we understood. She was making a shroud.

"Leah, help me move this table outside," she said when she was finished. It was the first time she'd spoken in more than half a day, to anyone, and I jumped to do as I was told. She moved Ruth May to her own bed while we moved the big, heavy table out into the center of the front yard. We had to turn it on end to get it out the door. When we set it down, the legs settled soundly into the dust so it did not wobble, as it had always done inside the house. Mother went back inside and returned with the shrouded body in her arms. Gently she laid Ruth May out on the table, spending a long time arranging her arms and legs within the sheer cloth. The shade of the mango stretched all the way across the yard, and I realized it must be afternoon, a fact that surprised me. I looked at several familiar things, one at a time: a striped green mango lying in the grass; my own hand; our dining table. All these things seemed like objects I hadn't seen before. I looked at the table and forced my mind to accept the words "This is my dead sister." But Ruth May was shrouded in so many misty layers of mosquito netting I could barely make out any semblance of a dead child inside. She looked more like a billowy cloud that could rise right up through the trees, whenever Mother finally let her go.

Nelson was weaving together palm fronds to make a funeral arch of leaves and flowers to set over the table. It looked something like an altar. I thought perhaps I ought to help him, but I couldn't think how. Several women from the village had already come. Mama Mwanza arrived first, with her daughters. A few at a time, the others followed. They fell down at the edge of our yard when they came, and walked on their knees to the table. All of them had lost children before, it dawned on me through my shock. Our suffering now was no greater than theirs had been, no more real or tragic. No different. They all knelt around the table silently for quite a while, and I knew I should join them, but I felt unaccountably afraid to get close to the table. I stayed at the back of the group.

Suddenly one woman shrieked, and I felt my skull would split open. All the others immediately joined in with the quivering, high *biläla*. I felt blood rushing through all the narrow parts of my body: the wrists, the throat, the backs of my knees. Adah was white-faced beside me, and looked into my eyes as if she were drowning. We'd heard this strange mourning song many times before, back during the heavy rains when so many children got sick. It had tricked us at first, more than once, sending us running to the windows to see what beautiful, exotic birds made such a strange call. Now, of course, we couldn't think of birds. The trilling of our neighbors' tongues set loose knives that cut the flesh from our bones and made us fall down with our shame and our love and our anger. We were all cut down together by the knife of our own hope, for if there is any single thing that everyone hopes for most dearly, it must be this: that the youngest outlive the oldest.

In our family, the last was first. I would like to believe she got what she wanted. I ground my knees in the dust and shook and sobbed and opened my mouth to cry out loud. I crossed my arms over my chest and held on to my own shoulders, thinking of Ruth May's sharp, skinny shoulder blades under her little white shirt. Thinking of ant lions and "Mother May I." Recalling her strange, transfigured shadow the last time I pushed her in the swing. The sounds of our voices rose up through the tree branches into the sky, but Ruth May did not.

When the wailing finally stopped, we were wrapped in silence and the buzzing of locusts. The air was thick and ponderous with humidity. It felt like a wet wool blanket you could not take off.

Mother had begun moving all of our furniture into the yard. First the chairs. Then our beds and my father's roll-top desk. These heavy things she dragged by herself, even though I know for a fact that two months ago she couldn't have moved them. I continued to watch without any particular expectation as she emerged, next, with our clothes and books. Then our cooking pots. She stacked these things on the chairs and desk. The women watched closely, as my sisters and I did, but no one moved. Mother stood looking at us all, waiting. Finally she took the good skillet we'd brought from home and pressed it into Mama Mwanza's hands. She offered our blouses and dresses to Mama Mwanza's children. They accepted them in both hands, thanked her, and left. Mama Mwanza balanced the skillet on her head, since she needed her hands for walking, and solemnly led her family away from our funeral. Tentatively the other women touched our things. Their initial reluctance gave way to excited chatter as they began to sort through the piles of our possessions, unabashedly holding our clothes up to their children's chests, scrutinizing such oddities as a hairbrush and fingernail clippers, thumping on the enamel pans with their knuckles to test their worth. Eventually they took what they needed, and left.

But the children soon came back, unable to resist the scene of such a spectacle. Just as they used to do when we first arrived here, they materialized one by one out of the moist air and the bamboo thickets until they'd formed a silent, watchful circle around the periphery of our yard. I suppose they were as astonished as we were that a member of our family was capable of death. Gradually they crept forward, closing their circle around the table, and there they remained for a very long time, staring at Ruth May.

Mother had gone back in the house, where we could hear her strange, tireless industry moving upon the empty rooms. Our father seemed to be nowhere. My sisters and I stayed outside with the children because they seemed to embrace our presence. Out of habit we knelt on the ground and prayed the dumb prayers of our childhood: "Our Father which art in heaven," and "Yea, though I walk through the valley of the shadow of death, I will fear no evil." I could not remotely believe any Shepherd was leading me through this dreadful valley, but the familiar words stuffed my mouth like cotton, and it was some relief to know, at least, that one sentence would follow upon another. It was my only way of knowing what to do.

Whenever I stopped praying, the buzz of the locusts grew horrible in my ears. So I didn't stop. Sometimes Rachel prayed with me, and sometimes the Congolese children also prayed in whatever words they knew. I recited the 23rd Psalm, the 121st Psalm, the 100th and 137th and 19th and 66th Psalms, the 21st chapter of Revelation, Genesis one, Luke 22, First Corinthians, and finally John 3:16: "For God so loved the world, that he gave his only begotten Son, that whosoever believeth in him should not perish but have everlasting life."

Then I stopped. It was very late in the afternoon, and I could think of no more prayers. I'd come to the end of all I knew. I listened to the world around me, but all other sound had ceased entirely. Not a single bird called. I felt terrified. The air seemed charged and dangerous but I couldn't pray anymore, and I couldn't get up and do anything else. To go back inside our empty house, where Mother was, especially, I couldn't make myself do. Not for anything. It seemed impossible. So I stayed where I was, kneeling beside my sisters with our heads bowed low beneath the crackling air.

The sky groaned and cracked, and suddenly the shrill, cold needles of rain pierced our hands and the backs of our necks. A thunderstorm broke open, and with a strength as mighty as the thirst of crops and animals, the rain poured down on our heads. It lashed us hard, answering months of prayers. Some of the smaller children rushed to break off elephant-ear leaves for umbrellas, but most of us simply stayed where we were, receiving the downpour. Lightning sang and hissed around our shoulders, and the thunder bellowed.

Our father came out of the house and stood looking at the sky, holding out his hands. It seemed to take him a long time to believe in the rain.

"The Lord spoke to the common people gathered at the well," he said at last, in his old booming voice that allowed no corner for doubt. He had to shout to be heard above the noise of the downpour. "And the Lord told them, Whosoever drinks of this ordinary water will be thirsty again, but the water I will give unto him will quench his thirst forever. It will become a spring within him, bubbling up for eternal life."

The children weren't paying much mind right then to my father or his bubbling spring of eternal life. They were so transfixed by the rain. They held up their faces and arms to the cold water, as if the whole of their skin were a manioc field that needed to be soaked.

"If anyone is thirsty," my father shouted, "let him come to me and drink! If anyone believes in me, streams of living water shall flow forth from his heart!"

He walked to a tall boy near me, Pascal's half brother. I'd spoken to him twice and knew his name was Lucien, though I'm sure my father didn't know it. Nevertheless, Father held out his large, white hand and spread his fingers wide over the boy's head. Lucien looked my father in the eye as if he expected to be struck, but he didn't flinch.

"I am a voice of one shouting in the desert, Straighten the Lord's way!" my father cried. "I am only baptizing in water, but someone is standing among you of whom you do not know. He is God's Lamb, who is to remove the world's sin."

My father lowered his hand and closed his fingers gently over the top of Lucien's head.

"In the name of the Father, the Son, and the Holy Ghost I baptize you, my son. Walk forward into the light."

Lucien didn't move. Father took his hand away and waited, I suppose, for the miracle of baptism to take hold. Then he turned to Lucien's tiny sister Bwanga, who held on to Lucien's hand for dear life. Their mother had died during the disease time, and their father's other wife—Pascal's mother—had taken them both into her house. Throughout this time of loss and salvation, Bwanga had remained Ruth May's most loyal playmate. Even that my father wouldn't have known. I felt an unspeakable despair. He knew nothing about the children. Under his cupped hand Bwanga's little bald head looked like an overripe avocado he was prepared to toss away. She stood wide-eyed and motionless.

"In the name of the Father, the Son, and the Holy Ghost," he repeated, and released her.

"Mah-dah-mey-I?" Bwanga asked.

Several other children remembered this game and echoed: "Mah-dah-mey-I?" Their eyes left Father and came to rest on Ruth May inside the drenched cloud of netting on the table. They all picked up the refrain, asking again and again in a rising plea: Mother May I? And though they surely knew no permission would be granted, they kept up their soft, steady chant for a very long time in the pouring rain. Water clung to their eyelashes and streamed in runnels down their open faces. Their meager clothes, imposed on them by foreigners, clung to their thin chests and legs like a second skin finally ready to accept the shape of their bodies. The dust on our feet turned blood-colored and the sky grew very dark, while Father moved around the circle baptizing each child in turn, imploring the living progeny of Kilanga to walk forward into the light.

Book Five

EXODUS

*. . . And ye shall carry up my bones
away hence with you.
And they took their journey . . . and encamped . . .
in the edge of the wilderness. . . .
He took not away the pillar of cloud by day,
nor the pillar of fire by night.*

EXODUS 13:19–22

Orleanna Price

SANDERLING ISLAND, GEORGIA

A S LONG AS I KEPT MOVING, my grief streamed out behind me like a swimmer's long hair in water. I knew the weight was there but it didn't touch me. Only when I stopped did the slick, dark stuff of it come floating around my face, catching my arms and throat till I began to drown. So I just didn't stop.

The substance of grief is not imaginary. It's as real as rope or the absence of air, and like both those things it can kill. My body understood there was no safe place for me to be.

A mother's body remembers her babies—the folds of soft flesh, the softly furred scalp against her nose. Each child has its own entreaties to body and soul. It's the last one, though, that overtakes you. I can't dare say I loved the others less, but my first three were all babies at once, and motherhood dismayed me entirely. The twins came just as Rachel was learning to walk. What came next I hardly remember, whole years when I battled through every single day of grasping hands and mouths until I could fall into bed for a few short hours and dream of being eaten alive in small pieces. I counted to one hundred as I rocked, contriving the patience to get one down in order to take up another. One mouth closed on a spoon meant two crying empty, feathers flying, so I dashed back and forth like a mother bird, flouting nature's maw with a brood too large. I couldn't count on survival until all three of them could stand alone. Together they were my first issue. I took one deep breath for every step they took away from me. That's how it is with the firstborn, no matter what kind of mother you are—rich, poor, frazzled half to death or sweetly content. A first child is your own best foot forward, and how you do cheer those little feet as they strike out. You examine every turn of flesh for precocity, and crow it to the world.

But the last one: the baby who trails her scent like a flag of surrender through your life when there will be no more coming after—oh, that's love by a different name. She is the babe you hold in your arms for an hour after she's gone to sleep. If you put her down in the crib, she might wake up changed and fly away. So instead you rock by the window, drinking the light from her skin, breathing her exhaled dreams. Your heart bays to the double crescent moons of closed lashes on her cheeks. She's the one you can't put down.

My baby, my blood, my honest truth: entreat me not to leave thee, for whither thou goest I will go. Where I lodge, we lodge together. Where I die, you'll be buried at last.

By instinct rather than will, I stayed alive. I tried to flee from the grief. It wasn't the spirit but just a body that moved me from one place to another. I watched my hands, heard my mouth give orders. Avoided corners and stillness. When I had to pause for breath I stood in the open, in the center of a room or out in the yard. The trees roared and danced as if they were on fire in the pouring rain, telling me to go on, go on. Once I'd moved our table outside, with my baby laid out upon it, I could see no sense in anything but to bring out the rest. Such a bewildering excess of things we had for one single family, and how useless it all seemed now. I carried out armloads of fabric and wood and metal put together in all their puzzling ways, and marveled that I'd ever felt comfort in having such things. I needed truth and light, to remember my baby's laughter. This stuff cluttered my way. What relief, to place it in the hands of women who could carry off my burden. Their industrious need made me light-headed: my dresses would be curtains, and my curtains, dresses. My tea towel, a baby's diaper. Empty food tins would be pounded into palm-oil lamps, toys, plowshares maybe—who could say? My household would pass through the great digestive tract of Kilanga and turn into sights unseen. It was a miracle to witness my own simple motion, amplified. As I gave it all up, the trees unrolled their tongues of flame and blazed in approval.

Motion became my whole purpose. When there was nothing left

to move but myself, I walked to the end of our village and kept going, with a whole raft of children strung out behind me. Nothing to do but take my leave, *Sala mbote!* I went on foot because I still had feet to carry me.

Plain and simple, that was the source of our exodus: I had to keep moving. I didn't set out to leave my husband. Anyone can see I should have, long before, but I never did know how. For women like me, it seems, it's not ours to take charge of beginnings and endings. Not the marriage proposal, the summit conquered, the first shot fired, nor the last one either—the treaty at Appomattox, the knife in the heart. Let men write those stories. I can't. I only know the middle ground where we live our lives. We whistle while Rome burns, or we scrub the floor, depending. Don't dare presume there's shame in the lot of a woman who carries on. On the day a committee of men decided to murder the fledgling Congo, what do you suppose Mama Mwanza was doing? Was it different, the day after? Of course not. Was she a fool, then, or the backbone of a history? When a government comes crashing down, it crushes those who were living under its roof. People like Mama Mwanza never knew the house was there at all. *Independence* is a complex word in a foreign tongue. To resist occupation, whether you're a nation or merely a woman, you must understand the language of your enemy. *Conquest* and *liberation* and *democracy* and *divorce* are words that mean squat, basically, when you have hungry children and clothes to get out on the line and it looks like rain.

Maybe you still can't understand why I stayed so long. I've nearly finished with my side of the story, and still I feel your small round eyes looking down on me. I wonder what you'll name my sin: Complicity? Loyalty? Stupefaction? How can you tell the difference? Is my sin a failure of virtue, or of competence? I knew Rome was burning, but I had just enough water to scrub the floor, so I did what I could. My talents are different from those of the women who cleave and part from husbands nowadays—and my virtues probably unrecognizable. But look at old women and bear in mind we are another country. We married with simple hopes: enough to eat and children who might outlive us. My life was a business of growing where planted and making good on the debts life gathered onto me. Companionship and joy came unexpectedly, mostly in small, exploding moments when I was apart from my husband and children. A kiss of flesh-colored sunrise while I hung out the wash, a sigh of indigo birds exhaled from the grass. An okapi at the water. It didn't occur to me to leave Nathan on account of *unhappiness*, any more than Tata Mwanza would have left his disfigured wife, though a more able woman might have grown more manioc and kept more of his children alive. Nathan was something that happened to us, as devastating in its way as the burning roof that fell on the family Mwanza; with our fate scarred by hell and brimstone we still had to track our course. And it happened finally by the grace of hell and brimstone that I had to keep moving. I moved, and he stood still.

But his kind will always lose in the end. I know this, and now I know why. Whether it's wife or nation they occupy, their mistake is the same: they stand still, and their stake moves underneath them. *The Pharaoh died*, says Exodus, *and the children of Israel sighed by reason of their bondage.* Chains rattle, rivers roll, animals startle and bolt, forests inspire and expand, babies stretch open-mouthed from the womb, new seedlings arch their necks and creep forward into the light. Even a language won't stand still. A territory is only possessed for a moment in time. They stake everything on that moment, posing for photographs while planting the flag, casting themselves in bronze. Washington crossing the Delaware. The capture of Okinawa. They're desperate to hang on.

But they can't. Even before the flagpole begins to peel and splinter, the ground underneath arches and slides forward into its own new destiny. It may bear the marks of boots on its back, but those marks become the possessions of the land. What does Okinawa remember of its fall? Forbidden to make engines of war, Japan made automobiles instead, and won the world. It all moves on. The great Delaware rolls on, while Mr. Washington himself is no longer even what you'd call good compost. The Congo River, being of a different temperament, drowned most of its conquerors outright. In Congo a slashed jungle quickly becomes a field of flowers, and scars become the ornaments of a particular face. Call it oppression, complicity, stupefaction, call it what you like, it doesn't matter. Africa swallowed the conqueror's music and sang a new song of her own.

If you are the eyes in the trees, watching us as we walk away from Kilanga, how will you make your judgment? Lord knows after thirty years I still crave your forgiveness, but who are *you*? A small burial mound in the middle of Nathan's garden, where vines and flowers have long since unrolled to feed insects and children. Is that what you are? Are you still my own flesh and blood, my last-born, or are you now the flesh of Africa? How can I tell the difference when the two rivers have run together so? Try to imagine what never happened: our family without Africa, or the Africa that would have been without us. Look at your sisters now. Lock, stock, and barrel, they've got their own three ways to live with our history. Some can find it. Many more never do. But which one among us is without sin? I can hardly think where to cast my stones, so I just go on keening for my own losses, trying to wear the marks of the boot on my back as gracefully as the Congo wears hers.

My little beast, my eyes, my favorite stolen egg. Listen. To live is to be marked. To live is to change, to acquire the words of a story, and that is the only celebration we mortals really know. In perfect stillness, frankly, I've only found sorrow.

What We Carried Out

Leah Price

BULUNGU, LATE RAINY SEASON
1961

WE ONLY TOOK what we could carry on our backs.

Mother never once turned around to look over her shoulder. I don't know what would have become of us if it hadn't been for Mama Mwanza's daughters, who came running after us, bringing oranges and a demijohn of water. They knew we'd get thirsty, even though the rain hammered our shirts to our backs and chilled us right through the skin, and being thirsty ever again seemed out of the question. Either we'd never known such rain, or we'd forgotten. In just the few hours since the storm broke, the parched road through our village had become a gushing stream of mud, blood-red, throbbing like an artery. We couldn't walk in it at all, and could barely keep our footing on the grassy banks beside it. A day ago we'd have given up our teeth for a good rain, and now we gnashed them in frustration over the deluge. If only we'd had a boat, it seemed possible we could ride the waves straight to Leopoldville. That's the Congo for you: famine or flood. It has been raining ever since.

Late that afternoon as we trudged along we spotted a bright bouquet of color up ahead, glowing dimly through the rain. Eventually I recognized the huge pink starburst across the rump of Mama Boanda. She, Mama Lo, and several others huddled together beside the road under elephant-ear leaves, waiting out a particularly fierce spell of the downpour. They motioned us into their shelter and we joined them, stupefied by the rain. It's hard to believe any water on earth could be so unequivocal. I put out my hand and watched it disappear at the end of my arm. The noise on our heads was a white roar that drew us together in our small shelter of leaves. I let my mind drift into a pleasant nowhere as I breathed the mamas' peanut-and-manioc scent. The upright sprigs of Mama Boanda's hair dripped from their ends, like a tiny garden of leaking hoses.

When it slowed back down to mere cloudburst, we set off together. The women carried leaf-wrapped packets of manioc and other things on their heads, food they were taking to their husbands in Bulungu, they said. A large political meeting was going on there. Mama Lo also had palm oil to sell in Bulungu. She balanced the immense rectangular can of oil on her head while she chatted with me, and looked so comfortable at it that I tried placing my plastic demijohn on my own head. To my great surprise I found I could keep it there as long as I had one hand on it. In all our time in the Congo I'd been awestruck by what the ladies could carry this way, but had never once tried it myself. What a revelation, that I could carry my own parcel like any woman here! After the first several miles I ceased to feel the weight on my head at all.

With no men around, everyone was surprisingly lighthearted. It was contagious somehow. We laughed at the unladylike ways we all sank into the mud. Every so often the women also sang together in little shouted bursts of call and response. Whenever I recognized the tune, I joined in. Father's mission had been a success in at least one regard: the Congolese loved our music. They could work miracles with "Soldiers of the Cross" in their own language. Even that most doleful of Christian laments—"Nobody Knows the Trouble I've Seen"—sounded snappy and upbeat through these women's windpipes as they sauntered along: "*Nani oze mpasi zazo! Nani oze mpasi!*" We *had* seen trouble beyond compare, but in that moment as we marched along with rain streaming off the ends of our hair, it felt like we were out on a grand adventure together. Our own particular Price family sadness seemed to belong to another time that we didn't need to think about anymore. Only once I realized I was looking around for Ruth May, wondering whether she was warm enough or needed my extra shirt. Then I thought with astonishment, Why, Ruth May is no longer with us! It seemed very simple. We were walking along this road, and she wasn't with us.

My mind wandered around a great deal, until it found Anatole. I had peculiar thoughts weighing on me that I badly needed to tell him. That the inside of a green mamba's mouth is pure sky-blue, for example. And that we'd strewn ashes on the floor like Daniel, capturing the six-toed footprints, which I had not mentioned to anybody. Anatole might not be safe in Kilanga, any more than we were. But perhaps nobody was safe, with so many things getting turned upside-down. What was the purpose of the political meeting in Bulungu? Who was the secretive man Adah had seen in Axelroot's shack, laughing about orders from President Eisenhower? Did they truly mean to kill Lumumba? As we passed through the forest we heard gunfire in the distance, but none of the women spoke of it, so we didn't either.

The road followed the Kwilu River upstream. I spent our year in Kilanga thinking of civilization as lying downstream from us, since that was the way the boats went to Banningville. But when Mother set out from the village on foot she'd asked some of our neighbors which way led to Leopoldville and they'd all agreed, upstream was the best. They said in two days we would get to Bulungu. There the path joined up with a larger road going west, overland, toward the capital. There would be trucks, the neighbor women said. Probably we could find a ride. Mother had asked the women, Did *they* ever take the road to Leopoldville? And they looked at each other, surprised at this odd question. No. The answer was no, they'd had no reason to go that way. But they were certain we would have a pleasant trip.

In fact our shoes filled with mud and our clothes turned to slime, and it was the farthest thing from pleasant. Mosquitoes that had lain dormant through the long drought now hatched and rose from the forest floor in clouds so thick they filled our mouths and nostrils. I learned to draw back my lips and breathe slowly through my teeth, so I wouldn't choke on mosquitoes. When they'd covered our hands and faces with red welts they flew up our sleeves and needled our armpits. We scratched ourselves raw. There were always more mosquitoes rising up from the road like great columns of smoke, always moving ahead of us, and we dreaded them. But by putting one foot ahead of the other we traveled farther in one day than we ever had thought to go before.

Some time after dark we arrived in the small village of Kiala. Mama Boanda invited us to come to the house where her mother and father lived with two unmarried sisters, who appeared to be twenty years older than Mama Boanda. We couldn't really get straight whether they were actually sisters, aunts, or what. But, oh, were we happy to come in out of the rain! Cows rescued from the slaughter could not have been happier. We squatted around the family's large kettle and ate *fufu* and *nsaki* greens with our fingers. Mama Boanda's ancient parents looked just alike, both of them tiny, bald, and perfectly toothless. The tata stared out the doorway with indifference, but the mama paid attention and nodded earnestly while Mama Boanda chattered on and on with a very long story. It was about *us*, we realized, since we heard the word *nyoka*—snake—many times, and also the word *Jesus*. When the story ended, the old woman studied my mother for a long time while she wrapped and rewrapped her faded blue *pagne* over her flat chest. After a time she sighed and went out into the rain, returning shortly with a hard-boiled egg. She presented it to my mother and motioned for us to eat it. Mother peeled the egg and we divided it, crumbling it carefully from hand to mouth while the others watched us closely, as if expecting immediate results. I have no idea whether this treasured egg was meant as a special cure for sorrow, or if they merely thought we needed the protein to sustain our dreadful journey.

We all shook from exhaustion. The rain and mud had made every mile into ten. Adah's weak side was overtaken by convulsive trembling, and Rachel seemed to be in a trance. The old woman worried aloud to her daughter that the guests might die in her house;

this kind of thing was felt to be bad luck. But she didn't throw us out, and we were grateful. With slow, deliberate movements of her bone-thin arms, she plucked up sticks from a pile near the door and started a fire to warm us, right inside the hut. The smoke made it hard to breathe but did give us relief from the mosquitoes. We wrapped ourselves in the extra *pagnes* offered to us as blankets, and settled down on the floor to sleep among strangers.

The night was pitch-dark. I listened to the pounding rain on the thatch and the quiet drips that leaked through, and only then did I think of Father. *"They say you thatched your roof and now you must not run out of your house if it rains."* Father was no longer with us. Father and Ruth May both, as simple as that. My mind ached like a broken bone as I struggled to stand in the new place I found myself. I wouldn't see my baby sister again, this I knew. But I hadn't yet considered the loss of my father. I'd walked in his footsteps my whole life, and now without warning my body had fallen in line behind my mother. A woman whose flank and jaw glinted hard as salt when she knelt around a fire with other women; whose pale eyes were fixed on a distance where he couldn't follow. Father wouldn't leave his post to come after us, that much was certain. He wasn't capable of any action that might be seen as cowardice by his God. And no God, in any heart on this earth, was ever more on the lookout for human failing.

Out of the thunderous rain the words came to my ears in Anatole's serene, particular voice: *You must not run out of your house if it rains.* Anatole translated the rage of a village into one quiet sentence that could pin a strong-willed man to the ground. It is surprising how my mother and father hardened so differently, when they turned to stone.

I imagined him still standing in our yard, frozen under the deluge, baptizing an endless circle of children, who would slip away and return with new faces requiring his blessing. I'd never understood the size of my father's task in the world. The size, or the terrible extravagance. I fell in and out of sleep under a strange dream of awful weight that I had to move to free myself. A mountain of hard-boiled eggs that turned into children when my hands touched them, dark-eyed children whose faces begged me for a handful of powdered milk, my clothes, whatever I had. *But I've brought nothing to give you,* I told them, and my heart took me down like a lead weight, for no matter whether these words were true or false, they were terrible and wrong. Each time I drifted off I sank down again through the feverish damp scent and dark blue hopelessness of this awful dream. Finally I shuddered it off and lay sleepless, hugging around my shoulders a thin cotton cloth that smelled of sweat and smoke. With exhaustion for company, I listened to the pounding rain. I would walk in no one's footsteps now. How could I follow my mother out of here now, and run away from what we'd done?

But after what we'd done, how could I stay?

We didn't reach Bulungu on the second day, and on the third we came down with a fever. Our bodies finally surrendered to the overpowering assault of mosquitoes. For all these months I'd imagined malaria as a stealthy, secret enemy, but now that it was fully upon me it was as real as anything. I could feel the poison move through my bloodstream like thick, tainted honey. I pictured it as yellow in color. At first I was terrified, shaking with the cold and the panicky flight of my heart, which seemed to be drowning as the poison rose up in my chest. But even if I could have attached words to my terror, there was no one to hear them. The rain on our heads dashed all other sound. On and on we walked, straight through fatigue and far, far beyond it. In time I arrived at a strange, sluggish calm. I imagined honey-colored parasites celebrating in my golden-tinted organs as I alternately froze and burned. When I discovered my face was hot as a stove, I happily used it to warm my freezing hands. The rain turned to ice as it lashed my arms. The trees began to burn with a pinkish aura that soothed my eyes. I lost one of my shoes in the mud, and failed to care. Then I lost the other. My legs began to fold strangely under me. At some point I lay down in an irresistible hollow at the base of a tree and urged Mother and the others to go on without me.

I have no recollection of arriving in Bulungu. I'm told I was carried on a pallet by some men who met us coming out of the jungle from a camp where they made charcoal during the dry season. I owe them my life, and regret that I can't recall a face or voice or even the rhythm of their step as they carried me. I worry that I might have been indecent to them, yelling insults as Ruth May sometimes did when she was delirious with malaria fever. I suppose I'll never know.

Bulungu was a whirl of excitement, which I took in gradually, thinking it must be due to our arrival. That we were an unlikely cause for celebration didn't occur to me, since I was surrounded by so many other entirely improbable things: men beating drums and dancing with the crowns of palm trees sprouting out of their heads, for example. Women with iridescent feathers on their heads and trailing down their spines. Eeben Axelroot's airplane with coronas of flame dancing around the wings as it touched down on a field of waving pink grass. Later on, in the dark shelter of someone's house where we were staying, I watched the man Axelroot bizarrely transformed. The Underwood devil's horns glowed through his slicked-down hair, as he sat in front of the window facing my mother. A living tail crept like a secretive velvet snake through the rungs of the chair behind him. I couldn't take my eyes off that sinister restlessness. He held the tail in his left hand, trying to quiet it down as he talked. Discussing Rachel. Mother's profile in the window turned to salt crystal, reflecting all light.

Other people came and went through the darkness where I lay under thatch, sheltered in my cave of dreams and rain. Sometimes I recognized Grandfather Wharton by my bed, patiently waiting for me to take my turn. With a guilty shock I saw we were playing checkers and I wasn't holding up my end. Grandfather told me in the most offhand manner that we'd both died.

My father came only once, with blue flames curling from his eyebrows and tongue: *Many are the afflictions of the righteous: but the Lord delivereth him out of them all*. The thin blue line of words rose straight up from his lips through the air. I watched, entranced. At the point where they touched the thatched ceiling, they became a line of ants. Morning and dusk and morning again I watched them trailing up to a hole in the peak of the roof, carrying their tiny burdens out into the light.

Nothing here has surprised me. Least of all, the presence of Anatole Ngemba. One morning he was here, and every day after that, holding a burning tin cup of bitter tea to my mouth and repeating my name: "Béene-béene." The truest truth. For my whole sixteen years I've rarely thought I was worth much more than a distracted grumble from God. But now in my shelter of all things impossible, I drift in a warm bath of forgiveness, and it seems pointless to resist. I have no energy for improving myself. If Anatole can wrap all my rattlebone sins in a blanket and call me goodness itself, why then I'll just believe him.

That is all I can offer by way of explaining our surprising courtship. As I wake up out of my months-long sleep, I find the course of my life has narrowed right down, and I feel myself rushing along it like a flood of rich, red mud. I believe I'm very happy.

I can't say how many weeks we were here before Mother left, or how many have passed since. I've had the good fortune of shelter; this hut belongs to a pupil of Anatole's, whose father lived here but is now deceased. Anatole left Kilanga soon after we did, and now spends a lot of time in neighboring villages, talking to people and organizing something large. He seems to have countless friends and resources in Bulungu, and I can stay here as long as I need to. But Mother couldn't. Mother could hardly sit still.

The day she left stands out in my mind as a drenched, sunny morning. The rain was letting up, and Anatole thought I was well enough to leave my mosquito tent for a few hours. We would go as far as the Kwenge to say good-bye. Rachel had already flown away with her devil saviour, and I was nailed down in Bulungu, since my body was still sunk so deep in poison it couldn't bear up to many more mosquito bites. But Mother and Adah were leaving. A *commerçant* had arrived by truck from Leopoldville, and in the rainy season that was a miracle not to be snubbed. He intended to return to the city with a cargo of bananas, and shook his stick fiercely at the Congolese women who tried to clamber onto his massively loaded truck for a ride. But perhaps, the *commerçant* decided, looking Mother up and down, avoiding her rigid blue gaze, perhaps he had room for the white woman. In the great green mountain of bananas he fixed a nest just big enough for Mother and one of her children. I thought Adah's lameness and Mother's desperation had purchased his sympathy. I didn't know until later there were rumors of huge rewards for white women delivered safely to the embassy in Leopoldville.

The truck was orange. I do remember that. Anatole and I rode along as far as the river to see them off. I vaguely heard Anatole making promises to Mother on my behalf: he would get me well, he'd send me when I felt ready to go home. It seemed he was speaking of someone else, as surely as the man with horns had flown away with someone other than Rachel. As we all bobbed precariously on the mountain of bananas, I just stared at Mother and Adah, trying to memorize what remained of my family.

As soon as we arrived at the mucky bank of the Kwenge, we spotted a problem. The old flatbed ferryboat had been functional just the day before, the *commerçant* claimed, but now it bobbed list-lessly on the opposite shore in spite of his piercing whistles and waving arms. Two fishermen turned up in a dugout canoe and informed us the ferry was stranded with no power. This was nor-mal, it seemed. Not insurmountable at any rate. Up came our truck's hood and out came the battery, which the fishermen would carry across the Kwenge to the ferry—for a price, of course. The *commerçant* paid it, muttering curses that seemed too strong for the early hour, since this was surely only the first irritation of a very long trip. (Or the third, if you counted my mother and Adah as the first two.) It was explained to us that the ferryman would jerry-rig the battery to start his ferry's engine and come back across to us. Then we could push the truck onto the ferry and reunite it with its battery again on the other side.

Right away, though, another problem. The immense truck battery was of an ancient type too large to be wedged down in the belly of the tiny canoe. After great discussion the fishermen found an answer: a pair of broad planks were set across the boat in a peculiar configuration that required the battery to ride on one side, with a counterweight on the other. There being no large rocks at hand, the fishermen eyed Adah and me. They decided either one of us would work for ballast, but feared Adah's handicap would prevent her holding on, and if she fell in the river the precious battery would also be lost. Mother, looking straight ahead, agreed I was the stronger one. No one mentioned I was dizzy with malaria fever, nor did it occur to me to raise this as an excuse. Anatole held his tongue, in deference to my family. We'd lost so much already, who was he to tell us how to risk what was left?

I went in that canoe. I could tell the river was receding from its rainy-season flood by its peculiar rank smell and all the driftwood stranded along its banks. I marveled that I'd learned so much about Congolese rivers. I thought of my mother's lifelong warning to us children whenever we entered a boat: if it overturns, grab hold for dear life! Yet Congolese pirogues are made of such dense wood if they capsize they sink like a rock. All these thoughts passed through me while the fishermen paddled urgently across the swift, boiling Kwenge. I clung to the rough plank, poised far out over the water, giving all my might to the service of balance. I don't remember letting out my breath until we were safely across.

Possibly I've imagined this; the whole episode seems impossibly strange. I mentioned it later and Anatole laughed at what he called my reconstructed history. He claims I rode inside the canoe, at my own request, because the weight of the oddly shaped battery tipped the boat dangerously. Yet the event keeps returning to me in my dreams exactly as I've described it, with all the same sights and smells occurring in sequence as I stretched my weight over the water. It's hard for me to doubt this is how it happened. I can't deny my brain was still muddled, though. I have only the haziest recollection of waving at my mother and sister in a rising cloud of diesel exhaust and mosquitoes as they began their slow, permanent exodus from the Congo. I wish I could remember their faces, Adah's especially. Did she feel I'd helped to save her? Or was it just more of the same parceling out of fortunes that had brought us this far, to this place where our path would finally divide into two?

I've compensated by remembering everything about Anatole in the days that followed. The exact green taste of the concoctions he boiled to cure me; the temperature of his hand on my cheek. The stitched patterns of light through thatch when morning entered the darkness where we slept, I against one wall, he against the other. We shared the fellowship of orphans. I felt it acutely, like a deep hunger for protein, and despaired for the flat-dirt expanse between Anatole and me. I begged him closer, inch by inch, clinging to his hands when he brought the cup. Now the bitterness of quinine and sweetness of kissing are two tastes perfectly linked on my soft palate. I had never loved a man before, physically, and I've read enough of both Jane Eyre and Brenda Starr to know every first love is potent. But when I fell into mine, I was drugged with the exotic delirium of malaria, so mine is omnipotent. How can I ever love anyone now but Anatole? Who else could make the colors of the aurora borealis rise off my skin where he strokes my forearm? Or send needles of ice tinkling blue through my brain when he looks in my eyes? What else but this fever could commute my father's ghost crying, "*Jezebel!*" into a curl of blue smoke drifting out through a small, bright hole in the thatch? Anatole banished the honey-colored ache of malaria and guilt from my blood. By Anatole I was shattered and assembled, by way of Anatole I am delivered not out of my life but through it.

Love changes everything. I never suspected it would be so. Requited love, I should say, for I've loved my father fiercely my whole life, and it changed nothing. But now, all around me, the flame trees have roused from their long, dry sleep into walls of scarlet blossom. Anatole moves through the dappled shade at the edges of my vision, wearing the silky pelt of a panther. I crave to feel that pelt against my neck. I crave it with a predator's impatience, ignoring time, keening to the silence of owls. When he's gone away for a night or two, my thirst is inconsolable. When he comes back, I drink every kiss down to its end and still my mouth aches like a dry cave.

Anatole didn't take me: I chose him. Once, long ago, he forbade me to say out loud that I loved him. So I'll invent my own ways to tell him what I long for, and what I can give. I grip his hands and don't let go. And he stays, cultivating me like a small inheritance of land where his future resides.

Now we sleep together under the same mosquito net, chastely. I don't mind saying I want more, but Anatole laughs and rubs his knuckles into my hair, pushes me playfully out of the bed. Tells me to go get my bow and hunt a bushbuck, if I want to kill something. The word *bàndika*, for "kill with an arrow," has two meanings, you see. He said it wasn't the time for me to become his wife, in the sense used by the Congolese. I was still mourning, he said, still sick, still living partly in another place. Anatole is a patient farmer. He reminds me that our arrangement is not at all unusual; he's known many men to take even ten-year-olds as brides. At sixteen I am worldly by some people's standards, and by anyone's I'm devoted. The fever in my bones has subsided and the air no longer dances with flames, but Anatole still comes to me at night in the pelt of a panther.

I'm well enough to travel now. It's been true for a while, really, but it was easy for me stay on here with Anatole's friends in Bulungu, and hard for us to speak of what comes next. Finally, this evening, he had to ask. He took my hand as we walked to the river, which surprised me, as he's normally reticent to show affection in public. I suppose it wasn't very public—the only people we could see were the fishermen mending their nets on the opposite shore. We stood watching them while the sunset painted the river with broad streaks of pink and orange. Islands of water hyacinths floated past in the drowsy current. I was thinking I'd never felt more content or known such beauty in all my life. And right then he said, "Béene, you're well. You can go, you know. I promised your mother I would see that you get home safely."

My heart stopped. "Where does she think home is?"

"Where you are happiest."

"Where do *you* want me to go?"

"Where you will be happy," he said again, and so I told him where that place is. Nothing could be easier. I've thought about it long and hard and decided that if he will tolerate me as I am, I'll decline to return to all familiar comforts in order to stay here.

It was an unusual proposal, by the standards of any culture. We stood on the bank of the Kwenge listing the things we'll have to abandon or relinquish. It's important information. For all I may be forsaking, he's giving up a good deal more: the possibility of having more wives than one, for instance. And that's only the beginning. Even now, I think Anatole's friends doubt his sanity. My whiteness could bar him outright from many possibilities, maybe even survival, in the Congo. But Anatole had no choice. I took him and held on. There's enough of my father in me that I had to stand my ground.

Rachel Price Axelroot

JOHANNESBURG, SOUTH AFRICA
1962

WANT SO LIEF HET GOD die wêreld gehad, dat Hy sy eniggebore Seun gegee het, sodat elkeen wat in Hom glo, nie verlore mag gaan nie, maar die ewige lewe kan hê.

How do you like that? Ha! That is John 3:16 in Afrikaans. For the last entire year I have worn my little white gloves and pillbox hat to the First Episcopal Church in Johannesburg and recited it right along with the best of them. And now one of my very close friends happens to be from Paris, France, and has taken me under her wings, so I can also go to the Catholic service with her and recite: *Car Dieu a tant aimé le monde qu'il a donné son Fils unique . . .* In French, another words. I am fluent in three languages. I have not remained especially close with my sisters, but I dare say that for all their being gifted and what not, they can't do a whole lot better than John 3:16 in three entire languages.

Maybe that won't necessarily guarantee me a front-row seat in heaven, but considering what all I have had to put up with from Eeben Axelroot for the last year, just for starters, that ought to at least get me in the door. His gawking at other women when I am still so young and attractive myself, and with my nerves shot already, I might add, since I have been through so much. Not to mention his leaving me alone while he goes on all his trips, getting rich on one crackpot scheme after another that never did pan out. I put up with him out of gratitude, mainly. I guess trading away your prime of life is a fair price for somebody flying you out of that hellhole. He did save my life. I promised him I would testify to those very words: *Rescued from imminent prospect of death.* And I did, too, in a whole slew of forms, so we could collect the money from the U.S. Embassy. They had emergency money available to help their citizens in reaching safety after the Communist crisis with Lumumba and all of that hubbub. Axelroot even got himself a little medal of honor for heroic service, which he is very vain of and keeps in a special box in the bedroom. For that reason we couldn't actually get legally married right away. The way he explained it was it wouldn't look right for him to collect money on saving his own wife. *That* kind of thing you would just naturally be expected to do on your own, without getting paid for it or winning any medals of honor.

Well, dumb me, I believed him. But it turns out Axelroot could collect medals galore in the department of avoiding holy matrimony. He has a hundred and one reasons not to marry the cow so he can buy the milk for free.

But I didn't think about that at the time, of course. Just imagine how it must have been for an impressionable young girl. There I was shivering in the rain, surrounded on every side by mud huts, mud roads, mud everything. People squatting in the mud, trying to cook over a fire in the pouring rain. Dogs going crazy, running through the mud. We walked practically halfway across the Congo. That was my chosen path to suffering, as our dear old dad would have put it, not that I had any choice. I got baptized by mud. I laid me down at night on filthy floors and prayed the Lord I wouldn't wake up dead from a snakebite as I had just seen happen tragically to my own sister, knowing full well it could just as soon have been me. Words cannot describe my mental framework. When we finally got to that village and there was Mr. Axelroot in his sunglasses leaning against his airplane, all smirking and Sanforized in his broad-shouldered khaki uniform, I only had one thing to say: "Enough already. Get me out of here!" I didn't care what kind of forms I had to sign. I would have signed a deal with the Devil himself. I swear I would have.

So that's how it was for me, one day standing there up to my split ends in mud, and the next day strolling down the wide, sunny streets of Johannesburg, South Africa, among houses with nice green lawns and swimming pools and gobs of pretty flowers growing behind their lovely high walls with electric gates. Cars, even! Telephones! White people just everywhere you looked.

At that time Axelroot was just in the process of getting set up in Johannesburg. He has a brand-new position in the security division of the gold-mining industry, near the northern suburbs, where supposedly we are soon to be living in high style. Although after an entire year all his promises are starting to show the telltale signs of age. Not to mention our furniture, which every stick of it has all been previously owned.

When I first got to Johannesburg I stayed for a brief time with a very nice American couple, the Templetons. Mrs. Templeton had separate African maids for her cooking, cleaning, and laundry. I must have washed my hair fifty times in ten days, and used a clean towel each and every time! Oh, I thought I'd died and gone to heaven. Just to be back with people who spoke the good old American language and understood the principle of a flush toilet.

Eeben's and my house is not nearly so grand, of course, but we certainly get by, and I supply the woman's touch. Axelroot did pretty well for himself as a pilot in the Congo, transporting perishable goods from the bush into the cities for retail sale, and he was also active in the diamond trade. He worked for the government, too, with his secret assignments and all, but he has never talked about it all that much since we started living together. Now that we have relations any old time we feel like it, which by the way I don't think is the worst sin there is when there's people getting hurt, cheated, or killed left and right in this world, well, now Mr. Axelroot doesn't have to show off his big secrets to the Princess to get a kiss out of her. So now his number-one secret is: I need another beer! Which just goes to show you.

But I was determined right off the bat to make the best of my situation here in my new home of Johannesburg, South Africa. I just started going by the name Rachel Axelroot, and no one had to be the wiser, really. I've always made sure I go to church with the very best people, and we get invited to their parties. I insist on that. I have even learned to play bridge! It is my girlfriends here in Joburg that have taught me how to give parties, keep a close eye on the help, and just overall make the graceful transition to wifehood and adulteration. My girlfriends, plus my subscription to the *Ladies' Home Journal*. Our magazines always arrive so late that we are one or two months out of style. We probably started painting our nails Immoral Coral after everybody sensible had already gone on to pink, but heck, at least we are all behind the times together. And the girls I associate with are very sophisticated in ways that you simply can't learn from a magazine. Especially Robine, who is Catholic and from Paris, France, and will positively not eat dessert with the same fork she used at dinner. Her husband is the Attaché to the Ambassador, so talk about good manners! Whenever we are invited to the better homes for dinner, I just keep my eye on Robine, because then you can't go wrong.

We girls stick together like birds of a feather, and thank goodness for that, because the men are always off on one kind of business or another. In Axelroot's case, as I have mentioned, it frequently turns out to be monkey business. For all I know, he's off somewhere saving some other damsel in distress with the promise of marriage someday after he's collected his reward money! That would be Axelroot all over, to turn up with an extra wife or two claiming that's how they do it here. Maybe he's been in Africa so long he has forgotten that we Christians have our own system of marriage, and it is called Monotony.

Well, I put up with him anyway. When I get out of bed every morning, at least I'm still alive and not dead like Ruth May. So I must have done something right. Sometimes you just have to save your neck and work out the details later. Like that little book said: Stick out your elbows, pick up your feet, and float along with the crowd! The last thing you want to do is get trampled to death.

As far as the actual day he flew me out of the Congo in his plane, it's hard for me even to remember what I thought was going to happen next. I was so excited to be getting out of that horrid mud hole I couldn't think straight. I'm sure I said good-bye to Mother and Adah and Leah, though I really don't remember giving a second thought to when I would ever see them again, if ever. I must have been in an absolute daze.

It's funny but I do recall just this one thing. Eeben's plane was hundreds of feet up in the air already, way over the clouds, when I suddenly remembered my hope chest! All those pretty things I'd made—monogrammed towels, a tablecloth and matching napkins—it just didn't seem right to be getting married without them. As befuddled as I was, I made him promise he'd go back someday and get those things from our house in Kilanga. Of course he hasn't. I realize now it was just plain foolish of me to think he ever would.

I guess you might say my hopes never got off the ground.

Adah Price

Emory University, Atlanta
1962

TELL ALL THE TRUTH but tell it slant, says my friend Emily
Dickinson. And really what choice do I have? I am a crooked
little person, obsessed with balance.

I have decided to speak, so there is the possibility of telling.
Speaking became a matter of self-defense, since Mother seems to
have gone mute, and with no one to testify to my place in the
world I found myself at the same precipice I teetered upon when
entering the first grade: gifted, or special education with the ear-
pulling Crawleys? Not that I would have minded the company of
simple minds, but I needed to flee from Bethlehem, where the walls
are made of eyes stacked in rows like bricks, and every breath of air
has the sour taste of someone's recent gossip. We arrived home to a
very special heroes' welcome: the town had been starving outright
for good scuttlebutt. So hip hip hooray, welcome home the pitiful
Prices! The astonishing, the bereft, bizarre, and homeless (for we
could no longer live in a parsonage without a parson), tainted by
darkest Africa and probably heathen, Orleanna and Adah, who have
slunk back to town without their man, like a pair of rabid dalma-
tions staggering home without their fire engine.

We were presumed insane. Mother took the diagnosis well. She
moved our things out of storage into a plywood cabin on the piney

outskirts of town, which she rented on the strength of a tiny legacy from Grandfather Wharton. She did not hook up the telephone. She took up a hoe instead, and began to put every square inch of her sandy two-acre rented lot under cultivation: peanuts, sweet potatoes, and four dozen kinds of flowers. She seemed determined to grow tragedy out of herself like a bad haircut. A neighbor down the road had a mean goose and hogs, whose manure Mother toted home daily like a good African in two balanced bushel pails. It would not have surprised me to see her put a third bucket on her head. By midsummer we could not see out the windows for the foxglove and the bachelor's buttons. Mother said she aimed to set up a plank shack by the road and sell bouquets for three-fifty apiece. I wondered what Bethlehem would say about that. The minister's wife gone barefoot to roadside commerce.

As earnestly as Mother had taken up seed catalogs, I took up the catalog of Emory University and studied my possibilities. Then I rode the Greyhound to Atlanta and limped into the admissions office. I was allowed to have an interview with a gentleman named Dr. Holden Remile, whose job I think was to discourage people such as myself from asking for interviews with people such as himself. His desk was immense.

I opened my mouth and waited for the sentence I hoped would arrive. "I need to go to your college here, sir. And when I am done with it, I will need to go to your medical school."

Dr. Remile was quite shocked, whether by my deformity or my audacity I can't say, but probably less shocked than I was by the sound of my own voice. He asked whether I had funds, whether I had high school transcripts, whether I had at least taken high school chemistry or advanced algebra. The only answer I had was "No, sir." But I did mention I had read quite a few books.

"Do you know what calculus is, young lady?" he asked, in the manner of a person who is hiding something frightening in one of his hands. Having grown up around the hands of Reverend Price, I am fairly immune to such fright.

"Yes, sir," I said. "It is the mathematics of change."

His telephone rang. While I waited for him to have his conversation, I worked out in my head both the sum and the product of the numbers on the large numbered set of files on his bookshelf, which were all out of order, and made up an equation for righting them, which I wrote down for him on paper. I had to use algebra, though, not calculus. I also observed that his name, backward, was the French verb for wearing one's clothes threadbare, so I told him that as well, with no offense intended as his clothes were fine.

Dr. Remile suddenly ascertained that I was due some government benefits, being the child of a veteran. He set me up for taking the entrance examinations, for which I returned to Atlanta one month later. I didn't miss any of the questions in mathematics. On the verbal portion I missed four questions, all having to do with choosing a word in a series that doesn't belong. I have always had trouble with that line of questioning. Given my own circumstances, I find that anything can turn out to belong nearly anywhere.

I had told the truth: I needed to go to his college. I needed to get out of Bethlehem, out of my skin, my skull, and the ghost of my family. It is not because I was ashamed of Mother—how could *I*, the village idiot, be ashamed of her? I somewhat enjoyed the company of her madness, and certainly I understood it. But Mother wanted to consume me like food. I needed my own room. I needed books, and for the first time in my life I needed schoolmasters who would tell me each day what to think about.

In organic chemistry, invertebrate zoology, and the inspired symmetry of Mendelian genetics, I have found a religion that serves. I recite the Periodic Table of Elements like a prayer; I take my examinations as Holy Communion, and the pass of the first semester was a sacrament. My mind is crowded with a forest of facts. Between the trees lie wide-open plains of despair. I skirt around them. I stick to the woods.

Since I can't call her, I take the bus back on weekends. We drink tea and she shows me her flowers. The odd thing is when Father was around she never gardened at all. That was his domain, and he directed us all in the planting of useful foods, all to the Glory of

God and so forth. We never had one flower in our yard the whole of my childhood. Not so much as a dandelion. Now Mother's shack is the mere peak of a roof surrounded by a blaze of pinks, blues, oranges. You have to bend under a wild arch of cosmos when you come up the walk, and use your whole right arm to push the holly-hocks aside to get in the front door. It turns out Mother has an extraordinary talent for flowers. She was an entire botanical garden waiting to happen.

When I visit her we never talk much, and are both relieved by the silence, I think. There are only the two of us now, and I owe her my very life. She owes me nothing at all. Yet I have left her, and now she is sad. I'm not used to this. I have always been the one who sac-rificed life and limb and half a brain to save the other half. My habit is to drag myself imperiously through a world that owes me unpayable debts. I have long relied on the comforts of martyrdom.

Now I owe a debt I cannot repay. She took hold of me with a fierce grip and pulled me through. Mother was going to drag me out of Africa if it was her last living act, and it very nearly was. This is how it happened: the *commerçant* whose truck showed up like a rusted-out angel in Bulungu promised us a ride to Léopoldville with his bananas, but he soon changed his mind and dumped us for more bananas. After a conference with some soldiers along the road, he became convinced that fruit was now bringing a higher price than white women in the city. So out we went.

We walked for two days without food. At night we crouched at the edge of the woods and covered ourselves with palm leaves so the soldiers wouldn't spot us. Late on the second evening an army truck pulled up beside us, and a man threw us suddenly into the back, where we landed across laps helmets rifles. No doubt the sol-diers planned to do us harm; I was numb with that expectation. But Mother's milk-glass eyes frightened them. Plainly she was possessed of some fierce evil that would enter these men if they touched her, or me. Especially me. So they kept their distance from both of us. We bumped along silently in the back of the truck, passing through dozens of military roadblocks, and were turned over to the Belgian

Embassy, which took us in until someone could sort out what ought to be done with us. We spent nineteen days in the infirmary, swallowing a variety of specialized poisons, since we had intestinal parasites, fungus growing on our feet and forearms, and more than the usual degree of malaria.

Then, on a hospital plane full of UN workers and sick white people, we were transported through a long thrumming darkness, in which we slept the sleep of the dead. When the droning stopped we all sat up and blinked like disturbed corpses. There was light at the round windows. The belly of the plane groaned open and we were delivered abruptly into the benign spring air of Fort Benning, Georgia.

It is impossible to describe the shock of return. I recall that I stood for the longest time staring at a neatly painted yellow line on a neatly formed cement curb. Yellow yellow line line. I pondered the human industry, the paint, the cement truck and concrete forms, all the resources that had gone into that one curb. For what? I could not quite think of the answer. So that no car would park there? Are there so many cars that America must be divided into places with and places without them? Was it always so, or did they multiply vastly, along with telephones and new shoes and transistor radios and cellophane-wrapped tomatoes, in our absence?

Then I stared for a while at a traffic light, which was suspended elaborately on wires above the intersection. I couldn't look at the cars themselves. My brain was roaring from all the color and orchestrated metal movement. From the open building behind me came a blast of neutral-smelling air and a high hum of fluorescent lights. Even though I was outdoors, I felt a peculiar confinement. One discarded magazine lay on the edge of the street, impossibly clean and unblemished. A breeze gently turned the pages for me, one at a time: here was a neatly coiffed white mother beside a huge white clothes dryer and a fat white child and a great mound of bright clean clothes that would be sufficient, it seemed to me, to clothe a whole village; here were a man and woman holding between them a Confederate flag on a vast lawn so flat and neatly trimmed their shadows stretched behind them for the length of a fallen tree; here was a blonde woman in a black dress and pearls and long red fingernails leaning over a blank white tablecloth toward a glass of wine; here was a child in many kinds of new clothes hugging a doll so clean and unrumpled it seemed not to belong to her; here was a woman in a coat and hat, hugging a bundle of argyle socks. The world seemed crowded and empty at the same time, devoid of smells, and extremely bright. I continued to stare at the traffic light, which glowed red. Suddenly a green arrow popped on, pointing left, and the row of cars like obedient animals all went left. I laughed out loud.

Mother, meanwhile, had moved on. She was walking in a trance toward a pay telephone. I hurried and caught up with her, a little timidly, because she had cut straight to the front of a long line of soldier boys waiting to call home. She demanded that someone give us the correct change to call Mississippi, which two boys did in such a hurry you would think Mother was their commanding officer. The unfamiliar American coins felt light in my hands. I passed them to Mother and she dialed some second cousins who promised to come collect us almost immediately, even though Mother had not spoken with them in nearly a decade. She still knew the telephone number by heart.

Tell all the truth but tell it slant. What secret is left in our family to tell? I may have to stop talking again, until I can be sure of what I know. I thought I had it settled long ago, you see. My hymn to God: *Evol's dog, dog ho!* My hymn for love: *Eros, eyesore!* Oh, I knew it all, backward and forward. I learned the balance of power in one long Congolese night, when the driver ants came: the bang on the door, the dark hustle and burning feet, and last of all Adah dragging the permanent singsong of her body *left . . . behind.* Out into the moonlight where the ground boiled and there stood Mother like a tree rooted motionless in the middle of a storm. Mother staring at me, holding Ruth May in her arms, weighing the two of us against one another. The sweet intact child with golden ringlets and perfectly paired strong legs, or the dark mute adolescent dragging a stubborn, disjunct half-body. Which? After hesitating only a second, she chose to save perfection and leave the damaged. Everyone must choose.

Live was I ere I saw evil I wrote in my journal. Alive one moment, dead the next, because that is how my divided brain divined the world. There was room in Adah for nought but pure love and pure hate. Such a life is satisfying and deeply uncomplicated. Since then, my life has become much more difficult. Because later on, she chose *me*. In the end she could only carry one child alive out of Africa and I was that child. Would she rather have had Ruth May? Was I the booby prize? Does she look at me and despise her loss? Am I alive only because Ruth May is dead? What truth can I possibly tell?

Recently I rifled through the history of Our Father. An old trunk full of his things. I needed to find his military discharge papers, which would provide for me some benefits in the domain of college tuition. I found more than I was looking for. His medal is not, as we were always told, for heroic service. It is simply for having been wounded and having survived. For escaping from a jungle where all others marched to their deaths. No more than that. The conditions of his discharge were technically honorable, but unofficially they were: Cowardice, Guilt, and Disgrace. The Reverend the sole survivor in a company of dead men who have marched along beside him all his life since then. No wonder he could not flee from the same jungle twice. Mother told me a part of the story, and I realized I already knew the rest. Fate sentenced Our Father to pay for those lives with the remainder of his, and he has spent it posturing desperately beneath the eyes of a God who will not forgive a debt. This God worries me. Lately He has been looking in on me. My sleep is visited by Ruth May and the many other children who are buried near her. They cry out, "Mother May I?" and the mothers crawl forward on hands and knees, trying to eat the dirt from their babies' fresh graves. The owls still croon and croon, and the air is thick with spirits. This is what I carried out of the Congo on my crooked little back. In our seventeen months in Kilanga, thirty-one children died, including Ruth May. Why not Adah? I can think of no answer that exonerates me.

Mother's reasons for saving me were as complicated as fate itself, I suppose. Among other things, her alternatives were limited. Once she betrayed me, once she saved me. Fate did the same to Ruth May, in the opposite order. Every betrayal contains a perfect moment, a coin stamped heads or tails with salvation on the other side. Betrayal is a friend I have known a long time, a two-faced goddess looking forward and back with a clear, earnest suspicion of good fortune. I have always felt I would make a clear-eyed scientist, on account of it. As it turns out, though, betrayal can also breed penitents, shrewd minor politicians, and ghosts. Our family seems to have produced one of each.

Carry us, marry us, ferry us, bury us: those are our four ways to exodus, for now. Though, to tell the truth, none of us has yet safely made the crossing. Except for Ruth May, of course. We must wait to hear word from her.

I rode on the ferry. Until that morning when we all went to the riverbank, I still believed Mother would take Leah, not me. Leah who, even in her malarial stupor, rushed forward to crouch with the battery in the canoe and counter its odd tilt. I was outshone as usual by her heroism. But as we watched that pirogue drift away across the Kwenge, Mother gripped my hand so tightly I understood I had been chosen. She would drag me out of Africa if it was her last living act as a mother. I think probably it was.

Leah Price

MISSION NOTRE DAME DE DOULEUR
1964

LA DRAGUEUSE, the nuns call me here. The Mine Sweeper. And not because my habit drags the ground, either. I wear trousers underneath and tuck it up half the time just to move faster or climb up a tree with my bow to shoot a little meat, which I'd say they're happy to have. But I can see in their eyes they think I have too much piss and vinegar for the present circumstances. Even Soeur Thérèse, who's the closest thing I have to a friend here in the Grand Silence, has marked me as the black sheep in this snowy flock by insisting I wear all brown below the shoulders. She's in charge of the hospital laundry and claims I'm a hopeless case where white is concerned.

"*Liselin!*" she scolds, holding up my scapular stained with the blood of something or other, some cat I have skinned.

"The monthly visit?" I'll offer, and she doubles over, pink-faced, declaring me *de trop*. Yet I look around me and wonder how, in the present circumstances, any amount of piss and vinegar could possibly be enough.

Liselin is me: Soeur Liselin, a mercy case smuggled in under cover of darkness, given refuge for the indefinite term of my fiancé's imprisonment, tucked for the meantime into too much cloth and married to the Lord to conceal my maiden name. I hope He understands when I pray that our marriage won't last forever. The sisters seem to forget I'm not one of them, even though they know how I came here. Thérèse makes me repeat the details while her gray eyes grow wide. Here she is, merely twenty years old and thousands of miles from the pastures of France, washing out the dressings of lepers and awful miscarriages, yet she's electrified by my narrow escape. Or maybe that I shared it with Anatole. When we're alone in the sweltering laundry room, she asks me how I know I'm in love.

"I must be. What else would make you stupid enough to put hundreds of people in danger?"

It's true, I did that. When I finally woke up from my drugged stupor in Bulungu I could see what a burden I'd been, not just for the *fufu* and fish sauce I'd eaten day after day, but for being a foreigner in the eye of a storm. Mobutu's army was known to be ruthless and unpredictable. Bulungu could be accused of anything for harboring me. Bulungu could also be burned to the ground for no reason at all. Everyone learned fast, the best strategy was to be invisible. Yet my presence was known throughout the region: I was a gaudy flag waving overhead during all those months of sickness and oblivion, just a girl in love, the center of my own universe. Finally, I sat up to see the sun still rose in the east, but everything else had changed. I begged Anatole to get me out to anyplace where I wouldn't be a danger to others, but he wouldn't send me alone. He insisted I had nothing to be ashamed of. He was risking his own pro-Lumumbist neck to stay near me, but many people were now taking risks for what they loved, he said, or simply for what they knew. Soon we'd go, he promised, and go together.

Plans were laid for us by friends, including some men from Kilanga I'd never dreamed would take such chances for Anatole. Tata Boanda, for one. Bright red trousers and all, he arrived late one night on foot, toting a suitcase on his head. He had money for us that he claimed was owed to my father, though this is doubtful. The suitcase was ours. In it were a dress and a coloring notebook of Ruth May's, pieces of our hope chests, my bow and arrows. Someone in Kilanga saved these precious things for us. I suppose it's also possible the women who went through our house didn't want these items, though the bow at least would have been valuable. A third possibility, then: dismayed by the failure of our Jesus to protect us, they opted to steer clear.

The news of Father wasn't good. He was living alone. I hadn't thought of this—who would cook for him? I'd never envisioned Father without women's keeping. Now he was reported to be bearded, wild-haired, and struggling badly with malnutrition and parasites. Our house had burned, with the blame going either to Mother's spirit or the mischief of village children, though Tata Boanda allowed it was probably Father trying to toast meat over a kerosene flame. Father ran off to a hut in the woods he was calling the New Church of Eternal Life, Jesus Is Bängala. As promising as that sounds, he wasn't getting a lot of takers. People were waiting to see how well Jesus protected Tata Price, now that he had to get by the same as everyone without outside help from the airplane or even women. So far, Father seemed to be reaping no special advantages. Additionally, his church was too close to the cemetery.

Tata Boanda told me with sincere kindness that Ruth May was mourned in Kilanga. Tata Ndu threatened to exile Tata Kuvudundu for planting the snake in our chicken house, which he was known to have done, since Nelson pointed out the footprints to many witnesses. Kilanga had fallen on trouble of every kind. The pro-Lumumbists among Anatole's schoolboys were having armed skirmishes with what was left of the National Army, now Mobutu's army, farther south along the river. We were warned that travel anywhere would be difficult.

It was harder than that. Even though the rain had stopped, we could barely walk as far as the Kwenge. From there we planned to travel by ferry all the way to Stanleyville, where Lumumba still has enormous popular support. There was work to be done, and Anatole felt we could be safe there. The money Tata Boanda brought us was our salvation. It was a small amount, but in hard Belgian francs. Congolese currency had become useless overnight. With a million pink Congolese bills we couldn't have bought our way onto the ferry.

Everything was like that: the ground shifted while we slept, and we woke up each day to terrible new surprises. In Stanleyville we quickly saw I was a liability, even more than in Bulungu. People were outraged by the sight of white skin, for reasons I had the sense to understand. They'd lost their hero to a bargain between the foreigners and Mobutu. Anatole wrapped me up in wax-print *pagnes*, hoping to disguise me as a Congolese matron while trying to keep me from staggering dazed in front of automobiles. I nearly swooned in the mill and flow of Stanleyville—people, cars, animals in the street, the austere gaze of windows in the tall concrete buildings. I hadn't stepped out of the jungle since my trip with Father to Léopoldville, a year ago or a hundred, I couldn't say.

Anatole lost no time arranging to get us out of the city. In the back of a friend's truck, covered with manioc leaves, we left Stanleyville late at night and crossed over into the Central African Republic near Bangassou. I was delivered to this mission deep in the jungle, where, amidst the careful neutrality of the sisters, a rumpled novice named Soeur Liselin might pass a few months unnoticed. Without asking a single question, the Mother Superior invited Anatole and me to spend our last night together in my little blank room. My gratitude for her kindness has carried me a long way on a difficult road.

Thérèse leans close and looks up at me, her eyebrows tilting like the accents above her name. "Liselin, of what do you accuse yourself? Has he touched you *everywhere*?"

We expected to be parted for no more than six or eight weeks, while Anatole worked with the Lumumbists to reassemble their fallen leader's plan for peace and prosperity. We were that naive. Anatole was detained by Mobutu's police before he even made it back to Stanleyville. My beloved was interrogated to the tune of a broken rib, taken to Léopoldville, and imprisoned in the rat-infested courtyard of what was once a luxurious embassy. Our extended separation has so far improved my devotion to Anatole, my French grammar, and my ability to live with uncertainty. Finally, I've confided to Thérèse, I understand the subjunctive tense.

I shudder to think what Father would say to me here, skulking among a tribe of papist females. I pass the days as productively as I can: trying to stay clean, sharpen my aim, and keep my lip buttoned from Vespers till breakfast. Trying to learn the trick of what passes for patience. Every few weeks I get a letter from Léopoldville, which holds me on track. My heart races when I see the long blue envelope in a sister's hand, delivered to me under her sleeve as if a man himself were inside. And, oh, he is! Still sweet and bitter and wise and, best of all, still alive. I squeal, I can't help it, and run outside to the courtyard to taste him in private like a cat with a stolen pullet. I lean my face against the cool wall and kiss its old stones in praise of captivity, because it's only my being here and his being in prison that saves us both for another chance at each other. I know he despises being useless, sitting still while war overtakes us. But if Anatole were free to do as he pleased right now, I know he'd be killed in the process. If captivity is damaging his spirit, I just hope for an intact body and will do what I can for the rest, later on.

The nuns spied me out there and told me I'm going to wear away their foundation. They are used to gunfire and leprosy but not true love.

Clearly I'm here to stay awhile, so Mother Marie-Pierre has put me to work in the clinic. If I can't quite get the hang of poverty-chastity-and-obedience, I can learn instead about vermifuges, breech deliveries, arrow wounds, gangrene, and elephantiasis. Nearly all the patients are younger than me. Preventatives for old age are rampant here. Our supplies come from the French Catholic Relief, and sometimes just thin air. Once a messenger on a bicycle came teetering up the jungle path bringing us twelve vials of antivenin, individually wrapped in tissue inside a woman's jewelry box—an astounding treasure whose history we couldn't guess. The boy said it came from a doctor in Stanleyville who was being evacuated. I thought of the Belgian doctor who'd set Ruth May's arm, and I decided to believe Ruth May herself was somehow involved in this gift. The sisters merely praised the Lord and proceeded to save a dozen people from snakebite; more than we've lost.

From talking with the patients I've gotten passably fluent in Lingala, which is spoken throughout northern Congo, in Léopoldville, and along most of the navigable rivers. If Anatole ever comes back for me, I'll be ready to go most anywhere. But then a month will pass with no letter and I'm sure he's slipped into death or recovered his clear ideals and the sense to steer clear of a badly misplaced white girl, he's gone forever. As lost to me as my sister, oh, sweet Jesus, Ruth May. And Adah, Rachel, Mother, and Father, all gone as well. What's the meaning of my still being here without name or passport, parroting "how-do-you-do" in Lingala? I am trying to get some kind of explanation from God, but none is forthcoming. At nights in the refectory we sit with our hands in our laps and stare at the radio, our small, harsh master. We hear one awful piece of news after another, with no power to act. The free Congo that so nearly came to pass is now going down. What can I do but throw my rosary against the wall of my cell and swear violence? The nuns are so patient. They've spent decades here prolonging the brief lives of the undernourished, accustomed completely to the tragedy playing out around us. But their unblinking eyes framed by their white starched wimples make me want to scream, "*This is not God's will be done!*" How could anyone, even a God distracted by many other concerns, allow this to happen?

"*Ce n'est pas à nous,*" says Thérèse, not ours to question. As convincing as Methuselah shouting, *Sister God is great! Shut the door!*

"I've heard that before," I tell her. "I'm sure the Congolese heard it every day for a hundred years while they had to forbear the Belgians. Now they finally get a fighting chance, and we're sitting here watching it get born dead. Like that baby born blue out of that woman with tetanus this morning."

"That is an awful comparison."

"But it's true!"

She sighs and repeats what she's told me already. The sisters take no position in war, but must try to hold charity in their hearts even for the enemy.

"But who *is* the enemy? Just tell me that much, Thérèse. Which side are you trying not to hate, white men or Africa?"

She snaps a sheet open wide in her hands and takes the center with her teeth to fold it in half. Also, I think, to stop up her mouth.

"I'd fight alongside the Simbas if they'd let me," I confessed to her once.

Thérèse has a way of looking at me sideways, and I wonder if she wasn't too hasty in taking her vows. She's attracted to mine sweeping. "You have a good aim and good nerves," she allowed behind the sheet she was folding. "Go join them."

"You think I'm joking."

She stopped to look at me seriously. *"Non, ce n'est pas une blague.* But it's not your place to fight with the Simbas, even if you were a man. You're white. This is their war and whatever happens will happen."

"It's no more their war than it is God's will be done. It's the doing of the damned Belgians and Americans."

"The Reverend Mother would wash your mouth with disinfectant."

"The Reverend Mother has more pressing needs for her disinfectant." And nowhere near enough, either, I thought. In the privacy of my little room I've damned many men to hell, President Eisenhower, King Léopold, and my own father included. I damn them for throwing me into a war in which white skin comes down on the wrong side, pure and simple.

"If God is really taking a hand in things," I informed Thérèse, "he is bitterly mocking the hope of brotherly love. He is making sure that color will matter forever." With no more to say between a devout farm girl and a mine sweeper, we folded our sheets and our different-colored habits.

The Simbas would shoot me on sight, it's true. They're an army of pure desperation and hate. Young Stanleyville boys and old village men, anyone who can find a gun or a machete, all banded together. They tie *nkisis* of leaves around their wrists and declare themselves impermeable to bullets, immune to death. And so they are, Anatole says, "For how can you kill what is already dead?" We've heard how they sharpened their teeth and stormed the invaders in northeastern Congo, feeding on nothing but rage.

Thirty whites killed in Stanley, two Americans among them—we heard that over the shortwave radio and knew what it meant. By nightfall the United Nations would launch their answer, an air and land attack. The Combined Forces, they're calling this invading army: the U.S., Belgium, and hired soldiers left over from the Bay of Pigs. Over the next weeks we heard a hundred more times about the whites killed by Simbas in Stanleyville. In three languages: Radio France, the BBC, and Mobutu's Lingala newscasts from Léopoldville, the news was all one. Those thirty white people, rest their souls, have purchased an all-out invasion against the pro-Independents. How many Congolese were killed by the Belgians and labor and starvation, by the special police, and now by the UN soldiers, we will never know. They'll go uncounted. Or count for nothing, if that is possible.

The night the helicopters came in, the vibrations pummeled us out of our beds. I thought the old stone convent was falling down. We ran outside with the wind from the blades tearing down on us from just above the trees, whipping our plain white nightgowns into a froth. The sisters registered their dismay, crossed themselves, and hurried back to bed. I couldn't. I sat on the ground, hugging my knees, and started to cry, for the first time since time began, it seems. Crying with my mouth open, howling for Ruth May and the useless waste of our mistakes and all that's going to happen now, everyone already dead and not yet dead, known or unknown to me, every Congolese child with no hope. I felt myself falling apart—that by morning I might be just bones melting into the moldy soil of the sisters' vegetable garden. A pile of eggless, unmothering bones, nothing more: the future I once foretold.

To hold myself together I tried to cry for something more manageable. I settled on Anatole. Kneeling before our little statue of the Virgin with an eroded face I endeavored to pray for my future husband. For a chance. For happiness and love and, if you can't pray for sex outright, the possibility of children. I found I could hardly remember Anatole's face, and couldn't picture God at all. He just ended up looking like my father. I tried to imagine Jesus, then, in the body of Brother Fowles. Tata Bidibidi, with his kind, pretty wife and their precarious boat dispensing milk powder and quinine and love to children along the river. Attend to Creation, was his advice. Well, the palm trees in our courtyard were ripped and flattened from the wind of the helicopters, and looked far too defeated by war to accept my prayers. So I focused on the sturdy walls of the compound and prayed straight to the black stones. I implored them, "Please let there be sturdy walls like these around Anatole. Please let them hold up a roof that will keep this awful sky from falling on him." I prayed to old black African stones unearthed from the old dark ground that has been here all along. One solid thing to believe in.

Rachel Axelroot

JOHANNESBURG
1964

IF I'D KNOWN WHAT MARRIAGE was going to be like, well, heck, I probably would have tied all those hope-chest linens together into a rope and hung myself from a tree!

It isn't living here in South Africa that I mind. It hardly even seems like a foreign country here. You can get absolutely anything you need in the stores: Breck Special Formulated Shampoo, Phillips' milk of magnesia, Campbell's tomato soup, honestly you name it! And the scenery is beautiful, especially taking the train down to the beach. My girlfriends and I love to pack up a picnic basket with champagne and Tobler biscuits (which actually are cookies, not biscuits—imagine my surprise when I bought some aiming to serve them with gravy!), and then we just head out to the countryside for a view of the green rolling hills. Of course you have to look the other way when the train goes by the townships, because those people don't have any perspective of what good scenery is, that's for sure. They will make their houses out of a piece of rusted tin or the side of a crate—and leave the writing part on the outside for all to see! But you just have to try and understand, they don't have the same ethics as us. That is one part of living here. Being understanding of the differences.

Otherwise this country is much like you'd find anywhere. Even the weather is very typical. I have always felt that people in other countries just don't have any idea that Africa could be this normal. The only bad thing is that with the equator being above us the change of seasons comes backwards, which does take some getting used to. But do I complain? Heck, no, I just slap up our Christmas tree in the middle of summer and sing "Deck the Halls" and have a martini on the patio and don't give it another thought anymore. I am a very adaptable kind of person. I don't even mind speaking Afrikaans to the maid, which is practically the same thing as English once you get the hang of it. As long as you're just giving orders, anyway, which are more or less about the same in any language. And if you hear the word "*Nuus*" on the radio, for example, why, any fool can figure out that means "News." So you just get up and switch over to the English station!

I have a good life, as far as the overall surroundings. I have put the past behind me and don't even think about it. Do I have a family? I sometimes have to stop and ask myself. Do I have a mother, father, and sisters? Did I even *come* from anywhere? Because it doesn't seem like it. It seems like I'm just right here and always was. I have a little tiny picture of my sisters and me cut out in a heart shape, which I happened to be wearing in a gold locket when I left our unfortunate circumstances in the Congo. Sometimes I get it out and stare at those teeny little sad white faces, trying to make out where I am in that picture. That's the only time I ever think about Ruth May being dead. Which I've said was all because of Leah, but really, mainly, it's probably Father's fault because the rest of us just had to go along with whatever he said. If it was up to me, I would never have stepped foot in that snake-infected place. I would have sat home and let other people go be missionaries if they wanted to, bully for them! But the picture is so small I have to hold it practically at the end of my nose to make out who is who. It hurts my eyes to focus on it, so mostly it stays in the drawer.

Like I said, I am content with my present circumstances for the most part. My misery comes from a different concern: my marriage. There is just no word bad enough for Eeben Axelroot. Who has still not made an honest woman out of me, I might add! He just treats me like his slave-girlfriend-housemaid, having a roll in the hay when he feels like it and then running off doing God knows what for months at a time, leaving me alone in my prime of life. But if I threaten to leave him, he calls me the poor little rich girl (which, if we actually were rich, would be a whole different story) and says I can't leave him because no man we know around here could afford the upkeep! That is completely unfair. Everyone we know has a nicer house than us. He received a large sum for his service in the Congo, a decent nest egg you might say, but have I seen it? No, sir, and believe you me I looked under the mattress, because that is the kind of person he is. Actually, there's a gun under there. He says he invested the money. He claims he's gotten back involved with the diamond business in the Congo and has many foreign partners, but you still have to remind him to take a bath on any given day. So if he has foreign partners, I don't think they are of a very high class. I told him so, too. Well, he raised up his head from his beer bottle just long enough to have a good laugh at my expense. He said, "Baby, your intellectual capacity is out of this world!" Meaning the vacuum of outer space, ha, ha. His favorite joke. He said my brain was such a blank slate he could tell me every state secret he knows and then march me straight down to the Damnistry International and not have a thing to worry about. He said the government should hire me to work for the other side. This is not lovey-dovey quarreling, mind you. He says these things and laughs in my face! Oh, I have cried till I threatened to ruin my own complexion, let me tell you.

But not anymore. I have abided my time and kept my eyes open, while in the meantime telling him off good in the bathroom mirror whenever I'm all alone and he's not there, just like I used to do to Father. "You just wait," I tell him. "I'll show you whose mind is a blank slate!"

And now Rachel Price is about to have her day. I have a trick up my sleeve which I haven't told a soul about, even though it's the God's honest truth and I know it: I have a good shot at the Ambassador.

Actually Daniel is the First Attaché, but the French are all so much of a higher class, regardless of their position. Like I said, we meet the best people through the Templetons, who have divine shindigs. "Come over for drinks and a *braai*," meaning a barbecue, is what we always say in Johannesburg. Those parties have a very international flair, what with the scotch whiskey, American LPs, and the embassy gossip. After that one time the Prime Minister got shot in the head, there was a big old crackdown on the blacks, which was absolutely necessary, but resulted in misunderstandings at many of the foreign embassies. The nation of France, especially, has gotten all high-and-mighty about threatening to remove their associations from South Africa. We've all been hearing for weeks now that Daniel is going to be reposted to Brazzaville. His little Frenchy wife Robine will never hack it, I can see that as plain as day. She's well known for just as soon firing her maids as looking at them, and as far as she is concerned, everything that lies outside the civilized boundaries of Johannesburg is Darkest Africa. She and Daniel were already on the verge of a breakup, even if they didn't know it. So I saw my opportunity, you might say. "She doesn't know how lucky she is," I whispered in his ear. "I'll tell you a little secret. If it was me, I'd go with you in two shakes of a lamb's tail." This was two Saturdays ago, over at the Templetons' when we were slow-dancing around the pool to "Big Girls Don't Cry" by the Four Seasons. I happen to remember that was the song. Because just that very morning I'd found out about another one of Axelroot's little piccadillies, but I'm a big girl so I just put my hair up, marched downtown, and bought me a brand-new siren-red bathing suit with a bare midriff. Keeping up the insurance is how I think of it. Like they say in the magazines, Just wear a smile and a Janzen! And that is exactly what I was doing two Saturdays ago at the Templetons' party.

"After what all I lived through in the Congo," I cooed to Daniel, "I could take Brazzaville and keep right on smiling."

And guess what: that is just what I'm going to do! I might as well get started packing my bags and getting measured for a Dior gown.

After what I know about that man, I can wrap him around my little finger. And what he did to me, boy! A man only does *that* kind of thing when he has certain feelings. I can tell you with absolute positivity that I am soon going to be Mrs. Daniel Attaché-to-the-Ambassador DuPrée. Eeben Axelroot will be high and dry with no one but the maid to pick up his socks. And Daniel, bless his heart, will never even know what hit him.

Leah Price Ngemba

BIKOKI STATION
JANUARY 17, 1965

IT CAN FEEL COLD HERE, in the early-morning haze of the dry season. Or maybe it's just me. Maybe my blood's gotten thin, a weakness Father used to accuse us of when we complained of the chill winters in north Georgia. Certainly there's no winter here: the equator just about runs smack-dab through our bed. Anatole tells me I'm passing from the northern to the southern hemisphere whenever I go out to poke up the fire in the kitchen house, so I should consider myself worldly, even though it's nearly impossible these days to leave the station.

The plain bitter truth is that this day chills me to the bone. I try not to pay attention to the month and date, but the blossoming poinsettias roar at me that it's coming anyway, and on January 17 I'll wake up too early, with an ache in my chest. Why did I have to crow, "Who's brave enough to go out there with me?" Knowing her as I did, that she'd never stand to be called a coward by anyone, least of all her sister.

It's a bleak anniversary in our household. I killed a snake this morning, just whacked it into pieces with my machete and flung all three of them up in the trees. It was the big black one that's been hanging around the back door since the end of the rains. Anatole came out and clucked his tongue at my handiwork.

"That snake was not doing us any harm, Béene."

"I'm sorry, but I woke up this morning craving an eye for an eye."

"What does this mean?"

"It means that snake crossed my path on the wrong day."

"He was eating a lot of rats. Now they will be into your manioc."

"Black rats or white ones? I'm not sure I can tell the difference."

He looked at me a long time, trying to work me out. Finally he asked, "Why do you think your sadness is so special? Children died every day in Kilanga. They are dying here and now."

"Oh, how could I *forget*, Anatole. She was just one of a million people who left the world that day, along with the great Prime Minister Patrice Lumumba. I'm sure in the long run Ruth May hardly mattered at all."

He came to me and touched my hair, which has gotten rather shaggy. When I can remember to be a good Congolese wife, I tie it up in a headcloth. Anatole carefully wiped my eyes with the tail of his shirt. "Do you think I can't remember Little Sister? She had the heart of a mongoose. Brave and clever. She was the chief of all children in Kilanga, including her big sisters."

"Don't talk about her. Just go to work. *Wenda mbote.*" I took his hand away and glared at him. *Don't mention her and I won't speak of your Lumumba shattered with machetes like this poor snake and thrown in pieces into an abandoned house in Elisabethville, with the blessings of my hateful homeland.* I stomped off to the kitchen house, where I could hear the rats already at the manioc, rewarding my spite.

This is a day Anatole and I simply have to get through. I've heard people say grief brings you closer, but the griefs he and I carry are so different. Mine are white, no doubt, and American. I hold on to Ruth May while he and the rest of Congo secretly hold a national day of mourning for lost Independence. I can recall, years ago, watching Rachel cry real tears over a burn hole in her green dress while, just outside our door, completely naked children withered from the holes burning in their empty stomachs, and I seriously wondered if Rachel's heart were the size of a thimble. I suppose that's how he sees me today. Any other day I might pray, like my old friends the Benedictine sisters, to lose my self-will in the service of greater glory. But January 17, in my selfish heart, is Ruth May's only.

Through a crack between the boards I watched him pick up his book bag and head off in his earnest, square-shouldered Anatole way down the road toward the school. Anatole, my first prayer to Creation answered. Both of us were spared, in body at least, by the stone walls of our different imprisonments, and altered in spirit, in ways we're struggling to understand. I've lost all the words to my childhood prayers, so my head rings with its own Grand Silence. And Anatole has found new words for shaping belief.

His circumstances were as bizarre as mine, and very lucky—we agree on that. Most dissidents now are executed, or held under conditions that make them wish for execution. But Mobutu was just getting organized in '61, and still given to peculiar omissions. Anatole got to spend his days playing bottle-cap checkers with a pair of lackadaisical guards, who let him read and write anything as long as he didn't escape. They liked Anatole, and apologized that they had to support their families on the handful of coins or rice they got when Mobutu's deputies came by to count the prisoners each morning. After that he could organize lessons under the courtyard's scabby mango, teaching literacy to any guard or fellow prisoner who felt like improving himself on a given day. The guards helped get books for Anatole, and went to a lot of trouble to get his letters posted to various countries. Right under Mobutu's nose, he discovered the writings of the great African nationalist Kwame Nkrumah, and the poetry of a young doctor in Angola, Agostinho Neto, with whom he started up a correspondence. Neto is about Anatole's age, also educated by missionaries. He'd already gone abroad to study medicine and returned home to open a clinic, where his own people could get decent care, but it didn't work out. A gang of white policemen dragged him out of his clinic one day, beat him half to death, and carted him off to prison. The crowds that turned up to demand his release got cut down like trees by machine-gun fire. Not only that, but the Portuguese army went out burning villages to the ground, to put a damper on Neto's popularity. Yet, the minute he got out of prison, he started attracting droves of people to an opposition party in Angola. Anatole is encouraged by his example and talks about Neto a good deal, hoping to meet with him somehow, somewhere. I can't feature it, when it's too dangerous now for them even to continue writing letters.

Of course, Anatole's most faithful prison correspondence was with a nun in Bangassou, which was a matter of great hilarity to his fellow prisoners. *Sa planche de salut!* they teased—his long plank to salvation—a slang expression meaning your last hope. Anatole still sometimes calls me his *planche de salut*. But by the time we were reunited last fall, I was unsure enough of God and too mad at everybody else to offer any kind of salvation. For sure, though, I'd had enough of poverty-chastity-obedience to trade it in on being Anatole's wife. A medical evacuation Jeep got me through disguised as a corpse all the way to Bikoki, an old rubber plantation settlement outside of Coquilhatville. My sweetheart, released after three years without formal charges, was waiting here to raise the dead.

We chose Bikoki expecting to find people Anatole knew here, former friends and employers in the rubber trade, but most are dead now or have left the country. A surprise, though, was Aunt Elisabet, his mother's youngest sister. She came looking for him here a decade ago. Anatole was already gone long before, but Elisabet took work at the mission station, had a child, and never left. It's a great change for Anatole to have relatives and a wife, after his lifelong status as an orphan.

The mission is a ghost town now, and the agricultural station also nearly deserted. The Simbas have cleared the place of Europeans without ever setting foot here. The plantation is mostly rubble. (I imagine it dismantled by the whacked-off ghost hands of all those rubber workers.) The one building left standing contains the very library where Anatole, as a young household servant, taught himself to read and write English. At my request we were married in that room by the village chief, in a ceremony that was neither quite Christian nor Bantu. I asked for God's blessing and carried red bougainvillea flowers for my mother. Aunt Elisabet draped around our shoulders the traditional marriage cloth called *nzole*, a beautiful double-sized *pagne* that symbolizes the togetherness of marriage. It also works as a bedspread.

Since its heyday as a planter's mansion, parts of the house had been used as an army bunker, a birthing hospital, and a goat barn. Now the plan was to use it for a school. The department chief in Coquilhatville admires Anatole, so turned a blind eye to his prison record and hired him as headmaster for the regional *école secondaire*. We're also trying to keep open the agricultural extension program, training former rubber workers to subsistence farming. And I volunteer at the clinic, where a Guinean doctor comes once a week from Coquilhatville to immunize and diagnose babies. In spite of all we'd been through, Anatole and I stood together last fall and declared the word *Independence* out loud. We said it with our eyes on the sky, as if it were some fabulous bird we could call down out of the air.

It's taken a lot to dampen our hopes. But everything has turned around so fast, like a magician's trick: foreign hands moved behind the curtain and one white King was replaced with another. Only the face that shows is black. Mobutu's U.S. advisors even tried to hold elections here, but then got furious when the wrong person won—Antoine Gizenga, Lumumba's lieutenant. So they marched the army into parliament and reorganized it once again in Mobutu's favor.

"If the Americans mean to teach us about democracy, the lesson is quite remarkable," Anatole observed.

"Breathtaking," I agreed.

He says I have different personalities: that my Lingala is sweet and maternal, but in English I'm sarcastic. I told him, "That's nothing—in French I'm a mine sweeper. Which personality annoys you the most?"

He kissed my forehead. "The most, I love my Béene." His absolute truth. Is that what I am? When the neighbors or students ask me my nationality, I tell them I came from a country that no longer exists. They can believe it.

In the last months our government paychecks have dwindled from almost nothing to nothing. We tell our coworkers that a mere

lack of funds mustn't discourage our hopes. We know that to criti-
cize Mobutu, even in private, is to risk having your head cracked
open like a nut, which naturally would discourage one's hopes
entirely. We live on what we can find, and when we're offered news
of friends, we take a deep breath first. My old friend Pascal and two
other former students of Anatole's were murdered by the army on
the road south of here. Pascal had a kilo of sugar cane and a defunct
World War II handgun in his backpack. We heard about it on
Christmas Day, when we had a visit from Fyntan and Celine
Fowles. They're now staying at Kikongo, the hospital mission on the
Wamba they told us about. I rejoiced to see them, but any reunion
brings awful news, and I cried myself to sleep when they left. I'd
nearly forgotten Pascal, his wide-set eyes and insolent smile, and
now he comes creeping around my dreams, throwing open windows faster than I can shut them. What little scrap of audacity
caught the attention of an army officer on the road? What if I
marked him with some English word I taught him, as stupidly as we
doomed our parrot?

This is the kind of crazy dread we live with. Our neighbors are
equally terrified of Mobutu's soldiers and their opposition, the Simbas, whose reputation is stalking northern Congo like a lion itself.
The Simbas' anger against all foreigners is understandable, but
increasingly their actions aren't. We hear of atrocities on the shortwave, then hear them exaggerated on Mobutu's official newscasts,
and it's hard to know what's real. I think about food, mostly, and
occupy my mind by watching children. I don't really fear the Simbas, even though I'm white. Anatole is very well respected; my
alliance with him will save me, or it won't. Justice moves in mysterious ways.

Father is still carrying on with his tormented Jesus Is Bängala
church. This was the Fowleses' other awful news: Father had walked
or hitchhiked all the way over to the Kikongo mission in an agitated state, bellowing that his guts were on fire with venom. He
claimed he'd swallowed a live snake. The mission doctor gave him
quinine and vermifuges, which would give pinworms a run for

their money, but likely not a green mamba. Poor Father. Now he's left Kilanga altogether, vanished into the forest, it seems, or melted under the rain. Sometimes at night I think about how he might be dead and I haven't heard yet. It's a hard thing to live with in the dark, and I lie awake cooking up plans to go hunt for him. But in daylight a wall of anger pushes me in a different direction, roaring that I must leave Father behind me. I couldn't strike out on my own, and even with help it's not worth the risk. I understand that he's dangerous to me now.

Dangerous to many people, and always was, I guess. Fyntan and Celine must have been alarmed by our misguided outpost in Kilanga, where we slept in their same house, antagonized their former friends, even turned their parrot out to nature's maw. And that mission doctor at Kikongo must have found Father a sight to behold: a wild-haired preacher with a snake in his belly. That doctor has stayed on with his family, in spite of the danger—they're from someplace in the South, Fyntan thought, Georgia or Kentucky. I wish I could go visit them and talk in my own language, the English I knew before I grew thorns on my tongue.

It's the only time I get homesick, when America lands on my doorstep in a missionary guise. There are others who didn't go back, like me. But they seem so sure of being right here where they are, so rooted by faith—Fyntan Fowles, for one, and the strangers who turn up every so often to ask if I can help get a message through or keep a box of medicines safe till a boat is found to take it upriver. I'll happily invent a meal and make up a bed on the floor, just to hear the kindness in their stories. They're so unlike Father. As I bear the emptiness of a life without his God, it's a comfort to know these soft-spoken men who organize hospitals under thatched roofs, or stoop alongside village mamas to plant soybeans, or rig up electrical generators for a school. They've risked Mobutu and every imaginable parasite in the backwater places where children were left to die or endure when the Underdowns and their ilk fled the country. As Brother Fowles told us a long time ago: there are Christians, and there are Christians.

But visitors of any stripe are rare, and most days are exactly like the ones before. Funny to speak of boredom, I guess. If I'd tried in childhood to imagine my present life in the jungle, I'd have been struck numb with the adventure of it. But instead I'm numb with the tedium of a hard life. We collapse into bed at night. I spend all day walking between the soybean fields, the kitchen house, the market, the clinic, and the nutrition class I teach at the agriculture school, wondering on any given day if I've given out more information than I've taken in. For sure that's the direction the calorie count is going. We have manioc and yams to fill our bellies, but protein is scarcer than diamonds. I bargain high and low for an egg or beans, a precious chicken, some fresh river fish, or I'll catch a ride into the Coquilhatville market to gaze at such treasures as tinned ham, for a king's ransom. Sometimes I even manage to pay it! But Anatole has lost weight this winter and I've lost even more, eight kilos, so fast I'm a little scared. Probably I have whipworm again. I'm pretty sure I was pregnant at Christmastime, but now I'm sure I'm not, so there must have been a loss in there, but it's easier not to mention it to Anatole. Easier not to count it, if that's possible.

I'm losing my family, piece by piece. Father is lost, wherever he is. Rachel I could only despise more if I knew for sure which way to direct my ire, presumably South Africa, where I guess she's finally hit paydirt with her exceeding whiteness and mercenary husband. I can't reliably get a letter to Mother or Adah. Mobutu's chief postal minister, a relative of Mobutu's wife, stopped paying all the postal workers for the last year so he could use the money to build himself a mansion in Thysville. Now it takes a huge bribe or a personal contact to get mail out of the country, and the letters incoming I can only suppose are piling up somewhere in Léopoldville, being sniffed for money or valuables.

If people are shocked by these unexplained losses—the post, their salary, a friend walking home on the road—they don't mention it. What do people here know but forbearance? They take one look at the expensive, foreign-made uniforms of Mobutu's police and know to keep their thoughts to themselves. They know who stands behind Mobutu, and that in some place as far away as heaven, where the largest rules are made, white and black lives are different kinds of currencies. When thirty foreigners were killed in Stanleyville, each one was tied somehow to a solid exchange, a gold standard like the hard Belgian franc. But a Congolese life is like the useless Congolese bill, which you can pile by the fistful or the bucketful into a merchant's hand, and still not purchase a single banana. It's dawning on me that I live among men and women who've simply always understood their whole existence is worth less than a banana to most white people. I see it in their eyes when they glance up at me.

January is a hard, dry month and I'm lonely, I think. Lonely for others of my kind, whoever that might be. Sometimes I imagine leaving, going home to see Mother and Adah, at least, but the logistics of money and travel and a passport are too laborious even to imagine. My daydream gets as far as the front gate and ends right there, looking back at Anatole, who's saying, Not *you*, Béene.

Tonight he'll come home worried and exhausted. There's hardly any way to keep the *école secondaire* open another term without funds, and parents are anxious that education is only putting their children at greater risk. The awful truth is they're right. But he won't talk about that. He'll sneak up behind me in the kitchen house and throw an arm across my chest, making me scream and laugh at the same time. He'll rub his knuckles into my hair and cry, "Wife, your face is as long as a crocodile's!"

I'll tell him it's just as ugly, too, and my skin is about that scaly. I say these things so he'll argue with me. I'm difficult in January. I know this. I need him to insist that I'm useful and good, that he wasn't out of his mind to marry me, that my white skin is not the standard of offense. That I wasn't part of every mistake that's led us to right now, January 17, with all its sins and griefs to bear.

He reminded me once that the first green mamba was meant for him. He aroused Tata Kuvudundu's anger by encouraging discussion about us, and white people in general. He blames his misjudgment of village politics. We all have that snake in our belly, I suppose, but Anatole can't take mine. If I can't yet mourn a million people who left this world in a single day, I'll start with one, and move from there. I don't have much left of my childhood beliefs I can love or trust, but I still know what justice is. As long as I'm carrying Ruth May piggyback through my days, with her voice in my ear, I still have her with me.

Adah Price

I AM LOSING MY SLANT.

In medical school I have been befriended by an upstart neurologist, who believes I am acting out a great lifelong falsehood. Adah's False Hood. In his opinion, an injury to the brain occurring as early as mine should have no lasting effects on physical mobility. He insists there should have been complete compensation in the undamaged part of my cerebral cortex, and that my dragging right side is merely holding on to a habit it learned in infancy. I scoffed at him, of course. I was unprepared to accept that my whole sense of *Adah* was founded on a misunderstanding between my body and my brain.

But the neurologist was persuasive, intimidatingly handsome, and the recipient of a fabulously coveted research grant. Mostly to prove him wrong, I submitted my body to an experimental program of his design. For six months he had me stop walking entirely, in order to clear my nervous pathways of so-called bad habits. Instead, I crawled. With the help of friends I rearranged my small apartment to accommodate a grown-up baby, and warily crept each morning from a mattress to my coffee maker and hotplate on the kitchen floor. I used only the lower half of the refrigerator. To preserve my dignity I went to work in a wheelchair. I was starting a rotation in pediatrics at the time—good luck, since children don't tend to hold the crippled responsible for their infirmities, as grown-ups do. Adults listen to you with half an ear, while the Biblical prescription "Physician, heal thyself!" rings in the other. But children, I found, were universally delighted by a doctor with wheels.

At home, while I set about memorizing the flaws in my carpet, my body learned to cross-coordinate. One day I felt the snap like a rubber band that drew my right leg up under me as my left arm moved forward. A week later I found I could easily balance on my hands and toes, push my rear end up into the air and fall over into a sit. Nobody was there to watch, praise be, as I spontaneously clapped my hands at the wonder of my accomplishment. Within a few weeks I had strength enough in both arms to pull myself up on the furniture, and from there I could release myself to a stand. Now, tentatively, I toddle in a straight line. I have taken each step in its turn. I was not learning it all over again but for the first time, apparently, since Mother claims I did none of these things as a baby. She insists I lay on my back for three years crying for Leah to stay close and play with me, until finally one day without prelude I rolled off the couch and limped after her. Mother says I never practiced anything but always watched Leah, letting her make the mistakes for both of us, until I was ready to do it myself with acceptable precision. Mother is kind to me, probably because I've stayed nearer at hand than her other children. But I disagree. I made plenty of my own mistakes. I just made them on the inside.

It has taken me so long to believe I am saved. Not from crookedness; I am still to some extent crooked and always too slow. But saved from the abandonment I deserved. It has taken until tonight, in fact.

Leah is in Atlanta now, and that is part of the problem if not the whole of it. Leah with Anatole and their little son Pascal and another child well in progress. Leah majoring in Agronomics and all of them making a noble attempt to plant themselves on American soil. I can see it will not last. When I go with them to the grocery, they are boggled and frightened and secretly scornful, I think. Of course they are. I remember how it was at first: dazzling warehouses buzzing with light, where entire shelves boast nothing but hair spray, tooth-whitening cream, and foot powders. It is as if our Rachel had been left suddenly in charge of everything.

"What is that, Aunt Adah? And that?" their Pascal asks in his wide-eyed way, pointing through the aisles: a pink jar of cream for removing hair, a can of fragrance to spray on the carpet, stacks of lidded containers the same size as the jars we throw away each day.

"They're things a person doesn't really need."

"But, Aunt Adah, how can there be so many *kinds* of things a person doesn't really need?"

I can think of no honorable answer. Why must some of us deliberate between brands of toothpaste, while others deliberate between damp dirt and bone dust to quiet the fire of an empty stomach lining? There is nothing about the United States I can really explain to this child of another world. We leave that to Anatole, for he sees it all clearly in an instant. He laughs aloud at the nearly naked women on giant billboards, and befriends the bums who inhabit the street corners of Atlanta, asking them detailed questions about where they sleep and how they kill their food. The answers are interesting. You might be surprised to know how many pigeons roosting in the eaves of Atlanta's Public Library have ended up roasting over fires in Grant Park.

I find an extraordinary kindred spirit in Anatole. We are both marked, I suppose. Freaks at first sight, who have learned to take the world at face value. He was marked early on by his orphaned state, his displacement, his zealous skeptical mind, his aloneness. I have noticed that he, too, reads things backward: what the billboards are really selling, for example. Also where poverty comes from, and where it goes. I shall not covet my sister's husband, but I shall know him, in my way, better. Anatole and I inhabit the same atmosphere of solitude. The difference between us is he would give up his right arm and leg for Leah, whereas I already did.

Will I lose myself entirely if I lose my limp?

How can I reasonably survive beyond the death of Ruth May and all those children? Will salvation be the death of me?

Here in the hospital I have too much time for questions like these. It occurs to me I have access to an infinite variety of narcotic drugs. Sleep is an absolute possibility. God can't see you when you're asleep, Ruth May used to insist. *Evil peels no eye on sleep. Live! Die.*

They see a great deal of Mother. Mother last year gave up her floral hermitage in Bethlehem and moved to an apartment in Atlanta, having found a new church of sorts. She marches for civil rights. They pay her to work in an office, but I know she lives for the marches. She is very good at it, and impervious to danger. She came over to my apartment one night, having walked nearly a mile through tear gas, so that I could check her eyes for damage to the cornea. Her eyes were not even red. I think bullets would pass right through her.

It crosses my mind that I may need a religion. Although Mother has one now, and she still suffers. I believe she talks to Ruth May more or less constantly, begging forgiveness when no one is around.

Leah has one: her religion *is* the suffering.

Rachel doesn't, and she is plainly the happiest of us all. Though it could be argued that she is, herself, her own brand of goddess.

I am sorry to say I do not see Leah and Anatole as much as I might. Being a medical student, of course, I have an inhuman schedule, and everyone makes allowances for that. Also I am in a different region of the university altogether from married student housing. They are making babies over there, while over here we merely save them.

It has been a difficult month: a rotation in neonatal intensive care. We lost two babies in the last week. And in this past day, Christmas Eve, while the clock made two complete rotations of its own, I watched over three tiny creatures whose lungs struggled like the flat, useless wings of butterflies prematurely emerged. Triplets. I considered Nelson's view of what ought to be done with twins, and the dreadful consequences of ignoring that tradition. What we had here was worse: a triple calamity fallen on the house of these poor parents. I spoke with the father, a boy of sixteen or so, who gave the clear impression, through the use of the conditional tense when speaking of the parental care required for these damaged children, that he might not stick around. So a plague on the mother alone. While the machines hummed softly in our hospital and white-soled shoes whispered up and down the halls, a catastrophe was roaring down upon this child of a mother. This is her Christmas gift. She will be indentured forever. Never again will her life be free of travail and disappointment in her three blind mice. She may cut off their tails with a carving knife, this husbandless wife, whose school friends are still promenading through their girlhoods.

Who is to say she should not have run to the forest with her hair and umbilical cords flying, and knelt to deposit each of these three at the base of its own pine tree? Who will argue that my drips and incubators are really the wiser plan?

Who could blame Mother if she had chosen to leave me so?

After midnight I fell asleep on my cot in the interns' lounge, but was battered by dreams. Entubed, damaged children of all colors danced on my head and arms and hands. *Live or die, live or die?* they chorused. *Mother May We?*

Africa has slipped the floor out from under my righteous house, my Adah moral code. How sure I always felt before, how smug, moving through a world that desired to cast me into the den of ear-pulling Crawleys. Adah the bridled entitled, Adah authorized to despise one and all. Now she must concede to those who think perhaps I should have been abandoned in the jungle at birth: well, they have a point. What I carried out of Congo on my crooked little back is a ferocious uncertainty about the worth of a life. And now I am becoming a doctor. How very sensible of me.

I struggled half awake and half asleep, and then suddenly, in the middle of my fevered, stolen nap, utterly awake. In dread, trembling. Lying on my side with my eyes open. I felt my cold hands. I was *afraid.* This is the new awful thing I cannot bear to feel. Afraid. *This is my letter to the World That never wrote to Me—The simple news that Nature told—With tender Majesty. Her message is committed to hands I cannot see—For love of her, sweet countrymen, judge tenderly of Me!*

In spite of myself I have loved the world a little, and may lose it.

I sat up on my cot, ran a hand through my damp, tangled hair, felt bruises all over my arms in the shape of small footprints. The second hand on the wall clock made its steady, ludicrous progress: *sluff, sluff, sluff* . . .

Afraid of what, exactly?

Suicidal idyll fratricidal. Afraid. That. Mother would choose Leah.

Perfect Leah with her adorable babe and husband. In a few hours it will be morning, they will dance around the tree with their little gifts from Mother, and they will stay, they will, after all. And the lure of grandsons will be too strong to resist, and Mother will be theirs. And then I will have to go to sleep. *Sleep oh sleep thou certain knot of peace.*

For many tedious seconds I sat on the edge of my cot, swallowing indecision and tears. Then I got up, wiped my face on the sleeve of my hospital coat, walked to the physicians' lounge, and dialed the number I knew by heart. I called her. It was the dead-flat middle of the night. The night before Christmas and all through the house I am Adah who expects no gifts, Adah who does not need or care what others say. Yet I woke up my mother and finally asked her why she chose me, that day at the Kwenge River.

Mother hesitated, understanding that there were many wrong answers. I did not want to hear that the others could take care of themselves, nor that she felt she had no other choice.

Finally she said, "After Ruth May you were my youngest, Adah. When push comes to shove, a mother takes care of her children from the bottom up."

That is the bedtime story my mother made up for me. It was not a question of my own worth at all. There is no *worth*. It was a question of position, and a mother's need. After Ruth May, she needs me most.

I find this remarkably comforting. I have decided to live with it.

Leah Price Ngemba

KINSHASA
1974

YOU CAN'T GO TO LÉOPOLDVILLE NOW, or to Stanleyville, Coquilhatville, or Elisabethville. The names of all those conquerors (and
their ladies) have been erased from our map. For that matter you can't
even go to the Congo; it's Zaire. We repeat these words as if we're trying to memorize a false identity: I live in Kinshasa, Zaire. The places
we've always used to position ourselves are suddenly unfamiliar—
cities, villages, even rivers. Elisabet worries genuinely, in spite of our
reassurances, that she and Anatole might have been assigned new first
names, since theirs are European and "colonialist." It wouldn't surprise
me, actually. Mobutu's edicts are that far-reaching. The old couple next
door seem to share her dread: they always forget and say
"Léopoldville," then cover their mouths with their hands as if they've
let slip a treason.

In the evenings we quiz each other, searching out more and more
obscure places on the map to trip each other up: Charlesville? Banningville? Djokupunda! Bandundu! The boys get them right more
often than I do, mainly because they like to show off. Anatole never
misses one, because his mind is that quick, and also I think the
indigenous names mean more to him. They're foreign to me, of
course. After the boys are asleep I sit at the table in the flickering
kerosene light, working my way slowly over the new map, feeling as

if Father had found me out here to give me The Verse. We're retraining our tongues to Mobutu's great campaign of *authenticité*.

But what is authentic about it, I keep asking Anatole. Kinshasa's main street is Boulevard the 30th of June, in memory of that great Independence Day carefully purchased by thousands of pebbles thrown into bowls and carried upriver. How authentic is that? What really became of that vote is another matter, not memorialized in any public place I can see. There is no Boulevard 17 Janvier Mort de Lumumba.

He points to the dirt path that runs between ours and our neighbors' houses, down through a ditch where we clutch up our skirts and tiptoe over the sewage on oil drums to reach the main road. "This boulevard needs a name, Béene. Put a sign here." Wise guy. He can't wait to see if I'll do it.

Our house is sturdy, with a concrete floor and a tin roof. We live in what would be called, in America, a slum, though here it's an island of relative luxury in the outskirts of *la cité,* where the majority have a good deal less in the way of roofing, to say the least. Under our roof, we're six: Anatole and me, our boys Pascal, Patrice, and the baby, Martin-Lothaire, and Aunt Elisabet, plus her daughter Christiane occasionally. After we came back from Atlanta we brought Elisabet down here from Bikoki, where things had gotten fairly desperate. I can't say they're any less desperate here, but she's good company. I thought I'd learned resourcefulness, but Elisabet has given me a higher education in making soup out of stones. *Mondele*, she calls me, I'm her white daughter. Yet she's hardly older than Anatole and looks just like him, minus the broad shoulders and narrow waist. (Her shape is somewhat the reverse.) With his same sweet patience, she works nonstop in our one-room house, singing in Lingala, her left hand always holding her outer *pagne* closed for modesty while her right does more alone than I could with three. She's told me everything she can recall of her older sister, Anatole's mother, and like a kid I make her repeat the stories. I'm hungry for any family I can get. I'm lucky if I hear from Mother and Adah twice a year. It's not their fault. I know they've sent countless packages that are piled up somewhere in the great, crumbling postal edifice downtown. I expect the Minister of Post could build himself a second or third home out of undelivered boxes.

By some miracle, we did get a package at Easter time. The boys hooted and ran the length of our *17 Janvier* lane brandishing their precious Mars bars. (Which, I heard Pascal boast to his friends, are manufactured on Mars.) I was tempted to do the same with my own loot: five books in English! Also clothing, aspirin, antibiotics, hand lotion, thick cotton diapers, batteries for our radio, and long letters. I buried my face in the clothes for the scent of my mother, but of course they came from some American child who's no kin to us. Mother does volunteer work in African relief. We're her pet project, you could say.

In every package there's one oddball thing from Adah, a sort of secret message is how I think of it. This time it was an old *Saturday Evening Post* she'd found in the bottom of Mother's closet. I leafed through it, wondering, Did Adah want me to read about how Jimmy Stewart got his start, or to know that when a Philco moves in, your TV troubles move out? Then I found it, an article called "Will Africa Go Communist?" Adah retains her eagle eye for irony. It was all about how the U.S. ought to take better charge of the maverick Congo; the two photographs stopped my heart. In one, a young Joseph Mobutu looks out imploringly above a caption declaring his position in jeopardy. Next to him is a smiling, rather crafty-looking Patrice Lumumba, with a caption warning: "He may be on his way back!" The magazine is dated February 18, 1961. Lumumba was already a month dead, his body buried under a chicken coop in Shaba. And Mobutu, already well assured of his throne. I can picture the Georgia housewives shuddering at the Communist challenge, quickly turning the page on that black devil Lumumba with the pointed chin. But I was hardly any less in the dark, and I was in Bulungu, the very village where Lumumba had been captured. My sister married a man who may have assisted in his death-sentence transport to Shaba, though even Rachel will never know that for sure. We have in this story the ignorant, but no real innocents.

Adah wrote at the bottom of the page, "Remember 'Devil One' and 'W. I. Rogue?' Our secret secrets?" She says there's talk now of an investigation, that the Congress may look into past wrongdoing in the Congo or "any possible link between the CIA, Lumumba's death, and the army coup that brought Mobutu to power." Are they joking? Adah says no one is giving it any credence; here, no one has ever doubted it. It's as if history can be no more than a mirror tipped up to show each of us exactly what we already knew. Now everyone's pretending to set the record straight: they'll have their hearings, while Mobutu makes a show of changing all European-sounding place names to indigenous ones, to rid us of the sound of foreign domination. And what will change? He'll go on falling over his feet to make deals with the Americans, who still control all our cobalt and diamond mines. In return, every grant of foreign aid goes straight to Mobutu himself. We read he's building himself an actual castle with spires and a moat near Brussels, to provide a respite, I guess, from his villas in Paris and Spain and Italy. When I open my door and look out, I see a thousand little plank-and-cardboard houses floating at every conceivable tilt on an endless ocean of dust. We hardly have a functional hospital in our borders, or a passable road outside Kinshasa. How can this be, a castle with spires and a moat? Why doesn't the world just open its jaws like a whale and swallow this brazenness in one gulp? is the question I'd pose to Father these days. "Who gave him charge of the whole world? If you have insight, hear this: Can one who hates right govern?" Job 34:13, thank you very much.

The latest news from Mobutu is that he's bringing two great American boxers, Muhammad Ali and George Foreman, to the stadium in Kinshasa. The announcement came on the radio this afternoon. I only listened with one ear because of a larger drama unfolding in our kitchen. I'd just put Martin down for a nap on his mat and was boiling the diapers while Elisabet crumbled a papery onion and hot *pili-pili* into a bowl. She fries this with mashed tomatoes into a thin red sauce for the manioc. That's the principal trick of Congolese cooking: rubbing two leaves together to give color and taste to another day's translucent, nutritionally blank ball of manioc.

The pot for boiling the *fufu* was waiting in line for the stove, after the diapers, and after that would come the big laundry kettle with the boys' shirts and our household's three sheets and two towels. Here in Kinshasa we have a "city kitchen," with the stove right inside the house, but it's only a little bottle-gas burner, maddeningly sluggish after my years of cooking over roaring wood fires. A lot of people in *la cité* do cook with wood, which they have to nibble secretively from each other's houses at night, like termites.

This was supposed to be a payday for Anatole, and at the school there's been talk about the *supplémentaire*, meaning the possibility of the government's starting back payments on the wages they've been stealing from all public schools for over a year. This "supplement" is supposed to be a sign of good faith, to forestall a nationwide strike of university students, but some students walked out anyway, and the signs of Mobutu's faith so far have been expressed with nightsticks. I worry constantly about Anatole. Although I know his capacity for self-restraint in a dangerous moment is uncanny.

Elisabet and I knew there would be no *supplémentaire* but were still greatly enjoying spending it at tomorrow's market. "A kilo of fresh eels and two dozen eggs!" I proposed, and she laughed at me. My craving for protein drives me to a singlemindedness she calls my *mondele*-hungries.

"Better, ten kilos of rice and two bars of soap," she said, which we do need badly, but I despaired for an imaginary windfall that would bring nothing but more white starch into this house.

"Nothing white," I declared.

"Brown soap, then," she offered. "Oh! And some nice pink *papier hygiénique!*" she added fervently, and we both laughed at that pipe dream. The last roll of toilet paper we'd seen, in any color, came from Atlanta.

"At least some *beans*, Elisabet," I whined. "Fresh green ones. *Mangwansi*, like we used to have in the country."

Pascal's best friend, a hearty girl named Elévée, had wandered in and sat down at the table opposite Elisabet, but was uncharacteristically quiet.

"What do you think?" Elisabet prodded her with the blunt end of her knife. "Tell Madame Ngemba she needs a new *pagne* with some color left in it. Tell her she is disgracing her sons with the washing rag she wears to the market."

Elévée picked at the short sleeve of her school uniform, evidently not desiring to talk about fashion. Her very black skin looked ashy, and she had the tired slump to her shoulders I recognize in my boys when they're getting hookworm. I carried the boiled diapers outside, washed my hands carefully with our sliver of soap, and interrupted the afternoon's procession of cookpots to make Elévée a cup of tea.

Suddenly she reported with a blank face that she was leaving school.

"Oh, Elévée, you can't," I said. She's a smart little girl, though this guarantees nothing, of course.

Elisabet simply asked her, "Why?"

"To work at night with Mother," she said flatly. Meaning, to work as a prostitute.

"How old are you?" I demanded angrily. "Eleven? Ten? This is a crime, Elévée, you're a *child*! There are laws to protect you from that kind of work. It's horrible, you don't know. You'll be scared and hurt and could get terribly sick."

Elisabet looked at me with dismay. "*Mondele*, don't frighten her. They have to have the money."

Of course that's true. And of course there are no laws to protect children from prostitution. Elisabet's daughter, Christiane, I'd guess to be seventeen, and I suspect she sometimes does night work in town, though we can't talk about it. Whenever we hit rock bottom, Elisabet somehow discovers a little cash in her purse. I wish she wouldn't. I just stared at Elévée, my son's little friend with skinned knees and her two braids sticking out like handlebars: a prostitute. It dawned on me that her childishness would increase her value, for a while anyway. That made me want to scream. I shoved the manioc pot onto the stove, slopping water all over everywhere.

I survive here on outrage. Naturally I would. I grew up with my teeth clamped on a faith in the big white man in power—God, the President, I don't care who he is, he'd serve justice! Whereas no one here has ever had the faintest cause for such delusions. Sometimes I feel like the only person for miles around who hasn't given up. Other than Anatole, who expresses his outrage in more productive ways.

We sat without speaking awhile, after Elévée's announcement. The radio informed us the two American boxers would be paid five million American dollars each, from our treasury, for coming here. And it will cost that much again to provide high security and a festival air for the match. "All the world will respect the name of Zaire," Mobutu declared in a brief taped interview at the end of the broadcast.

"Respect!" I practically spat on the floor, which would have horrified Elisabet more than the ill-considered use of twenty million dollars.

"Do you know what's under the floor of that stadium?" I asked.

"No," Elisabet said firmly, though I'm sure she does know. Hundreds of political prisoners, shackled. It's one of Mobutu's most notorious dungeons, and we're all aware Anatole could end up there, any day. For what he teaches, for his belief in genuine independence, for his loyalty to the secret Parti Lumumbist Unifié, he could be brought down by one well-bribed informant.

"The prisoners might make a lot of noise during the boxing match," Elévée suggested.

"Not improving the general respectability of Zaire," I said.

"*Likambo te*," Elisabet shrugged. "Pascal and Patrice will be very excited. *Mondele,* just think, *Muhammad Ali*. He is a hero! Little boys in the streets will cheer for him."

"No doubt," I said. "People from the world over will come watch this great event, two black men knocking each other senseless for five million dollars apiece. And they'll go away never knowing that in all of goddamned Zaire not one public employee outside the goddamned army has been paid in two years."

For a woman to curse in Lingala is fairly abominable. Elisabet puts up with a lot from me. "Stanleyville," she commanded, to change the subject.

"Kisangani," I responded without enthusiasm. Elévée ran off to play with Pascal, rather than be trapped into this drear exercise.

"Parc National Albert?"

"Parc de la Maiko."

Neither of us knew or cared if I was right.

I'm learning that Elisabet's sudden conversational turns are always for a good reason—usually someone's safety, probably mine. I watch her in the marketplace, too, well aware that no schoolroom has ever taught me as much. The Congolese have an extra sense. A social sense, I would call it. It's a way of knowing people at a glance, adding up the possibilities for exchange, and it's as necessary as breathing. Survival is a continuous negotiation, as you have to barter covertly for every service the government pretends to provide, but actually doesn't. How can I begin to describe the complexities of life here in a country whose leadership sets the standard for absolute corruption? You can't even have a post office box in Kinshasa; the day after you rent it, the postmaster may sell your box to a higher bidder, who'll throw your mail in the street as he walks out the door. The postmaster would argue, reasonably, he's got no other way to support his family—his pay envelope arrives empty each week, with an official printed statement about emergency economic measures. The same argument is made by telephone operators, who'll place a call outside the country for you only after you specify the location in Kinshasa where you'll leave *l'enveloppe* containing your bribe. Same goes for the men who handle visas and passports. To an outsider it looks like chaos. It isn't. It's negotiation, infinitely ordered and endless.

As a white woman in Kinshasa I present possibilities, but even a black woman with my same purse and leather shoes would be approached on the street. It's taking me forever to get used to this. Last week a young man walked up and asked me outright for three thousand zaires, and once again my jaw dropped.

"*Mondele*, he wasn't asking for three thousand zaires," Elisabet said quietly when we'd moved on to coveting the pineapples. He was opening the door for a transaction, she explained. He has something to offer, maybe inside information on black-market goods or the name of a telephone operator with unauthorized (therefore cheap) access to long distance. She's explained this to me a dozen times, but it only sinks in as I come to see for myself what it is, this life. Anybody who needs *anything* in Kinshasa—a kidney-stone operation or a postage stamp—has to bargain for it, shrewdly. The Congolese are used to it and have developed a thousand shortcuts. They sum up prospects by studying each other's clothing and disposition, and the bargaining process is well under way before they open their mouths to speak. If you're deaf to this subtle conversation, it comes as a shock when the opening bid seems to be, "Madame, I request from you three thousand zaires." I've heard foreign visitors complain that the Congolese are greedy, naive, and inefficient. They have no idea. The Congolese are skilled at survival and perceptive beyond belief, or else dead at an early age. Those are the choices.

I got some inkling of this from Anatole long ago, I suppose, when he explained why he translated Father's sermons. It wasn't evangelism, just full disclosure. Opening up the bargaining table to a would-be congregation. I multiplied my perception of Anatole's intelligence by ten that day, and now looking back I have to do the same for everyone we knew. The children who hounded us daily for money and food weren't dim-witted beggars; they were accustomed to the distribution of excess, and couldn't fathom why we held ourselves apart. The chief who proposed to marry my sister surely didn't dream Father would actually hand over his whining termite! I think Tata Ndu was gently suggesting we'd become a burden to his village in a time of near famine; that people here accommodate such burdens by rearranging families; and that if we found such an idea impossible we were perhaps better off somewhere else. Tata Ndu certainly had his arrogance in the ways of command, even calling down a vote in church to humiliate my father, but in matters of life and death, I can see now, he was almost incomprehensibly polite.

It's a grief to see the best of Zairean genius and diplomacy spent on bare survival, while fortunes in diamonds and cobalt are slipped daily out from under our feet. "This is *not* a poor nation," I remind my sons till they hear it in their sleep. "It is only a nation of poor."

No paycheck tonight, of course, let alone the *supplémentaire*. But Anatole came home excited about the general strike and spoke of it quietly through dinner, careful as always to use code words and false names. Any such knowledge could endanger the boys. Though I believe Pearl Harbor itself would have passed by them tonight, intent as they were on devouring the manioc. To make it last longer I pinched up little bites with my left hand while I nursed Martin on the right. With every gulp he drew, I felt more ravenous.

"One of these days," I announced, "I am going to take my bow and sneak through the bars of the *Résidence*." Mobutu's Kinshasa mansion is surrounded by a park, where some zebras and one pitiful elephant paw at the grass.

Pascal was all for it. *"Oh, Mama! Abattons l'éléphant!"*

Patrice soberly informed us he didn't think an arrow could pierce an elephant's hide.

Pascal was unconcerned. "Have you seen that thing? Mama's arrow will knock it over, *plaf! Kufwa!"*

Elisabet asked thoughtfully, *"Mondele*, how would you *cook* an elephant?"

What we eat is manioc, manioc, manioc. Whether it's tinted pink with a tomato skin or green with a leaf of cress, it's still manioc. Rice and soy meal help when we can get them, to balance our amino acids and keep our muscle tissue from digesting itself in the process known picturesquely as kwashiorkor. When we first moved to Kilanga, I remember thinking the children must get plenty to eat because their bellies all bulged out. Now I know their abdominal muscles were too weak to hold their livers and intestines in place. I see signs of it in Patrice. Any food that reaches us in Kinshasa has to come over impossible roads in dilapidated trucks from the interior, so it costs too much even if you can find it. Sometimes Anatole reminds me of our long-ago conversation when I tried to explain how we grew food back home, in huge fields far from the people who eat it. Now I understand his dismay. It's a bad idea, at least for Africa. This city is a foreigner's premise of efficiency planted on this

soil, and it's a very bad idea. Living in it, no one could think otherwise. It's a vast congregation of hunger, infectious disease, and desperation, masquerading as opportunity.

We can't even grow any food of our own. I did try it, right at the
metal flank of our back door, under the clothesline. Pascal and
Patrice helped me scratch up a little plot that eventually produced a
few bleak, dusty bouquets of spinach and beans, which were gobbled
up one night by our neighbor's goat. The children of that household
looked so starved (as did the goat), I couldn't regret this donation.

We, at least, have the option of leaving. In the back of my mind I
think this—we could try again in Atlanta. And while we stay here
for Anatole's teaching and organizing, and live on the next-to-noth-
ing that work earns, we still have a measure of privilege incomprehensible to our neighbors. I've taken my sons to the States for vaccinations that aren't available anywhere in Zaire. I've seen them all
born alive, and not one lost to smallpox or tuberculosis. We're luckier than most. That's what's hardest to bear: the view out the window. La cité is a grim, dust-colored homeland, and I suffer nostalgia
for our life in the interior. In Bikoki and Kilanga we could always
pick something off a tree, at least. We never passed a day without
seeing flowers. Epidemics sometimes devastated the village, but they
always ended, not far from where they began.

I can have a good laugh at my former self, remembering how my
sisters and I nervously made our list of prospects: oranges, flour,
even eggs! At our low point as missionaries, we were still fabulously
wealthy by the standards of Kilanga. No wonder any household
item we carelessly left on our porch quietly found a new home in
the night. No wonder the neighbor women frowned in our doorway when we pulled out the linings of our pockets as evidence of
our poverty. Not another soul in town even had pockets. They must
have felt exactly as I do now glaring at Mobutu on the doorstep of
his fairy-tale palaces, shrugging, with his two hands thrust deep into
the glittering loot of his mines.

"I thought you said the Congolese don't believe in keeping riches
to themselves," I told Anatole once, inclined toward an argument.

But he just laughed. "Who, Mobutu? He is not even African now."

"Well, what is he, then?"

"He is the one wife belonging to many white men."

Anatole explained it this way: Like a princess in a story, Congo was born too rich for her own good, and attracted attention far and wide from men who desire to rob her blind. The United States has now become the husband of Zaire's economy, and not a very nice one. Exploitive and condescending, in the name of steering her clear of the moral decline inevitable to her nature.

"Oh, I understand that kind of marriage all right," I said. "I grew up witnessing one just like it."

But it dawns on me now that, in the end, Mother carried every last one of our possessions outside as a farewell gift to Kilanga. There are wives, and then there are wives. My pagan mother alone among us understood redemption.

The rest of us are growing into it, I suppose. God grants us long enough lives to punish ourselves. *Janvier 17, Mort de Lumumba* and Ruth May, that's still the bleak day at our house. Anatole and I grow wordless and stare into the distance at our own regrets, which aren't so far apart anymore. On January nights I'm visited by desperate dreams of stretching myself out over the water, reaching for balance. When I look back at the shore, a row of eggs become faces of hungry children, and then comes the fall into blue despair, where I have to move a mountain that crumbles in my hands. It's a relief to wake up drenched in sweat and find Anatole's body next to me. But even his devotion can't keep this weight off my shoulders. "*Have mercy upon me, O God, according unto the multitude of thy tender mercies,*" I catch myself praying, before I've fully awakened to a world where I have no father, and can count on no tender mercies.

Anatole says recurring dreams are common to those who've suffered seriously from malaria. When I'm nervous or sad I also fall prey to the awful itch from *filaires*, tiny parasites that crawl into your pores and cause a flare-up every so often. Africa has a thousand ways to get under your skin.

★   ★   ★

Our life here in Kinshasa contains more mercies than most can hope for. I haven't yet had to bump off Mobutu's elephant. I even got to bring home a nice fat paycheck, for a time. I signed on to an American payroll, rationalizing that I'd scatter dollars over the vendors in my little corner of *la cité*, at least, as it's certain no foreign relief will reach them any other way.

Mrs. Ngemba, English teacher, was my new identity. It chafed me as much as the Benedictine habit, as it turns out. I taught at a special school in the compound for Americans who came to work on the Inga-Shaba power line. This was the great nuptial gift from the U.S. to the Congo—financing the construction of the Inga-Shaba. It's an enormous power line stretching across eleven hundred miles of jungle, connecting hydroelectric dams below Léopoldville to the distant southern mining region of Shaba. The project brought in Purdue engineers, crews of Texas roughnecks, and their families, who lived outside Léopoldville in a strange city called Little America. I rode the bus out there every morning to teach grammar and literature to the oddly unpoetic children of this endeavor. They were pale and displaced and complained of missing their dire-sounding TV shows, things with *Vice* and *Cop* and *Jeopardy* in their titles. They'd probably leave the Congo never knowing they'd been utterly surrounded by vice, cops, and the pure snake-infested jeopardy of a jungle. The compound was like a prison, all pavement and block, enclosed by razor wire. And like any prisoners, these kids fought with anything sharp they could find. They mocked my style of dress and called me "Mrs. Gumbo." I pitied them, despised them, and silently willed them back home on the first boat. I got warnings time and again, for "attitude" as the superintendent put it, but he tolerated me for want of a replacement. I quit at the end of the second term.

The place spooked me. I'd step up onto the bus at my street corner at the end of *17 Janvier,* doze bumpily through half an hour of predawn, then open my eyes in another world. The compound had row after row of shining metal houses and dozens of liquor bars glittering at daybreak with an aura of fresh vomit and broken glass.

The bus would hiss to a stop just inside the gate for a bizarre shift change: we teachers and maids would step down, and the bus would take on the weary, disheveled whores. Congolese girls, with bleached orange hair and a crude phrase or two of English, and the straps of expensive American bras sliding down their shoulders from under skimpy blouses. I could just imagine them getting home, folding this uniform, and wrapping themselves in *pagnes* before going to the market. As we all stood blinking at each other, getting our bearings, the compound trucks would roar past us into the jungle, carrying crews of men who apparently (judging from the whores) never slept.

In the course of a year I watched these rough-and-ready foreigners go out to build thousands of miles of temporary roads for carting cable, machine tools, and sheet metal, past villagers who'll live out their days without electricity, machine tools, or sheet metal. The Shaba Province, incidentally, roars with waterfalls, more than enough to generate its own electricity. But with all the power coming from the capital, the mines could be lit up by Mobutu's own hand, and shut down at the first sign of popular rebellion. Katanga had once tried to secede, after all. At the time I was working there, we believed that was the justification for this strange project.

Since I quit, we've learned more, enough for me to curse my small contribution to the Inga-Shaba. It was not merely a misguided project; it was sinister. The power line was never meant to succeed at all. With no way to service a utility stretching across the heart of darkness, the engineers watched the monster's tail crumble as fast as the front was erected. The whole of it was eventually picked clean in the way a forest tree gets gleaned by leaf-cutter ants: nuts, bolts, and anything that might serve for roofing material trailed off into the jungle. Anyone could have predicted that exact failure. But by loaning the Congo more than a billion dollars for the power line, the world Export-Import Bank assured a permanent debt that we'll repay in cobalt and diamonds from now till the end of time. Or at least the end of Mobutu. It's a popular game, wondering which will come first. With a foreign debt now in the billions, any hope that was left for our Independence is handcuffed in debtor's prison. Now the black market is so much healthier than the legitimate economy I've seen people use zaires for repairing cracks in their walls. Foreign bootlegging of minerals is so thorough that our neighbor the French Congo, without a single diamond mine in its borders, is the world's fifth-largest exporter of diamonds.

And whatever hasn't left the country is in the King's pantry. If my sister Rachel and Mr. William Shakespeare put their heads together to invent an extravagant despot, they couldn't outdo Mobutu. Now he's building a palace modeled on the one his friend the Shah has got in Iran. It's in his native village of Gbadolite. They say he's got fat peacocks strutting around in a courtyard, protected by high walls, pecking up grain from silver plates inscribed with Moorish designs. The gasoline generator that lights up the palace makes such a horrid bellowing, day and night, that all the monkeys have fled the vicinity. The air-conditioning has to run all the time so the jungle heat won't damage the gold leaf on his chandeliers.

I can just imagine. Outside the palace walls, the women of Gbadolite are squatting in their yards, boiling manioc in salvaged hubcaps, and if you asked them the meaning of Independence they'd scowl and shake a stick at you. What a nuisance, they'd say. The towns all have new names, and if that weren't enough to remember, now we're supposed to call one another *citoyen*.

In downtown Kinshasa, where a lot of the bars have television sets, Mobutu in his leopard-skin hat blinks on every evening at seven o'clock for the purpose of unifying our nation. "How many fathers?" he asks again and again in this recorded pageant, and his recorded audience responds, *"One!"*

"How many tribes? How many parties?" he continues. "How many masters?"

Each time his loyal congregation screams, *"Mookoo! One!"*

The image flickers and the *citoyens* drink their beer or go on about their business. Mobutu is speaking in his own tribal language. Most people out there can't even understand.

Rachel Axelroot DuPrée Fairley

THE EQUATORIAL
JANUARY 1978

LISTEN, don't believe in fairy tales! After that happy-ever-after wedding, they never tell you the rest of the story. Even if you get to marry the prince, you still wake up in the morning with your mouth tasting like drain cleaner and your hair all flat on one side.

That was poor little me, suddenly a diplomat's wife on the edge of the forest prime evil, wearing my Dior gown and long black gloves to embassy parties in Brazzaville, French Congo. That was the fairy-tale part, and sure, it was fun while it lasted. I felt like a true-life Cinderella. My hair did just wonderfully in the humidity, and I had my own personal French hairdresser (or so he said, but I suspected him of being Belgian), who'd come to our home every Tuesday and Saturday. Life could not have been better. Never would anyone have believed that merely a few short years before I had been living with my family over on the other side of the river—*me*, the very self-same Rachel, slogging through the filth! Ready to sell my soul for a dry mohair sweater and a can of Final Net hairspray. Hoo, boy! I received quite an education about politics, as an embassy wife. The French Congo and the newly independent Republic of Congo are separated by one mere river and about a million miles of contemporaneous modern thinking. It's because they tried to go and do it all for themselves over there, and don't have the temperament. They're still struggling to get decent telephone service. Whereas in my duration of diplomatic service in Brazzaville, French Congo, the worst I ever had to do was fuss at the servants to cut back the scraggly hibiscus on the lawn, and clean the mold off the crystal.

Well. That is all water under the bridge now. Diplomatic service or not, a man who leaves his wife for his mistress is no catch, I was sorry to find out. Well, live and learn. Like they always say, the rear-view mirror is twenty-twenty.

Remy, my third husband, was very devoted. He was an older man. My life has been 101 calamities with at least half of them in the marriage department, but finally I got lucky in love, with Remy Fairley. *He* at least had the decency to die and leave me the Equatorial.

With Remy resting in peace I was free to express my talents, and I have built this place up from what it was, let me tell you. The Equatorial is now the nicest hotel for businessmen along the whole northern route from Brazzaville to Owando. We are about a hundred miles north of the city, which is considerably farther in kilometers, but still we get the tourist trade. There are always French and Germans and what not stopping in on their way up north to oversee one project or another, or just escaping from the city to see a little of true-life Africa before they finish up their foreign assignment in Brazzaville and go back home to their wives. They usually tend to be oil men or interpreners.

We're on the premises of what was formerly a plantation, so the house is surrounded by lovely groves of orange trees and coconut palms. The mansion itself has been converted to twelve comfortable rooms of various sizes, all quite luxurious, with two full baths on each floor. The restaurant is in a large open portico on the ground floor shaded by bougainvilleas. There is nearly always a breeze. We recently put in a second small covered patio with a bar so that while my guests are enjoying a meal, their chauffeurs will have a pleasant place to bide their time. The restaurant is for paying guests only, which is, needless to say, whites, since the Africans around here wouldn't earn enough in a month to buy one of my *prix-fixe* dinners. But I certainly am not one to leave anyone sitting out in the rain! So I built them that shelter, so they wouldn't be tempted to come in and hang about idly in the main bar. I'm famous for my love of animals, too, and have created quite a little menagerie in the compound between the garden and the restaurant for everyone's amusement. Any time of day you can hear the parrots chattering in their cages. I taught them to say "Drink up now! Closing time!" in English, French, and Afrikaans, though I have to admit they've picked up a few depictable phrases from my guests, over the years. The clientele at the Equatorial is always the highest caliber but, nevertheless, they are men.

My proudest achievement is the swimming pool, patio, and gardens, which I put in entirely by myself. The pool took the most spectacular effort. I got it dug by paying a whole troop of local boys for each and every basket of earth they moved. And of course, watching like a hawk to be sure they didn't stuff the bottom of the basket with leaves. It is hard work running a place like this, don't you believe it. My help would rob me blind if I didn't keep every single thing locked down, and punish the culprits with a firm hand. Most women would not last a week in my position. My secret is: I like it! I really do. In spite of everything, I stroll through the restaurant in my bikini with my platinum-blonde hair piled high, jingling my big bunch of keys, cheerfully encouraging my guests to drink their martinis and forget about their workaday cares back home. And I think: Finally, Rachel, this is your own little world. You can run it exactly however you please. Who needs a husband when I have more handsome gentlemen around than you can shake a stick at? And yet, if ever I don't like the way someone behaves, out he goes! If I want chicken curry for dinner, I simply say to the cooks: Chicken curry! If I want more flowers, I snap my fingers and have them planted. Just like that. Oh, I work myself to the bone, keeping this business open seven days a week and the weekends. My rates might be a little higher than average, but my guests do not have a single complaint. Why should they go and get swindled at some other establishment when they can come here!

I will probably grow very rich and very old at the Equatorial before any member of my family ever visits me here. It's true! They never have. Leah is right over there in Kinshasa, which is just a hop, skip, and jump away. When they had that fight down there with Muhammad Ali and George Foreman we had *tons* of tourists from that. They came over to Africa for the fight and then crossed the river and toured around in French Congo, since the roads and everything are so much nicer in general over here. I knew we'd get a slew of people, the minute they announced they were having that fight. I've always had a sixth sense for spotting a trend coming, and I was right on the ball. I finished up the second-floor bathroom I'd been having trouble with, and redecorated the bar with a boxing theme. I even went through hell and high water trying to get an authentic advertising poster from the fight, but sometimes you just have to make do with what you have. I got one of the boys to fashion little miniature boxing gloves out of dried plantain leaves sewn together, which turned out very realistic, and had them dangling down from all the lights and fans. I hate to brag but if I do say so myself they were cute as a button.

I kept thinking, everyone is in such a festive mood, and Leah is just not that far away, in miles. Mother and Adah keep saying they might come over to visit, and if they could cross an entire ocean, you would think Leah could stoop to taking a bus. Plus, supposedly Father is still over there wandering about in the jungle, and honestly, what else does *he* have to do? He could get cleaned up and pay a visit on his eldest daughter. Oh, I dreamed of a true class reunion of our family. Just imagine all their faces, if they saw this place. Which, I might add, none of them came.

I suppose I should just give up, but in the back of my mind I still think about it. I picture myself taking Leah and Adah on the grand tour, sweeping my hand over the elegant mahogany paneling in the bar, Ta-dah! Or grandly opening the door to the upstairs bathrooms, which have mirrors edged in faux gold (I could afford real, but it would peel right off in this humidity!) and give the overall effect of appearing very continental, with toilet *and* bidet. How astonished my sisters would be to see what all I have accomplished, starting with practically nothing. I don't care if they're gifted and know every word in the dictionary, they still have to give credit for hard work. "Why, Rachel," Leah would say, "you run this place with such genialness and vivacity! I never knew you had such an exemplary talent for the hospitality business!" Adah would, of course, say something more droll, such as "Why, Rachel, your interest in personal hygiene has truly become a higher calling."

If you ask me, that's exactly why they don't come—they're afraid they would have to start respecting me finally. I'm sure they'd rather go on thinking they are the brains of the family and I am the dumb blonde. They have always been very high up on their horses, which is fine, although if you ask me they have shot their own career ladders in the foot. Adah evidently got famous for being a brain in college and going to medical school (Mother sent me newspaper clippings for Adah winning some prize practically every time she took a crap), and she could have done very well for herself as a lady doctor. But what I gather from what Mother writes me now is that she works night and day wearing a horrid white coat in some dreary big-deal place in Atlanta where they study disease organisms. Well, fine! I guess somebody has to do it!

Now, Leah, though. That one I will never understand. After all this time I can certainly work with the Africans as well as anybody can, mainly by not leading them into temptation. But to *marry* one? And have children? It doesn't seem natural. I can't see how those boys are any kin to me.

I wouldn't say so to her face, of course. I swear I haven't said a word in all these years. Not that it's hard, since we don't write all that often. She only sends Christmas cards, which generally get here just in the nick of time for Easter. I think the mailmen over in Zaire must be lazy or drunk half the time. And when I do get a letter, it's always a great disappointment. Just: Oh how are you, I had another baby named whatsit or whosis. She could at least give them names in plain English, you would think. She never asks about the hotel at all.

We're all keeping our hopes up for family relations, I guess, but our true family fell apart after Ruth May's tragic death. You could spend your whole life feeling bad about it, and I get the idea Mother especially is still moping around. And Leah's decided to pay for it by becoming the Bride of Africa. Adah, now she could probably get her a halfway decent boyfriend since she's finally gotten her problem fixed, but no, she has to throw her prime of life down the test tube of a disease organism.

Well, that's their decision. What happened to us in the Congo was simply the bad luck of two opposite worlds crashing into each other, causing tragedy. After something like that, you can only go your own way according to what's in your heart. And in my family, all our hearts seem to have whole different things inside.

I ask myself, did I have anything to do with it? The answer is no. I'd made my mind up all along just to rise above it all. Keep my hair presentable and pretend I was elsewhere. Heck, wasn't I the one hollering night and day that we were in danger? It's true that when it happened I was the oldest one there, and I'm sure some people would say I should have been in charge. There was just a minute there where maybe I could have grabbed her, but it happened so fast. She never knew what hit her. And besides, you can't possibly be in charge of people who will not give you the time of day, even in your own family. So I refuse to feel the slightest responsibility. I really do.

In the evenings here at the Equatorial I usually wind up the day by closing down the bar all by myself, sitting in the dark with my nightcap and one last cigarette, listening to the creepy sounds of a bar with no merriment left in it. There are creepy little things that get into the thatch of the roof, monkey squirrels or something, that you only notice at night. They scritch around and peep down at me with their beady little eyes till I just about lose my mind and scream, "Shut the hell up!" Sometimes I have to slip off my thongs to throw at them before they'll pipe down. Better to keep this place filled up with businessmen and keep the liquor flowing, is what I always say. Honestly, there is no sense spending too much time alone in the dark.

Leah Price Ngemba

KINSHASA
RAINY SEASON, 1981

ANATOLE IS IN PRISON. Maybe for the last time. I get out of bed and put on my shoes and force myself to take care of the children. Outside the window the rain pours down on all the drenched, dark goats and bicycles and children, and I stand here appraising the end of the world. Wishing like hell we hadn't come back from Atlanta.

But we had to. A person like Anatole has so much to offer his country. Not, of course, in the present regime, whose single goal is to keep itself in power. Mobutu relies on the kind of men who are quick with guns and slow to ask questions. For now, the only honorable government work is the matter of bringing it down. So says Anatole. He'd rather be here, even in prison, than turning his back on an outrage. I know the dimensions of my husband's honor, as well as I know the walls of this house. So I get up and put on my shoes and curse myself for wanting to leave in the first place. Now I've lost everything: the companionship of his ideals, and the secret escape I held in reserve, if my own failed completely. I always thought I could fly away home. Not now. Now I've pulled that ace out of the hole, taken a good look, and found that it's useless to me, devalued over time. An old pink Congolese bill.

How did this happen? I've made three trips back now, more as a stranger each time. Did America shift under my feet, or did it stand still while I stomped along my road toward whatever I'm chasing, following a column of smoke through my own Exodus? On our first trip, America seemed possible for us. Anything did. I was pregnant with Patrice then—1968, it would have been. Pascal was almost three, picking up English like the smart little parrot he is. I studied agricultural engineering at Emory, and Anatole was in political science and geography. He was an astonishing student, absorbing everything in the books, then looking past them for things his teachers didn't know. The public library he mistook for heaven. "Béene," he whispered, "for everything that has ever come into my mind, there is already a book written about it."

"Watch out," I teased him. "Maybe there's one in here about you."

"Oh, I fear it! A complete history of my boyhood crimes."

He came to feel derelict about sleeping at night, for the sake of all the books he'd miss reading in those hours. He retained some reticence about speaking English, refusing for example ever to say the word *sheet* because to his ear it's indistinguishable from *shit*, but he read with a kind of hunger I'd never witnessed. And I got to be with my family. Adah was well along in medical school then, so was terribly busy, but we practically lived with Mother. She was so good to us. Pascal prowled over her furniture and napped on her lap like a cat.

I went back the second time to recover from Martin's birth, since I'd gotten dangerously anemic, and to get the boys their booster shots. Mother raised the money to fly us over. It was just the boys and me that time, and we stayed on longer than we'd planned, for the exquisite pleasure of enough food. Also to give Mother a chance to know her only grandchildren. She took us to the ocean, to a windswept place of sandy islands off the Georgia coast. The boys were wild with all their half-composted discoveries and the long, open stretches for running. But it made me homesick. The shore smelled like the fish markets in Bikoki. I stood on the coast staring across an impossible quantity of emptiness toward Anatole, and whatever else I'd left behind in Africa.

It's a funny thing to complain about, but most of America is perfectly devoid of smells. I must have noticed it before, but this last time back I felt it as an impairment. For weeks after we arrived I kept rubbing my eyes, thinking I was losing my sight or maybe my hearing. But it was the sense of smell that was gone. Even in the grocery store, surrounded in one aisle by more kinds of food than will ever be known in a Congolese lifetime, there was nothing on the air but a vague, disinfected emptiness. I mentioned this to Anatole, who'd long since taken note of it, of course. "The air is just blank in America," I said. "You can't ever smell what's around you, unless you stick your nose right down into something."

"Maybe that is why they don't know about Mobutu," he suggested.

Anatole earned a stipend from student teaching, an amount the other graduate students called a "pittance," though it was much more than he and I had ever earned together in any year. We lived once again in married student housing, a plywood apartment complex set among pine trees, and the singular topic of conversation among our young neighbors was the inadequacy of these rattletrap tenements. To Anatole and me they seemed absurdly luxurious. Glass windows, with locks on every one and two on the door, when we didn't have a single possession worth stealing. Running water, *hot*, right out of a tap in the kitchen, and another one only ten steps away in the bathroom!

The boys alternated between homesickness and frenzy. There were some American things they developed appetites for that alarmed me, and things they ignored, which alarmed me even more. For example, the way well-intentioned white people spoke to my trilingual children (they fluently interchange French, Lingala, and English, with a slight accent in each) by assaulting them with broad, loud baby talk. Anatole's students did essentially the same, displaying a constant impulse to educate him about democracy and human rights—arrogant sophomores! With no notion of what their country is doing to his. Anatole told me these stories at night with a flat resignation, but I cursed and threw pillows and cried while he held me in the vast comfort of our married-student double bed.

The citizens of my homeland regarded my husband and children as primitives, or freaks. On the streets, from a distance, they'd scowl at us, thinking we were merely the scourge they already knew and loathed—the mixed-race couple, with mongrel children as advertisement of our sins. Drawing nearer they would always stare at Anatole as contempt gave way to bald shock. His warrior's face with its expertly carved lines speaks its elegance in a language as foreign to them as Lingala. That book was closed. Even my mother's friends, who really did try, asked me nothing of Anatole's background or talents—only, in hushed tones when he left the room, "What happened to his face?"

Anatole claimed the stares didn't bother him. He'd already spent so much of his life as an outsider. But I couldn't stand the condescension. Anatole is an exquisitely beautiful and accomplished man in his own country, to those who appreciate intellect and honor. I already spent a whole childhood thinking I'd wrecked the life of my twin sister, dragged after me into the light. I can't drag a husband and sons into a life where their beauty will blossom and wither in darkness.

So we came home. Here. To disaster. Anatole's passport was confiscated at the airport. While Pascal and Patrice punched each other out of exhausted boredom and Martin leaned on me crying that his ears hurt, my husband was brought down without my notice. He was a wanted man in Zaire. I didn't understand this at the time. Anatole told me it was a formality, and that he had to give our address in Kinshasa so they'd know where to bring his passport back to him the next day. I laughed, and said (in front of the officials!) that, given our government's efficiency, it would be the next year. Then we crammed ourselves into a battered little Peugeot taxi that felt like home at last, and came to Elisabet's house, to fall into sleep or the fitful wakefulness of jet lag. I had a thousand things on my mind: getting the boys into school, finding a place to live, exchanging the dollars from Mother at some Kinshasa bank that wouldn't give us old zaires or counterfeit new ones, getting food so we wouldn't overwhelm poor Elisabet. Not one of my thoughts was for my husband. We didn't even sleep together, since Elisabet had borrowed the few small cots she could find.

It would have been our last chance. The *casques-bleus* came pounding on the door right at dawn. I wasn't completely awake. Elisabet was still modestly wrapping her *pagne* as she stumbled to the door, and four men entered with such force they shoved her against the wall. Only Martin was really awake, with his huge black eyes on the guns in their belts.

Anatole behaved calmly, but his eyes were desperate when he looked at me. He mentioned names of people I should find right away—to help us get settled he said, though I knew what he meant—and an address that seemed to be backward.

"The boys," I said, having no idea how I meant to finish the sentence.

"The boys love you more than their own eyes. *Planche de salut.*"

"They're African, for always. You know."

"Béene. Be kind to yourself."

And he is gone. And I have no idea how to be kind to myself. Living, as a general enterprise, seems unkind beyond belief.

At least I know where he is, which Elisabet says is a blessing. I can't agree with her. They took him immediately to Thysville, which is about a hundred kilometers south of Léopoldville over the best road in this nation, repaved recently with a grant of foreign aid. The prison is evidently that important. I had to go to eight different government offices to get information, submitting like an obedient dog to carry a different slip of onionskin paper from one office to the next, until I met my master with his chair tipped back and his boots on his desk. He was startled to see a white woman, and couldn't decide whether to be deferential or contemptuous, so he alternated. He told me my husband would be in detention until formal charges were filed, which could take six months to a year. The charges are in the general nature of treason, which is to say anti-Mobutism, and the most likely sentence will be life imprisonment, though there are other possibilities.

"At Camp Hardy," I said.

"Le Camp Ebeya," he corrected me. Of course. Camp Hardy has been renamed, for *authenticité*.

I knew not to be encouraged about the so-called "other possibilities." Camp Hardy happens to be where Lumumba was held, and
beaten to within an inch of his life, before his death flight to
Katanga. I wonder what comfort my husband will get from this bit
of shared history. We've known several other people, including a fellow teacher of Anatole's, who've been detained more recently at
Camp Hardy. It's considered a prolonged execution, principally
through starvation. Our friend said there were long periods when
he was given one banana every two days. Most of the cells are solitary, with no light or plumbing or even a hole in the floor. The
buckets are not removed.

I was told I couldn't visit until Anatole was formally charged.
After that, it would depend on the charges. I glared at the empty
blue helmet sitting on the desk, and then at my commandant's
unprotected head, wishing I might cause it to explode with the
force of my rage. When he had no more to tell me, I thanked him
in my politest French, and left. *Forgive me, O Heavenly Father, according to the multitude of thy mercies. I have lusted in my heart to break a
man's skull and scatter the stench of his brains across several people's back
yards.*

At least he isn't shackled under the stadium floor, Elisabet keeps
saying, and I suppose even my broken heart can accept that as good
fortune.

I've never known such loneliness. The boys are sad, of course, but
Pascal and Patrice at fifteen and thirteen are nearly men, with men's
ways of coping. And Martin is so confused and needs such comfort
he has nothing to give me.

We did find a house right away, recently vacated by a teacher's
family who've left for Angola. It's a long way from the center, in
one of the last little settlements on the road out toward the interior,
so we have at least the relief of flowering trees and a yard for growing vegetables. But we're far from Elisabet and Christiane, who
work long hours cleaning a police station and attached government
warehouse. I don't have the solace of daily conversation. And even
Elisabet isn't truly a kindred spirit. She loves me but finds me baf-

fling and unfeminine, and probably a troublemaker. She may lose her job because of familial association with treason.

I never bothered to notice before how thoroughly I've relied on Anatole to justify and absolve me here. For so many years now I've had the luxury of nearly forgetting I was white in a land of brown and black. I was Madame Ngemba, someone to commiserate with in the market over the price of fruit, the mother of children who sought mischief with theirs. Cloaked in my *pagne* and Anatole, I seemed to belong. Now, husbandless in this new neighborhood, my skin glows like a bare bulb. My neighbors are deferential and reserved. Day after day, if I ask directions or try to chat about the weather, they attempt nervously to answer me in halting English or French. Did they not notice I initiated the conversation in Lingala? Do they not hear me hollering over the fence at my sons every day in the habitual, maternal accents of a native-born fishwife? The sight of my foreign skin seems to freeze their sensibilities. In the local market, a bubble of stopped conversation moves with me as I walk. Everyone in this neighborhood knows what happened to Anatole, and I know they're sympathetic—they all hate Mobutu as much, and wish they were half as brave. But they also have to take into account his pale-skinned wife. They know just one thing about foreigners, and that is everything we've ever done to them. I can't possibly improve Anatole's standing in their eyes. I must be the weakness that brought him down.

I can't help thinking so myself. Where would he be now, if not for me? Dancing with disaster all the same, surely; he was a revolutionary before I met him. But maybe not caught. He wouldn't have left the country twice, listening to my pleas of an aging mother and fantasies of beefsteak. Wouldn't even have a passport, most likely. And that's how they got him.

But then, where would his children be? This is what we mothers always come back to. How could he regret the marriage that brought Pascal, Patrice, and Martin-Lothaire onto the face of Africa? Our union has been difficult for both of us in the long run, but what union isn't? Marriage is one long fit of compromise, deep and wide. There is always one agenda swallowing another, a squeaky wheel crying out. But hasn't our life together meant more to the world than either of us could have meant alone?

These are the kinds of questions I use to drive myself to distraction, when the boys are out and I'm crazed with loneliness. I try to fill up the space with memories, try to recall his face when he first held Pascal. Remember making love in a thousand different darknesses, under a hundred different mosquito nets, remember his teeth on the flesh of my shoulder, gently, and his hand on my lips to quiet me when one of the boys was sleeping lightly next to us. I recall the muscles of his thighs and the scent of his hair. Eventually I have to go outside and stare at my plump, checkered hens in the yard, trying to decide which one to kill for supper. In the end I can never take any of them, on account of the companionship I would lose.

One way of surviving heartache is to stay busy. Making something right in at least one tiny corner of the vast house of wrongs— I learned this from Anatole, or maybe from myself, the odd combination of my two parents. But now I'm afraid of running out of possibilities, with so many years left to go. I've already contacted all the people he advised me to find, to warn them, or for help. The backward address turned out after several mistakes to be the under-secretary to Étienne Tshisekedi, the one government minister who might help us, though his own position with Mobutu is now on the outs. And of course I've written to Mother's friends. (At the "Damnistry International," as Rachel probably still calls it.) I begged them to send telegrams on Anatole's behalf, and they will, by the bushel. If Mobutu is capable of embarrassment at all, there's a chance his sentence could be reduced from life to five years, or less. Meanwhile, Mother is raising money for a bribe that will get him some food, so five years and "life" won't be the same sentence. I've gone down to the government offices to find out where the bribe should go when we have it ready. I've nagged about visitation and mail until they all know my face and don't want to see it. I've done what I can, it seems, and now I have to do what I can't. Wait.

By lamplight when the boys are asleep I write short letters to

Anatole, reporting briefly on the boys and our health, and long letters to Adah about how I'm really faring. Neither of them will ever see my letters, probably, but it's the writing I need, the pouring out. I tell Adah my sorrows. I get dramatic. It's probably best that these words will end up suffocating in a pile, undelivered.

I might be envious of Adah now, with no attachments to tear her heart out. She doesn't need children climbing up her legs or a husband kissing her forehead. Without all that, she's safe. And Rachel, with the emotional complexities of a salt shaker. Now *there's* a life. Sometimes I remember our hope chests and want to laugh, for how prophetic they were. Rachel fiercely putting in overtime, foreshadowing a marital track record distinguished for quantity if not quality. Ruth May exempt for all time. My own tablecloth, undertaken reluctantly but in the long run drawing out my most dedicated efforts. And Adah, crocheting black borders on napkins and tossing them to the wind.

But we've all ended up giving up body and soul to Africa, one way or another. Even Adah, who's becoming an expert in tropical epidemiology and strange new viruses. Each of us got our heart buried in six feet of African dirt; we are all co-conspirators here. I mean, all of us, not just my family. So what do you do now? You get to find your own way to dig out a heart and shake it off and hold it up to the light again.

"Be kind to yourself," he says softly in my ear, and I ask him, How is that possible? I rock back and forth on my chair like a baby, craving so many impossible things: justice, forgiveness, redemption. I crave to stop bearing all the wounds of this place on my own narrow body. But I also want to be a person who stays, who goes on feeling anguish where anguish is due. I want to belong somewhere, damn it. To scrub the hundred years' war off this white skin till there's nothing left and I can walk out among my neighbors wearing raw sinew and bone, like they do.

Most of all, my white skin craves to be touched and held by the one man on earth I know has forgiven me for it.

Rachel Price

THE EQUATORIAL
1984

THIS WAS THE FIRST and the absolute last time I am going to participate within a reunion of my sisters. I've just returned from a rendezvous with Leah and Adah that was simply a sensational failure.

Leah was the brainchild of the whole trip. She said the last month of waiting for her husband to get out of prison was going to kill her if she didn't get out of there and do something. The last time he was getting let out, I guess they ended up making him stay another year at the last minute, which would be a disappointment, I'm sure. But really, if you commit a crime you have to pay the piper, what did she expect? Personally, I've had a few husbands that maybe weren't the top of the line, but a criminal, I just can't see. Well, each to his own, like they say. She's extra lonely now since her two older boys are trying out school in Atlanta so they won't get arrested, too, and the younger one is also staying there with Mother for the summer so Leah could be free to mastermind this trip. Which, to tell you the truth, she mostly just arranged for the sole purpose of getting a Land Rover from America to Kinshasa, where she and Anatole have the crackpot scheme of setting up a farm commune in the southern part and then going over to the Angola side as soon as it's safe, which from what I hear is going to be no time this century. Besides, Angola is an extremely Communistic nation if you ask me. But does Mother care about this? Her own daughter planning to move to a communistic nation where the roads are practically made of wall-to-wall land mines? Why no! She and her friends raised the money and bought a good Land Rover with a rebuilt engine in Atlanta. Which, by the way, Mother's group has never raised one red cent for me, to help put in upstairs plumbing at the Equatorial, for example. But who's complaining?

I only went because a friend of mine had recently died of his long illness and I was feeling at loose odds and ends. Geoffrey definitely was talking marriage, before he got so ill. He was just the nicest gentleman and very well to do. Geoffrey ran a touristic safari business in Kenya, which was how we met, in a very romantic way. But he caught something very bad over there in Nairobi, plus he was not all that young. Still, it shouldn't have happened to a better man. Not to mention me turning forty last year, which was no picnic, but people always guess me not a day over thirty so who's counting? Anyway I figured Leah and I could tell each other our troubles, since misery loves company, even though she has a husband that is still alive at least, which is more than I can say.

The game plan was for Adah to ride over on the boat to Spain with the Land Rover, and drive to West Africa. Adah driving, I just couldn't picture. I still kept picturing her all crippled up, even though Mother had written me that no, Adah has truly had a miracle recovery. So we were all to meet up there in Senegal and travel around for a few weeks seeing the sights. Then Adah would fly home, and Leah and I would drive as far as Brazzaville together for safety's sake, although if you ask me two women traveling alone are twice as much trouble as one. Especially my sister and me! We ended up not speaking through the whole entirety of Cameroon and most of Gabon. Anatole, fresh out of the hoosegow, met us in Brazzaville and they drove straight back home to Kinshasa. Boy, did she throw her arms around him at the ferry station, kissing right out in front of everybody, for a lot longer than you'd care to think. Then off they went holding hands like a pair of teenagers, yakety-yak, talking to each other in something Congolese. They did it expressly to exclude me from the conversation, I think. Which is not easy for someone who speaks three languages, as I do.

Good-bye and none too soon, is what I say. Leah was like a house on fire for the last hundred miles of the trip. She'd made a long-distance call from Libreville to make sure he was getting let out the next day *for sure*, and boy, did she make a beeline after that. She couldn't even bother herself to come up and see the Equatorial—even though we were only half a day's drive away! And me a bereaved widow, practically. I can't forgive that in my own sister. She said she would only go if we went on down to Brazzaville *first,* and then brought Anatole with us. Well, I just couldn't say yes or no to that right away, I had to think. It's simply a far more delicate matter than she understands. We have a strict policy about who is allowed upstairs, and if you change it for one person then where does it end? I *might* have made an exception. But when I told her I had to think about it, Leah right away said, "Oh, no, don't bother. You have your standards of white supremacy to uphold, don't you?" and then climbed up on her high horse and stepped on the gas. So we just stopped talking, period. Believe me, we had a very long time to listen to the four-wheel-drive transmission and every bump in the road for the full length of two entire countries.

When it was finally over I was so happy to get back to my own home-sweet-home I had a double vodka tonic, kicked off my shoes, turned up the tape player and danced the Pony right in the middle of the restaurant. We had a whole group of cotton buyers from Paris, if I remember correctly. I declared to my guests: "Friends, there is nothing like your own family to make you appreciate strangers!" Then I kissed them all on their bald heads and gave them a round on the house.

The trouble with my family is that since we hardly ever see each other, we have plenty of time to forget how much personality conflict we all have when it comes right down to it. Leah and Adah and I started bickering practically the minute we met up in Senegal. We could never even agree on where to go or stay or what to eat. Whenever we found any place that was just the teeniest step above horrid, Leah felt it was too expensive. She and Anatole evidently have chosen to live like paupers. And Adah, helpful as always, would chime in with the list of what disease organisms were likely to be present. We argued about positively everything: even communism! Which you would think there was nothing to argue about. I merely gave Leah the very sensible advice that she should think twice about going to Angola because the Marxists are taking it over.

"The Mbundu and the Kongo tribes have a long-standing civil war there, Rachel. Agostinho Neto led the Mbundu to victory, because he had the most popular support."

"Well, for your information, Dr. Henry Kissinger himself says that Neto and them are followers of Karl Marx, and the other ones are pro-United States."

"Imagine that," Leah said. "The Mbundu and Kongo people have been at war with each other for the last six hundred years, and Dr. Henry Kissinger has at long last discovered the cause: the Kongo are pro-United States, and the Mbundu are followers of Karl Marx."

"Hah!" Adah said. Her first actual unrehearsed syllable of the day. She talks now, but she still doesn't exactly throw words away.

Adah was in the back, and Leah and me up front. I was doing most of the driving, since I'm used to it. I had to slow way down for a stop sign because the drivers in West Africa were turning out to be as bad as the ones in Brazzaville. It was very hard to concentrate while my sisters were giving me a pop quiz on world democracy.

"You two can just go ahead and laugh," I said. "But I read the papers. Ronald Reagan is keeping us safe from the socialistic dictators, and you should be grateful for it."

"Socialistic dictators such as?"

"I don't know. Karl Marx! Isn't he still in charge of Russia?"

Adah was laughing so hard in the backseat I thought she was going to pee on herself.

"Oh, Rachel, Rachel," Leah said. "Let me give you a teeny little lesson in political science. Democracy and dictatorship are *political* systems; they have to do with who participates in the leadership. Socialism and capitalism are *economic* systems. It has to do with who owns the wealth of your nation, and who gets to eat. Can you grasp that?"

"I never said I was the expert. I just said I read the papers."

"Okay, let's take Patrice Lumumba, for example. Former Prime Minister of the Congo, his party elected by popular vote. He was a socialist who believed in democracy. Then he was murdered, and the CIA replaced him with Mobutu, a capitalist who believes in dictatorship. In the Punch and Judy program of American history, that's a happy ending."

"Leah, for your information I am proud to be an American."

Adah just snorted again, but Leah smacked her forehead. "How can you possibly say that? You haven't set foot there for half your life!"

"I have retained my citizenship. I still put up the American flag in the bar and celebrate every single Fourth of July."

"Impressive," Adah said.

We were driving along the main dirt road that followed the coast toward Togo. There were long stretches of beach, with palm trees waving and little naked dark children against the white sand. It was like a picture postcard. I wished we could quit talking about ridiculous things and just enjoy ourselves. I don't know why Leah has to nag and nag.

"For your information, Leah," I informed her, just to kind of close things off, "your precious Lumumba would have taken over and been just as bad a dictator as any of them. If the CIA and them got rid of him, they did it for democracy. Everybody alive says that."

"Everybody alive," Adah said. "What did the dead ones say?"

"Now, look, Rachel," Leah said. "You can get this. In a *democracy*, Lumumba should have been allowed to live longer than two months as head of state. The Congolese people would have gotten to see how they liked him, and if not, replaced him."

Well, I just blew up at that. "These people here can't decide *anything* for themselves! I swear, my kitchen help still can't remember to use the omelet pan for an omelet! For God's sakes, Leah, you should know as well as I do how they are."

"Yes, Rachel, I believe I married one of them."

I kept forgetting that. "Well, shut my mouth wide open."

"As usual," Adah said.

For the entire trip I think the three of us were all on speaking terms for only one complete afternoon. We'd got as far as Benin without killing each other, and Adah wanted to see the famous villages on stilts. But, wouldn't you know, the road to that was washed out. Leah and I tried to explain to her how in Africa the roads are here today, gone tomorrow. You are constantly seeing signs such as, "If this sign is under water the road is impassable," and so forth. *That* much we could agree on.

So we ended up going to the ancient palace at Abomey, instead, which was the only tourist attraction for hundreds of miles around. We followed our map to Abomey, and luckily the road to it was still there. We parked in the center of town, which had big jacaranda trees and was very quaint. It was a cinch to find the ancient palace because it was surrounded by huge red mud walls and had a very grand entryway. Snoozing on a bench in the entrance we found an English-speaking guide who agreed to wake up and take us through on a tour. He explained how in former centuries, before the arrival of the French, the Abomey kings had enormous palaces and very nice clothes. They recorded their history in fabulous tapestries that hung on the palace walls, and had skillful knives and swords and such, which they used to conquer the neighboring tribes and enslave them. Oh, they just killed people right and left, he claimed, and then they'd put the skulls of their favorite enemies into their household decor. It's true! We saw every one of these things—the tapestries depicting violent acts and the swords and knives and even a throne with human skulls attached to the bottoms of all four legs, plated with bronze like keepsake baby shoes!

"Why, that's just what I need for my lobby in the Equatorial," I joked, although the idea of those things being the former actual heads of living people was a bit much for three o'clock in the afternoon.

This was no fairy-tale kingdom, let me tell you. They forced women into slave marriage with the King for the purpose of reproducing their babies at a high rate. One King would have, oh, fifty or a hundred wives, easy. More, if he was anything special. Or so the guide told us, maybe to impress us. To celebrate their occasions, he said, they'd just haul off and kill a bunch of their slaves, grind up all the blood and bones, and mix it up with mud for making more walls for their temples! And what's worse, whenever a King died, forty of his wives would have to be killed and buried with him!

I had to stop the guide right there and ask him, "Now, would they be his favorite wives they'd bury with him, or the meanest ones, or what?"

The guide said he thought probably it would have been the prettiest ones. Well, I can just imagine that! The King gets sick, all the wives would be letting their hair go and eating sweets day and night to wreck their figures.

Even though Leah and I had been crabbing at each other all week, that afternoon in the palace at Abomey for some reason we all got quiet as dead bats. Now, I have been around: the racial rioting in South Africa, hosting embassy parties in Brazzaville, shopping in Paris and Brussels, the game animals in Kenya, I have seen it all. But that palace was something else. It gave me the heebie-jeebies. We walked through the narrow passages, admiring the artworks and shivering to see chunks of bone sticking out of the walls. Whatever we'd been fighting about seemed to fade for the moment with those dead remains all around us. I shook from head to toe, even though the day was quite warm.

Leah and Adah happened to be walking in front of me, probably to get away from the guide, because they like to have their own explanations for everything, and as I looked at them I was shocked to see how alike they were. They'd both bought wild-colored wax-cloth shirts in the Senegal market, Adah to wear over her jeans and Leah to go with her long skirts (I personally see no need to go native, thanks very much, and will stick to my cotton knit), and Adah really doesn't limp a bit anymore, like Mother said. Plus she *talks*, which just goes to show you her childhood was not entirely on the up-and-up. She's exactly as tall as Leah now, too, which is simply unexplanatory. They hadn't seen each other for years, and here they even showed up wearing the same hairstyle! Shoulder-length, pulled back, which is not even a regular fashion.

Suddenly I realized they were talking about Father.

"No, I'm sure it's true," Leah said. "I believe it was him. I think he really is dead."

Well! This was news to me. I walked quickly to catch up, though I was still more or less of a third wheel. "You mean Father?" I asked. "Why didn't you say something, for heaven's sake."

"I guess I've been waiting for the right time, when we could talk," Leah said.

Well, what did she think we'd been doing for the last five days but *talk*. "No time like the present," I said.

She seemed to mill it over, and then stated it all as a matter of fact. "He's been up around Lusambo for the last five years, in one village and another. This past summer I ran into an agricultural agent who's been working up there, and he said he very definitely knew of Father. And that he's passed away."

"Gosh, I didn't even know he'd moved," I said. "I figured he was still hanging around our old village all this time."

"No, he's made his way up the Kasai River over the years, not making too many friends from what I hear. He hasn't been back to Kilanga, that much I know. We still have a lot of contact with Kilanga. Some of the people we knew are still there. An awful lot have died, too."

"What do you mean? Who did we know?" I honestly couldn't think of a soul. We left, Axelroot left. The Underdowns went all the way back to Belgium, and they weren't even really *there*.

"Why don't we talk about this later?" Leah said. "This place is already full of dead people."

Well, I couldn't argue with that. So we spent the rest of our paid-for tour in silence, walking through the ancient crumbling halls, trying not to look at the hunks of cream-colored bones in the walls.

"Those are pearls that were his eyes," Adah said at one point, which is just the kind of thing she would say.

"Full fathom five thy father lies," Leah said back to her.

What the heck that was about I just had to wonder. I sure didn't see any pearls. Those two were always connected in their own weird, special way. Even when they can't stand each other, they still always know what the other one's talking about when nobody else does. But I didn't let it bother me. I am certainly old enough to hold up my head and have my own personal adventures in life. I dreamed I toured the Ancient Palace of Abomey in my Maiden-form Bra!

Maybe once upon a time I was a little jealous of Leah and Adah, being twins. But no matter how much they might get to looking and sounding alike, as grown-ups, I could see they were still as different on the inside as night and day. And I am different too, not night or day either one but something else altogether, like the Fourth of July. So there we were: night, day, and the Fourth of July, and just for a moment there was a peace treaty.

But things fall apart, of course. With us they always do, sooner or later. We walked into the little town to get something cool to drink, and found a decent place where we could sit outside at a metal table watching the dogs and bicycles and hustle-bustle go by, every-body without exception carrying something on their heads. Except the dogs weren't, of course. We had a few beers and it was pleasant. Leah continued her news report about the all-important boon-docks village of our childhood fame, which in my opinion is better off to forget. I was waiting for the part about what Father died of. But it seemed impolite to push. So I took off my sunglasses and fanned myself with the map of West Africa.

Leah counted on her fingers: "Mama Mwanza is still going strong. Mama and Tata Nguza, both. Tata Boanda lost his elder wife but still has Eba. Tata Ndu's son is chief. Not the oldest one, Gbenye—they ran him out of the village."

"The one that stole your bushbuck," Adah said.

"Yep, the one. He turned out to be the type to constantly pick a fight, is what I gather. Lousy for a chief. So it's the second son, Kenge. I don't remember him very well. Tata Ndu died of fever from a wound."

"Too bad," I said sarcastically. "My would-be husband."

Adah said, "You could have done worse, Rachel."

"She *did* do worse," Leah declared. Which I do not appreciate, and said so.

She just ignored me. "Nelson is married, can you believe it? With two daughters and three sons. Mama Lo is dead; they claimed she was a hundred and two but I doubt it. Tata Kuvudundu is gone, dead, a long time now. He lost a lot of respect over the . . . what he did with us."

"The snake, you mean?" I asked.

She took a deep breath, looked up at the sky. "All of it."

We waited, but Leah just drummed her fingers on the table and acted like that was the end of that. Then added, "Pascal is dead, of course. That's been forever. He was killed by the blue-helmets on the road near Bulungu." She was looking away from us, but I could see she had tears in her eyes! Yet I had to rack my brains to remember these people.

"Oh, Pascal, your *son*?"

Adah informed me I was an imbecile.

"Pascal our childhood *friend*, who my son is named after. He died eighteen years ago, right before my Pascal was born, when we were in Bikoki. I never told you, Rachel, because I somehow had the impression you wouldn't care. It was when you were in Johannesburg."

"Pascal our friend?" I thought and thought. "Oh. That little boy with the holes in his pants you ran around with?"

Leah nodded, and kept on staring out at the big jacaranda trees that shaded the street. They dropped their huge purple flowers every so often, one at a time, like ladies dropping their hankies to get your attention. I lit another cigarette. I had expected two cartons of Lucky Strikes to last me the whole trip, but, boy, what with all the nervous tension those suckers were *gone*. I dreaded to think about it. Here on the street there were plenty of grimy little boys who'd sell you cigarettes one at a time with brand names like Black Hat and Mr. Bones, just to remind you they had no filter tips and tasted like burning tar and were going to kill you in a jiffy. African tobacco is not a pretty picture.

"So," I finally said, nudging Leah. "Dear old Dad. What's the scoop?"

She continued looking out at the street, where all kinds of people were going by. It was almost like she was *waiting* for somebody. Then she sighed, reached over and shook out one of my last precious cigarettes and lit up.

"This is going to make me sick," she said.

"What, smoking? Or telling about Father?"

She kind of laughed. "Both. And the beer, too. I'm not used to this." She took a puff, and then frowned at the Lucky Strike like it was something that might bite her. "You should hear how I get after the boys for doing this."

"Leah, tell!"

"Oh . . . it's kind of awful. He'd been up there for a while on the north bend of the Kasai, in the area where they grow coffee. He was still trying to baptize children, I know this for a fact. Fyntan and Celine Fowles get up that way every few years."

"Brother *Fowles*," I said. "You still keep in touch with him? Jeez Louise, Leah. Old home week. And he still knows Father?"

"They actually never got a look at him. I guess Father had reached a certain point. He hid from strangers. But they always heard plenty of stories about the white witch doctor named Tata Prize. They got the impression from talking to people that he was really old. I mean *old*, with a long white beard."

"*Father*? Now I can't picture that, a beard," I said. "How old would he be now, sixty?"

"Sixty-four," Adah said. Even though she talked now, it was like she was still handing over her little written announcements on notebook paper.

"He'd gotten a very widespread reputation for turning himself into a crocodile and attacking children."

"Now *that* I can picture," I said, laughing. The Africans are very superstitious. One of my workers swears the head cook can turn himself into a monkey and steal things from the guest rooms. I believe it!

"Still trying to drag the horse to water," Adah said.

"What horse?"

"So there was a really horrible incident on the river. A boat full of kids turned over by a croc, and all of them drowned or eaten or maimed. Father got the blame for it. Pretty much hung without a trial."

"Oh, *Jesus.*" I put my hand on my throat. "Actually *hung*?"

"No," Leah said, looking irritated but getting tears in her eyes at the same time. "Not hung. Burned."

I could see this was hard for Leah. I reached out and took hold of her hand. "Honey, I know," I told her. "He was our daddy. I think you always put up with him better than any of us. But he was mean as a snake. There's nothing he got that he didn't deserve."

She pulled her hand out of mine so she could wipe her eyes and blow her nose. "I know that!" She sounded mad. "The people in that village had asked him to leave a hundred times, go someplace else, but he'd always sneak back. He said he wasn't going to go away till he'd taken every child in the village down to the river and dunked them under. Which just scared everybody to death. So after the drowning incident they'd had enough, and everybody grabbed sticks and took out after him. They may have just meant to chase him away again. But I imagine Father was belligerent about it."

"Well, sure," I said. "He was probably still preaching hell and brimstone over his shoulder while he ran!" Which is true.

"They surrounded him in an old coffee field and he climbed up on one of those rickety watchtowers left over from the colonial days. Do you know what I'm talking about? They call them *tours de maître.* The boss towers, where in the old days the Belgian foreman would stand watching all the coffee pickers so he could single out which ones to whip at the end of the day."

"And they burned him?"

"They set the tower on fire. I'm sure it went up like a box of matches. It would have been twenty-year-old jungle wood, left over from the Belgians."

"I'll bet he preached the Gospel right to the very end," I said.

"They said he waited till he was on fire before he jumped off. Nobody wanted to touch him, so they just left him there for the animals to drag off."

I thought, Well, nobody around there's going to be drinking any coffee for a while! But it seemed like the wrong moment for a joke. I ordered another round of Elephant beers and we sat pondering our different thoughts.

Then Adah got a very strange look and said, "He got The Verse."

"Which one?" Leah asked.

"The *last* one. Old Testament. Second Maccabees 13:4: 'But the King of Kings aroused the anger of Antiochus against the rascal.'"

"I don't know it," Leah said.

Adah closed her eyes and thought for a second and then quoted the whole thing out: "'The King of Kings aroused the anger of Antiochus against the rascal. And when Lysias informed him this man was to blame for all the trouble, he ordered them to put him to death in the way that is customary there. For there is a tower there seventy-five feet high, filled with ashes, and there they push a man guilty of sacrilege or notorious for other crimes to destruction. By such a fate it came to pass that the transgressor died, not even getting burial in the ground.'"

"Holy shit!" I declared.

"How come you know that verse?" Leah asked.

"I must have gotten that one fifty times. It's the final 'The Verse' in the Old Testament, I'm trying to tell you. One-hundred-count from the end. If you include the Apocrypha, which of course he always did."

"And what's at the finish of it?" I asked. "The take-home lesson?"

"The closing statement of the Old Testament: 'So this will be the end.'"

"So this will be the end," Leah and I both repeated, in complete amazement. After that we were speechless for approximately one hour, while we listened to each other's throat sounds every time we took a swallow of beer. And Leah smoked the last two Lucky Strikes in West Africa.

Finally she asked, "Why would he give you that verse so many times? I *never* got that one." Which if you ask me is really not the point.

But Adah smiled, and answered like it mattered, "Why do you think, Leah? For being slow."

After a while I smelled wood smoke. Some vendors were setting up to grill meat along the side of the street. I got up and bought some for everyone with my own money, so I wouldn't have to hear Leah gripe that it was too expensive, or Adah telling us what exact germs were living on it. I got chicken on wooden skewers and brought it back to the table wrapped in wax paper.

"Eat up and be merry!" I said. "Cheers."

"In memory of the Father," Adah said. She and Leah looked at their shish kebabs, looked at each other, and had another one of their private little laughs.

"He was really his own man, you have to give him that," Leah said, while we munched. "He was a history book all to himself. We used to get regular reports from Tata Boanda and the Fowleses, when he was still around Kilanga. I probably could have gone to see him, but I never got up the nerve."

"Why not?" I asked her. "I would, just to tell him where to get off."

"I guess I was scared of seeing him as a crazy person. The tales got wilder and wilder as the years went by. That he'd had five wives, who all left him, for example."

"That's a good one," I said. "Father the Baptist Bigamist."

"The Pentecostal Pentigamist," Adah said.

"It was really the best way for him to go, you know? In a blaze of glory," Leah said. "I'm sure he believed right up to the end that he was doing the right thing. He never did give up the ship."

"It's shocking he lasted as long as he did," Adah said.

"Oh, true! That he didn't die fifteen years ago of typhus or sleeping sickness or malaria or the combination. I'm sure his hygiene went to hell after Mother left him."

Adah didn't say anything to that. Being the doctor, of course, she would know all about tropical diseases and wouldn't care for Leah sounding like the expert. That's how it always is with us. Step too far one way or the other and you've got on your sister's toes.

"For gosh sakes," I said suddenly. "Did you write to Mother? About Father?"

"No. I thought Adah might want to tell her in person."

Adah said carefully, "I think Mother has presumed him dead for a long time already."

We finished our shish kebabs and talked about Mother, and I even got to tell a little about the Equatorial, and I thought for once in our lives we were going to finish out the afternoon acting like a decent family. But then, sure enough, Leah started in about Mobutu putting her husband in prison, how the army terrorizes everybody, what was happening with the latest payola schemes in Zaire, which between you and me is the only reason I have any customers at all on my side of the river, but I didn't say so. Then she moved on to how the Portuguese and Belgians and Americans have wrecked poor Africa top to bottom.

"Leah, I am sick and tired of your sob story!" I practically shouted. I guess I'd had one too many, plus my cigarettes were gone, and it was hot. I'm so extremely fair the sun goes straight to my head. But really, after what we'd just seen in that palace: wife murdering and slave bones in the walls! These horrible things had nothing to do with us; it was all absolutely hundreds of years ago. The natives here were ready and waiting when the Portuguese showed up wanting to buy slaves, I pointed out. The King of Abomey was just delighted to find out he could trade fifteen of his former neighbors for one good Portuguese cannon.

But Leah always has an answer for everything, with vocabulary words in it, naturally. She said we couldn't possibly understand what their social milieu was, before the Portuguese came. "This is sparse country," she said. "It never could have supported a large population."

"So?" I examined my nails, which were frankly in bad shape.

"So what looks like mass murder to us is probably misinterpreted ritual. They probably had ways of keeping their numbers in balance in times of famine. Maybe they thought the slaves were going to a better place."

Adah chimed in: "A little ritual killing, a little infant mortality, just a few of the many healthy natural processes we don't care to think about." Her voice sounded surprisingly like Leah's. Although I presume Adah was joking, whereas Leah *never* jokes.

Leah frowned at Adah, then at me, trying to decide which one of us was the true enemy. She decided on me. "You just can't assume that what's right or wrong for us is the same as what was right or wrong for them," she said.

"Thou shalt not kill," I replied. "That's not just our way of thinking. It happens to be in the Bible."

Leah and Adah smiled at each other.

"Right. Here's to the Bible," Leah said, clinking her bottle against mine.

"Tata Jesus is *bängala!*" Adah said, raising her bottle too. She and Leah looked at each other for a second, then both started laughing like hyenas.

"Jesus is poisonwood!" Leah said. "Here's to the Minister of Poisonwood. And here's to his five wives!"

Adah stopped laughing. "That was *us*."

"Who?" I said. "What?"

"Nathan's five legendary wives. They must have meant *us*."

Leah stared at her. "You're right."

Like I said: night, day, and the Fourth of July. I don't even try to understand.

Adah Price

FULL FATHOM *five thy father lies;*
  Of his bones are coral made:
Those are pearls that were his eyes:
Nothing of him that doth fade,
But doth suffer a sea-change
Into something rich and strange.

This is no mortal business. The man occupied us all in life and is still holding on to his claim. Now we will have to carry away his sea-changed parts rich and strange to our different quarters. Estranged, disarranged, we spend our darkest hours staring at those pearls, those coral bones. Is this the stuff I came from? How many of his sins belong also to me? How much of his punishment?

Rachel seems incapable of remorse, but she is not. She wears those pale white eyes around her neck so she can look in every direction and ward off the attack. Leah took it all—bones, teeth, scalp—and knitted herself something like a hair shirt. Mother's fabrication is so elaborate I can hardly describe it. It occupies so much space in her house she must step carefully around it in the dark.

Having served enough time in Atlanta with her volunteer work, Mother has moved to the Georgia coast, to a hamlet of hoary little brick houses on Sanderling Island. But she carried the sunken treasure along to her little place by the shore. She stays outdoors a lot, I think to escape it. When I go to visit I always find her out in her walled garden with her hands sunk into the mulch, kneading the roots of her camellias. If she isn't home, I walk down to the end of the historic cobbled street and find her standing on the sea wall in her raincoat and no shoes, glaring at the ocean. Orleanna and Africa at a standoff. The kids flying by on bicycles steer clear of this barefoot old woman in her plastic babushka, but I can tell you she is not deranged. My mother's sanest position is to wear only the necessary parts of the outfit and leave off the rest. Shoes would interfere with her conversation, for she constantly addresses the ground under her feet. Asking forgiveness. Owning, disowning, recanting, recharting a hateful course of events to make sense of her complicity. We all are, I suppose. Trying to invent our version of the story. All human odes are essentially one. "My life: what I stole from history, and how I live with it."

Personally I have stolen an arm and a leg. I am still Adah but you would hardly know me now, without my slant. I walk without any noticeable limp. Oddly enough, it has taken me years to accept my new position. I find I no longer have *Ada*, the mystery of coming and going. Along with my split-body drag I lost my ability to read in the old way. When I open a book, the words sort themselves into narrow-minded single file on the page; the mirror-image poems erase themselves half-formed in my mind. I miss those poems. Sometimes at night, in secret, I still limp purposefully around my apartment, like Mr. Hyde, trying to recover my old ways of seeing and thinking. Like Jekyll I crave that particular darkness curled up within me. Sometimes it almost comes. The books on the shelf rise up in solid lines of singing color, the world drops out, and its hidden shapes snap forward to meet my eyes. But it never lasts. By morning light, the books are all hunched together again with their spines turned out, fossilized, inanimate.

No one else misses *Ada*. Not even Mother. She seems thoroughly pleased to see the crumpled bird she delivered finally straighten up and fly right.

"But I liked how I was," I tell her.

"Oh, Adah. I loved you too. I never thought *less* of you, but I wanted better for you."

Don't we have a cheerful, simple morality here in Western Civilization: expect perfection, and revile the missed mark! Adah the Poor Thing, hemiplegious egregious besiege us. Recently it has been decided, grudgingly, that dark skin or lameness may not be entirely one's *fault*, but one still ought to show the good manners to act ashamed. When Jesus cured those crippled beggars, didn't they always get up and dance off stage, jabbing their canes sideways and waggling their top hats? Hooray, all better now, hooray!

If you are whole, you will argue: Why wouldn't they rejoice? Don't the poor miserable buggers all want to be like me?

Not necessarily, no. The arrogance of the able-bodied is staggering. Yes, maybe we'd like to be able to get places quickly, and carry things in both hands, but only because we have to keep up with the rest of you, or get The Verse. We would rather be just like *us*, and have that be all right.

How can I explain that my two unmatched halves used to add up to more than one whole? In Congo I was one-half *benduka* the crooked walker, and one-half *bënduka,* the sleek bird that dipped in and out of the banks with a crazy ungrace that took your breath. We both had our good points. Here there is no good name for my gift, so it died without a proper ceremony. I am now the good Dr. Price, seeing straight. Conceding to be in my right mind.

And how can I invent my version of the story, without my crooked vision? How is it right to slip free of an old skin and walk away from the scene of the crime? We came, we saw, we took away and we left behind, we must be allowed our anguish and our regrets. Mother keeps wanting to wash herself clean, but she clings to her clay and her dust. Mother is still *ruthless*. She claims I am her youngest now but she still is clutching her baby. She will put down that burden, I believe, on the day she hears forgiveness from Ruth May herself.

★   ★   ★

As soon as I came back, I drove down to see her. We sat together on her bony couch with my photographs of Africa, picking through and laying them out, making a tidepool of shiny color among the seashells on her coffee table.

"Leah's thin," I reported, "but she still walks too fast."

"How is Rachel holding up?"

That is a good question. "In spite of remarkable intervening circumstances," I said, "if Rachel ever gets back to Bethlehem for a high school reunion she will win the prize for 'Changed the Least.'"

Mother handled the photos with mostly casual interest, except for the ones that showed my sisters. Over these she paused, for an extremely long time, as if she were listening to small, silent confessions.

Finally I made mine. I told her he had died. She was strangely uncurious about the details, but I gave her most of them anyway.

She sat looking puzzled. "I have some pansies I need to set out," she said then, and let the screen door bang as she walked out to the back porch. I followed, and found her in her old straw gardening hat, a trowel already in one hand and the flat of pansies balanced in the other. She ducked under the tangled honeysuckle toward the garden path, using her trowel like a machete to hack through some overgrown vines that crowded her jungly little porch. We marched purposefully down her little path to the lettuce bed by the gate, where she knelt in the leaf mold and began punching holes in the ground. I squatted nearby, watching. Her hat had a wide straw brim and a crown completely blown out, as if whatever was in her head had exploded many times.

"Leah says he would have wanted to go that way," I said. "A blaze of glory."

"I don't give a damn what he would have wanted."

"Oh," I said. The damp ground soaked the knees of her jeans in large dark patches that spread like bloodstains as she worked.

"Are you sorry he's dead?"

"Adah, what can it possibly mean to me now?"

Then what are you sorry about?

She lifted seedlings out of the flat, untangling their nets of tender white roots. Her bare hands worked them into the ground, prodding and gentling, as if putting to bed an endless supply of small children. She wiped the tears off both sides of her face with the back of her left hand, leaving dark lines of soil along her cheekbones. *To live is to be marked*, she said without speaking. *To live is to change, to die one hundred deaths. I am a mother. You aren't, he wasn't.*

"Do you want to forget?"

She paused her work, resting her trowel on her knee, and looked at me. "Are we *allowed* to remember?"

"Who's to say we can't?"

"Not one woman in Bethlehem ever asked me how Ruth May died. Did you know that?"

"I guess."

"And all those people I worked with in Atlanta, on civil rights and African relief. We never once spoke of my having a crazy evangelist husband still in the Congo somewhere. People knew. But it was embarrassing to them. I guess they thought it was some awful reflection on me."

"The sins of the father," I said.

"The sins of the father are not discussed. That's how it is." She returned to her business of stabbing the earth.

I know she is right. Even the Congo has tried to slip out of her old flesh, to pretend it isn't scarred. *Congo* was a woman in shadows, dark-hearted, moving to a drumbeat. Zaire is a tall young man tossing salt over his shoulder. All the old injuries have been renamed: *Kinshasa, Kisangani.* There was never a King Léopold, no brash Stanley, bury them, forget. You have nothing to lose but your chains.

But I don't happen to agree. If chained is where you have been, your arms will always bear marks of the shackles. What you have to lose is your story, your own slant. You'll look at the scars on your arms and see mere ugliness, or you'll take great care to look away from them and see nothing. Either way, you have no words for the story of where you came from.

"I'll discuss it," I said. "I despised him. He was a despicable man."

"Well, Adah. You could always call a spade a spade."

"Do you know when I hated him the most? When he used to make fun of my books. My writing and reading. And when he hit any of us. You especially. I imagined getting the kerosene and burning him up in his bed. I only didn't because you were in it too."

She looked up at me from under her hat brim. Her eyes were a wide, hard, granite blue.

"It's true," I said. I pictured it clearly. I could smell the cold kerosene and feel it soaking the sheets. I still can.

Then why didn't you? Both of us together. You might as well have.

Because then you would be free too. And I didn't want that. I wanted you to remember what he did to us.

Tall and straight I may appear, but I will always be Ada inside. A crooked little person trying to tell the truth. The power is in the balance: we are our injuries, as much as we are our successes.

Leah Price Ngemba

KIMVULA DISTRICT, ZAIRE
1986

I HAVE FOUR SONS, all named for men we lost to war: Pascal, Patrice, Martin-Lothaire, and Nataniel.

'Taniel is our miracle. He was born last year, a month early, after his long, bumpy upside-down ride in the Land Rover that moved our family from Kinshasa to the farm in Kimvula District. We were still ten kilometers from the village when my chronic backache spread to a deep, rock-hard contraction across my lower belly, and I understood with horror that I was in labor. I got out and walked very slowly behind the truck, to subdue my panic. Anatole must have been worried sick by my bizarre conduct, but it's no use arguing with a woman in labor, so he got out and walked with me while the boys bickered over who would drive the truck. I can vaguely recall its twin red taillights ahead of us on the dark jungle road, bumping along tediously, and the false starts of an afternoon thundershower. After a while, without saying anything, I went to the side of the road and lay down on a pile of damp leaves between the tall, buttressed roots of a kapok tree. Anatole knelt next to my head and stroked my hair.

"You should get up. It's dark and damp here, and our clever sons have gone off and left us."

I raised my head and looked for the truck, which was indeed

gone. There was something I needed to explain to Anatole, but I couldn't be bothered with it at the peak of a contraction. Straight overhead was the tree, with its circle of limbs radiating out from the great, pale trunk. I counted my way around that circle of branches like numbers on the face of a clock, slowly, one deep breath for each number. Seventeen. A very long minute, maybe an hour. The contraction subsided.

"Anatole," I said. "I mean to have this baby right here and now."

"Oh, Béene. You have never had any patience at all."

The boys drove on for some time before stopping and backing up, by the grace of God and Martin-Lothaire. He'd lost the argument about driving and was pouting out the back window when it dawned on him to shout for his brother to stop: "Wait, wait, Mama must be having the baby!"

Anatole threw things around madly in the truck before finding an elephant-grass mat and some shirts (at least we had with us everything we owned, and it was clean). He made me sit up so he could tuck these things under me. I don't remember it. I only remember my thighs tensing and my pelvis arching forward with that sudden thunderous urge that is so much more powerful than any other human craving—the need to push. I heard a roar, which I suppose was me, and then Nataniel was here with us, bloodying a clean white shirt of Anatole's and an old, soft *pagne* printed with yellow birds.

Anatole did a laughing, backward-hopping dance of congratulation. It wasn't yet quite a year since his release from Camp Hardy, and he was sympathetic to his son's eager escape from solitary confinement. But the baby was weak. Anatole immediately settled down to driving us anxiously through the dark while I curled around our suckling boy in the backseat, alarmed to see he wasn't even that—he couldn't nurse. By the time we arrived in Kimvula he felt feverish. From there he wasted very quickly to a lethargic little bundle of skin-covered bones and a gaunt, skin-covered skull. He didn't even cry. The next many days and nights ran together for me because I was terrified to put him down at all, or even to fall asleep holding him, for fear he'd slip away. Anatole and I took turns rocking his limp little body, talking to him, trying to coax him into the world of the living. Martin insisted on taking his turn, too, rocking and whispering boy secrets into the little printed blanket. But Nataniel was hard to convince. Twice he stopped breathing altogether. Anatole blew into his mouth and massaged his chest until he gasped faintly and came back.

After a week he began to eat, and now seems to have no regrets about his decision to stay with us. But during that terrible first week of his life I was racked with the miseries of a weak, sore body and a lost soul. I could recollect having promised some God or other, more than once, that if I could only have Anatole back I would never ask for another thing on this earth. Now here I was, banging on heaven's door again. A desolate banging, from a girl who could count the years since she felt any real presence on the other side of that door.

One night as I sat on the floor rocking, sleepless, deranged by exhaustion, cradling this innocent wreck of a baby, I just started to talk out loud. I talked to the fire: "Fire, fire, fire, please keep him warm, eat all the wood you need and I'll get more but just don't go out, keep this little body I already love so much from going cold!" I spoke in English, fairly certain I'd gone mad entirely. I spoke to the moon outside and the trees, to the sleeping bodies of Anatole and Patrice and Martin, and finally to the kettle of boiled, sterile water and tiny dropper I was using to keep the baby from dehydrating. Suddenly I had a fully formed memory of my mother kneeling and talking—praying, I believe—to a bottle of antibiotics when Ruth May was so sick. I could actually hear Mother's breath and her words. I could picture her face very clearly, and feel her arms around me. Mother and I prayed together to whatever it is that we have. This was enough.

If God is someone who thinks of me at all, he must think of me as a mother. Scraping fiercely for food and shelter, mad entirely for love, by definition. My boys all cry, "*Sala mbote!*" as they run out the door, away from my shelter and advice but never escaping my love.

Pascal has gone farthest—for two years he's been in Luanda, where he studies petroleum engineering and, I sincerely believe, chases girls. He reminds me so much of his namesake, my old friend, with similar wide-set eyes and the same cheerful question breaking like a fresh egg upon every new day: "*Beto nki tutasala?* What are we doing?"

Patrice is just the opposite: studious, sober, and an exact physical copy of his father. He wants to study government and be a Minister of Justice in a very different Africa from this one. I go weak in the knees with dread and admiration, watching him sharpen his hopes. But it's Martin-Lothaire who's turning out to be the darkest of my sons, in complexion and temperament. At twelve, he broods, and writes poetry in a journal like his father's hero Agostinho Neto. He reminds me of his Aunt Adah.

Here in Kimvula District we're working with farmers on a soybean project, trying to establish a cooperative—a tiny outpost of reasonable sustenance in the belly of Mobutu's beast. It's futile, probably. If the government catches wind of any success here, the Minister of Agriculture will rob us out of existence. So we quietly plant our hopes out here in the jungle, just a few kilometers from the Angolan border, at the end of an awful road where Mobutu's spies won't often risk their fancy cars.

We count our small successes from day to day. Anatole has reorganized the secondary school, which had been in pure collapse for ten years—hardly a young adult in Kimvula village can read. I'm busy with my ravenous Taniel, who nurses night and day, riding in his sling on one side or the other so he won't have to pause while I boil his diapers. Patrice and Martin have been commandeered by their father to teach French and mathematics respectively, even though this puts Martin in charge of children older than himself. Myself, I'm just happy to be living among fruit trees and cooking with wood again. I don't mind the satisfying exhaustions of carrying wood and water. It's the other exhaustion I hate, the endless news of Mobutu's excesses and the costs of long-term deprivation. People here are instinctively more fearful and less generous than they were twenty years ago in Kilanga. Neighbor women do still come calling to offer little gifts, a hand of bananas or an orange for the baby to suck on and make us laugh at his puckery face. But their eyes narrow as they look around the room. Never having known a white person before, they assume I must know Mobutu and all important Americans personally. In spite of my protests, I think they worry I'll report to someone that they had an orange to spare. There's nothing like living as a refugee in one's own country to turn a generous soul into a hard little fist. Zaireans are tired to death, you can see it anywhere you look.

Our house here is mud and thatch, plenty large, with two rooms and a kitchen shed. A happier place, for sure, than the tin-and-cement box that packaged us up with all our griefs in Kinshasa. There, the cranky indoor plumbing constantly grumbled at us like God to Noah, threatening the deluge, and Anatole swore if he lived through ten thousand mornings in Kinshasa he would never get used to defecating in the center of his home. Honestly, a latrine does seem like a return to civilization.

But our life in this village feels provisional. We have one foot over the border into the promised land, or possibly the grave. Our plan is to pack up our truck again and drive from here to Sanza Pombo, Angola, as soon as we possibly can. There we'll keep our hands busy in a new, independent nation, whose hopes coincide with our own. We've been leaning toward Angola for ten years now—Anatole had a chance to serve in the new government there in 1975, right after the treaty that gave Neto the presidency. But Anatole wasn't yet ready to abandon the Congo. And then Neto died, too young. In 1982 another invitation came from the second President, José dos Santos. Anatole was prevented from accepting that post by the inconvenience of living in a two-meter-square room with a bucket of his excrement for company in the Thysville penitentiary.

I don't believe Anatole has many regrets, but he would have been proud to work with Neto or dos Santos. Thanks to those remarkable men, plus others uncounted who died on the way, Angola has wrested itself free of Portugal and still owns its diamonds and oil wells. The industry of Angolans doesn't subsidize foreigners, or any castles with moats, and their children are likely to get vaccinations and learn to read. They're still desperately poor, of course. They kept their diamonds and oil at a horrific cost. None of us predicted what came to pass there. Least of all Neto, the young doctor-poet who just meant to spare his people from the scarring diseases of smallpox and humiliation. He went to the U.S. looking for help and was shown the door. So he came home to try to knock down Portuguese rule on his own and create a people's Angola. *Then* he got some attention from the Americans. For now he was a Communist devil.

Ten years ago, when Anatole received that first letter stamped with the new, official seal of the Presidency of Independent Angola, it looked like dreams could come true. After six hundred years of their own strife and a few centuries of Portuguese villainy, the warring tribes of Angola had finally agreed to a peace plan. Agostinho Neto was President, in an African nation truly free of foreign rule. We so nearly packed up and went, that very day. We were desperate to move our sons to a place where they could taste hope, at least, if not food.

But within two weeks of the peace agreement, the United States violated it. They airlifted a huge shipment of guns to an opposition leader, who vowed personally to murder Neto. On the day we heard this I sat sobbing in our kitchen, flattened with shame and rage. Patrice came and sat on the floor by my chair, patting my leg with a little boy's solemn endurance. *"Mama, Mama, ne pleure pas. Ce n'est pas de la faute de Grand-mère, Mama."* It didn't even occur to him to connect *me* with American disgrace; he thought I was angry at Mother and Adah. He looked up at me with his narrow little face and almond eyes and there was his father years and years and *years* ago saying, "Not you, Béene."

But who, if not me, and for how many generations must we be forgiven by our children? Murdering Lumumba, keeping Mobutu in power, starting it all over again in Angola—these sound like plots between men but they are betrayals, by men, of children. It's thirty million dollars, Anatole told me recently, that the U.S. has now spent trying to bring down Angola's sovereignty. Every dollar of it had to come from some *person*, a man or woman. How does this happen? They think of it as commerce, I suppose. A matter of hardware, the plastic explosives and land mines one needs to do the job. Or it's a commerce of imagined dreads, the Bethlehem housewives somehow convinced that a distant, black Communist devil will cost them some quarter in their color-matched living rooms.

But what could it possibly have mattered to them that, after the broken treaty and Neto's desperate plea for help, the Cubans were the only ones to answer it? We cheered, the boys and Anatole and our neighbors all jumping and screaming in our yard, when the radio said the planes had come into Luanda. There were teachers and nurses on board, with boxes of smallpox vaccine. We imagined them liberating Angola and marching right on up the Congo River to vaccinate us all!

Rachel informs me I've had my brains washed by a Communist plot. She's exactly right. I've been won to the side of schoolteachers and nurses, and lost all allegiance to plastic explosives. No homeland I can claim as mine would blow up a struggling, distant country's hydroelectric dams and water pipes, inventing darkness and dysentery in the service of its ideals, and bury mines in every Angolan road that connected food with a hungry child. We've watched this war with our hearts in our throats, knowing what there is to lose. Another Congo. Another wasted chance running like poisoned water under Africa, curling our souls into fists.

But with nothing else to hope for, we lean toward Angola, waiting, while the past grows heavy and our future narrows down to a crack in the door. We're poised on the border with everything we might need for an eventual destiny assembled around us. We have cots, the table and chairs we acquired in Kinshasa, a collection of agriculture books and teaching tools from Bikoki, my ancient suitcase of family treasures salvaged from Kilanga. Anatole has even kept the globe I gave him for a wedding present, painted by my own hand on a calabash while the nuns prayed their novenas. Their weird library had St. Exupéry but nothing so secular as an atlas of the world, so I had to work from memory. Later my sons set upon it like apprentice palm readers, trying to divine the fate of their world from the lengths and curves of its rivers. Miraculously it survives the humidity and our moves, with only a few unwarranted archipelagos of gray mold dotting its oceans. Anatole cherishes it, and the astonishing fact that I was the first to tell him the shape of our world. But when I see it on his table I'm taken aback by what I overlooked at age eighteen: the Caspian Sea, for example. The Urals, Balkans, Pyrénées—whole mountain ranges vanished under my negligence. But the Congo is exactly the right shape and size, in relation to Europe and the Americas. Already I was determined, I guess, to give Africa a fair shake.

We are all still the children we were, with plans we keep secret, even from ourselves. Anatole's, I think, is to outlive Mobutu and come back here when we can stand on this soil and say "home" without the taste of gold-leaf chandeliers and starvation burning bitter on the backs of our tongues. And mine, I think, is to leave my house one day unmarked by whiteness and walk on a compassionate earth with Ruth May beside me, bearing me no grudge. Maybe I'll never get over my grappling for balance, never stop believing life is going to be *fair*, the minute we can clear up all these mistakes of the temporarily misguided. Like the malaria I've never shaken off, it's in my blood. I anticipate rewards for goodness, and wait for the ax of punishment to fall upon evil, in spite of the years I've rocked in this cradle of rewarded evils and murdered goodness. Just when I start to feel jaded to life as it is, I'll suddenly wake up in a fever, look out at the world, and gasp at how much has gone wrong that I need to fix. I suppose I loved my father too much to escape being molded to at least some part of his vision.

But the practice of speaking a rich, tonal language to my neighbors has softened his voice in my ear. I hear the undertones now that shimmer under the surface of the words *right* and *wrong*. We used to be baffled by Kikongo words with so many different meanings: *bängala*, for *most precious* and *most insufferable* and also *poison-*

wood. That one word brought down Father's sermons every time, as he ended them all with the shout "Tata Jesus is *bängala!*"

Way back then, while Rachel could pull words out of thin air to mean what she pleased, and Ruth May was inventing her own, Adah and I were trying to puzzle out how everything you thought you knew means something different in Africa. We worried over *nzolo*—it means *dearly beloved*; or a white grub used for fish bait; or a special fetish against dysentery; or little potatoes. *Nzole* is the double-sized *pagne* that wraps around two people at once. Finally I see how these things are related. In a marriage ceremony, husband and wife stand tightly bound by their *nzole* and hold one another to be the most precious: *nzolani*. As precious as the first potatoes of the season, small and sweet like Georgia peanuts. Precious as the fattest grubs turned up from the soil, which catch the largest fish. And the fetish most treasured by mothers, against dysentery, contains a particle of all the things invoked by the word *nzolo*: you must dig and dry the grub and potatoes, bind them with a thread from your wedding cloth, and have them blessed in a fire by the *nganga* doctor. Only by life's best things are your children protected—this much I surely believe. Each of my peanut-brown babies I called my *nzolani*, and said it with the taste of fish and fire and new potatoes in my mouth. There is no other possibility now.

"Everything you're sure is right can be wrong in another place. Especially *here*." I say this frequently, while I'm boiling diapers in the kitchen house and having my imaginary arguments with an absent Rachel. (Which are not so different from arguments with Rachel in person.) She reminds me once again of the Communist threat. I walk outside to dump the water and wave at my neighbor, who's boiling peanuts in a hubcap. Both of us cower at the sound of tires. It might be the black Mercedes of the *casque-bleus*, Mobutu's deputies come to take our measly harvest to help finance another palace. And then it comes to me suddenly, from childhood, my first stammering definition of communism to Anatole: They do not fear the Lord, and they think everybody should have the same kind of house.

From where I'm standing, sister, it's hard to fathom the threat.

I live in a tiny house piled high with boys, potatoes, fetishes and books of science, a wedding cloth, a disintegrating map of the world, an ancient leather suitcase of memories—a growing accumulation of *past* crowding out our ever-narrowing future. And our waiting is almost over. It's taken ten years and seems like a miracle, but the Americans are losing in Angola. Their land mines are still all over the country, they take off the leg or the arm of a child every day, and I know what could happen to us if we travel those roads. But in my dreams I still have hope, and in life, no safe retreat. If I have to hop all the way on one foot, damn it, I'll find a place I can claim as home.

Book Six

SONG OF THE
THREE CHILDREN

*All that you have brought upon us
and all that you have done to us,
You have done in justice . . .
Deliver us in your wonderful way.*

SONG OF THE THREE CHILDREN, 7–19
THE APOCRYPHA

Rachel Price

THE EQUATORIAL

I AM FOREVER GETTING COMPLIMENTS on my spotless complexion, but let me tell you a little secret. It takes more work than anything in this world to keep yourself well preserved.

Jeez oh man, nothing like turning fifty to make you feel a hundred years old. Not that I was about to put candles on a cake and burn the place down. I got through that day without telling a soul. Now I've closed the bar and here I sit with my Lucky Strike and my sandal hanging off my toe and I can always look back on it as just one more day like any other. But it sure gives you something to compensate upon.

Did I ever think I would wind up here getting old? Not on your life. But here I am. I've walked off more marriages and close calls than you can shake a stick at, but never got out of the Dark Continent. I have settled down here and gotten to be such a stick-in-the-mud I don't even like to go out! Last week I was forced to drive down to Brazzaville for the liquor order because I honestly could not find a driver trustworthy to come back with the liquor and car in one piece, but there was a flood on the way and two trees across the road, and when I finally got back here I kissed the floor of the bar. I did, I swear. Mostly I kissed it for still being there, since I still expect every plank of this place to be carried off by my own help during my absence. But so far, so good.

At least I can say that I'm a person who can look around and see what she's accomplished in this world. Not to boast, but I have created my own domain. I call the shots. There may be a few little faults in the plumbing and minor discrepancies among the staff, but I'm very confident of my service. I have a little sign in every room telling guests they are expected to complain at the office between the hours of nine and eleven A.M. daily. And do I hear a peep? No. I run a tight ship. That is one thing I have to be proud of. And number two, I'm making a killing. Three, there's no time to get lonely. Like I said, same old face in the mirror, fifty years old and she doesn't look a day over ninety. Ha, ha.

Do I ever think about the life I missed in the good old U.S.A.?

Practically every day, would be my answer. Oh, goodness, the parties, the cars, the music—the whole carefree American way of life. I've missed being a part of something you could really believe in. When we finally got TV here, for a long while they ran Dick Clark and the *American Bandstand* every afternoon at four o'clock. I'd lock up the bar, make myself a double Singapore Sling, settle down with a paper fan and practically swoon with grief. I *know* how to do those hairstyles. I really could have been something in America.

Then why not go back? Well, now it's too late, of course. I have responsibilities. First there was one husband and then another to tie me down, and then the Equatorial, which isn't just a hotel, it's like running a whole little *country*, where everybody wants to run off with a piece for themselves the minute you turn your back. The very idea of my things being scattered over hill and down dale through the jungle, my expensive French pressure cooker all charred to tarnation boiling manioc over some stinky fire, and my nice chrome countertops ending up as the roof of somebody's shack? No thank you! I can't bear the thought. You make something, seems like, and spend the rest of your days toiling so it won't go all unraveled. One thing leads to another, then you're mired in.

Years ago, when things first started going sour with Axelroot, *that* was probably when I should have gone home. I didn't have anything invested in Africa yet but a little old apartment boudoir decorated to the best of my abilities in blush pink. Right then I could have tried to talk him into moving back to Texas, where he supposedly had some kind of ties, according to his passport, which turned out to be almost entirely false. Better yet, I could have gone by myself. Hell's bells! I could have sashayed out the door without so much as a howdy-do, since technically speaking we were only married in the Biblical sense. Even back then I knew some gentlemen in high places that could have helped me scrounge up the plane fare, and then before you could say Jack Robinson Crusoe I'd have been back in Bethlehem, sharing a shack with Mother and Adah with my tail between my legs. Oh, sure, I'd have to hear them say I told you so about Axelroot. But I have swallowed my pride before, that's for sure. I've done it so many times I am practically lined with my mistakes on the inside like a bad-wallpapered bathroom.

I had my bags packed more than once. But when push came to shove I was always afraid. Of what? Well, it's hard to explain. Scared I wouldn't be able to fit back in is the long and short of it. I was only nineteen or twenty at that time. My high school friends would still have been whining over boyfriends and fighting for carhop jobs at the A&W. Their idea of a dog-eat-dog world was Beauty School. And now here comes Rachel with stained hair and one dead sister and a whole darn marriage behind her already, not to mention hell and high water. Not to mention the Congo. My long tramp through the mud left me tuckered out and just too worldly-wise to go along with the teen scene.

"What was it like over there?" I could just hear them asking. What would I say? "Well, the ants nearly ate us alive. Everybody we knew kept turning up dead of one disease and another. The babies all got diarrhea and plumb dried up. When we got hungry we'd go shoot animals and strip off their hides."

Let's face it, I could never have been popular again at home. The people I'd always chummed around with would stop speaking to you if they so much as suspected you'd ever gone poo behind a bush. If I wanted to fit in I'd have to pretend, and I'm no good at play-acting. Leah could always do that—she'd take the high road to please Father, or her teachers, or God, or maybe just to prove she could do it. And Adah of course play-acted at not talking for years and years, merely to be ornery. But if it was me, I'd never remember who I was trying to be. Before the day was out I'd forget, and blurt out my own true feelings.

This is off the subject but do you know who I always really felt for? Those soldier boys that went back to the States after Vietnam. I read about that. Everybody was crying, "Peace, brother!" And here they'd been in the jungle watching fungus eat up the dead bodies. I know just how they felt.

Personally, I didn't need that. I'm the type of person where you just never look back. And I have become a success in my own right. I've had opportunities as a woman of the world. An ambassador's wife—imagine that! Those girls back in Bethlehem must be getting old and gray, still loading their Maytags and running after their kids or even grandkids by now and still wishing they were Brigitte Bardot, whereas I have actually been in the Foreign Service.

I never was able to have children. That is one thing I do regret. I have had very bad female problems on account of an infection I contracted from Eeben Axelroot. Like I said, I paid my price with *him*.

There is never a dull moment here at the Equatorial, though. Who needs children when you have monkeys rushing into the dining room to steal the very food off your guests' plates! This has happened on more than one occasion. Among the variety of animals I keep in cages in the garden I have four monkeys and a bat-eared fox that will escape on the slightest pretense from the boy who cleans out the cages. Into the restaurant they'll run screaming, the poor fox running for his life but the monkeys all too easily diverted by the sight of some fresh fruit. They'll even pause to grab a bottle of beer and drink it down! One time I returned from a trip to the market to find my two vervet monkeys, Princess Grace and General Mills, teetering drunk on a table while a group of German coffee-plantation owners sang "Roll Out the Barrel!" Well, I'll tell you. I tolerate just about any kind of good times my guests wish to have, since that's how we keep our heads above the water in this business. But I made those German gentlemen pay for the damage.

Every so often a group of fellows will stop by in the afternoon on a sightseeing tour, and receive a mistaken impression of my establishment. This only happens with newcomers who are unfamiliar with the Equatorial. They take one look at me stretched out by the pool with all the keys on a chain around my neck, and one look at my pretty young cooks and chambermaids on their afternoon break, lounging against the patio wall between the geraniums. And guess what: they'll take me for the madam of a whorehouse! Believe you me, I give them a piece of my mind. If this looks like a house of prostitution to you, I tell them, that just shows the quality of your own moral fiber.

I have to admit, though, it's funny in a certain way. I am no longer as young as I might have been, but if I do say so, I have never let myself go. I guess I should be flattered if some fellow peeks around the garden wall and thinks he spies Jezebel. Oh, if Father could see me now, wouldn't he give me The Verse!

I'm afraid all those childhood lessons in holiness slid off me like hot butter off the griddle. I sometimes wonder if dear old Dad is turning in his grave (or whatever he's in). I'm sure he expected me to grow up as a nice church lady with cute little hats, organizing good deeds. But sometimes life doesn't give you all that many chances at being good. Not here, anyway. Even Father learned that one the hard way. He came on strong, thinking he'd save the children, and what does he do but lose his own? That's the lesson, right there. If you take a bunch of practically grown, red-blooded daughters to Africa, don't you think at least some of them are going to marry or what have you, and end up staying? You can't just sashay into the jungle aiming to change it all over to the Christian style, without expecting the jungle to change you right back. Oh, I see it time and again with the gentlemen who come through here on business. Some fellow thinks he's going to be the master of Africa and winds up with his nice European-tailored suit rumpled in a corner and his wits half cracked from the *filaires* itching under his skin. If it was as easy as they thought it was going to be, why, they'd be done by now, and Africa would look just like America with more palm trees. Instead, most of it still looks exactly how it did a zillion years ago. Whereas, if you think about it, the Africans are running all over America right now, having riots for their civil rights and predominating the sports and popular-music industries.

From the very first moment I set foot in the Congo, I could see we were not in charge. We got swept up with those people that took us to the church for all their half-naked dancing and goat meat with the hair still on, and I said to myself: this little trip is going to be the ruin of the Price family as we know it. And, boy, was it ever. Father's mistake, see, was to try to convert the whole entire shebang over into just his exact way of thinking. He always said, "Girls, you choose your path and stick to it and suffer your consequences!" Well. If he's finally dead now and laid to rest in some African voodoo cemetery, or worse yet eaten up by the wild animals, well, amen. I guess that is about as consequential as it gets.

The way I see Africa, you don't have to like it but you sure have to admit it's out there. You have your way of thinking and it has its, and never the train ye shall meet! You just don't let it influence your mind. If there's ugly things going on out there, well, you put a good stout lock on your door and check it twice before you go to sleep. You focus on getting your own one little place set up perfect, as I have done, and you'll see. Other people's worries do not necessarily have to drag you down.

I amaze myself sometimes at what I have personally been through and still remain in one piece. Sometimes I really do think I owe the secret of my success to that little book I read long ago called *How to Survive 101 Calamities*. Simple remedies for dire situations, that's the lesson. In a falling elevator, try to climb up on the person nearby so their body will cushion your landing. Or in a crowded theater when everybody's hightailing it for the fire exit, stick your elbows hard into the ribs of your neighbors to wedge yourself in, then pick up your feet so you won't get trampled. That is how people frequently lose their lives in a riot: somebody steps on your heel, then walks right up till you're flat and they're standing on you. That's what you get for trying to stand on your own two feet—you end up getting crushed!

So that's my advice. Let others do the pushing and shoving, and you just ride along. In the end, the neck you save will be your own. Perhaps I sound un-Christian, but let's face it, when I step outside my own little world at night and listen to the sounds out there in the dark, what I feel down in my bones is that this is not a Christian kind of place. This is darkest Africa, where life roars by you like a flood and you grab whatever looks like it will hold you up.

If you ask me, that's how it is and ever shall be. You stick out your elbows, and hold yourself up.

Leah Price

Sanza Pombo, Angola

"ONCE UPON A TIME," Anatole says in the dark, and I close my eyes and fly away on his stories. It's almost a shock to be alone together in our bed, practically elderly, after almost thirty years of little elbows and heels and hungry mouths. When Taniel turned ten he abandoned us for a cot of his own, full of rocks that fall out of his pockets. Most boys his age still sleep on the pile of their families, but Taniel was adamant: "My brothers have beds to themselves!" (He doesn't realize they've moved on from solitude—even Martin now at college has a girlfriend.) With his curly head cocked forward bent on keeping up and trying to eat the world in one bite, he takes my breath away. He's so much like Ruth May.

And in our bed, which Anatole calls the New Republic of Connubia, my husband tells me the history of the world. Usually we start with five hundred years ago, when the Portuguese came poking the nose of their little wooden ship into the mouth of the Congo River. Anatole peers from side to side, pantomiming Portuguese astonishment.

"What did they see?" I always ask, though I already know. They saw Africans. Men and women black as night, strolling in bright sunlight along the riverbanks. But not naked—just the opposite! They wore hats, soft boots, and more layers of exotic skirts and tunics than would seem bearable in the climate. This is the truth. I've seen the drawings published by those first adventurers after they hurried back home to Europe. They reported that the Africans lived like kings, even wearing the fabrics of royalty: velvet, damask, and brocade. Their report was only off by a hair; the Kongo people made remarkable textiles by beating the fibrous bark of certain trees, or weaving thread from the raffia palm. From mahogany and ebony they made sculpture and furnished their homes. They smelted and forged iron ore into weapons, plowshares, flutes, and delicate jewelry. The Portuguese marveled at how efficiently the Kingdom of Kongo collected taxes and assembled its court and ministries. There was no written language, but an oral tradition so ardent that when the Catholic fathers fixed letters to the words of Kikongo, its poetry and stories poured into print with the force of a flood. The priests were dismayed to learn the Kongo already had their own Bible. They'd known it by heart for hundreds of years.

Impressed as they were with the Kingdom of Kongo, the Europeans were dismayed to find no commodity agriculture here. All food was consumed very near to where it was grown. And so no cities, no giant plantations, and no roads necessary for transporting produce from the one to the other. The kingdom was held together by thousands of miles of footpaths crossing the forest, with suspension bridges of woven vines swinging quietly over the rivers. I picture it as Anatole describes it: men and women in tiers of velvet skirts, walking noiselessly on a forest path. Sometimes, when I have relapses of my old demon, I lie in the crook of his arm and he comforts me this way, talking to me all night long to stave off the bad dreams. Quinine just barely keeps my malaria in check, and there are resistant strains here now. The fever dreams are always the same, the first warning that I'll soon be knocked on my back. The old blue hopelessness invades my sleep and I'm crossing the river, looking back at the faces of children begging for food, "*Cadeaux! Cadeaux!*" But then I wake up in our nation of two, enclosed in our mosquito tent's slanted planes lit silver by moonlight, and always think of Bulungu, where we first lay together like this. Anatole cradling me into forgiveness, while I rattled and shook with fever. Our marriage has been, for me, a very long convalescence.

Now they are walking home, Béene. With baskets of palm nuts and orchids from the forest. They're singing.

Songs about what?

Oh, everything. The colors of a fish. And how well behaved their children would be if they were all made of wax.

I laugh. *Who are they? How many?*

Just a woman and a man on the path. They are married.

And their troublesome children aren't with them?

Not yet. They have only been married one week.

Oh, I see. So they're holding hands.

Of course.

What does it look like there?

They are close to the river, in a forest that has never been cut down. These trees are a thousand years old. Lizards and little monkeys live their whole lives up above without coming down to the ground. Up in the roof of the world.

But down on the path where we are, it's dark?

A nice darkness. The kind your eyes can grow to like. It's raining, but the branches are so thick that only a little mist comes down. New mbika vines are curling up from the ground behind us, where the water pools in our foot-steps.

What happens when we come to the river?

We'll cross it, of course.

I laugh. *As easy as that! And what if the ferry is stuck without a battery on the other side?*

In the Kingdom of Kongo, Béene, no batteries. No trucks, no roads. They declined to invent the wheel because it looked like nothing but trouble in this mud. For crossing the river they have bridges that stretch from one great greenheart tree to another on the opposite bank.

I can see this couple. I know they're real, that they really lived. They climb up to a platform in the greenheart where the woman pauses for balance, bunches her long skirts into one hand, and prepares to walk out into the brighter light and rain. She touches her hair, which is braided in thick ropes and tied at the back of her neck with little bells. When she's ready she steps out over the water on the swaying vine-bridge. My heart rushes and then settles into the rhythm of her footsteps along the swinging bridge.

"But what if it's a huge river," I asked him once—"like the Congo, which is much broader than the reach of any vine?"

"This is simple," he said. "Such a river should not be crossed."

If only a river could go uncrossed, and whatever lay on the other side could live as it pleased, unwitnessed and unchanged. But it didn't happen that way. The Portuguese peered through the trees and saw that the well-dressed, articulate Kongo did not buy or sell or transport their crops, but merely lived in place and ate what they had, like the beasts of the forest. In spite of poetry and beautiful clothes, such people were surely not fully human—were *primitive;* that's a word the Portuguese must have used, to salve their conscience for what was to come. Soon the priests were holding mass baptisms on shore and marching their converts onto ships bound for sugar plantations in Brazil, slaves to the higher god of commodity agriculture.

There is not justice in this world. Father, forgive me wherever you are, but this world has brought one vile abomination after another down on the heads of the gentle, and I'll not live to see the meek inherit anything. What there *is* in this world, I think, is a tendency for human errors to level themselves like water throughout their sphere of influence. That's pretty much the whole of what I can say, looking back. There's the possibility of balance. Unbearable burdens that the world somehow does bear with a certain grace.

For ten years now we've been living in Angola, on an agricultural station outside of Sanza Pombo. Before independence, the Portuguese had a palm-oil plantation here, cleared out of virgin jungle a half-century ago. Under the surviving oil palms we grow maize, yams, and soybeans, and raise pigs. Every year in the dry season, when travel is possible, our cooperative gains a few new families. Mostly young children and women with their *pagnes* in tatters, they come soundlessly out of the forest, landing here as lightly as weary butterflies after years of fleeing the war. At first they don't speak at all. Then after a week or two the women usually begin to talk, very softly but without cease, until they've finished the accounting of places and people they've lost. Nearly always I learn they've made a circular migration in their lifetimes, first having fled their home villages for the city, bluntly facing starvation there, and now returning to this small, remote outpost, where they have some hope of feeding themselves. We manage to produce a little extra palm oil for sale in Luanda, but most of what we grow is consumed here. The cooperative owns a single vehicle, our old Land Rover (which has had such a life it would tell its own history of the world if it could), but our rains start in September and the road doesn't become passable again until April. Most of the year, we look at what we have and decide to get along.

We're not far from the border, and the people of this region look and speak so much as they did in Kilanga I was dumbstruck when we first came here by a sense of childhood returned. I kept expecting someone I knew to come around the corner: Mama Mwanza, Nelson, Tata Boanda in his red trousers, or most eerily, my father. Obviously, the boundary between Congo and Angola is nothing but a line on a map—the Belgians and Portuguese drawing their lots. The ancient Kongo used to stretch across all of central Africa. As a nation it fell, when a million of its healthiest citizens were sold into slavery, but its language and traditions did not. I wake up to the same bubbling *mbote!* shouted outside the open window of our station house. The women wrap and rewrap their *pagnes* in the same way, and press the palm-oil harvest in the same kind of contraption that Mama Lo used. Often I hear ghosts: the upward slant of Pascal's voice in the question *Beto nki tutasala?* What are we doing?

I don't hear it often, though. In our village there are very few boys of an age to climb trees for birds' nests, or girls stomping self-importantly down the road with a sibling clutched sideways like an oversized rag doll. I notice their absence everywhere. The war cost most of its lives among children under ten. That great, quiet void is moving slowly upward through us. A war leaves holes in so much more than the dams and roads that can be rebuilt.

I teach classes in nutrition, sanitation, and soybeans, to women who respectfully call me Mama Ngemba and ignore nine-tenths of what I tell them. Our hardest task is teaching people to count on a future: to plant citrus trees, and compost their wastes for fertilizer. This confused me at first. Why should anyone resist something so obvious as planting a fruit tree or improving the soil? But for those who've lived as refugees longer than memory, learning to believe in the nutrient cycle requires something close to a religious conversion.

I ought to understand. I've been as transient in my adult life as anyone in our cooperative. And only now, after working this same land for ten years, am I coming to understand the length and breadth of outsiders' failure to impose themselves on Africa. This is not Brussels or Moscow or Macon, Georgia. This is famine or flood. You can't teach a thing until you've learned that. The tropics will intoxicate you with the sweetness of frangipani flowers and lay you down with the sting of a viper, with hardly room to breathe in between. It's a great shock to souls gently reared in places of moderate clime, hope, and dread.

The Portuguese were so shocked, evidently, that they stripped the gentle Kongo and chained them down in rows, in the dark, for the passage. Condemned for their lack of cash crops. The Europeans couldn't imagine a reasonable society failing to take that step, and it's hard for us to imagine even now. In a temperate zone it's the most natural thing in the world, right as rain, to grow fields of waving grain. To grow them year after year without dread of flood or plague, in soil that offers up green stems that bend to the scythe again and again, bread from a bottomless basket. Christians could invent and believe in the parable of the loaves and fishes, for their farmers can trust in abundance, and ship it to burgeoning cities, where people can afford to spend their lives hardly noticing, or caring, that a seed produces a plant.

Here you know what a seed is for, or you starve. A jungle yields no abundance to feed the multitudes, and supports no leisure class. The soils are fragile red laterite and the rain is savage. Clearing a rain forest to plant annuals is like stripping an animal first of its fur, then its skin. The land howls. Annual crops fly on a wing and a prayer. And even if you manage to get a harvest, why, you need roads to take it out! Take one trip overland here and you'll know forever that a road in the jungle is a sweet, flat, impossible dream. The soil falls apart. The earth melts into red gashes like the mouths of whales. Fungi and vines throw a blanket over the face of the dead land. It's simple, really. Central Africa is a rowdy society of flora and fauna that have managed to balance together on a trembling geo-logic plate for ten million years: when you clear off part of the plate, the whole slides into ruin. Stop clearing, and the balance slowly returns. Maybe in the long run people will persist happily here only if they return to the ways of the ancient Kongo, traveling by foot, growing their food near at hand, using their own tools and cloth near the site of production. I don't know. To be here without doing everything wrong requires a new agriculture, a new sort of planning, a new religion. I am the un-missionary, as Adah would say, beginning each day on my knees, asking to be converted. *Forgive me, Africa, according to the multitudes of thy mercies.*

If I could reach backward somehow to give Father just one gift, it would be the simple human relief of knowing you've done wrong, and living through it. Poor Father, who was just one of a million men who never did catch on. He stamped me with a belief in justice, then drenched me in culpability, and I wouldn't wish such torment even on a mosquito. But that exacting, tyrannical God of his has left me for good. I don't quite know how to name what crept in to take his place. Some kin to the passion of Brother Fowles, I guess, who advised me to trust in Creation, which is made fresh daily and doesn't suffer in translation. This God does not work in especially mysterious ways. The sun here rises and sets at six exactly. A caterpillar becomes a butterfly, a bird raises its brood in the forest, and a greenheart tree will only grow from a greenheart seed. He brings drought sometimes, followed by torrential rains, and if these things aren't always what I had in mind, they aren't my pun-ishment either. They're rewards, let's say, for the patience of a seed.

The sins of my fathers are not insignificant. But we keep moving on. As Mother used to say, not a thing stands still but sticks in the mud. I move my hands by day, and by night, when my fever dreams come back and the river is miles below me, I stretch out over the water, making that endless crossing, reaching for balance. I long to wake up, and then I do. I wake up in love, and work my skin to darkness under the equatorial sun. I look at my four boys, who are the colors of silt, loam, dust, and clay, an infinite palette for children of their own, and I understand that time erases whiteness altogether.

Adah Price

ATLANTA

A TOAD CAN DIE OF LIGHT! Emily warned us, as she peered out at the street from between her drawn curtains. *Death is the common right of Toads and Men. Why swagger, then?*

My colleagues in medical school accused me of cynicism but they had no idea. I am a babe in the woods, abandoned at the foot of a tree. On the day I swore to uphold the Hippocratic oath, the small hairs on the back of my neck stood up as I waited for lightning to strike. Who was I, vowing calmly among all these necktied young men to steal life out of nature's jaws, every old time we got half a chance and a paycheck? That oath never felt safe to me, hanging around my neck with the stethoscope, not for a minute. I could not accept the contract: that every child born human upon this earth comes with a guarantee of perfect health and old age clutched in its small fist.

The loss of a life: unwelcome. Immoral? I don't know. Depends perhaps on where you are, and what sort of death. Hereabouts, where we sit among such piles of leftover protein we press it into cakes for the pets, who usefully guard our empty chairs; here where we pay soothsayers and acrobats to help lose our weight, then yes, for a child to die from hunger is immoral. But this is just one place. I'm afraid I have seen a world.

In the world, the carrying capacity for humans is limited. History holds all things in the balance, including large hopes and short lives. When Albert Schweitzer walked into the jungle, bless his heart, he carried antibacterials and a potent, altogether new conviction that no one should die young. He meant to save every child, thinking Africa would then learn how to have fewer children. But when families have spent a million years making nine in the hope of saving one, they cannot stop making nine. Culture is a slingshot moved by the force of its past. When the strap lets go, what flies forward will not be family planning, it will be the small, hard head of a child. Overpopulation has deforested three-quarters of Africa, yielding drought, famine, and the probable extinction of all animals most beloved by children and zoos. The competition for resources intensifies, and burgeoning tribes itch to kill each other. For every life saved by vaccination or food relief, one is lost to starvation or war. Poor Africa. No other continent has endured such an unspeakably bizarre combination of foreign thievery and foreign goodwill. Out of sympathy for the Devil and Africa, I left the healing profession. I became a witch doctor. My church is the Great Rift Valley that lies along the eastern boundary of Congo. I do not go there. I merely study the congregation.

This is the story I believe in: When God was a child, the Rift Valley cradled a caldron of bare necessities, and out of it walked the first humans upright on two legs. With their hands free, they took up tools and beat from the bush their own food and shelter and their own fine business of right and wrong. They made voodoo, the earth's oldest religion. They engaged a powerful affinity with their habitat and their food chain. They worshiped everything living and everything dead, for voodoo embraces death as its company, not its enemy. It honors the balance between loss and salvation. This is what Nelson tried to explain to me once, while we scraped manure from the chicken coop. I could not understand how *muntu* could refer to a living person or a dead one with equal precision, but Nelson just shrugged. "All that is being here."

God is everything, then. God is a virus. Believe that, when you get a cold. God is an ant. Believe that, too, for driver ants are possessed, collectively, of the size and influence of a Biblical plague. They pass through forest and valley in columns a hundred meters across and many miles long, eating their way across Africa. Animal and vegetable they take, mineral they leave behind. This is what we learned in Kilanga: move out of the way and praise God for the housecleaning. In a few days the dark brigade will have passed on through—those ants can't stop moving. You return to find your houses combed spotless of spoiled crumbs, your bedding free of lice, your woodlots cleansed of night soil, your hen coops rid of chicken mites. If by chance a baby was left behind in a crib, or a leopard in a cage, it would be a skeleton without marrow, clean as a whistle. But for those prepared to move aside for a larger passage, it works. Loss and salvation.

Africa has a thousand ways of cleansing itself. Driver ants, Ebola virus, acquired immune deficiency syndrome: all these are brooms devised by nature to sweep a small clearing very well. Not one of them can cross a river by itself. And none can survive past the death of its host. A parasite of humans that extinguished us altogether, you see, would quickly be laid to rest in human graves. So the race between predator and prey remains exquisitely neck and neck.

As a teenager reading African parasitology books in the medical library, I was boggled by the array of creatures equipped to take root upon a human body. I'm boggled still, but with a finer appreciation for the partnership. Back then I was still a bit appalled that God would set down his barefoot boy and girl dollies into an Eden where, presumably, He had just turned loose elephantiasis and microbes that eat the human cornea. Now I understand, God is not just rooting for the dollies. We and our vermin all blossomed together out of the same humid soil in the Great Rift Valley, and so far no one is really winning. Five million years is a long partnership. If you could for a moment rise up out of your own beloved skin and appraise ant, human, and virus as equally resourceful beings, you might admire the accord they have all struck in Africa.

Back in your skin, of course, you'll shriek for a cure. But remember: air travel, roads, cities, prostitution, the congregation of people for efficient commerce—these are gifts of godspeed to the virus. Gifts of the foreign magi, brought from afar. In the service of saving Africa's babies and extracting its mineral soul, the West has built a path to its own door and thrown it wide for the plague.

A toad can die of light! Death is the common right of toads and men. Why swagger, then? My colleagues accuse me of cynicism, but I am simply a victim of poetry. I have committed to memory the common rights of toads and men. I could not swagger if I tried. I don't have the legs for it.

My work is to discover the life histories of viruses, and I seem to be very good at it. I don't think of the viruses as my work, actually. I think of them as my relations. I don't have cats or children, I have viruses. I visit them daily in their spacious glass dishes, and like any good mother I cajole, I celebrate when they reproduce, and I take special note when they behave oddly. I think about them when I am not with them. I have made important discoveries about the AIDS and Ebola viruses. As a consequence, I must sometimes appear at public functions where I am lauded as a saviour of the public health. This startles me. I am nothing of the kind. Certainly I'm no mad exterminator bent on killing devil microbes; on the contrary, I admire them. That is the secret of my success.

My life is satisfying and ordinary. I work a great deal, and visit my mother on Sanderling Island once a month. I enjoy my time there, which we mostly pass without speaking. Mother lets me be. We take long walks on the beach, where she watches those namesake shore-birds, the sanderlings, leaving no stone unturned. Sometimes in mid-January when she seems restless we'll take the ferry and drive up the coast highway, passing through the miles of flat, uninhabited palmetto scrub and the occasional stick shack, where old, dark women sit weaving beautiful sweetgrass baskets. Late in the evening we will sometimes pull into the dirt parking lot of a clapboard praise house and listen to old, dark Gullah hymns rising out the windows. We never go inside. We know our place. Mother keeps her head turned the whole time toward Africa, with her eye on the ocean, as if she expects it might suddenly drain away.

But on most of my visits we go nowhere. We sit on her porch, or I watch while she works her small jungle, snapping off dead leaves, forking rotted manure into her camellias, talking under her breath. Her apartment is the ground floor of one of those century-old brick boxes with earthquake bolts, remarkable pieces of giant hardware that run right through the building from east to west, capped off on the outside with iron washers the size of end tables. I think of them as running through Mother too. It would take something on this order, really, to hold her together.

She inhabits her world, waiting for forgiveness, while her children are planted in or upon the four different nations that have claimed us. "Lock, stock, and barrel," she calls us. Rachel is clearly the one with locks on every possible route to defenestration. And Leah barrels forward, setting everything straight. So I am the one who quietly takes stock, I suppose. Believing in all things equally. Believing fundamentally in the right of a plant or a virus to rule the earth. Mother says I have no heart for my own kind. She doesn't know. I have too much. I know what we have done, and what we deserve.

She still suffers from the effects of several diseases she contracted in the Congo, including schistosomiasis, Guinea worms, and probably tuberculosis. When she sticks out her tongue and allows me to treat her small maladies, I can see that every one of her organs has been compromised in some way. But as the years pass and she bends over more and more, she seems to survive in her narrowing space. She never married again. If anyone asks, she says, "Nathan Price was all the marriage I needed." I can see this is true. Her body was locked up tight, years ago, by the boundaries of her costly liberty.

I have not married either, for different reasons. The famous upstart neurologist wanted to be my lover, it turned out, and actually won me to his bed for a time. But slowly it dawned upon my love-drunk skull: he had only welcomed me there after devising his program to make me whole! He was the first of several men to suffer the ice storms of Adah, I'm afraid.

This is my test: I imagine them back there in the moonlight with the ground all around us boiling with ants. Now, which one, the crooked walker, or the darling perfection? I know how they would choose. Any man who admires my body now is a traitor to the previous Adah. So there you are.

Sometimes I play chess with one of my colleagues, an anchorite like myself, who suffers from post-polio syndrome. We can pass whole evenings without need for any sentence longer than "Checkmate." Sometimes we go out to a restaurant in the Atlanta Underground, or see a film at a theater that accommodates his wheelchair. But the racket always overwhelms us. Eros is not so much an eyesore, it turns out, as just too much noise. Afterward we always have to drive out of town toward Sandy Springs or the Chattahoochee, anywhere that is flat and blank and we can park the car in a red dirt road between peanut fields and let moonlight and silence reclaim us. Then I go home by myself and write poems at my kitchen table, like William Carlos Williams. I write about lost sisters and the Great Rift Valley and my barefoot mother glaring at the ocean. All the noise in my brain. I clamp it to the page so it will be still.

I still love to read, of course. I read differently now that I am in my right mind, but I return to old friends. *No Snickidy Lime*: "This is my letter to the World That never wrote to Me—" What more satisfying lines for a brooding adolescent? But I only saw half, and ignored the other side of the poem: "The simple News that Nature told—With tender Majesty." At Mother's house I recently found my dusty *Complete Emily Dickinson* with its margins littered shockingly by my old palindromes: *Evil deed live!* croaked that other Adah, and I wonder, Which evil was it, exactly?

Such childhood energy I spent on feeling betrayed. By the world in general, Leah in particular. Betrayal bent me in one direction while guilt bent her the other way. We constructed our lives around a misunderstanding, and if ever I tried to pull it out and fix it now I would fall down flat. Misunderstanding is my cornerstone. It's everyone's, come to think of it. Illusions mistaken for truth are the pavement under our feet. They are what we call civilization.

Lately I've started collecting old books that are famous for their misprints. There's a world of irony in it. Bibles, in particular. I've never actually seen any of these in original editions, but back in the days when print was scarce, only one printing of the Bible was widespread at any given time, and people knew it by heart. Its mistakes became celebrated. In 1823 when the Old Testament appeared with the verse "And Rebekah arose with her *camels*"—instead of *damsels*—it was known as the Camel's Bible. In 1804, the Lions Bible had sons coming forth from lions instead of loins, and in the Murderers' Bible of 1801, the complainers in Jude 16 did not murmur, they murdered. In the Standing Fishes Bible, the fishermen must have looked on in such surprise when "the fish stood on the shore all the way from Engedi to Eneglaim." There are dozens of these: the Treacle Bible, the Bear Bible, the Bug Bible, the Vinegar Bible. In the Sin-On Bible, John 5:14 exhorted the believers not to "sin no more," but to "sin on more!" *Evol's dog! Dog ho!*

I can't resist these precious Gospels. They lead me to wonder what Bible my father wrote in Africa. We came in stamped with such errors we can never know which ones made a lasting impression. I wonder if they still think of him standing tall before his congregation shouting, "*Tata Jesus is bängala!*"

I do. I think of him exactly that way. We are the balance of our damage and our transgressions. He was my father. I own half his genes, and all of his history. Believe this: the mistakes are part of the story. I am born of a man who believed he could tell nothing but the truth, while he set down for all time the Poisonwood Bible.

Book Seven

THE EYES
IN THE TREES

THE GLIDE OF BELLY ON BRANCH. The mouth thrown open wide, sky blue. I am all that is here. The eyes in the trees never blink. You plead with me your daughter sister sister for release, but I am no little beast and have no reason to judge. No teeth and no reason. If you feel a gnawing at your bones, that is only yourself, hungry.

I am *muntu* Africa, *muntu* one child and a million all lost on the same day. I am your bad child now gone good, for when children die they were only good. That is our gain in the great long run, and your loss. A mother cries for what she remembers, but she remembers the precious infant harvested already by time, and death is not to blame. She sees innocence, the untouched kingdom the great leader slain the great empty hole shaped like the child growing large and becoming grand. But this is not what we are. The child might have grown to be wicked or goodness itself but almost surely ordinary. Would have made mistakes caused you pain eaten the world in one bite. But you send us to the kingdom of somewhere else, where we move untouched through the forest and no trees fall to the ax and everything is as it could never be.

Yes, you are all accomplices to the fall, and yes, we are gone forever. Gone to a ruin so strange it must be called by another name. Call it *muntu*: all that is here.

Mother, be still, listen. I can see you leading your children to the water, and you call it a story of ruin. Here is what I see: First, the forest. Trees like muscular animals overgrown beyond all reason. Vines strangling their kin in the wrestle for sunlight. The glide of snake belly on branch. A choir of seedlings arching their necks out of rotted tree stumps, sucking life out of death. I am the forest's conscience, but remember the forest eats itself and lives forever.

Away down below single file on the path comes a woman with four girls, the pale doomed blossoms. The mother leads them on, blue-eyed, waving a hand in front of her to part the curtain of spiders' webs. She appears to be conducting a symphony. Behind her back the smallest child pauses to break off the tip of every branch she can reach. She likes the stinging green scent released by the broken leaves. As she reaches to snatch a leaf she spies a plump, orange-bodied spider that has been knocked to the ground. The spider is on its back and fatly vulnerable, struggling to find its pointed feet and scurry back into the air. The child delicately reaches out her toe and squashes the spider. Its dark blood squirts sideways, alarmingly. The child runs to catch up.

At the river they eat their picnic lunch, then move downstream to shriek in the cool water. The noise they make frightens away a young okapi. He had just lately begun to inhabit this territory on the edge of the village. If the children had not come today, the okapi would have chosen this as his place. He would have remained until the second month of the dry season, and then a hunter would have killed him. But instead he is startled today by the picnic, and his cautious instincts drive him deeper into the jungle, where he finds a mate and lives through the year. All because. If the mother and her children had not come down the path on this day, the pinched tree branches would have grown larger and the fat-bodied spider would have lived. Every life is different because you passed this way and touched history. Even the child Ruth May touched history. Everyone is complicit. The okapi complied by living, and the spider by dying. It would have lived if it could.

Listen: being dead is not worse than being alive. It is different, though. You could say the view is larger.

On another day the same woman leads her children through a market. Now she has white hair and only three daughters. None of them walks with a limp. They do not stay in line, as they did before. One of the daughters often strays away to handle bolts of fabric and talk with the merchants in their own language. One of the daughters touches nothing, and clutches her money to her breast. And one daughter keeps her hand on the mother's arm, guiding her away from dusty craters in the pavement. The mother is bent and betrays the pain in her limbs. They are all surprised to be here, surprised at themselves and each other. These four have not been together in one place since the death of the other. They have come here to say good-bye to Ruth May or so they claim. They wish to find her grave. But in truth they are saying goodbye to their mother. They love her inordinately.

The market around them is crowded with sellers and buyers. Women from the villages have walked for days to narrow their eyes at this city market. They stack their oranges into careful pyramids, then squat on thin legs, resting their angular wrists between their knees. And the city women, who wrap their skirts only a little differently, come to bargain on feeding their families. Hoping to lower the price they scatter insults over their sisters' wares, like irritating handfuls of harmless gravel. *What horrible oranges, I paid half as much for better last week.* The orange vendor deflects this nonsense with a yawn. She knows that, in the end, every need finds purchase.

The mother and daughters move like oil through the clear dark fluid of this crowd, mingling and then coming back to itself. Foreign visitors are rare here but not unknown. Narrowed eyes follow them, summing possibilities. Little boys chase with hands extended. One daughter opens her purse and finds coins, another daughter clutches her purse more tightly. Older boys with colorful stacks of T-shirts collect and follow in a swarm like bottleflies. They leap in front of each other to attract attention to their goods, but the visitors ignore them, stooping instead to examine ordinary wood carvings and beaded jewelry. The boys are baffled and shove each other more noisily.

Drowning out all other noise is the music that blares from many sidewalk shops of the cassette vendors. This music is so familiar it does not seem foreign. The little boys, the visitors, the village women all move their heads to the tightly strung voices of three different singers, popular ones from America, whose wrecked ancestors, captive and weeping, were clamped in iron bracelets in the hold of a ship at a seaport very close by. Their music has made a remarkable, circular trip. That fact is lost on everyone present. This ruin must be called by another name. What would have been is this instead.

The woman and her daughters are looking for something they will not find. Their plan was to find a way back to Kilanga and finally to the sister's grave. It is the mother's special wish to put a grave marker there. But they are stalled. It's impossible to cross the border. In the six months since they began to plan their trip, the Congo has been swept by war. A terrible war that everyone believes will soon have been worth the price. A good boil, they say here, a good boil purifies the rotten meat. After thirty-five years the man Mobutu has run away in the night. Thirty-five years of sleep like death, and now the murdered land draws a breath, moves its fingers, takes up life through its rivers and forests. The eyes in the trees are watching. The animals open their mouths and utter joyful, astonishing words. The enslaved parrot Methuselah, whose flesh has been devoured now by many generations of predators, is forcing his declaration of independence through the mouths of leopards and civet cats.

On this same day at this hour of early morning the man Mobutu lies in bed in his hiding place. The shades are drawn. His breath is so shallow the sheet drawn across his chest does not rise or fall: no sign of life. The cancer has softened his bones. The flesh of his hands is so deeply sunken the bones of his fingers are perfectly revealed. They have assumed the shape of everything he stole. All he was told to do, and more, he has done. Now in his darkened room, Mobutu's right hand falls. This hand, which has stolen more than any other hand in the history of the world, hangs limp over the side of the bed. The heavy gold rings slide forward to the knuckles, hesitate, then fall off one at a time. They strike the floor with five separate tones: a miraculous, brief song in an ancient pentatonic scale. A woman in white hurries to the door, believing against all reason that she has just heard the ailing President playing a song on the *kalimba*. When she sees him, she covers her mouth with her hand.

Outside, the animals sigh.

Soon the news will reach every city and lodge like a breath or a bullet in all the different breasts. The flesh of General Eisenhower consumed by generations of predators will speak aloud. The flesh of Lumumba, also consumed, will speak aloud. For a time the howl will drown out everything. But right now the world is caught in that small blank space in which no one has yet heard the news. Lives proceed for one last moment unchanged. In the marketplace they buy and sell and dance.

The mother and her daughters are stopped short by the sight of a woman they seem to recognize. It is not the woman herself they know, but her style of dress and something else. Her benevolence. They cross the street to where she sits on the sidewalk with her back to a cool north wall. Spread out around her on a bright cloth are hundreds of tiny animals carved from wood: elephants, leopards, giraffes. An okapi. A host of tiny animals in a forest of invisible trees. The mother and daughters stare, overtaken by beauty.

The woman is about the age of the daughters, but twice as large. Her yellow *pagne* is double-wrapped and her ornate bodice cut low on her large bosom. Her head is bound in sky blue. She opens her mouth, smiles broadly. *Achetez un cadeau pour votre fils*, she orders them sweetly. There is not a trace of pleading in her voice. She cups her hand as if it were full of water or grain as she points to the small, perfect giraffes and elephants. Having used up her single French phrase, she speaks Kikongo unabashedly, as though there were no other language on earth. This city is far from the region where that language is spoken, but when one of the daughters answers her in Kikongo, she does not seem surprised. They chat about their children. Too old for toys, all of them, á *bu*. Grandchildren, then, the woman insists, and so after more deliberation they pick out three ebony elephants for the children of the children. It is the great-grandmother, Orleanna, who buys the elephants. She studies her handful of unfamiliar coins, then holds all of them out to the vendor. The woman deftly plucks out the few she needs, and then presses into Orleanna's hand a gift: the tiny wooden okapi, perfectly carved. *Pour vous, madame*, she says. *Un cadeau.*

Orleanna pockets her small miracle, as she has done for the whole of her life. The others stand half-turned but unwilling to go. They wish the woman good luck and ask if she comes from the Congo. Of course, she says, *Á bu*, and to come here with her carvings to sell she must walk all the way, more than two hundred kilometers. Sometimes if she is lucky she can buy a ride on a truck. But lately without the black market not so many *commerçants* cross the border and it will be difficult. It may take her a month to get back to her family in Bulungu.

Bulungu!

Eé, mono imwesi Bulungu.

On the Kwilu River?

Eé—of course.

Have you heard any news lately from Kilanga?

The woman frowns pleasantly, unable to recall any such place.

They insist: *But surely.* It is Leah who does the talking now, in Kikongo, and she explains again. Maybe the name was changed during the *authenticité*, though it's hard to imagine why. *The next village down the river, only two days' walk on the road that goes through there. The village of Kilanga! Years ago, there was an American mission there.*

But no, the woman says. There is no such village. The road doesn't go past Bulungu. There is only a very thick jungle there, where the men go to make charcoal. She is quite sure. There has never been any village on the road past Bulungu.

Having said all that needs to be said, the woman closes her eyes to rest. The others understand they must walk away. Walk away from this woman and the force of her will, but remember her as they move on toward other places. They will recall how she held out her hand as if it were already full. Sitting on the ground with her cloth spread out, she was a shopkeeper a mother a lover a wilderness to herself. Much more than a shopkeeper, then. But nothing less.

Ahead of them, a small boy hunched with a radio to his ear is dancing down the street. He is the size of Ruth May when last seen alive. Orleanna watches the backs of his knees bending in the way of little children, and she begins once more—how many times must a mother do this?—begins to work out how old I would be now.

But this time will be the last. This time, before your mind can calculate the answer it will wander away down the street with the child, dancing to the African music that has gone away and come home changed. The wooden animal in your pocket will soothe your fingers, which are simply looking for something to touch. Mother, you can still hold on but forgive, forgive and give for long as long as we both shall live I forgive you, Mother. *I shall turn the hearts of the fathers to the children, and the hearts of the children to their fathers.* The teeth at your bones are your own, the hunger is yours, forgiveness is yours. The sins of the fathers belong to you and to the forest and even to the ones in iron bracelets, and here you stand, remembering their songs. Listen. Slide the weight from your shoulders and move forward. You are afraid you might forget, but you never will. You will forgive and remember. Think of the vine that curls from the small square plot that was once my heart. That is the only marker you need. Move on. Walk forward into the light.

Bibliography

Achebe, Chinua, *Things Fall Apart*. Doubleday, N.Y., 1959.

Boivin, Michael, *The Accidental Anthropologist*. Spring Arbor College Press, Spring Arbor, Mich., 1995.

Clark, Dora Jane Armstrong, *Congo Trails*. Vantage Press, N.Y., 1961.

Conrad, Joseph, *Heart of Darkness*. London, 1899.

Dugauquier, D. P., *Congo Cauldron*. Jarrolds, London, 1961.

Forbath, Peter, *The River Congo*. Houghton Mifflin, Boston, 1977.

Guide du Voyageur au Congo Belge et au Ruanda-Urundi. Édité par L'Office du Tourisme du Congo Belge et du Ruanda-Urundi, Bruxelles, 1954.

Heinz, G., and H. Donnay, *Lumumba: The Last Fifty Days*. Grove, N.Y., 1969.

Jahn, Janheinz, trans. Marjorie Grene, *Muntu: African Culture and the Western World*. Grove Weidenfeld, N.Y., 1958.

Joris, Lieve, trans. Stacey Knecht, *Back to the Congo*. Macmillan, London, 1987.

Kalb, Madeleine G., *The Congo Cables*. Macmillan, N.Y., 1982.

Kingsley, Mary, *Travels in West Africa*. Orion, London, 1897.

Kwitny, Jonathan, *Endless Enemies: The Making of an Unfriendly World*. Congdon & Weed, N.Y., 1984.

Laman, K. E., *Dictionnaire Kikongo-Français*. Brussels, 1936.

Livingstone, David, *Thirty Years' Adventures and Discoveries of Dr. David Livingstone and the Herald-Stanley Expedition*. Hubbard Bros., Philadelphia, 1872.

Merriam, Alan P., *Congo: Background of Conflict*. Northwestern University, Evanston, 1961.

Meyers, Margaret, *Swimming in the Congo*. Milkweed, Minneapolis, 1995.

Schweitzer, Albert, *On the Edge of the Primeval Forest*. A. and C. Black, London, 1921.

Smith, Alexander McCall, *Children of Wax: African Folk Tales*. Interlink Books, N.Y., 1991.

Somé, Malidoma Patrice, *Of Water and the Spirit: Ritual, Magic, and Initiation in the Life of an African Shaman*. G. P. Putnam, N.Y., 1994.

Stanley, H. M., *À Travers le Continent Mystérieux, Le Tour du Monde: Nouveau Journal des Voyages*. Vol. XXXVI, No. 913, 1874–1877, texte et dessins inédits.

U.S. Congress, *Senate Select Committee to Study Governmental Operations with Respect to Intelligence Activities*, Frank Church, chair, final report of Select Committee, United States Senate. Congressional Record, 1976.

Visser, John, and David S. Chapman, *Snakes & Snakebite: Venemous Snakes and Management of Snakebite in southern Africa*. Purnell, Capetown, 1978.

Wagner, Michael R., *Forest Entomology in West Tropical Africa: Forest Insects of Ghana*. Dordrecht, Kluwer Academic Publishers, Boston, 1991.

Weissman, Stephen R., "The CIA Covert Action in Zaire and Angola," *Political Science Quarterly,* Summer 1979.

Williams, John G., *A Field Guide to the Birds of East and Central Africa*. Houghton Mifflin, Boston, 1964.

Williams, John G., *A Field Guide to the Butterflies of Africa*. Houghton Mifflin, Boston, 1969.

Winternitz, Helen, *East Along the Equator: A Journey Up the Congo and into Zaire*. Atlantic Monthly Press, N.Y., 1987.

Quotations from the Apocryphal Books are taken from *The Complete Bible: An American Translation,* trans. J. M. Powis Smith and Edgar J. Goodspeed. University of Chicago Press, Chicago, 1939.

BARBARA KINGSOLVER's previous books include the novels *Pigs in Heaven*, *Animal Dreams*, and *The Bean Trees*; the bestselling essay collection, *High Tide in Tucson*; as well as collected works of short fiction and poetry. She was trained as a biologist before becoming a full-time writer, and has lived and worked in Europe, Africa, and the United States. Her articles on culture, politics, and natural history have appeared in the *New York Times* as well as *The Nation*, *Smithsonian*, *National Geographic*, and many other magazines. She lives with her husband and two daughters in Arizona and the southern Appalachian mountains.

 HarperPerennial

Books by Barbara Kingsolver:

ANIMAL DREAMS
ISBN 0-06-092114-5

Codi Noline, a dreamless woman at the end of her rope, discovers the unexpected when she returns home to Grace, Arizona, to confront her past and face her ailing father.

THE BEAN TREES
ISBN 0-06-091554-4

A novel about the peculiarities of family introduces Taylor Greer, a spirited young woman who finds an abandoned child in her car while on the road to Tucson, Arizona.

HIGH TIDE IN TUCSON
Essays from Now or Never
ISBN 0-06-092756-9

Twenty-five essays focus on Kingsolver's favored literary themes of family, community, and the natural world.

HOMELAND AND OTHER STORIES
ISBN 0-06-091701-6

A rich and emotionally resonant collection of twelve stories explore the twin themes of family ties and the life choices one must ultimately make alone.

PIGS IN HEAVEN
ISBN 0-06-092253-2

The contested adoption of a Native American child raises powerful questions about individual rights and the need for community.

THE POISONWOOD BIBLE
ISBN 0-06-093053-5

Kingsolver's bestselling epic novel which chronicles three decades in the life of an American family who travel to the Belgian Congo as missionaries in 1959.

Available at bookstores everywhere, or call 1-800-331-3761 to order.

Visit Barbara Kingsolver's website at www.kingsolver.com